Essence

Nectar Trilogy, Volume 3

DD Prince

Published by DD Prince, 2018.

DD PRINCE
ESSENCE
A DARK VAMPIRE ROMANCE
Standard vampire romance?
Nope. Not even close.
Wait 'till you see where this story goes!
NECTAR
TRILOGY,
BOOK
3

Essence

Nectar, Book Three

by DD Prince

This book is for adults only. It deals with dark subject matter contains subject matter that may be triggers for some readers. Please proceed with caution.

This book is NOT standalone. You need to read Nectar and Ambrosia first.

Kyla's Prologue:

I HEAR HIM CALLING me, urging me, but all these particles keep swirling around me and around his voice. He sounds so far away.

It feels a bit like floating. It's as if I'm weightless and everything around me keeps going from hazy to dark to hazy again. Like someone keeps messing with the lenses of my eyes, bringing things almost, but not quite, into focus.

But, every so often his voice rouses me, like a distant whisper, sometimes urging me, sometimes pleading with me.

Tristan's Prologue:

EVERYTHING IS FUCKED.

Every. Fucking. Thing.

Fucked.

Vacant. Her eyes are vacant.

And it's my fault.

How the hell did this happen?

The arrogance drilled into me for ten years meant that I had this blind and stupid notion that I could control everything around me. My arrogance was my downfall. Her downfall. Somehow I managed to fail every test, every trial. Was I so blood drunk? How did it all go so fucking wrong?

Did I underestimate my enemies and overestimate my importance? Was I so full of arrogance about my birthright, my foretold importance, omnipotence?

Was I so up my own goddamn ass that I just had no idea what I was up against, no idea that everyone around me wasn't just there to keep doing my bidding as they'd done for a decade?

After they gave her to me, it was no longer about me and my wants. They were all about their own agendas.

She said,

"Maybe all this is what'll help you learn to lead."

What a way to learn, build character, melt away the arrogance, losing the only thing that truly matters to me. Does this punishment fit my crimes? Probably. I can blame *them*, I can blame the blood, but it's all on me. I'm to blame. I failed.

Does it even matter now why?

It all boils down to the fact that I've lost her. She's in front of me but I *have* lost her. And it's pretty fuckin' fitting because I never deserved to have something *that* good.

There were so many crimes I committed. I felt entitled to take what I wanted. I went against every moral I'd been raised with. Because that's what vampires are told to do. We're told to forget everything we know and believe that we're not only at the top of the food chain but that we're weak if we don't take what's on offer.

And *this* vampire was told he was at the top of that top. So many violent acts, there's so much blood, on my hands. She'd fall right out of love with me if she had the full picture.

The one thing I ironically succeeded at was getting her to admit that she loves me. And that was fucked, too, because it meant that she came to trust me. She had instincts all the way along that made her second guess things every step of the way, but because she loved me and because I made promises to her she ultimately trusted me to keep her safe.

And I fucking failed her every single time.

And now she's here, beside me, empty. My little cherry bomb now has vacant eyes, just like all the rest. Kyla is empty. *My* Kyla who was so full of life, of fire, of fireworks. I can't feel her. And the silence, the emptiness is loud.

I wish *I* were empty, devoid of emotion. But no. I'm overflowing with it, spilling over with cold emptiness and regret.

Because of me she got violated by that motherfucking asshole. Because I was stupid enough to think I had my impulses under control, she gets pregnant, and then because I underestimated Adrian Constantin that was ripped away.

That piece of us... of the both of us... I *felt* it the minute it happened. It existed and it was real.

Before it happened, all I could think of was how I didn't want it because it'd put her at risk but as soon as conception happened I felt the shift and wanted to find some way to protect them both. But, now it's gone. All of it. The life our love created along with everything in Kyla that made her Kyla.

The more I think about what they did, all they did, the more I wish I'd taken my time with Claude, the more I want to get my fingers around Constantin's heart. I want him to pay for what he's done. I want him to pay for what I haven't been able to do.

She's empty and she's been fed on by not one but two vampires who wanted to take her from me. Two. Fuck. Almost drained. Cluster fucking fail.

The idea of any other teeth on her drove me to where I wanted out of my skin, wanted to bury anyone who touched her that way, the way that was only supposed to be for me, send them straight to the fiery hot pits at the centre of the earth. And it happened because I didn't stop it.

Even my own goddamn fucking mother fed on her. The entire thing makes me physically ill, fills my guts with black boiling rage. My insides are warring between rage and absolute anguish and it's anyone's guess which side will win. I'll either shrivel up and cease to exist or I'll become an inferno that melts everything in sight.

How should I feel about the fact that she's this empty shell instead of a cold and heartless scheming she-vamp bitch? What would be worse? I don't know. Maybe that, instead of this, and maybe I really *did* get off easy here.

I can barely look at her. She's just what I expected her to be before I looked into her beautiful green eyes the night she used those eyes to brand my soul and bring it back from the dead. She's lovely, gorgeous. Mine.

So fucking much hair, soft curly hair past her tits that feels amazing all over me when we fuck, when I wake up beside her, when she cuddles into me with light in her eyes and all those curls spilled all over me. She's got warm skin that smells and tastes like the most beautiful ambrosia. Kyla's beautiful outside but I also got to see so much beauty also radiating from the inside, the inside that started to seriously fucking shine as I melted her walls away.

But no more. Now, she's an empty vessel. After having her zest, her essence, her life force underneath me, beside me, wrapped around me, deep inside me... and then losing it?

The sun won't rise again for me without her. I'm doomed to live in the dark, watching her exist, watching her subsist.

I'm forced to feel this pain because she revived my soul and now that she's empty I want it to fucking die.

And *I* want to inflict pain. I can't even yet acknowledge the rising need to make those who are responsible for this feel pain. No pain delivered to them will even touch *my* pain but I need an outlet for this rage.

So far, I've had to play things carefully due to the political tight rope royal vampires have to constantly walk on, but I am done playing. Fucking finished! Soon the rage will bubble over and surpass the anguish and that's when things will get fucking scary. I'll find out who's involved in this and I'll make those responsible pay.

But the most responsible of all is me. We're in this mess because I didn't do what I promised: protect her.

My gut twisted as I remembered her words not long after we first met.

"Who's gonna protect me from you?"

Too bad no one did.

Part 1

Tristan

1

The Constantin Center, Near Phoenix, AZ

TRISTAN WAS IN THE master bedroom of the cottage with Kyla. She was asleep in the sleigh bed, looking peaceful, looking pure and angelic, her beautiful curly hair fanned out over the pillow.

It was morning, but he hadn't slept yet.

He'd sat in a chair beside the bed watching her sleep...just like he'd done that first night she came to him. But this time for very different reasons and with very different emotions inside of him.

It'd been hours since he'd realized that turning her had gone wrong and he'd been in agony ever since. Agony because of *all* that had gone wrong. It played like a bad movie in his head all night long, the reel getting stuck, ticking at the end with empty green eyes staring up at him.

He'd carried her from that room off the lab back to the cottage and she'd just held onto him, looking off, staring at nothing.

He'd walked to the cottage without noticing whether or not anyone was watching, whether anyone was even there. Nothing existed during that time but a palpable emptiness. When it stopped, and he got a chance to think, when things sank in and became real, it'd undoubtedly be time for vengeance.

For now, he was in freefall. He was reeling, trapped in a dark elevator that was plummeting toward the bowels of the earth.

He'd put her in the bed and told her to sleep. She'd closed her eyes and immediately obeyed.

For fuck sakes.

He'd rolled his eyes at that. She'd always argued with him, hardly ever did what he'd asked of her without a bloody battle. He wanted with every ounce of his being for her to look at him challengingly, ready to fight about being bossed around.

When her eyes finally did open, hours later, he felt a spark of hope light at the sight of her beautiful emerald green cat eyes, but that spark quickly burned out because it was evident, as soon as their eyes met, that she was still empty. It wasn't even that she was herself and then went empty when she focused on his eyes like they typically did.

She woke up empty. And it gutted him.

"You can go to the bathroom and take a shower," he muttered, looking away, not wanting to see her nod vacantly at him.

There was a knock on the bedroom door.

"Wait Kyla," he told her without looking at her. She'd swung her feet, so they were dangling off the bed. She waited.

He got up and opened the door. Sam stood there, looking pensive.

"What?"

Sam took a step back, clearly reading Tristan's body language.

"Sorry. You didn't answer the door. Adrian gave me a key. Can we talk? I need some direction."

"Talk."

"Can I step in?"

"No."

"Downstairs, then?"

"Negative."

He wasn't leaving her. Every time he took his eyes off her something bad'd happened. Fuck, it'd happened right under his nose back in that lab. He wasn't letting her out of his sight right now.

"Alright, well update, then. Liam: still daggered. What'll we do? Want any moves made yet?"

"Not yet."

Tristan's lip curled. That fucker would be history; shredded into ribbons by the time Tristan was done with him. He wasn't ready. He needed to get his head together first or else the bloodshed might not stop there. It might go far; it might go way fuckin' wide. That might happen anyway, but for now he needed a minute to think.

"Alright. He's still secure. He'll stay that way. What can I do? Need food? Booze? Blood? Anything? She manageable?"

"Where the fuck were you when everything went down?"

"Liam must've snuck up on me and knocked me out. From what we can tell he used my print while I was unconscious along with someone else to get into the lab. He left me in the hall."

Tristan let out a long breath but assessed Sam, looked for signs of whether or not he was telling lies.

"Need anything?

"Blood bags. Jack Daniels. Gimme that key."

"More O-neg for her, too?" He handed over the key.

"AB-neg for me, or whatever, doesn't matter."

"AB-neg and O-neg." He moved to go.

"Just AB for me."

"She's fed, then? I heard you'd carried her here, so I assumed she hadn't woken but the feeder was untouched and most of the bags were still on the—-"

"She woke."

"And she's been manageable? She's had enough?"

"The bags are for me."

"Pardon?"

"Not now. Haven't slept. Haven't fed. Blood bags. Jack. Alright?"

"Yeah, 'course. Be back soon as I can. But..."

"Not now."

"You want a feeder instead of a bag?" Sam asked.

Tristan shook his head, "Bags."

WHEN SAM RETURNED WITH an armful of blood bags and a bottle of JD, he followed Tristan upstairs. Tristan stopped at the top step and sat, blocking Sam from following further.

Sam took two steps back and started,

"Adrian wants to know if—-"

"Keep him the fuck away from me or he's done."

Sam raised his hands defensively.

Tristan thrust both hands into his hair; he needed to think. Right now he wanted to rip Adrian's guts out with his bare hands.

If he did he'd have a lot of people to answer to. He almost didn't give a fuck. Almost. Something miniscule somewhere deep stopped him from ending the fucker. But it was only for now, only until he could get his head straight and make some decisions.

"I mean it," he glared at Sam, "He gets near me or her, especially her, I'll won't be able to stop myself. I don't even fuckin' know if I *can* stop myself. I might get a wild hair and decide I need to hunt him down."

It was the truth. His self-control was hanging on by a thread.

He lifted a bag from the step beside him, cracked it open and then took a swig and grimaced, "Tell him he doesn't leave this property. I want him here, close. In case I decide to gut him. Watch him."

"Tri—-" Sam started.

"Go," Tristan grunted, "and keep Taryn away from me, too. Everyone needs to stay the FUCK away from me. If you can't handle it and wanna fuck off, feel free. Tell me now and I'll find someone else to—-"

"Naw, Tris. I'm still with you. That hasn't changed. You tell me what you need and I'll backflip to make it happen, man. Truth."

"Fine. Then watch Constantin. He leaves, *you'll* answer to me, too."

Tristan didn't waver, just kept his eyes on Sam. Sam shifted uncomfortably, then continued,

"Taryn's just said she's heading down here soon. I managed to ward her off. I'll try..." Sam winced, looking like he'd tasted something unpleasant.

Attempting to stop Taryn from doing anything would definitely be unpleasant.

"I'll come back in a few hours and see if you need anything. And if you need me, call or text. I called Leonard and Jeff when things went down last night. They caught a red eye and they're here, on duty. I had them hit your condo first and bring more clothes for you both, as well as your other laptop. Some Kovac shit needs your attention. Check your emails when you can. They got a locksmith and I'll get new keys for you. They're both outside, watching this house."

"You still wearin' a patch?"

"I am."

"Patch them, too."

He didn't know if anyone would have effects from Kyla or not but he wasn't taking any chances.

"So, she's not vamp."

"No."

"But you're not feeding from her?"

"She's not the same."

Pain twisted in his gut. He took another swig of the blood bag and then glared at the bag as he choked it down. Piss wouldn't have been much less appetizing. He swallowed the last mouthful with a wince as Kyla came out of the bathroom and stopped in front of him. She swayed a little.

"Go, Sam. Now." Sam glanced in Kyla's direction and then, probably feeling the warning coming off Tristan, turned and descended the stairs. Tristan heard the front door close.

He stood up and took her eyes in for a second.

She was looking at him, but she wasn't herself. Her eyes were a little glassed over and she was swaying ever so slightly. Her face was expressionless. She wore black yoga pants that came to just below the knee and a black tank top. Her wet hair had been combed straight and was over one shoulder.

He forced himself to look her in the eye.

"Stay close to me unless I tell you different. I go downstairs, you follow unless I say to stay. You don't leave this house without me. I want you to make sure you eat when you're hungry, go to the bathroom when you need to. Take care of yourself. Tell me if there's something you need. You go nowhere or do nothing else without my permission except you take care of yourself. Eat, drink, shower, bathroom. Alright? You have questions or are unsure about what to do, you ask me. You follow no one else's directions. No one but me. No one touches you but me. And tell me if you're hurt. Got me?"

She blinked a few times and nodded. Her reactions were delayed. He hated that he had to stare into her eyes to make sure she got it. It was painful to stare so deep and yet see nothing resembling what'd been there before.

"Hey?"

She stood expressionless.

"Hey?" he repeated.

She blinked.

"Yes?"

His Kyla probably would've said "Hey" back to him.

"What's your name?"

She blinked a few times and then answered.

"Kyla Spencer."

"You know me?"

A few more blinks and then "Yes."

"What's my name?"

Silence.

He felt his body slump but then she finally said, "Tristan."

Fuck.

Every time I hear your voice call my name it

sounds

so

sweet...

It still sounded sweet.

"You love me, Kyla?" Emotion gripped him. At least she knew his name.

No answer.

"Do you love me, Kyla?"

"Yeah."

"Do you love anyone else?"

"No."

He took a step forward and put his hand to her cheek. She felt warm. She felt like Kyla. She remained still. She didn't lean into his hand. She would've. Even before she'd admitted she loved him she'd leaned into it, his touch, when he'd touched her. Yet another thing that made him start tumbling head over heels from that very first night. She'd been different from the others from the start.

He leaned in and took a whiff at her throat. It was already healed from Claudio, from Liam. That was fast. Was it because she'd consumed his blood? She smelled freshly showered but underneath it, she smelled like his Kyla. She didn't smell like a vamp.

Had she smelled this way the night before? He couldn't recall. He stroked where the bite wounds had been with his thumb. There was no trace of them but that didn't change the fact that they'd been there.

Other vampires' fucking teeth marks on her!

"Look at me."

She lifted her gaze to his but... nothing. There was no spark, zero fire. Just glassy green cat eyes under thick black lashes. Lashes so thick she looked like she had mascara on, even when she didn't.

"Open your mouth," he ordered. She swayed a little and then she complied. He again applied pressure on her gum with his thumb. Nothing descended. He wanted to taste her again, see if she tasted any different, but he didn't.

He might've been holding onto a strand of hope and didn't want that bubble to burst yet, didn't think he could stomach more despair right now.

He put his lips to her forehead for a moment and then let go of her, took a big swig of the Jack, and descended the stairs with the blood and the booze in hand. She followed.

IT WAS LATER THAT DAY. Tristan was talking to Sam at the threshold of the cottage.

"Adrian's here," Sam said, raising his hands defensively, "I warned him not to come but he—-"

Tristan stormed out the door, plowing past Sam, past Leonard and Jeff. The two guys were both trusted employees and he felt a small amount of relief at seeing them, but he'd need to talk to them to make sure they weren't programmed by anyone to get up to no good.

He glanced back, making the door slam with just a glance and then he got to Adrian, who was slightly off to the side, out of the view of the front door, but shouted, "Don't go in there!" pointing at Sam and his guys.

Kyla was in there, sitting on the sofa, staring at the empty fireplace and he didn't want anyone near her. He'd told her to stay when Sam had knocked on the door.

It was dusk, and it'd been a long day. A long day of nothing but agony. Until now. Now the other emotions were beginning to surpass the agony. The day had dragged. Watching her eat food he'd prepared for her, watching her stare off into space in what could only be described as a catatonic state. He was watching her while wallowing, while drinking Jack, while hating himself.

Adrian was standing on just the other side of the thigh-height stone fence that surrounded the cottage, eyes filled with fear and beyond wearing that fear, he was exuding it; Tristan could smell it.

He moved toward him, with purpose, with his fists clenched, radiating rage. He was about to reach to grip Adrian's throat but just as he reached, Adrian held up a dagger but in a surrender-like stance. Tristan felt the guy's fear as clear as the way he used to feel Kyla.

"Don't make me use this. I just want to talk to you. Tristan," he gulped, "I just want to help."

Tristan felt his guys move in to flank him and he stopped an inch away from the vamp's face. A growl rumbled up from his gut.

"I just want to help." Adrian repeated. He looked petrified, despite having a dagger in his hand.

"Like you've done so far?"

"I know," Adrian said, looking visibly shaken, looking upset, "I know. Please. Sam's said she's not vampire but she's not the same. Let's go inside. Let me examine her. Tell me—-"

"You don't fucking breathe her air you motherfucking liar!" he clipped, "You. Dead vamp walking. And you!" He looked to Sam, "You're done sharing information about me and Kyla. Understand?"

Sam gave a nod and then looked at his feet.

"Tristan?" A disapproving female voice cut in.

Tristan's neck jerked to the side as he saw his mother, her dark hair loose, dressed in a long black coat. She quickly moved in from another direction. She looked ghostly pale, though. She looked upset. She put her hand on his forearm.

He shrugged her off, "Get the fuck away from me," he snapped.

"Darling, please. Let Adrian help you. We need to talk. Let's all sit so you can—-"

"Not now," Tristan stalked back toward the door, snarling, "Not at all. I'll consider talking to *you* tomorrow, Constantin; I may also eat your heart. Could go either way."

"Tristan, I think that we should—-" That was his fucking mother again. He was done.

"Taryn, fuck off. I don't want to see you. At all. Go home. I fuckin' mean it. Go. The fuck. Home."

He slammed the door and threw the lock across.

Kyla was on the sofa, still staring at the fireplace, although there was no fire burning.

Seeing her there like that made his gut ache, his chest burn. He dropped to his knees on the floor in front of her and stared at her. She didn't even acknowledge his presence.

He swallowed what felt like a mouthful of dust.

He closed his eyes and absorbed the pain that surrounded him. It was inside his gut, his throat, his veins, his lungs, and in the air around him. He needed to feel her, ached for it. He put his head on her lap, his lips to the top of her hand, which was resting on her thigh. Her hand twitched, but other than that there was no reaction.

This feeling of disconnection from her was so fucking painful, more acute than pain from any physical blow he'd ever withstood.

Hairs rose on the back of his neck. He felt like he was being watched. He looked toward the door and saw a form at the long rectangular stained glass pane that was adjacent to the front door. His eyes narrowed to a glare and the glass shattered and blew out at the figure. He heard a feminine yelp.

Taryn.

Fuck her.

A fist was pounding on the door. He willed it to swing open, standing protectively in front of Kyla, fangs out, eyes black and menacing, and saw that Jeff and Adrian were helping Taryn down the pathway back toward the main building. Sam and Leonard were at the door.

"Uh, Tris..." Sam started.

"Get that boarded. Immediately," Tristan told him.

Sam nodded on a hard swallow and left.

"Up to bed, Kyla. Close the bedroom door behind you," he said and she blinked a few times, then got up and moved up the stairs. He stood, watching the back of her and when he heard the bedroom door close, he thrust his hands through his hair, then walked to the kitchen and took another swig of the nearly-empty bottle of Jack that sat there. He lifted it, turned and carried it up the stairs to the bedroom. He stood over the bed. She was lying there, looking at the ceiling.

"Kyla?"

"Yes?"

He swallowed hard.

"Hungry?"

She didn't answer.

"Do you need anything?"

Her lips parted but no words came out.

He didn't know how much more of this he could take, "Snap out of it."

She continued to stare at the ceiling.

"Look at me," he demanded.

She complied.

"Snap out of it. Come back to me." He said this staring deep, hoping he had the power to mesmerize her back.

She blinked at him. An eternity passed while he searched her eyes, looking deep, looking for the girl he loved.

“Please, baby,” he pleaded in a whisper.

Nothing.

“Go to sleep,” he muttered, finally.

She blinked slowly, twice, and then her eyes closed and stayed that way. Not even a moment later her breathing evened out, like a fucking Stepford wife.

He walked downstairs and drank the rest of the bottle while standing in the kitchen and then found a half empty bottle of whisky in a kitchen cupboard and drank that, too.

Hours later he fell asleep slumped over in the chair by the fireplace.

2

Three Days Later

TRISTAN GLARED AT THE door, willing whoever it was on the other side knocking to fuck right off.

"Tristan?" Sam called out.

He supposed he had to meet the asshole's eyes to will him away. He was pretty sure he now had that power.

Tristan glanced at the lock, willed it to turn and then made it open. Both happened instantly. This was new, since he'd turned her. He hadn't done that, removing or creating barriers with anyone other than her, and only when he'd been tweaked. He felt like he was in a permanent state of tweaked, of pissed, of ready to fucking snap at any second. The only thing keeping him subdued was the need to protect her.

Sam stood, hesitantly, in the doorway, staring at Tristan sitting in a chair that faced the door.

"Food already came, man. What?"

There had been a daily delivery of supplies. Pre-cooked meals that just needed to be heated, blood bags, and booze. The day before, someone had come in to clean, which he'd allowed but kept Kyla beside him while the housekeeper was in, his fangs descended the entire time. Other than that, he'd been left alone.

"Where is she?" Sam stepped in cautiously.

"Upstairs."

"Any chance you want to talk?"

Tristan shook his head.

"Man, I see that you're hurting. But see, if you could—-"

"Dead."

"Pardon?"

"Dead inside. Not hurting. Dead."

"Bro."

Fuck that pity.

"What do you want?"

"What's goin' on, Tris? Talk to me." Sam shut the door.

"Fuck no. Go." He said this without looking at Sam.

"I'm on your side here. I—-"

Tristan was suddenly in Sam's space, "Oh yeah? How exactly are you on my side? You were honest with me? You didn't lie to me for years about shit? You didn't use your subtle programming skills to influence my actions, decisions I made?"

Sam winced.

"Yeah, I know. I know your fucking game. You find your opportunities, usually when I'm frazzled and that's when you get in my fuckin' ear. That's when you drop your suggestions. It's all crystal clear now, man. What if I were to get in your ear and suggest that you slit yourself straight up from your belly to your chin?"

"Is that what you want me to do?"

"If it is?"

"Honest to Christ I'm on your side. I've told you this. I know that I have things to be sorry for and guilty of lies of omission? Yeah, I know. But, I was given a directive. I've always tried to walk the line between being your friend and doing my job. It wasn't easy. Believe me when I tell you this has been a much harder gig than I ever expected. I respect you. Always have. All I did was follow directions. I kept an eye on her and then delivered her and I reported on what I saw. I'm sorry that you see it as betrayal. I get it. I'd feel the same, I'm sure. It's how things are done with royals. Every royal gets their concierge who arranges their enchanted pet and that's what I did, arranged it for you but according to directions, according to protocol, protocol that's followed for every single royal and protocol that was watched extra-closely due to just how royal you are. The caveat was her. She isn't just an average enchanted pet. She was chosen for you before she was even born. I was kept on a need-to-know basis, but I tried to help wherever I could, when you needed me to, nudged when I saw the need to. But always with your best interests at heart. Truth, man. Serious. I think I may even be able to help you *here* but first I think maybe if you talk to Adrian, let him run a few tests, and then we get home and there I can research a few things. See how I can help..."

Tristan took a swig of booze from a near-empty bottle that sat beside another empty bottle.

"What're you doin', Tris? You look like shit. You not feeding?"

Tristan didn't answer.

Sam sat down on a chair, "You need to feed. You know you do. Looks like you're not getting enough."

Tristan shook his head, "It's shit."

"Yeah?"

"After her... like drinking piss."

"I'm sure. But you need to drink the piss, man. Or get a new feeder. You need to do it fast; you look like hell."

"Cheers," he replied with a sneer and took another swig from the bottle.

"What's up with her? Her blood's different?"

Tristan leaned forward in the chair and put his head in his hands, balancing his elbows on his knees, "She's empty. Gone. She's breathing, she's got a heartbeat, but nothing else. Looks like she's permanently zoned out."

"You try turning her again?"

"Probably wouldn't work. And even if it would, why? So she can go from being an empty shell to being an evil she-vamp bitch? At least she isn't dead. Now I'll just pay my penance."

"Penance?"

"Fuck off, Sam. I'm not doin' this. We don't do heart to heart shit, you and I. It ain't starting now. And your bullshit nudging won't fucking work on me anymore."

"I can feel that, Tristan. And I'm not nudging. I can feel that I can't nudge. But I'm still here for you. You're not just my assignment, you're my friend. First things first. Let's get you fed. I'll bring you a new feeder. Drink from a live one. You're drunk. You're feeling the booze extra hard due to lack of blood. I'm sensing you don't want to try feeding from Kyla again. So I'll get someone down here. Claudio's two are still here and we've used one's blood in those bags. Since it's piss to ya, we'll try the other one. They're both enchanted blood and if it's a direct feed—-"

"No." The blood bags he'd been drinking may have been from enchanted pets, but they still tasted like piss to him.

He wouldn't put his mouth on anyone else. He'd promised her.

"I won't drink directly from anyone but you ever again. Ever."

"You tappin' her at least?"

Tristan snarled and shot to his feet, "Watch your mouth."

Sam raised a hand, "That's obviously a *no*. If not a live feed then you need a release, Tris. Go up and get it. If you don't wanna do that, let me bring a feeder for you to feed from while tapping it. You know that's how you feed best, what gives you the rush. Or if you wanna leave human blood out of it, pick a vamp from the main house. Faye's still here. She's leaving in three days. You could hang with her, bang her, work out some frustration, maybe? Then she'll be gone and out of your hair and maybe your head'll be clearer. She's always been sweet on you and she's mildly tolerable for a she-vamp. Want me to fetch her?"

"No. Go." Tristan spat sourly, not looking him in the face.

"I'm going. But at least consider meeting with Adrian. He's remorseful, Tristan; frazzled as shit. Never seen anything like this with him and I've known the guy all my life. He's concerned about Kyla ovulating and menstruating. Her cycles have been unpredictable. She could ovulate soon. And he wants to run some tests to see—-"

"Get. The. Fuck. Out. Last warning or I rip your fucking head off. I don't give a fuck."

Sam backed away, "I believe you. I believe that you're nearly past caring. But you're still here so that's something. We need to talk, Tris, bro. We need to analyze her blood. Check levels. And we need a plan. You need to feed. You need to get laid. Then maybe your head'll clear so we can talk."

"Not interested in talking. Just getting my bearings. Then taking her home in a few days."

"Not to overload you here but Kovac, man, it needs your attention. Everything's cool. I've been in touch with Rick, with a few of the other execs and all is in hand. That's why I got your company laptop here. With Claudio gone you're acting CEO and if you play your cards right the board'll drop the *acting* instead of making you report to someone else for the next few years. Brandt reached out today for a conversation since word is getting round about Claudio and his council chairs now sit empty, too. I suspect they'll wanna put things to a vote for the CEO position as well as replace him on his councils. Some you're a member on, some you are not but would be a good candidate. I made an excuse, but we won't wanna leave him hanging long. You'll be under a microscope by the board for Kovac, by councils for North America in general. And I have an idea that I want to check out a little bit for Kyla and I can do that better once we're back home."

"What idea?"

"I don't wanna create any false hope or anything, so until I do some research it's pointless to—-"

"Then get the fuck out."

Tristan knew there wasn't even a spark of hope in his eyes at Sam's mention of an idea. Sam stood there a minute, about to speak, looking like he was measuring his words.

Tristan's eyes finally met his and he stared deep, "Go."

Sam backed out.

Tristan now had confirmation he could influence Sam against Sam's will. He'd suspected he'd done it a few times in the last few days but now he was sure.

That was another something new. He'd always had exceptionally strong skills to mesmerize people, animals, even. He hadn't mastered it with other vamps yet but based on how Sam's pupils reacted, dilated, and the way the air moved around him, Tristan was fairly certain he had another new talent. Perhaps before everything...her blood had accelerated other talents. And this talent obviously made him oblivious to Sam's *nudging*.

He glanced at the lock and willed it to turn again, to block the outside world out. And it was effortless again. There were new things he couldn't do before but were now easy. Things he *could* do when tweaked or really focused were now effortless.

He lifted the bottle of whisky that was on the table beside him by the neck and when he got it to his lips he realized it was empty. He released his grip, letting it fall and shatter. Without so much as a flinch at the sound of the glass smashing on the wood floor, he got to his feet and strode outside, willing the lock and then the door on the way, as well as willing it shut behind him so he could get some air but doing it thinking that he didn't have the capacity to dedicate headspace to thinking about the fact that Brandt, essentially Claudio's American counterpart, wanted to talk.

Tristan had no idea what'd been told about Claudio's demise. Tristan could be called before a council to answer for that. Brandt and Claude were tight. Brandt was a reasonable guy, a respected leader, on some high-level councils, but who knew what other things had been hidden? Kovac Capital was so far off his radar right now it wasn't even a blip.

But, maybe work would help him. Maybe the distraction would help him get his emotions under control.

He inhaled the night air for a few minutes and then headed back inside, seeing Leonard near the fence on his way in.

"Everything okay, boss?" Leonard asked from about 50 feet away.

"Yeah, man," Tristan called back and as he opened the door, he caught the aroma of blood. Her blood? Kyla's blood?

What the fuck?

"Stay there 'till I shut the door," he called out, looking him right in the eye, "Don't try to get in unless I tell you to come in."

His body jerked to a halt as he took in the room. He saw blood on the floor by all the shattered glass from the whisky bottle and then a few smudges of it leading toward the kitchen. He locked the door manually and rushed into the kitchen. She was standing by the fridge, drinking from a bottle of water.

His fangs dropped out of reflex, hunger gnawing at his gut, but he pulled them back. It was as if it was her blood, but it was diluted. No; it must be his mind playing tricks. He was feeling a little drunk. It took a lot to get him drunk but then again he'd been drinking a fuck of a lot of booze and very little blood, sub-par blood, plus had eaten virtually nothing food-like in days.

"I'm hurt," she said, looking dazedly in his direction.

He looked down and saw that her foot was wrapped with paper towel but it had bled through.

More negligence.

He moved swiftly to her and lifted her by putting both hands to her waist and sat her on the counter. Her foot was sliced on her heel. He twisted her so that her foot was hovering over the sink and he peeled away the paper towel and began to rinse it, feeling like there was a giant boulder sitting in the middle of his chest as he did it.

He was salivating, wanting to taste the blood but couldn't bring himself to do it, couldn't bring himself to try knowing the disappointment he'd feel when it didn't taste like it was supposed to taste. He'd only be able to seal it if he'd bitten, which he hadn't, it so he applied pressure.

He pulled his fangs back in, not even realizing they'd again dropped at the mouthwatering scent. He tried to shake off the drunken haze, wanting the bleeding to stop. As if by his silent command, it did.

"Stay here," he said softly and headed upstairs. He found a first aid kit in a drawer in the bathroom vanity and went down and applied first aid cream after making sure there wasn't any glass in it, and then he bandaged her heel and carried her up to the bedroom. He put her on the bed.

"Mess on the floor," she mumbled.

"Sorry, baby. That was my fault. I'll go clean it. Sleep."

That was certainly a somewhat lucid thing to notice. He looked at her eyes.

No. Still vacant.

She put her head on the pillow and closed her eyes. He pulled the blankets up over her and went back downstairs and cleaned up the glass, avoiding the almost overwhelming urge to taste the blood on his hands.

A while later he opened the bedroom door and found her, asleep. He'd felt drawn to her, couldn't stop thinking about the scent of her blood and whether or not it'd been a mirage.

He sat on the edge of the bed and pulled the blankets down.

She was wearing that red racerback tank top that'd brought them all the grief on their flight to Phoenix and black silky shorts that showed a lot of cheek under a short terrycloth robe that was gathered up around her waist. It was a white robe. He looked closer and spotted the white on white embroidered monogram from the hotel where she'd gotten attacked by Liam. He bared his teeth at that thought. Sam must've thrown it in with their bags. He wanted that off her.

Her mass of dark curls was fanned out over the pillow, her hands in prayer position under the cheek that was on the pillow.

He undid the sash and put the back of his hand against her and his knuckles trailed a path from her thigh up to her hip. Goosebumps rose on her leg and her arm. She shifted, still sleeping, and a lock of her hair fell over her cheek.

He reached for it and tucked it behind her ear. Emotion gripped his heart like a vice.

He leaned over and put his nose to her throat. She smelled like Kyla. She was warm like Kyla. He wanted to get lost in her.

But then he saw her eyelids flutter and then her eyes opened, and the beauty of the moment completely fucking died.

She moistened her lips slowly with the tip of her tongue and blinked a few times at him.

"I miss you already," he told her, "I miss you so much, sweet girl."

She nodded robotically. Her lips parted like she was about to say something. But then after an eternity she sealed them again.

"Sit up and gimme that robe. I don't want you wearing it."

She obliged. He took the robe from her and threw it on the floor.

"Put your hand on my face. Touch my chin." He closed his eyes and absorbed her touch. With his eyes closed, he could pretend. But not totally because although she'd followed his order, there was no emotion coming at him. And there was also that she'd started a habit of twirling her finger on the cleft on his chin when she touched his face. She didn't do that now. He flicked the lamp off. Maybe in the dark it'd be easier to pretend that her eyes weren't blank.

"I'm gonna kiss you. Respond. Kiss me back. Softly. Slowly. Okay?"

"Oh. Kay," she answered dazedly.

He leaned forward, and their lips touched. He felt hers part. His tongue dipped in and he tasted her. She tasted like his Kyla. The tip of her tongue touched his lower lip and he groaned and deepened the kiss.

He couldn't help it, emotion gripped him, and he tangled his fingers into her hair and his nose moved to the curve in her throat and he felt hope spark as he ran his nose along the soft warm skin, feeling her pulse against his cheek. She gasped and then went lax as if he'd bitten. But he didn't bite. And his Kyla had never, not once before all this shit, gone lax at being bitten, anyway. She would tense, she would gasp, she would become aroused or bewildered or try to fight. She never just went limp like the others.

Her skin was so soft, so warm and smooth. He wanted her. He wanted her blood and he wanted inside her with a fierceness that made his own blood pump harder. He backed up and looked down at her, eyes adjusting and seeing her in the dark. She was on her back, looking up in his direction, but not really looking *at* him, not the way *his Kyla* did, she'd done it even in the dark before this. Her lips were parted.

He backed away, thinking he couldn't look at her any longer, didn't think he could stand the pain that had replaced desire.

He was about to leave her there and go back downstairs, where he'd been sleeping a few hours here and there, but exhaustion washed over him. He suddenly felt bone tired, exhausted, and the darkness, her scent, and the bed were too inviting to deny.

He was beyond exhausted, probably almost as exhausted as he was when he'd found her in that trailer park except that this time it was a broken exhausted, not a relieved exhausted where he felt like he could finally sleep.

He kicked off his shoes and socks, dropped his jeans, threw his t-shirt off, rounded the bed and climbed in. She was just lying there, doing nothing.

He pulled the covers over them and pulled her close, "Hold me, baby. I need you to wrap yourself around me."

She wrapped her arms around him. He buried his nose in her hair and absorbed her scent and the feel of her wrapped around him. He didn't deserve it but at that moment he really fucking needed it. He hooked her leg over his hip and nuzzled in. He fell straight to sleep thinking that at least he had this. Even if he didn't deserve it.

THE BED WAS SHAKING; it jolted him awake. It was morning. It was shaking because her body was jerking, as if she was having some sort of seizure.

"Kyla!" he shouted. Her eyes opened at hearing her name, but she kept shaking, jerking, eyes to the ceiling, neck arched, back bowed.

"Hurt," she said with a hard T, pain punctuating the word.

"What hurts, sweet girl?" He tucked her in closer to him but she was still shaking hard.

"Me," she whimpered.

"Your foot?" He threw the blanket back over and reached down for her foot and lifted it, removed the bandage, and saw it was 100% healed. No sign whatsoever of the crescent shaped cut that'd been on her heel at bedtime. He put pressure against it and couldn't feel any trapped glass.

"Does your foot hurt?"

"No," she answered.

"What hurts?"

"Me."

He threw the bandage to the side and got back under the covers and pulled her tight against him. Her teeth were chattering, and her body was burning up with fever. He put one hand around the back of her head and held her close, kissing her forehead.

"Stop shaking, okay? It's okay. I've got you. What do you need?"

"Got me?" she asked in a whisper and he felt her body relax, sink into him, even. Her forehead was wedged into his throat. Her mouth against his skin. He felt her breath warm him. He closed his eyes and absorbed the feel of her. One of her tears hit the concave part of his throat.

"You still hurting?"

Her shaking paused.

"Yeah." Another tear began to trail its way down her cheek. He caught it with his lower lip and sucked it in. It tasted like her tears had before. And it landed like a lump in the centre of his chest. Her shaking resumed.

"How do I make it stop?"

He heard her teeth chatter.

"I don't know."

"Where does it hurt?"

"I..."

"Where?"

"Don't know."

Fuck.

"Close your eyes, baby. Go to sleep, okay?"

"Okay."

"Who am I? You still know who I am?"

Silence. She'd been answering quickly up until then, way quicker than she had been.

"Baby?"

"Tristan."

"Yeah. Say my name sometimes when you talk to me. Okay? Okay, baby?" He needed to know she knew him.

"Okay, Tristan."

"I love you. No one'll hurt you again, sweet girl. I'm so sorry, baby."

"M'kay, Tristan."

He felt her body relax further. He closed his eyes, gritted his teeth, and tried to find sleep. Every few minutes for a good hour her body would jerk.

He woke every time she did it. Fuck but she felt so good in his arms. He was worried, didn't know what was going on, but every time she jolted awake, making him jolt alert, his first thought was worry but his second thought was about how right it was to hold her while they slept.

The last few days he'd been sleeping slumped in a chair, avoiding having this because he was avoiding the pain associated with having her beside him without her being herself, but the alternatives? Not having her at all because she was dead? Or not having her willing to do this because she'd look at him with a sour and completely repulsed expression at the mere idea of a snuggle?

All of this sucked, but for right now, with just the two of them there, it'd do.

He didn't know what hurt or how he could make it stop. A voice nagged that Adrian might be able to help and that was probably the only reason Adrian wasn't already dead, because Tristan didn't yet know what he was dealing with here, but he fell asleep with a scowl being the last thing he remembered doing because the idea of letting Adrian Constantin anywhere near Kyla when the motherfucker could do even more harm? Right now, it was unfathomable.

THAT EVENING WAS MUCH the same. He left her upstairs all day. He told her to exercise for an hour after lunch, thinking that she needed to do more than sit around staring off into space. He'd found an exercise video online and played it on the tablet that was in the bedroom and left her to follow it. She did but sort of in a delayed reaction slow motion sort of way, like her brain wasn't registering what she was seeing immediately. Like it had to pass through a filter first. He left as she got into a plank position on the floor beside the bed.

He delivered food to the bedroom at dinner time and found her sitting on the bed. Just sitting. Her complexion was pale.

"Eat," was all he'd said when he put the tray down.

He'd waded through some of his work email in the afternoon, wanting the distraction and happy to have his own laptop, rather than the loaner that Adrian had provided, but hadn't gotten very far as he had zero passion for anything at the moment, so delegated a lot of things he'd normally take care of himself to associates back home.

That night he climbed in with her again. She was awake but lying in the bed, in night clothes, looking off into space, smelling like she usually did, making him so fucking thirsty but not remotely interested in the disappointment of feeding when it probably wouldn't taste like her. He wanted, down deep, to believe that since she was smelling like herself that she could come back in every way but he was afraid to hope.

He put his arm around her and hauled her back against his front. He fell asleep, playing with her hair, ignoring the almost overpowering urge to taste her, to take her.

Again, he woke up to her shaking, like she was having a seizure. She kept jerking and crying out, and then she was scratching up and down her arms and legs, frantic. He flicked the light on to get a better look at her skin. It looked fine, other than her nail marks.

"Kyla, stop! Stop scratching."

She was on her back, scratching as if she was in withdrawals from him not feeding.

She stopped scratching.

"I'm hurt," she whimpered.

"What hurts?"

"Me."

Damn it.

"What hurts, Kyla?"

"Me."

"What part of your body?"

She froze, mouth agape, looking dumbfounded, like she didn't know how to answer.

Fuck.

"What can I do?"

"I don't know."

"Need medicine?"

"I don't know."

"Tylenol?"

"No."

"Not that kind of hurt?"

She grunted painfully.

"Baby, I wanna help you but I don't know how."

She went back to raking her nails up and down her thighs. He grabbed her wrists and held them still, pinned over her head.

"Stop. Don't scratch!"

He transferred her wrists to one hand while he sniffed her throat, her hair, put his free hand on her belly and felt to see if she felt bloated or if she expressed pain at being touched. She didn't. He couldn't sense anything wrong with her.

She started to squirm a little and he felt her tits pressing into his chest. He ignored the stirring in his groin.

"Is it worse?"

"No."

"Is it better?"

"Yes."

He let go of her and moved away.

Then after a beat she said, "No."

"I wish you'd tell me what."

She didn't answer. She started to tremble again.

He grabbed her and pinned her underneath him and she stilled.

"Better?"

"Yes."

"I wish I knew what was hurting you, Kyla. I wish I could make it better."

She squirmed and he could smell arousal from her. Like the scent of citrus and melons but musky. He frowned.

"You."

"You? Me what? Do I make it better?"

There was a lump clogging his throat. Was she expressing the need to be comforted? She was aroused. His feeders rarely got aroused. They'd respond to commands, many would even get off, but he often had to lube them. Most of the time they were just like blow-up dolls. He felt guilt now about that, guilt he'd never before felt about taking what he'd been told he was entitled to.

Mesmerized women could typically function better than this. They were on autopilot. They couldn't have elaborate conversations but they were generally able to express themselves. But Kyla was worse than the average mesmerized woman. She was barely more than catatonic.

He let go of her and rolled over, his back to her. He was testing.

"Tristan," she breathed and she started trembling again. He rolled back her way and pulled her tight against him. The trembling stopped.

"Do you feel better when I hold you?" His voice was gruff.

She didn't answer.

He jiggled her shoulders, "Do you?"

She nodded.

"Does it still hurt?"

"Yeah."

"But it's a little better?"

"Uh huh."

"So you feel things."

No answer.

"Kyla?"

"Mm?" Her brows were furrowed.

"Are you in there?"

Silence.

He stared deep into her eyes, so deep that he could've sworn he saw something like a tiny spark of light deep in there.

Then, "Think so."

Hope bloomed in his chest, he kept staring, "Should I take you to Adrian? Should I let him run tests? I don't want him near you but if he can help..."

Fuck. Would that help? Or would it be more deceit, more games?

He let that hang. He waited a long time. She didn't reply. He looked to the ceiling and let out a long breath in despair. He felt her forehead move down and nuzzle down his jaw to behind his earlobe. Then he felt her eyelashes caressing his throat as she blinked every so often.

He held her tight and tried to find sleep. It took a long while. But she had stopped shaking and scratching and eventually she stopped blinking, so he finally closed his eyes.

HE WOKE. SHE WASN'T in the bed.

He knifed up and frantically bolted out of the room. The door had been shut and that did not sit well. The bathroom door was open and it was empty. The other room was empty.

He couldn't track her. Couldn't sense her. Couldn't even smell her.

Instead of going down the stairs he sailed over the banister and landed softly on his feet on the main floor, fear gripping his chest. He found her in the kitchen, staring out the window over the kitchen sink.

Relief flooded his veins. But then he spotted Adrian Constantin.

Constantin stood outside on the other side of the back patio and spotted Tristan behind Kyla. He waved at him hesitantly and then held both hands up defensively.

"Stay here," Tristan told her. He heard her delayed answer of "Okay," as he was shutting the door.

He was fucking pissed.

He stepped outside, giving no fucks that he was in boxers and nothing else. He folded his arms across his chest and leveled his gaze on him.

"Can we talk? I have a dagger. I don't want to use it but want you to know I'm armed." Constantin motioned to a dagger sheathed and clipped to his belt. It was ridiculous; Tristan knew he could disarm Adrian before the other vamp'd even blink.

"What do you want?"

"To run tests. Find out what's happened with her. Figure out how to help."

"You ever see a woman not turn after being fed vampire blood?"

"Never. I can see that the light has died in her eyes. I'm sorry."

"She's mesmerized. Completely. Doesn't seem to regain lucidity when she's alone, so far. I've watched for it. It's like she's in a permanent state."

"It might not be permanent. Have you fed from her? What does her blood taste like?"

"Not since right after she turned. I only tasted my blood."

"Can I examine her?"

"I have zero trust for you so thinkin' no."

The fucker stroked his chin thoughtfully.

"She was acting last two nights like she was in withdrawals," Tristan added, accusingly. Did Adrian know this'd happen? Was this another game?

"Try feeding now. See if there's a change. If that doesn't work, try feeding her your blood again."

"To turn her?" Tristan felt disgust bubble up.

Maybe she's better like this. But was she? Would she want to be an empty shell or something evil? What would Kyla think was worse?

"If it didn't work, it most likely wouldn't. Scrap that idea," Constantin scratched his temple, looking contemplative.

"Right." He turned to go back inside, not sure he believed the sonofabitch and not caring to stand around while the fucker pondered things. The emotions coming off him were a little confusing. Fear, desperation. Tristan wasn't sure what to think. He wanted to gut the bastard but in case he was able to help with Kyla, for now, he was watching.

Constantin's voice stopped him.

"I need to check her. If you can't detect ovulation, Tristan, it could come without warning. Or menstruation. I gather that with the fact that you're still here that it's not out of the question. But ovulation could happen soon."

Tristan shot him a dirty look.

"I have *always* put my work first. I always will. Kyla is part of that work. I want all of this to work out. She wasn't ready to be pregnant, not when we didn't know if it'd kill her. I want you two to breed. I want her blood to make you strong. I want to see *how* strong she gets as this bond deepens with you. I didn't want any of *this* to happen. I didn't want her to turn this soon and I certainly didn't think it'd fail. So we need to assess her blood, determine if she's fertile, we need to—-"

"How did he get your dagger? Why wasn't it better secured?" Tristan snapped.

"Liam hacked into my systems remotely and found vulnerabilities. That dagger was in a hidden compartment in my desk. I'm in there a lot. He had camera feeds on me. I've had it out, as you know."

It jived. Liam was VP of Information Technology for Kovac.

"He still daggered?"

"Yes."

"I'm gonna want access."

"You're planning to kill him."

Tristan didn't hesitate, "Of course."

"I could have him disposed of..."

"No. I do it. What about Claudio? Tell me what the fuck went wrong there."

Adrian sighed.

"Answers. Now," Tristan looked into his eyes.

"He knew I still had an untouched vial of her blood. He obviously let his curiosity get the better of him. His pets are no match for Kyla's blood. And he's had fertility issues. He wants his line carried on. I think he thought she was an alternate opportunity for that. I think that small taste of her blood made him want more and he became power-hungry. It's the only logical conclusion. He was ready to retire. I had many conversations with him about that, about your future. But then just the few days before everything went wrong he was talking long term plans again, as if retirement wasn't even on the horizon. I checked security feeds and he'd taken that blood a few days before things went wrong. It obviously altered his perception. He has used my lab before. He dabbles in chemistry still, was a chemist before he was turned. He knew I was equipped with a variety of gases. I'd commented about a gas that works through the ocular cavity that takes some vampires down but it didn't take you down. It doesn't work on me either and Liam was unaffected by it. I don't even know if he used the right one because it's odourless and there was a scent in the room that should not have been there. He was off. I think he wasn't able to help himself. After tasting her blood, it called to him *that* strongly."

Tristan folded his arms across his chest.

"I want to help. Let me help. This has been my life's work. She's from my line and I want this to work. I won't be careless, regarding anything, including your preferences. I assure you. I know you have no reason to trust me but please...let me try to help. I am *not* your enemy. I want the Constantin line to carry on. I want the work Alexander and I dedicated years toward to bear fruit. I am on your side. And I like her. Very much."

Tristan snickered, "You're wrong. You *are* my enemy. The only reason I'm keepin' you alive right now is in case you're of use to me. But my patience is running thin."

He turned his back on Adrian and went back inside.

She was still in front of the window.

"Did you go out? Did he come in?" Tristan demanded.

She shook her head and then said, "No."

"What was he doing?" He poured a coffee from the pot, which she'd obviously made. If there was one thing his girl couldn't do without, it was her coffee. Clearly that transcended being in the midst of her own zombie land. She hadn't poured any for herself, so he poured her a cup.

After a beat she said softly but without emotion, "Staring at me with a sad face."

"What do you see when *I* stare at you? Do I look sad?" He approached her and looked into her eyes. She met his gaze. It wasn't lucid, but she was searching his face, almost dazed, or drugged-looking, but clearly she was attempting to read and interpret.

"Hurt. Or mad."

"When you said you were hurt were you feeling hurt or were you hurting with body pain?"

"Yes."

"Both?"

She blinked at him.

"Are you hurt right now?"

"Um... yes?"

"Why were you shaking and scratching?"

A long pause.

"Hurts."

This was useless.

"Stay here."

He left the kitchen in a state of exasperation. He stepped outside to assess Leonard and Jeff's states of mind and to program the right sorts of results if things went wrong or if Adrian approached again.

THAT NIGHT SHE WOKE up screaming and crying while scratching again.

"Lemme out!" He heard her cry.

He'd been downstairs, in the midst of drafting an email to Brandt after having checked her a few moments earlier and seeing that she appeared restless, like she was dreaming, but he didn't know what to do for her, so he'd just gone back downstairs. Now, at her sounds of despair, he had immediately run up and reached for her and pulled her tight against him, "Out of where?"

She whimpered.

"Shhh, baby. It's okay."

"Okay, Tristan." But she hadn't stopped scratching and shaking.

"Kyla, it's okay." He rocked her back and forth.

"No," she whimpered, "Can't stop..." she was scratching hard and he could smell her blood.

"No," she cried out.

She felt hot; she had a fever.

He put his lips to her forehead, "Shit, you're burning up, princess."

"Princess," she started sobbing hard, looking like she was in intense pain and like the nickname had some sort of affect.

What the fuck? Does she comprehend me?

"What can I do?"

She kept sobbing into his chest, "It hurts. Get me out!"

"What hurts?"

"Me."

"Fuck. Kyla, I don't know what to do!"

He wanted to spit nails, smash something, wanted to fuck off away from this madness with her, take her somewhere safe, take her back to when she was safe. He was close to his breaking point.

"Try to sleep, baby, please," He told her through clenched teeth because he didn't know what else to do.

She kept jerking in his arms and she was getting hotter. He caught a few winks here and there but was too worried about her to catch any real sleep. By dawn she felt even hotter. He'd tried to help by wiping her body down with a cool cloth, but it didn't work so he'd taken her into a tepid bath and sat with her, holding her. She'd been trembling even harder and started scratching her legs, so he'd taken her back to bed, fed her Advil, and held her some more, holding her hands so she couldn't scratch. The medicine wasn't helping. She was like a fireplace.

He spied the phone on the nightstand, so he finally let out a breath and lifted it, feeling more helpless and hopeless despair than he'd ever felt in his life. He pressed zero and was answered by one of Adrian's minions who transferred him.

"Tristan?"

"She's been burning up all night. Having seizures or something. Worse than the previous two nights and her fever is at least 103. Advil, cool bath, nothing's helping."

"I'm coming."

"No! Just tell me how I can help her."

"T-t-take it..." she breathed. Goosebumps rose on him.

Take it? What the fuck did that mean?

"Have you fed from her, checked her blood?" He asked.

"No."

"Try. If it doesn't work you'll have to let me take vitals, do blood-work and see if I can figure out what this is."

"Right."

He didn't fucking like it.

"Keep me posted?"

He hung up without responding.

She was asleep, plastered against him, but shivering and burning up.

He pried her off, sat on the edge of the bed, and shifted her damp hair off her neck. He could see her pulse in her neck and sensation transcended into him. He envisaged her blood pumping through her, as if it was pumping through him.

Even if he hated how she tasted, he had to do it to try to help her, see if feeding could take these withdrawal-like symptoms away.

He leaned over and ran his nose along her throat. It hurt to do that, to do something so familiar with her, but something that meant so much to him.

He leaned in and his fangs elongated. He braced as he pierced her throat and felt the liquid surge into his mouth. Her body stiffened. It washed over him, how she tasted, and he was as surprised as the first night he'd tasted her. She tasted like nectar.

Not just her blood but it tasted like that other blood, her nectar, but maybe even better. It was a taste that he hadn't been aware of until now, other than when he found it on his face the day she took off on him. The knowledge of this flavour, it'd been there, under the surface for him, because he'd been blacking out when he'd tasted it before, but it slammed into conscious awareness now that it was just like that other blood.

Fuck.

Euphoria swept through every inch of him as her beautiful sweet ambrosia blood flooded his mouth and went down his throat.

And then POW!

His eyes went wide as he felt her emotions rush into him with the force of a levy breaking. Pain, fear, loss. She was lost. She was in a barren wasteland and she was groggy, disoriented, confused, in intense fucking pain.

She needed something. She needed something, but he didn't know what it was and she needed it desperately.

He let go of her throat; he had to. The emotions coming at him were so fucking intense!

He swallowed what was in his mouth. He put his hand on her face. Her face was already considerably cooler. She closed her eyes, blowing out breath rapidly over and over, winded.

She's in there.

Elation flooded him.

"You're in there."

He put his teeth on her again and took another small amount and for another split second, he felt her, felt more of the same. He released her throat from his mouth and looked to see she was empty-eyed.

"Come back, princess," he pleaded and then his fangs retracted.

He put his mouth to hers and kissed her passionately. She didn't respond.

He let out a pained moan and collapsed half on top of her.

A split second later he was off her, so he wouldn't crush her, and looking down. He felt better than he had in days, maybe weeks; maybe ever. In a physical way, anyway.

He felt like he could run marathons, climb mountains, conquer. He felt strong. He looked at how listless she was. He'd taken all she could give right now. She needed to recover. But he was so fucking relieved because she was in there, somewhere deep, but she was there.

He felt something else rising with his inner strength, inner strength that felt like it rose in him, like it was rising because Kyla's blood made him emerge into who he was meant to be. And besides that, something else that was rising was his wrath. He was ready to fucking kill. It wouldn't wait. There were vampires that needed to pay and at least one of them would pay right the fuck now.

He stood and spied his phone on top of the dresser. He caught a glimpse of his reflection in the mirror over that dresser and as he moved closer to get a better look he saw that his eyes were black, his skin was grey, and the whites of his eyes had broken blood vessels in them. He snarled at his own reflection and then reached for his phone.

He phoned Sam, who he could tell he'd woken.

"Get here. Now."

"Yeah, brother. Right there."

Sam was accustomed to middle-of-the-night requests. He had explained to Tristan, before things went wrong, that he'd been appointed his concierge specifically because of Sam's bloodline.

Tristan was the third royal Sam had played the role to. When royals who were in succession for an important role hit their 25th birthday, they were first turned and soon after they did a little stint with another royal in a mentor/protégée role, they were assigned a right hand man, someone who played a role of concierge, a guardian, someone to teach, to provide for, to protect, as well as to report back to other senior leaders on personality, shortcomings, strengths.

When royals hit their 35th human birthday, that's when they typically got their enchanted blooded pet. Their concierge stayed with them about five additional years, some permanently.

Sam had said he came from a specific line of vamps that made ideal concierges due to their talents and that was his explanation for his behaviour. Tristan had accepted this, knowing that royals often were appointed to specific positions based on their bloodline because of specific strengths that bloodline would generally suggest.

He said he'd had allegiance to Tristan all along but said he'd been merely doing what he had been trained to do, what he'd been bred to do, balance on a tightrope between serving the vamp he was assigned to and reporting to higher-ups. Before the lab, Tristan had accepted this, not blindly, but whatever Sam had yammered on about had placated him.

Sam said that he had no idea that things would be *this* different this assignment, the anomaly being Kyla's lack of mesmerization and the addition of the extra close eyes on their situation.

Tristan wasn't following Sam's word blindly. Not now. He was not ever going to follow anything blindly again, especially when it could put Kyla in jeopardy. He now knew that Sam had been supernaturally influencing him over the years. Sam had nudged things as his right-hand man, he'd had ample opportunity to influence Tristan. Sam had often weighed in on issues and he'd weighed in on handling the Kyla situation repeatedly, leading up to the attempt at turning her.

Tristan knew that Sam was someone he needed right now. Instinctively, he felt it. Being able to influence him would certainly help matters. So would being able to read intentions and he felt like that was a skill that had sharpened significantly.

He knew he wouldn't be susceptible to Sam's nudges any longer. He could feel things changing in him. Her blood was changing him yet again or maybe even further. Maybe each feed wasn't a change, it was more like part of an ongoing evolution, but it didn't feel like he was gaining new things, rather that barriers were being peeled away so that he'd become whole, become who he was meant to be.

Tristan felt less and less disconnected from himself each day. The monster, the grey hulk that Kyla had been afraid of wasn't to be feared any longer. Not for Kyla, anyway. Only for anyone who put her in jeopardy.

Now the only thing left for him to feel whole again was to get her back. And keep her safe for good.

3

SAM AND TRISTAN WERE in the living room of the cottage.

"Liam Donavan. Where is he?"

"Liam is in a holding cell off the hall where Adrian's lab is. Get him?"

"Bring Adrian, too."

"Tris, you're not gonna..." Sam looked concerned.

"Now. I'll leave the front door open. Quick."

"If you give him any reason to dagger you then she is out of your control. Now, I know you don't want *that.* As I said before things went awry, should anything else ever happen to you, you have my word, my vow, that I'll care for her until you're back or you're conscious but—-"

"Get him. Leave the dagger in Liam. I'm the one to remove it. Don't let anyone stop you." He'd said this as he looked deep into Sam's eyes.

Adrian's dagger wouldn't matter because he'd pull Kyla's dagger out of Liam and then he'd be as armed as Adrian.

Sam gave a chin jerk and left.

Tristan ran up the stairs and checked on her. She was asleep, and her temperature felt normal. He looked at her throat. His teeth marks were gone. Fuck, she'd healed already.

"Kyla?"

She opened her eyes and they focused on his shirt. She reached out and grabbed the wine-coloured material and started trembling.

"Kyla?"

She looked up at him, eyes roving his face, blinking rapidly, but not letting go of his shirt. He looked down at it. Was she regaining lucidity?

"Princess? You with me?"

Please. Fuck, please.

"C-c-cold."

Nope. Fuck.

He pulled the covers over her. Her teeth chattered.

His heart sank as he held her for a minute, stroking her hair, his eyes closed. She buried her face into his neck and began sobbing. It fucking killed, pulled hard at his heart because it felt like she was responding to him. Her nose was in the crook of his throat and she was shaking and crying. He wished he could feel her inside.

He heard the front door.

"I'll be back, baby." He hated to let go of her.

She continued to cling to him for a minute and then she began scratching at her arms. He let go and tipped her chin up to meet her eyes.

"Sleep, princess. Just have a little nap. Don't scratch."

She stopped scratching.

He kissed her forehead, "Good girl," and left her, closing the door tight, before heading down the stairs.

He willed the door unlocked on his way down and then spotted Sam and Adrian as well as an unconscious-looking Liam over Sam's shoulder. Liam was dropped on the floor, dagger still planted in his back from when Kyla had put it there. Constantin came to a stop beside him.

Tristan strode to them and it immediately hit him that Kyla's grandfather smelled like fear.

"How is she?" Adrian asked while taking a step back.

Tristan raised his index finger to signal *one sec*, reached over, yanked the dagger out of Liam's back and immediately plunged it into Adrian's chest before Adrian had a chance to react. Tristan then leaned over and retrieved the other dagger from the sheath attached to Adrian's belt.

"Fuck, Tris..." Sam reacted, "You're lightning fast, man. And you're pretty fucking close to his heart."

"Back up and shut the fuck up," Tristan clipped, looking Sam right in the eye, resulting in Sam following those orders instantly.

He stood over Liam, chest rising and falling rapidly, as he waited for the motherfucker to wake up. The rage burned and churned in him and then as the blond vamp came to, Tristan felt cold descend over his skin like a blanket of frost.

Liam's bloodshot eyes were brimming with fear. He looked groggy; the first few minutes after waking from being daggered were like that and Tristan knew that he'd felt weak from recovering, knew that waking after being daggered for a few days didn't just leave a vamp weak, they left a vamp depleted due to hunger. There'd be nausea, too. But Liam wasn't just coming to, Liam knew he was done.

Done, *done*.

Tristan's rage took over; he felt the change in himself. The chill crept deeper into his veins, over his bones, and rose up in his gut and then he quickly reached into Liam's mouth, pressing onto his gums until his fangs dropped and then Tristan punched him in the mouth, full force. The vamp spat his left incisor and two other non-canine teeth out and let out a sob. Tristan then reached, lightning fast, into Liam's gut, feeling the flesh split, feeling the vamp's panic bubble up and over. As he gripped, he twisted 180 degrees and then let go, gripped again, and did the other 180 degrees but held on.

He got an inch away from Liam's face, looked right into his eyes, then said in a low growl, "You'll bleed out before I rip your head off. You will bleed out in case you've still got even a drop of her blood inside you. You don't die until you're completely empty. Burn in hell." And then he yanked and watched, chest rising and falling, his eyes stone cold, until he saw that the vamp had bled nearly all out and was barely there. He then flicked the handful of flesh and whatever-the-fuck from his guts onto the bastard's face before his fingers gripped then separated his head from his neck.

He pulled the dagger from Adrian and held both jewel-handled knives in midair, looking over Adrian Constantin while waiting for him to wake. When that fucker's eyes opened he took in the grisly scene of Liam Donavan's headless body on the floor in a large pool of blood, the head torn off and insides all over his face while his guts were still attached to his body.

Adrian's eyes moved to see that Tristan had both the smaller dagger that'd been made for Kyla as well as his own and shook his head, pleading, "Don't kill me. You need me. I have information that *might* help you get her nectar back."

Tristan's eyes narrowed, "I have it. It's back. I don't need this steel to stop you. I could kill you a lot of different ways, man."

Adrian raised one eyebrow, "It's back?"

Adrian looked beyond Sam, who was standing, quietly. Tristan glanced over his shoulder and then looked up and saw Kyla, hands on the banister, looking down at them. She started to descend the stairs.

"Stop, Kyla," Tristan ordered.

She stopped. Her eyes appeared to be on the grisly scene on the floor.

He felt a little sick. Had she seen and comprehended what he'd just done? He didn't show a reaction. Neither did she. She must not have absorbed it.

"You need something, Kyla?"

She looked pale. Really pale.

"Thirsty."

"There's water in the bedroom on the dresser. Did you see it?"

"Grape," she said dazedly.

He almost smiled. Almost.

"I'll find you some. Wait in bed for me, baby."

"Okay, Tristan."

She turned and slowly walked back up.

"I *can* be useful to you. What do you want? What'll convince you to let me live?" Adrian asked, and Tristan's gaze swung back to him.

"I want her back," he growled, "With her essence, with everything that made her Kyla. Can you give me that? Unless you can give me that, I say you deserve to die the same death as him." Tristan's gaze moved to the massacre on the floor.

"I have a cocktail that might help a little and I can assemble a team to program her—-"

Tristan ignored that asinine comment, "Actually, no. Uh uh. You deserve worse. He did what he did because he was driven by urges after tasting enchanted blood. You're much more dangerous and evil than that. Maybe I'll punish you for a whole lot longer before I end *you*."

Adrian swallowed hard, looking shaky. "I might be able to help, no guarantees, but..."

"You're of no use to me..."

"I am! I have information. It's not a guarantee but it's ... it's possible. And I could have her worked on so that we can get her functional maybe..."

"Talk. Fuck functional. That's not good enough."

"Can I at least get off the floor, Tristan?" Adrian looked him in the eye and his expression, his words, they were laced with venom.

Tristan's eyes narrowed at him and won the stare down, then turned his attention to Sam's s eyes.

"Get him up. Watch him. Don't let him leave." He passed Sam Adrian's dagger, "You don't use one of these on me. Ever. Neither do you, Constantin; not that you'll ever get the opportunity."

Sam nodded. Adrian nodded.

Tristan went to the kitchen and washed his hands thoroughly in the sink. Liam's blood would get nowhere near Kyla, so he scrubbed as meticulously as a surgeon heading into surgery would. He opened the refrigerator door and assessed the contents. The fridge was well-stocked but there were no grape-flavoured soft drinks. He moved a bottle of ginger ale aside to get to a bottle of Coke. He poured a glass of it and carried it up to her, passing them along the way, saying, "Put that mess outside.," he climbed the stairs, "Let Jeff and Leonard take care of it. No one else steps inside. No one climbs these stairs."

"Roger, that," Sam said from the sofa where he and Adrian had been in conversation.

She was sitting in bed, a bottle of water in her hand.

"No grape, princess. I have Coke. You want Coke?"

He waited what seemed like forever for her to answer. He put the smaller dagger under the pillow her head was on.

"No," she said softly, finally. She looked weak. Dangerously weak.

He passed her the glass. "Try it." He sat beside her as she drank, then put his lips to her forehead. Her temperature was fine, but her colouring was wrong. So pale.

"How ya feelin'?" He caressed her face.

"Fuzzy?" she asked instead of answered after a few beats and put the three quarters full glass on the table beside the bed. She did it a little shakily and the glass was precariously on edge. He leaned over to her to move it back, resulting in her leaning into him.

His chest burned. He reached and lifted her legs and swung them into the bed and pulled her close. She burrowed into him and he took a big breath and basked in it.

"You're hurt?" she asked.

"No, baby, I'm okay," His heart twinged.

He heard the front door open and close. He wanted to stay with her but had to deal with shit downstairs, so he tucked her under the blankets.

"Stay up here. If you need me, call my name."

"Tristan."

"Yeah, baby." He felt that. It was musical the way she said his name. He closed his eyes and felt it deep and then kissed her lips.

She blinked at him, her eyes bloodshot.

"Tristan," she repeated.

"Yeah?"

She just lay there.

"I'll make you some food in a bit and bring it up. Hungry?" He caressed her face with the back of his hand.

She shook her head.

"Okay, but will you try for me? You need to replenish your strength."

He wanted her strong. And he wanted to feed and feel her again. As soon as possible.

She nodded and took what looked like a painful swallow.

He kissed her forehead, "Rest, baby. I'll bring you food soon. Stay here until I come back." He headed back downstairs.

Sam was mopping the floor. All traces of Liam Donavan were gone. Adrian Constantin was on the sofa, watching Sam, expression grim.

"Talk," Tristan said to Constantin while pouring a glass of whiskey.

"She's not lucid but she tastes like nectar? I'd like one of those." Adrian jerked his chin at the bottle of booze.

"I didn't say ask. I said talk. And I didn't offer you any."

"I'll talk, but I'm just surprised. The more I know, the more I can potentially help."

Tristan swallowed the equivalent of probably about 3 shots of whiskey by tossing the contents of his half-full glass down his throat.

"She's worse than 'not lucid'. She's a space cadet, zombie. She has her motor skills, but she's dazed, zoned out, slow responses. She was burning up and I tried feeding and it tasted not just like her but like her nectar. Her fever finally broke after I fed but she's still off. Off beyond the zombie thing. Uncomfortable; in pain. Now talk. Tell me why I shouldn't end you right here, right now."

"This information... it's..." Adrian looked to Sam and then back to Tristan and said, "Why don't you make yourself comfortable?"

Tristan folded his arms across his chest and glared.

"Indulge me. Please. Could I have a drink? You know, of the booze *I* supplied to you while hosting you on *my* property?"

Tristan snickered.

Constantin let out a huff of impatience, trying to act superior, but Tristan knew how freaked the asshole was.

Tristan sat on the edge of the coffee table in front of him. He felt serious anxiety waves rolling off Sam. He looked at him and jerked his chin toward the bottle of booze. Sam's face was impassive, but Tristan could feel the tension. Sam moved to the booze and poured a glass for Adrian and then one for himself.

"Spit it out," Tristan said.

"You're reading and programming Samuel. And myself?"

Tristan glanced at Sam again. Sam shrugged and then said "I'm aware. I'm on your side, Tris. Mesmerize away..."

"It's new," Tristan admitted.

"Since you fed today?" Adrian asked.

"No," Tristan answered.

"He nudged hard yesterday, too," Sam said, "And I now have no influence over him."

Adrian's brows shot up in surprise.

"None," Tristan confirmed.

Tristan glared at Sam and understanding passed between them. Sam pretty much admitted he'd been working Tristan. Maybe not blatantly, full out, but Tristan knew for certain that Sam had been subtly working Tristan all this time. It wasn't the same as mesmerizing, not as hypnotic, but it was a charisma some vamps used to their advantage on other vamps. Tristan now knew he had the ability to do it, with Adrian, even, and it wasn't easy for younger vamps, royal or not, to influence elders.

"What else is new? Anything since feeding from her today?"

"You'll get no more information from me, Constantin. You start giving *me* information. Now."

Adrian shrugged, "The scientist in me. I'd really like to assess how different her blood composition is."

"Talk," he said, through clenched teeth, "For the last time. I lost patience with you and your bullshit a long time ago, so I suggest you start fuckin' talking."

Adrian took a big breath, "The way I think I can help is through her brother."

Tristan did a double take.

"Her brother?"

"She has a twin. We'll need to find him. And perhaps Samuel can help with that. Find him for me, Samuel, and I might be able to help."

Sam let out a big breath and then muttered, "Fuck me."

The panic ceased coming from Sam. The guy was now resigned; it was like he knew this was coming and now that it had, he was just resigned to whatever it was. Sam downed the last swallow of his drink and poured another.

"How does Sam help?" Tristan tilted his head at Adrian and felt anger rising at Sam. More secrets?

"Sam, too, is a twin. He and his sister were products of another breeding program. True vamp, as you know, and a very specific bloodline. Lower level royals. Many in Samuel's bloodline have been used extensively as concierges to royals. All royal vamps are assigned a concierge chosen from specific blood lines that tend to be highly protective, strong, and very intelligent vampires with protective instincts..."

"I'm aware," Tristan interrupted impatiently.

Adrian nodded and continued, "He's aware of your programming, can't stop it, but unlike most, he is aware. He has some distinct abilities, problem-solving skills, physical strength, influence, the ability to wipe memories. This twin split is generally divided between what becomes a concierge and a breeder female vamp. Few female vamps are able to breed but this line has been resulting in virile twins, both genders. Sam's twin, she wasn't successfully bred. She was barren, but she was *so* precocious, such intelligence, that I chose to make her my protégé and was investigating ways to give her the full strengths of her vampire DNA without losing her 'essence' as you'd call it. When Samuel was turned, Samantha was not. I couldn't find a way and she began to age, began to become impatient. Things went wrong."

"Shocker," Tristan mumbled.

This vampire royalty hierarchy was a fucking caste system, for fuck sakes.

Constantin blathered on, "She wasn't happy. Things were different with her after that. She was resentful. We looked for solutions, but she ran out of patience and two years ago she had herself turned, against my wishes, and as you know, female vampires are unruly, true and royal vamps particularly so."

"Get to the fucking point," Tristan rolled his hand forward.

"Samuel had turned Jackson, Kyla's boyfriend, when he was brought here brain dead and Samantha was in charge of caring for him. Once he recuperated, given that he was newly vamp she wasn't mesmerized so she was able to convince him to turn her. We had a tough time with her for a time but then she vanished and with her, she took Kyla's brother. She knew his blood was enchanted and I suspect that she's used him as her pet all this time. If he's alive and unturned we could possibly do a blood transfusion, play with DNA, perhaps. Test some options to see if we can bring her back. His and Kyla's genetic make-up are very close, or was the last time I tested. When Kyla was abducted we had Kyle taken and wiped Katya and Lyle's memories at that point. He was raised here and sequestered until Samantha took him. I had tests planned for them both for when Kyla would've hit puberty, but I didn't have access to her so had very little knowledge of the way things would be split DNA-wise."

Constantin went quiet for a moment while Tristan moved around the room, in contemplation.

"Samuel and his sister share a link, as all twins do. Royal twins often have a supernatural link and they are driven to reunite when separated and often have tracking skills once they're turned. Perhaps he can help us find her. If she still has Kyla's twin, maybe something can be done."

Tristan looked at Sam and felt frustration and something else, perhaps trepidation, coming off him, coming off in waves.

"Sam and Samantha. Kyla and Kyle? Fuckin' ridiculous," Tristan said.

"Kyla also has other siblings, triplets, female, twenty-one years old. Two are still alive and they're with Katya. They're already turned so I highly doubt they'd be of assistance."

"So females with Kyla's exact lineage were turned?"

"Two. Yes. The third died in childbirth last year. She was never turned, but the child could be helpful. Not as likely as Kyle but..."

Tristan raised his hand to silence him, pushing down emotion that threatened to show itself at that news, "So there's no reason why Kyla shouldn't have turned?"

"Nothing I've been able to isolate. The triplets' blood composition was enchanted but not as strong, plus being triplets rather than twins, it wasn't as concentrated. They've all had their uses. The first-born of the triplets had the most vampire DNA; as is the usual. But I performed many experiments on Kyle before Samantha took him and he was not only mesmerized but it seems that Kyla's vampire genes were somehow stronger. She was the smaller of the two babies, born second, but she took more vampire genes than her brother and that could be the key to a lot of the mysteries surrounding her. He's got strong vampire traits. She's much stronger. In most male-female twin sets the male is more dominantly vampire even before turning, but that didn't happen here. I had planned to continue sampling and comparing them throughout their lives but as you know, Kyla vanished. And then Kyle was taken soon after Kyla was discovered. I suspect Samantha joined the militia that was responsible for moving Kyla before we could bring her in. So you can see even further why I've been so enamored with the science where Kyla is concerned. She's different. Her differences have fascinated me since her birth."

Tristan took a big breath, "You don't know where Samantha Jasper is?"

"No," Adrian replied, "As I said, I believe she's part of that militia, but I don't have proof and they've been elusive. Samuel here, hasn't been real cooperative. I haven't pushed hard, mind you. Twin allegiances are usually unbreakable, so I knew that'd be fruitless. Until now. *You* have the capability to break it."

Tristan looked deep into his eyes. "You're telling me the truth?"

"Yes."

He sensed no lies and knew that he had the ability to influence Adrian Constantin, too. Adrian clearly knew it too, felt it. Adrian's heartrate spiked, and he shook his head, "You're the most, *the most*, powerful vampire I've encountered. Even your mother can't come near to influencing me. Yet you can influence a vamp over a hundred years older than you are. You got the double dose of vampire DNA that should've been split with a twin. Most royal vamps nowadays are twins or triplets, so I believe you should have been a twin. But with you, there was no twin born, so we believe you absorbed all of it. Add that to the bloodline you come from and it's incredible. The feed you took from Kyla since the nectar returned? I can sense it has done even more to strengthen you. It's very promising that her blood has regenerated. I want to help you. Please. Let me help you. It would thrill me to see you at your full potential. Her as well. I need to help you breed with her, to see the results of—-"

Tristan reached toward Sam with an outstretched hand and Sam handed him the dagger. Tristan then fluidly thrust the steel of it into Adrian's gut, making him flop off the sofa onto the floor, face first.

Sam let out a chuckle, "Had enough of his verbal diarrhea?"

"More than enough." Tristan turned to Sam.

"You know where your sister is?" Tristan looked deep.

Sam nodded and jerked his chin toward the kitchen. Tristan followed him.

"I do," Sam replied, "I don't want him to hear."

Tristan knew that a daggered 'out' vamp could hear everything going on around him from his own time daggered.

"Is Kyla's brother alive?"

"He is."

"Is he vampire?"

"He is not."

"Was this the idea you had?"

"It was. I don't know if it'll work. Sasha trained under Adrian for years. She's a genius, an awkward slightly scatter-brained genius but a genius nonetheless. She gives Adrian a run for his money; she may know how to help, and I knew of Kyla's brother so thought he might be part of this puzzle. I'd have said she may be able to do whatever it is that he could do so you wouldn't have to be susceptible to his potential deception, but it seems with your newfound powers he couldn't deceive you anyway."

"Sasha?"

Sam shrugged, "Apparently an adorable mispronunciation of mine as a tot. It stuck. Better than Boy Sam and Girl Sam. Only Adrian still calls her Samantha and because of that, she detests it."

"Where is she?"

"I'll take you to her. Let me go see her first, please? I'll need to smooth things out. I haven't seen her since shortly after she turned, just before she left. We've spoken on the phone a few times; that's it. She knew I was your concierge and she reached out to me after your last birthday. She knew you'd have Kyla, knew that she was your intended, and knew why, and she's interested in discussing her. I've been avoiding her due to the fact that I'd be in a position where I'd have to choose. But I'm fairly sure she'd help you."

"Why would she help me?"

"She has a connection with Kyle, with them both. Trust me, she'll want to help. She may want something in return, but you've got all the power, Tris."

"Road trip then. You see her first, you can enlighten her, but I'll be close, and I need to suss things out before I let her near Kyla. You don't let her out of your sight until I get an opportunity to assess her and influence her, ensure she doesn't put things at a bigger risk."

"You can trust me, Tristan. Her as well."

That remained to be seen.

"Trust Kyla near a royal vampress? Right." Tristan rolled his eyes.

Sam let out a big breath, "I have no choice but to tell you this, I know you'll extract it from me whether I want to give it to you or not, but I have to tell you, this is top secret. My sister trusts me and while I'm not a double agent of any sort, I'm aware of secrets on both sides of the coin between powerful vamps such as Adrian, Brandt, and others as well as aware of some facts to do with the group Sasha is involved with."

"Give it to me."

"Kyle Kelly's blood. It makes Sasha even."

"Even?"

"Flips off the bitch switch. She's not like other female vamps. When she was un-turned, studying under Adrian, Adrian gave her some sort of cocktail and heavy programming to keep her above functional. Though some elders and blue bloods *could* program her and she was heavily influenced she was still very much an individual when she wasn't around him and she worked alone a lot, retained her memories. She had the free will to want and what she wanted was to be at her full potential as vampire. She couldn't fathom that she'd be evil; like other females we know. They never seem to think it'll happen to them, right?" He shook his head. "When she was first turned, she was hell on wheels. Fuck, she was one of the worst I've seen. But his blood... you can believe it based on having his twin's blood and seeing that for yourself. She's herself. Kyle is protected because his blood has literally erased the typical female vamp effect. She's vampire but she's a lot like her former self. She has empathy. She is again like she was before she was turned. It's like the evil was erased. She experienced reverse aging as well. She was aging as human, not having been turned in her 20's, but soon after she was turned she tasted Kyle's enchanted blood and the reversal of the female vamp effect started to happen. She experienced similar age reversal to your mother."

Feeding from Kyla gave *him* a conscience. Something about being with Kyla made him want to be better. Hope rose at the belief that her sibling's blood could have a strong effect on female vamps. Kyla's blood had done nothing to Taryn. Taryn was as evil as ever. Adrian said the make-up between twins wasn't necessarily identical, but could it be close enough to get Kyla's essence back?

"She'll be very protective of him," Sam said.

Tristan exhaled hard and nodded. "Get in touch. Talk to her about me, about Kyla. Do it in person only and tell her everything but ensure she tells no one. I want to be on the road tomorrow. Where are they?"

"An island off the pacific coast. We can get there by boat or flight from Washington. What about him?" Sam gestured to the direction of the room the daggered Adrian was in.

"Chuck 'em in the closet back there for tonight," he gestured over his shoulder with his chin, "I don't wanna look at his face, but I want him close. He's comin' with us. Where's Taryn?"

"She left after you told her to go."

"Find out if she's up to anything. Have her watched. Get Hunter on the job. He's not so easy for her to trace. And dig to see if you can find out if anything is happening here that Constantin's needed for within the next week. Assemble his team for me here in thirty minutes, so I can question them and then tell them how to handle his absence."

"Got it." Sam went and fetched Adrian, hefted him over his shoulder and moved toward the dining room.

TRISTAN CHECKED ON Kyla. She was asleep. Her skin was pale, and she was twitching, restless, as if she was having a bad dream. He put his hand on her face. She stilled.

"Wake up, little cherry bomb."

He kissed her eyelids one after the other and ran his hand up her arm.

She opened her eyes. They were bright sparkling green, but the whites of her eyes looked pinkish. She had dark circles under her eyes. He really wished he had the ability to use his diagnostic skills with her, so he'd know what the fuck was going on with her.

He wasn't sensing a thing; it was bewildering after having the ability to feel medical conditions from any ill person he met. All he had to do for some was be near them and certain conditions were emitted like radio waves he could easily decipher. In other circumstances he recognized illnesses by scent, much like a chef recognizes aromas for what food they represent. The taste of blood had always been very telling as well. Tristan's pre-vamp life as a chef may have contributed to giving him very attuned scenting and tasting abilities. Or perhaps that inherent talent in him was what made him seek out his career in the culinary arts before he'd been turned.

Those talents were failing him now, now when he really, *really* needed them.

"Princess, I've put a dagger under the mattress here, right by your pillow, okay? If any vamp but me comes in here and gets near you, you plunge it into them and leave it there. Except Sam. Unless you feel threatened by him. Okay, baby?"

She nodded.

Would she even comprehend a threat? He had no idea. He caressed her cheek with his palm,

"I love you. If you're in there and you can comprehend this, I'm working on things. Don't give up. I'm gonna do everything I can do to bring you back to me, okay? I've got what might be good news. I'm tryin', baby. I'm trying so hard to get you back."

She nodded solemnly. "Grape." it was a plea.

"I'll find you some grape." He kissed her lips and caressed her face.

THAT EVENING HE COULD barely get her to eat. She was even weaker, even more lethargic. He spoon-fed her some chicken stew and a bit of buttered bread and he'd gotten someone to track down some grape pop and she'd had a few mouthfuls but it didn't seem to do anything to boost her spirits.

"Does that taste good?" he'd asked.

She'd nodded and moistened her lips with her tongue but only had a second mouthful at his urging.

"Where's the dagger, baby?"

She blinked.

"The dagger, Kyla?"

"Under the mattress."

"Good girl, take another bite of bread."

"Liam's back," she muttered.

"He's not back." Tristan was tweaked.

"Dagger in his back."

"Not anymore, princess. Liam's gone. He won't hurt you again."

"Okay, Tristan."

He hoped she wouldn't have anyone close enough to have to need it but felt marginal comfort knowing she'd comprehended those directions.

The meeting with the compound employees had gone off without a hitch. He'd influenced them all to believe Adrian had gotten called away on an urgent out-of-town meeting and then he'd gotten an update from each of them. Nothing particularly nefarious had been happening beyond regular business and none of them had a clue about any experiments with Kyla so Adrian had been heading that project up without any assistance, of anyone here, at least.

Tristan's assistant, back home, was making flight arrangements to get them to Seattle and doing it quietly. Then they'd board a boat to take them to the nearby island Sasha was on. Sam said he had had spoken to his sister briefly to say that he wanted to meet and she was expecting him but didn't know yet that Tristan and Kyla would be nearby.

He was hungry for a feed. But more than nourishment, he was hungry to feel her. He had complete control over cravings, this wasn't about her blood nearly as much as it was about their connection and his desire to feel her and try to wade through her confusion to find out what she needed to make her feel well.

The fact that she tasted like what he wanted and needed was amazing but strange. He needed to feel her and see if he could figure anything out but with how weak and ill she seemed he didn't want to lose control and put her at even further risk.

Her scent came back; her blood came back. How could he get the rest of her to come back?

He climbed into bed with her that night and she wasn't looking any better; in fact, maybe a little worse. He pulled her close and put his nose and mouth to her throat. He felt her pulse move against his lips. When he sank in he braced and was hit with a tidal wave of her emotions, which were exactly the same as earlier that day. She was lost, confused, and in extreme pain.

She didn't go lax.

Her hands reached up and were in his hair an instant after he started to feed. His chest burned with emotion at feeling that response from her. He wanted to devour her, to feel her everywhere forever. Love burst through him and he hoped she could feel it the way she'd always felt him when he fed. Before everything went wrong she'd started to feel him whenever they were in close proximity.

"Can you feel me?" he asked, letting go of her throat and sealing it with a kiss.

She started writhing underneath him, as if she wanted him. He looked at her face. The emotions coming at him evaporated and her eyes were just blank but now his hips had fallen between her widened legs and his cock was pressed right against the triangle of her silky little pink panties. The writhing under him had woken his cock up.

The t-shirt she wore had ridden up and her bare stomach was under him. He ran his hand across it. He felt heat coming from her body, all over, extra heat between her legs.

Without even calculating the move, he grinded against her. Her lips parted and then her ankles were hooked around his thighs. Her hands were still in his hair. But her eyes were still blank.

He reached down and dipped a finger into her panties and fuck; she was wet for him. She closed her eyes, seeming to absorb his touch.

This isn't right. Is this right? Do I take her? Or would she think I was a filthy pig for it?

"If they're hypnotized it's not consensual, you asshole!"

That's what she'd said to him the first night, the night she was given to him, the night he'd first started falling, falling for her and falling, no plummeting, into who she was helping him become.

A man who wanted to be worthy of love.

A man who'd failed at becoming that but who would fucking try so fucking hard to be worthy, to keep her safe, if only he could have her back.

Her hips bucked against his hand in her panties and she closed her eyes and rotated her pelvis.

He pulled his hand away.

She arched her pelvis further, seeking it.

He backed off her and sat on the edge of the bed.

He felt her juices on his finger, his finger was tingling. He couldn't help it; he put his finger to his tongue and groaned. She tasted like herself, too.

That taste brought him back to the very first night, the first time he'd tasted her. He'd never tasted anything like her. Truth be told, he rarely went down on a woman since becoming vampire, and it'd probably only happened with female vamps, since they were a whole lot more present than the typical human female, but the minute he caught her scent he'd been drooling. She was appetizing from head to toe.

He wanted to fuck her with his tongue, wanted it bad.

If he gave her pleasure, instead of taking pleasure from her, would that make him a filthy pig?

He couldn't help it. He wanted, no needed, to know if he could make her come.

"Forgive me, princess, but I need to try."

He leaned forward and grabbed both her feet at the arches and pulled her down toward him. Her tee slid all the way up to her armpits, exposing her breasts. He kissed each perfect pink nipple and looked to her face. Her cheeks were a rosy shade of pink. Not pale. Pink. Flushed.

She was looking at the ceiling and chewing her bottom lip.

"Kyla?" he called out and her eyes moved to his face and then she blinked a couple of times and he knew she was definitely still in lala land. Despite being out of it she was turned on.

"Close your eyes, princess. Just feel me."

She closed her eyes and he trailed kisses toward her pelvis. He hooked his thumbs into her panties at the hips and pulled them down and off and buried his tongue in her silky wetness.

She tasted so fucking good. She was like sweet hot silk and the sound of her breath quickening, it alone had the power to undo him.

He lifted her legs over his shoulders and made love to her sweet pussy with his mouth, his hands running up and down her thighs, her hips, up to the underside of her breasts.

In only seconds she was panting. Eyes closed, arms over her head limp, and her hair fanned out over the pillow.

"You're fucking beautiful, princess," he told her and then flattened his tongue over her clit and then sucked hard as he rolled his tongue up and flicked it, then rammed it inside.

She let out a scream and came, hard. Her legs were shaking, her mouth was wide, and she had goosebumps everywhere, and he felt her pussy convulsing beautifully around his tongue.

He lifted his head but kept his hand on her, working her with two fingers inside, thumb on her clit.

Her eyes were wide, on him, and he could swear that for a split second they looked completely fucking lucid.

He got up on an elbow, sank his fangs into her wrist, and she screamed out in passion, grabbing his hair at the ear with her free hand. She rode another wave, bucking against his hand. And he felt her and saw light in her eyes. He felt it crystal clear. Need, want, and then she whimpered aloud,

"Tristan. Help me."

Her eyes were on him, fiery, real, staring deep, and fuck...completely KYLA.

He had to release her, she needed him to let go, couldn't safely give him any more blood. He released her wrist and the fire went out of her eyes, shifting away like a moving shadow. She went limp.

"What do you need?"

No answer.

"Tell me what you fucking need!" He shook her limp body, pleading, looking so deep into her glassed over eyes than he felt real strain behind his own. "Fucking tell me!"

He lifted her wrist, wanting to bite again, wanting her back, but he knew it'd be too much. She wouldn't be able to hack it.

Icy cold rage rose, pulsed inside. He crawled backwards away from her until he was standing at the foot of the bed, his fists clenched at his sides.

He needed to push it back. He needed to push back the urge to go downstairs, haul Adrian Constantin outta the closet in the dining room, yank that dagger out and use it on him extensively. He wanted to drag the knife from his gut up to his throat and then slice and dice the fucker like an onion, into a thousand pieces, starting at the asshole's ankles, letting him feel every single slice of the knife until he got to his chest and then he'd carve that useless heart out slowly, a millimeter at a fuckin' time.

Instead, he put his fist into the mirror, hating his reflection with a passion because this was all his fucking fault and then he took a few deep breaths and then found a way to cool it. He texted Sam, who came down to the cottage a few minutes later.

TRISTAN CLEANED UP the broken mirror and then went downstairs and let Sam in. He told him to put Adrian in the pit that he'd been put in after Constantin fucked them over, and then went back upstairs and did dozens of push-ups on the floor beside the bed, at least 50 chin-ups on the door frame of the bedroom, and then he crawled into the bed and closed his eyes after pulling her to his chest and tangling his fingers into her long soft hair.

Sam texted him after he was back, telling him Adrian was in the pit, that he'd done as Tristan had asked and gotten help from one of Adrian's security guys.

> **"Weird, man. I was waiting for him ages and then found out he was at the wrong pit. He said there was a mix-up and he was waiting 4 me at the other pit on the property. I don't know who's in it but he says there are 2 desecrated and daggered vamps in it."**

Tristan didn't know who they were, but he didn't give a shit right now. He texted back,

> **"Out of scope for tonight man. Hit the hay, after you help him forget."**

Tomorrow they'd leave this fucking place and, he hoped, get them on the road to getting her back.

She slept like an angel that night. She was curled up against him, almost as if she was herself, her colouring looking almost normal. She didn't make a peep all night.

But Tristan didn't sleep a wink.

4

Seattle, WA

THE TRIP TO SEATTLE was thankfully uneventful. Tristan had spoken to Adrian's team and ensured they were all ready for business as usual. Sam deposited Adrian in the pit that Tristan had been kept in, was having it guarded, and he had stocked up on several dozen patches that were in Adrian's lab that would allow him to be around Kyla. No one seemed to know anything about the other pit. Tristan would check it out later.

Kyla was a little pale and sickly and not real quick on her responses to questions so it took a little bit of influence at the airport. He decided they'd charter planes after this to make things simpler if they needed to travel again before he could get her well.

Getting her well felt possible. He desperately wanted to believe it wasn't a lost cause.

He gave her some natural nausea medicine for the plane ride as she'd vomited just before they left the compound and then again on the ride to the airport. She slept against his shoulder during the flight and then he got her into bed when they'd gotten into a hotel room and she went back to sleep after he'd spoon-fed her some pureed vegetable soup and got her to drink some of a protein smoothie. She didn't seem well enough for him to feed from, so he let her rest and he paced, did some work on his laptop, answering some emails to try to create the illusion of normalcy among vampire business and council peers, and stared out the window.

His heart was heavy, like it was a giant brick sitting in his chest. What if she kept getting worse? What if this was her slowly dying?

Would Sam's sister be able to help? If the worst happened, what the fuck would he do without her?

No.

He couldn't think of that. The very notion made him want to paint everything with blood.

But she was losing weight that she couldn't afford to lose. She was pale. Yet her blood tasted amazing. He'd had just a little, not nearly enough for a feed and not wanting to make her feel worse, and he had no signal of that. When he fed she perked up for a bit. Her blood levels were fine, better than fine; it was just something else that wasn't. But what?

In the past, he had tasted illness in people. He didn't taste it in her. He felt fucking helpless and that made him angry. Furious. Because this feeling was completely foreign to him before he met this girl. But there was nothing to do about it. All he could do was wait to hear from Sam. He hated this feeling of powerlessness. If he got her back he'd make sure he never felt this way again.

AFTER MIDNIGHT, HE heard from Sam, who phoned. Finally.

"Tris, we'll be there tomorrow morning. Sasha wants to meet you."

"I'd rather travel to her. Get Kyla help as quickly as possible."

"She okay?"

"No better, man. I don't like it."

"Well, Sasha's got trust issues, man. She is mostly on board with doing a blood transfusion, but..."

"Fuck." He felt sick. He knew that might be the plan but what if it not only failed but fucked her blood up?

"Hang tight. I'll see you tomorrow, as early as I can manage. You and she can talk and we go from there. Yeah?"

"Yeah, man." He hung up, hoping that Sam's sister was as capable as Sam had suggested.

SASHA WAS VERY MUCH a female version of Sam. She was tall, curvy, attractive, a brunette with wavy hair to her shoulders, big light brown eyes, and an olive complexion. She wore eyeglasses and looked very much the sexy doctor type. She looked about forty, a foxy librarian-type, although Tristan knew that wasn't the case. She'd be in her late seventies but experienced reverse aging just as his mother had, when she'd been turned. Taryn looked 35 or 40, when in reality she was in her late 50's.

Kyla was asleep behind the closed bedroom door. She hadn't woken yet; it was early and Tristan had decided that the door wouldn't open if she woke and tried to come out. The door didn't have a lock, but he knew, without having tested it, that this would be so.

He felt like he was getting stronger by the day. His lungs felt like they took in more air. His heart felt stronger. He felt his body working at enhanced efficiency. He knew he'd be able to deadlift more, run for longer, jump higher, that he'd reap more benefits than before from even a little bit of exercise. He could just *feel* that he was stronger, broken heart and ravaged soul notwithstanding.

He had one of the two daggers with him, in case he needed to incapacitate one while taking care of the other. He really didn't think Sam wasn't on his side, but he knew that vampire twins had an intense bond. He also knew that although he could influence Sam, someone who was generally not real easy to influence, due to the strength of his bloodline, he didn't know if Sam was at a disadvantage with his own sister, if she'd be able to sway him to double-cross Tristan, and he didn't know if she'd have any advantages over him.

There was no way Kyla would be harmed. He wouldn't let her be in the same vicinity as Samantha Jasper unless he was 100% confident in her abilities as well as her intentions.

"I can't guarantee that it'll work," she said, while he, her, and Sam sat over coffee in the sitting room of the hotel suite.

He'd filled her in on the basics, all of them, and so far his senses were telling him that he could believe in what she was telling him. She knew some of what he'd said, likely via Sam, but she listened patiently until he was done.

"I'd like to test her with a trickle-feed of Kyle's blood, watching to ensure it's not harming her in any way. You can be there for every facet of the testing process. I won't do a thing without your consent. My brother has explained that Dr. Constantin did things without your consent. I can understand how that would affect you. I assure you that I would proceed cautiously, whatever the case."

Sam had explained that he'd shared information with his sister about what sort of man Tristan was, about how he explained to Sasha that although he was a high-ranking member of some influential vampire councils, the sorts of councils Sasha had problems with, being with Kyla had restored his humanity somewhat.

Sasha was reading him. He was well aware of that. She was gauging him as a person, deciding if she might be able to trust him.

Sasha explained that a big element of the so-called militia was embracing more humanity. It wasn't a rebellion in the way of a violent uprising that aimed to maim. This, instead, was a collaborative group of vampires who were in a coalition that strived to have equal rights with royal vamps. Many of them wanted to embrace humanity, live lives that weren't necessarily altruistic but also that weren't pure hedonism. Instead of lording over the world at the top of the food chain, this collaborative alliance tried to live without being megalomaniacs and worked together to try to live a more symbiotic existence with others. They sought to live without "power-hungry blue-bloods" and hedonistic turned vamps who wanted to make all the decisions and control everyone.

She was contrite when he asked, "Vamps such as me?"

Sam's behaviour was peculiar and when Tristan questioned it, he admitted that he had some ideals from his sister drilled into him the last 18 hours and a lot of what she'd said had been sinking in. Sam claimed to be processing a lot of things. Tristan didn't quite know what to make of it. He wasn't sensing betrayal in Sam. Just that the man was warring with himself.

Tristan wasn't necessarily skeptical, merely planning to keep an eye on Sam, ensure he wasn't under someone's influence. He wanted to work hard at reading Sam's sister so that he could determine whether or not she was safe to deal with, but knowing she had a problem with Adrian Constantin's dubious moral code was a good sign.

Sasha was definitely different. She wasn't a screaming bitch; she seemed decent.

"So, you grew a conscience after drinking Kyle Kelly's blood?" Tristan asked.

"Seems so," she shrugged.

"Tell me, was your coalition involved in removing Kyla from her parents?"

"Yes. Before I had anything to do with them. Major efforts were taken to stop the breeding program run by Dr. Constantin.

But it was unsuccessful. Two individuals worked to make Kyla Kelly safe. The two were in separate locations, an effort taken to safeguard her whereabouts. Only three people knew where she was but two of them died, one as punishment for their involvement, the other of a freak unrelated accident so for years no one knew how to find her. Dr. Constantin found the third individual, a vampire who was incapacitated for so long he was desecrated in punishment for coalition involvement. Once he was located her new identity was revealed and my brother became involved for your end. Once things changed for me, I wanted to be involved for our end. But Sam wouldn't return my calls. There have been some bad eggs in our alliance over the years but most of us want the same outcome, democracy and freedom among vampires, to live our lives on our own terms."

"Why did you want to be involved at this level?"

"A few reasons. One, because the ongoing intentional breeding of royal bloodlines is a practice perpetrates the ongoing problem among our kind."

"Meaning?' Tristan was affronted.

"People like you, like your father, your grandfather; it's an ongoing cycle of dictatorship. These councils that exist for a variety of things may have many members, but they're mostly based on the illusion of a democracy. For the most part, the top three royals on each council make the decisions. Metes out the punishments. Keeps things from progressing. They opt to imprison, program, or exterminate vamps that they don't feel meet their criteria, try to control breeding and turning. They treat females like baby-making machines. They call us a militia, but we're merely a group of vampires including some of mixed race, some royal, some turned, from all walks of life who are looking to give people, turned vampires, and so-called blue-blooded vamps equality. We want to decide who to mate with, whether or not we want to try to be bred, to be able to decide *how* we want to live our lives. People have been indentured servants, chosen to bleed and breed for vampires and this is wrong. In the last two hundred years the upper echelon of the royals have been trying to micromanage our race. They don't have that right. There is a similar breeding program in Europe. The last large organized program is on the verge of being dismantled. There's an elder coming to the states next week to meet here for a small gathering. If things go well between now and then, perhaps you'd consider being a part of that meeting."

Tristan scratched his head, "Yeah, uh, all this isn't kind of hypocritical of you?"

"Oh, because Kyle is what you'd consider my pet? Absolutely. But Kyle Kelly has been in a coma for almost two years due to something brought on by Dr. Constantin's experiments so either his blood feeds me and keeps me sensible and able to help people, or I don't feed on him and that leaves me the sort who does nothing to contribute to society. Instead I go back to being another hedonistic psychotic vampress who gives no one anything, only takes. I knew Kyle before I was turned, from the time he was relocated to The Constantin Center and I think he would be happy to feed me if he knew how much it could help. And that's the second reason why I've been trying to reach out to my brother. Maybe Kyla can help me get Kyle conscious again."

Tristan quirked his eyebrows up, "Explain your relationship with him."

"I cared for him for years. Working with Dr. Constantin brought a lot of other people in front of me. I was not vampire; I was just their doctor so they were themselves with me. Many of them knew they were incarcerated. I was there for many of their moments of lucidity so I had many productive conversations with Kyle. He knows he has a sister, remembers her vividly even though they were separated very young. He knew she'd been found and that she'd been your intended. We talked at length about how much we wished that wasn't so. He wanted out of there so he could save her from you. I had suspicions about how to turn off the so-called bitch switch and I was wrong. I stumbled onto Kyle, who was unconscious, and I fed on him in a fit of hunger and felt the difference instantly. I was pissed at Dr. Constantin for treating me the way he did, for making me perform medical experiments like he did. When I was younger those experiments were done on me. I wanted to get away. I knew I had to take Kyle with me so I could *be me* and so I could help.

Luckily, I was programmed and medicated in such a way benefited me. I couldn't be mesmerized by a new vamp. I was in a high-level functional trance around vampires but I spent a lot of time with feeders and breeding program participants at The Constantin Center. When I took care of Jackson Curtis's preliminary testing, he was so new that I was immune to mesmerisation by him. Because of his brain-dead state, he had to be carefully monitored after being turned. In some cases, new vamps exhibit characteristics that because of that, require them to be put in custody, or that may need them to be destroyed.

When Jackson Curtis was brought in and turned by my brother, I wasn't rendered entranced, so I talked him into turning me. He did. My transformation was bad. I was exhibiting signs of severe left sided vampress tendencies. If you don't know, there are far left and far right vampresses. Dr. Constantin developed a scale that measured this. I measured far left. With this discovery, what Kyle's blood does, there could be a new way of measuring this scale. Left, centre, and right; right being a female vampire that has zero vamp-bitch temperament. I have had four other female vampires and three males tested on Kyle's blood. They don't know it's his blood, only that it's a potion I've come up with. No one knows about his blood but my brother and now you. Males aren't affected by it but all females were. All of them. Royal and turned." She took a sip of her coffee and then looked him in the eye.

"So, can I see her?" Sasha asked.

Tristan hesitated but then stared deep into her eyes, "You won't hurt her."

"I won't."

"You'll be 100% up front with me with anything you want to do. You're completely forbidden from being deceptive with me in any way, shape, or form where Kyla is concerned, where Kyle is concerned, where anything is concerned. Do you understand?"

"I understand. I have no desire to deceive you. We want you in our coalition. If I help you, maybe you'll consider it. I want Kyla to help Kyle. And I want her to be okay, too."

Tristan released his mental hold on the bedroom door and it swung open. Kyla was already standing there. Her hand out, cupped. She'd been trying to turn the knob and he hadn't even heard. She was in a nightgown that was like a long tank top, her curls were everywhere. The whites of her eyes were almost pink, the green of her eyes was washed-out looking, a milky green rather than a striking emerald green. Her expression was grim.

"I'm hurt."

She'd scratched her arms so hard that she was bleeding.

Sasha went to stand and Tristan halted everything. Both Sasha and Sam were frozen in place, immobile. Tristan's heart was racing as he moved to Kyla in the doorway, ushered her back a step, and then made the door slam and willed it to stay shut. He walked her back to the bed.

"What hurts, princess?"

"Hurt," she sobbed and crumpled, falling toward the floor; he caught her before she landed, lifted, then carried her to the bed and held her close.

"Princess," she whispered.

"Yeah, Princess. You're my princess. I love you so much. Please stop scratching, Kyla. Is that why you're hurt? Because you've scratched yourself raw?"

He kissed her arms tasting the blood on his tongue. He licked again and watched the scratch disappear. That was strange. He frowned and licked a scratch on her other arm and it vanished, like drying vanishing ink. In the past, the only time he could heal was if his own fangs had done the damage and it was never this quickly. He looked at her face. She was blankly staring off, looking so fucking frail.

"Why are you in such withdrawals when I fed only yesterday? This feeling, does it feel like when you hadn't been fed on?"

Her eyelids fluttered and then she passed out in his arms.

He rocked her for a minute, holding her close, chills in his gut, fucking hating every goddamn minute of this shit. He heard noise outside the door so put her into the bed and put his head against her chest for a minute and listened. Her heart was beating steadily. Her breathing was normal. So he tucked her into the blankets and went back out into the living space. Sasha was gone. Sam sat at the table, waiting.

"Where is she?"

"She wanted to give you space. I know you didn't get a lot of time in, but she is happy to have you attend her facility, meet Kyle, decide if you want her to try to help your girl and if you might want to help Kyle, too. She wasn't affected by the scent of Kyla's blood but she didn't want you uncomfortable, so she wanted to leave. She said Kyla's blood smells very similar to Kyle's but she's not a threat. She says she has zero urge to feed on Kyla."

Tristan's eyes moved to Sam's eyes, trying to read him.

"You can trust her, Tris. She has a set of morals and beliefs that, I'm telling you, you can trust. We can try patching her, too, if you like, but she believes she's fine around Kyla. The scent is close but not exact."

"Haven't had a whole lot of success in the trust arena, Sam."

"I know. Believe me, I know. Read me. Read any part of me or her next time you see her. Program away. But I'm telling you, this is real. I don't know if she can help you or not, but I know she'll try. She believes that vampires can be good, not just inherently evil. She's restoring my own faith, man, with the things she's told me, shown me, in just a day so far."

Tristan wasn't entirely convinced.

"Tris, my sister and I were born for a purpose. Our parents were set up just like Kyla's, just like yours. Adrian tried to orchestrate that purpose. He was successful with me to a certain point but there was a problem. No, there were a few problems. First, I'm royal but I don't get access to all the same rights and privileges as other blue bloods because I was bred to be a concierge. I don't get an enchanted pet. I don't get to sit on councils. Instead, I got to do others' bidding. I do your bidding; I do his. I constantly walk a line where I can't build real true bonds. As a vampire, I shouldn't want them. But a few intriguing things have happened. First, I've seen your transformation. I've seen how your pet has gotten to you. I crave that kind of connection all of a sudden. I wondered when I had that girl brought to the house that Rebecca killed what it'd feel like to have an actual conversation with her. It started to happen when I cared for Kyla while you had her separated from you back at the house, before the fire. When I got patched, it intensified. Why? Because my natural vampire urges were suppressed and those have brought round some new emotions. I think you can relate because her blood has suppressed some of your inclinations."

Tristan shook his head, "No. They haven't suppressed a thing. They've heightened who I truly am. She just helps me be better."

Sam inclined his head to the side. "Yeah, well, there's been a shift. I've been avoiding my sister because I knew she was unhappy before she turned, and she was real unhappy with me and the role I was playing. She tried to communicate with me but who I was, as vampire, wasn't who I was before I was turned, and she said it broke her heart. Spending the last day with her, I felt different. More receptive to what she was telling me. I couldn't work it out. I thought I missed her, seeing her youthful and beautiful and happy again may've been responsible. But then I got in the shower last night and realized I hadn't taken my patch off even though Kyla wasn't near. So whatever was suppressing my urges to feed on your pet was also suppressing some sort of filter that kept me indifferent. Don't you see? We have something very fucking wrong inside us. I've asked Sasha to try to analyse what's in those patches. Replicating them could be a game-changer. And I've had a few instances in my life where I've stopped and questioned things. I've generally avoided those emotions because they didn't feel natural. But now they do."

"Listen," Tristan said, "I know there's something wrong in me, in us. Of course I fucking know that. I've been fighting that for the past few months, since I first laid eyes on Kyla. She's collateral fucking damage for whatever it is that's fucking wrong with us! I've been fighting who I am for weeks. I've been fighting to protect her and fucking failing because I've been under your influence, Constantin's influence, because I've been under the influence of my own fucking ego, because I've been fuckin' blood drunk."

Sam had a glazed over look, "Whatever's in that patch dulls that wrong for me. Whatever's in her blood, it dulls that wrong for you, her brother's blood, for my sister. I want what I never got but I also wanna stop playing the mind fuck games that go along with the councils, the royals. Maybe we can fix this and then I can go and find *my* Kyla out there somewhere."

Tristan shook his head, "There isn't another one of her."

"Maybe not for you, but for me, maybe *my* girl is out there. A girl with blood that strengthens me, with a personality that makes me want to be worthy. Someone I can have a future with, a family..."

"Fuck," Tristan grunted. He could hardly believe it, but he felt Sam. Sam meant this.

Sam cleared his throat. His voice was thick, "So, Sasha has an errand and then she's willing to take us back. If you wanna think it over, you can stay here and do that. If you want to get her there, which I believe is a safer place, we can go in about 3 hours. She has a big house, plenty of room, and the facilities to do what she thinks could help. All private. Security systems. And respect from the others to give her space when she asks for it. No one needs to know you're there."

"Give me the location and the lowdown on the place. If I decide to come, I'll meet you there. If I need more time, I'll text you."

"Alright." Sam slapped him on the shoulder. "I'll head out. I'll be there."

"Gimme more facts on the place before you go."

"It's a small island, real small. Slice of paradise, actually. Just a few hundred acres and it's one of the coalition's Pacific settlements. Picture a bit of a modern-day hippie commune. They're not radicals man, they're like the tree-huggers of the vampire world. They share resources. They have their own councils, affiliations with others who are likeminded. On this island there are a dozen males ¾ of them are turned the others true but none are royal. Sasha is one of five females, she and one other are royal, and save one or two who are on what she'd describe as the centre area of the scale as she micro-doses them with Kyle's blood. They're a medical commune, of sorts. She has a mini hospital and research facility there. As she's royal she's done a little programming on all but the other female royal. They've volunteered to be programmed in a way that will protect secrets if they're apprehended by vamps outside their coalition. They leverage humans when they must but their approach is blood bags most of the time. They're trying to transition to where they don't need to deceive humans in order to feed. That's their ultimate goal. And Sasha has a few formulas that look promising. They do have firepower on the island in case anyone who's against them finds them. There are settlements like theirs in a number of places."

"What sorts of numbers are we talking outside this island?"

"A couple thousand members globally. They're not huge but they are growing and they've got a handful of elders who are on board for change."

TRISTAN DECIDED TO meet Sam down at the pier. He and Kyla took a cab down there after he'd planned for a few contingencies. He wouldn't board the boat with Sam and his sister and he had a plan b and a plan c for if things went wrong on this trip.

"I've chartered my own ride," Tristan told him when Sam met him at the pier, a sickly Kyla on his arm, his duffle bag over his other shoulder and he was pulling a wheeled suitcase with his free hand.

"They won't know how to get there."

"Then tell them."

"I'm not sure Sasha would—-"

"I'll influence them to guard the information accordingly as well as to forget it."

"She might suspect that you've already put orders in place that'll.."

"I'll do it, in front of her. I'm not coming without having a ride. I've also got additional reinforcements that'll be close to the island. I'll take care of programming them, too. My ride will stay on the water, anchored far enough out to be safe and close enough to evacuate us if need be."

Sam nodded and agreed. "Alright."

His sister poked her head out from the boat that Sam was in front of and gave a little wave.

Kyla waved at her. Tristan tipped her chin to meet his gaze. She was pretty out of it and just responding to the wave as, probably, a matter of reflex.

Sam jogged over to his sister and they spoke for a few minutes. Tristan could read them both, despite being a few hundred feet away. He sensed nothing deceitful. Sasha was rigid, slightly concerned, but Sam was giving her placations.

Tristan waited, stroking Kyla's forearm, which was linked with his arm. She was swaying a little, staring out at the water. But there was a little smile on her face.

Sam returned and gave him a nod.

"Anything happens, Sam; I get the slightest inkling of any sort of ploy..."

"Tristan, I'm telling you..."

"I'm supposed to believe you towed the line all this time and you're suddenly on my side completely? On your twin's side at the same time but won't double cross me if she turns out to have a hidden agenda? Yeah, right."

"You've already programmed me to be on your side," Sam said, "You're the strongest programming talent I've come across. It's probably unbreakable. Stronger than a twin bond. But I'm telling you, Tris bro, something about this patch..." Sam shook his head, "When I help get you two squared away and know I've done all I can to redeem myself with you and you're set with your happily ever after? I'm going off to get my own. I want a different life. I want to be your friend, but I will be asking that you release me from my current duties. My sister and I got drunk last night and spent hours talking. Today I can't stop thinking about how *my* story will end. I'm 78 years old, brother, and I look like I'm 28. I'm gonna find me a sweet young thing with sweet blood and buy a little place on the beach somewhere tropical. I'm gonna enjoy her a few years and then if she suits me, turn that sweet thing into a vampire and my sister will de-bitchify her, if all goes well with her research and ability to replicate a synthetic version of whatever is in Kyla's brother's blood that makes female vamps even-steven and then I'm gonna spend the rest of my days fucking my she-vamp under the stars with an occasional sexy human vixen on the menu between us. You know how fuckin' awesomely wild vamp on vamp sex is, right? You, yourself know wild a vamp-vamp-human female threesome is. Anyway, maybe have a coupla kids. We'll see."

Tristan half smiled. It was a good story. Time would tell if it'd turn out that way.

"I have a feeling you'll get her back. And never know, my sister could help you get her turned and de-bitchified so that she'll live maybe as long as you."

"I hope to God you're right, Sam but I don't want her to be a vamp. I just want her." Tristan didn't ever wanna show weakness but this was the honest truth just spilling from his lips like verbal diarrhea.

"I'm sure you want her for more than the next 50-60 odd years though, man..."

"One hurdle at a time."

5

TRISTAN DISMISSED SEVERAL of the men who were on the boat he'd chartered, some who were there as decoys. They went off in different directions, two in a small speedboat, a few in a canoe, and a few on jet skis. One was a co-pilot heading to a nearby parked amphibious helicopter where a pilot would scan the island, get him a report, and then wait on standby.

Tristan had also grabbed a satellite phone, as he didn't know what sort of signal would be available at the island. He'd be able to get them to swoop in if things went awry and something happened to the boat.

He had Kyla on deck during the boat ride. She smiled through the whole ride, looking under the weather but yet pretty, hair floating in the breeze as she gazed out at the waves.

He kept her close. He reached into the duffle bag and handed her a sports drink.

"Drink that, baby. Slowly. Small sips until you're done. We'll be there soon."

Within a short time, they were docking on a small island with a beachy front.

Sam helped one of the two remaining guys on the charter tie off and Tristan told Kyla to stay put a second while he spoke briefly to the captain to confirm his directions to be anchored within five minutes of the island until further notice.

Tristan grabbed their luggage, her hand, and they got off the boat. She stumbled over the rocky beach and seemed unsteady on her feet, so he scooped her up and carried her the rest of the way.

Ahead, up a narrow wooden staircase, was a three-level chalet style home with a high-peaked roof built into a rock face. There were satellite dishes on the slopes, solar panels galore, and there was a large deck straight across the face of the place on the top two levels. Young fruit trees and bushes brimming with peppers and tomatoes in large planters were lined up across the middle level. A good-sized glass solarium jutted off to the side and that, he could see, was filled with greenery.

"Welcome to my home and clinic," Sasha said in greeting from the doorway of the middle level, the only level accessible from the staircase, "Please come in. I'll just show you to your room first."

Tristan put Kyla on her feet but held her close to his side as they entered the bright and airy home, far too large for just one person. The decor had a cabin feel to it while being bright and cheerful at the same time. He was wary but sensed nothing unusual and no other vamps in the vicinity. No vamps had been in this house for a long while and that was slightly reassuring.

They followed her up a few stairs and then down a long hallway with several doors. Sasha opened the door at the end.

"Your room." She handed him two keys and said, "I had Sam put a lock on it just now. Make yourself comfortable, please. I don't have servants here. I keep the refrigerator stocked with ready-to-consume things: salads, sandwich fixings, fruit, cheese, the like. Blood bags are stocked as well; help yourself."

She gestured toward a wine fridge that was stocked with bags, "They're all labeled. Plenty of frozen entrees in the freezer for the microwave or oven. I'm busy and I really don't cook much but if you'll allow me to share that you're here and you're here more than a day or two, you'll meet some of the others and many of them would be happy to host dinners. One of our residents loves to cook and I visit her regularly and she's always sending me home with casseroles for my freezer so there's plenty of food here. If you don't want anyone to meet you, that's fine, too. I'm not expecting company for the next few days.

I *will* tell you that if you choose to meet others that there is absolutely zero elitism here. I know you're the Kovac crown prince and all but... yeah...no airs or titles here. If you permit me to share that you're visiting, that you're receptive to the possibility of joining our coalition, they'll treat you like they treat everyone else, as an equal.

If you want your visit kept quiet, fine. Nobody will bother us unless I invite them to. I have a Do Not Disturb flag out front for when I'm in the midst of research-intense projects and if it's up, which is it right now, people stay away unless there's an emergency. We have good privacy on this end of the island so if you want to walk the beach, go for a swim, take a canoe or pedal boat out, there's little chance of privacy being disturbed."

"Got it," Tristan said. He dropped their bags on the floor. The bedroom was large and airy with a wall of windows and a view of the water. A queen bed, nightstands, and a large armoire plus a long chest of drawers furnished the space. There wasn't an adjoining bathroom, which didn't make him too happy as he didn't like the idea of Kyla wandering in and out to use the washroom.

"My brother is also on this floor on the other end of the hall. My bedroom is the first down the hall from the kitchen on the middle level but I'm usually on the ground level, where my clinic is. I'll be staying close to Kyle while you're here in my office or my lab downstairs. Why don't you two get settled and we can talk in the kitchen some more, get refreshments, and then we'll head down there?"

Tristan gave her a chin jerk.

Sasha smiled and backed out of the room.

"How're you feeling, princess?" he turned to Kyla and asked, "You okay?"

"No," she said, belatedly.

"Do you want something?"

"Yes."

"What?"

"I don't know."

He pinched the bridge of his nose.

"Grape," she added.

"I'll get you a drink. They might not have that here. Need to use the bathroom? Tired?"

"No."

All that had been like pulling teeth, taking three times as long as those answers should've taken.

He took her hand, "Come with me." He wasn't about to leave her alone while he toured Sasha's clinic and lab.

In the kitchen Sam and his sister sat at a long butcher's block-like table that'd seat a dozen. They were drinking from mugs.

"Meh," Sam was saying as Tristan and Kyla arrived.

Sasha filled a third mug with blood from a large glass decanter "Try this," she urged.

Tristan leaned over and sniffed blood in the mug, "What is it?"

Whatever it was, it didn't smell right.

Sam gave him a foul look of warning.

Sasha answered, "It's a cocktail of several small animals' blood with a vitamin infusion."

"'Tis foul, is what it is!" Sam declared, putting his mug down hard on the tabletop, shooting his sister a look of disdain.

"We've had good feedback with this, particularly from turned vamps," she informed him, "It's very nutritionally balanced."

"Blech!" Sam replied, "Vampires need human blood. We're vampires, not vampire bats."

"Try it?" she asked Tristan, throwing a glare at her brother.

"I'll take a human and chase it with a Flintstone vitamin," Sam declared.

Tristan shook his head, "I'm good. Can I get some water or juice for Kyla? Grape juice if you have it."

Sasha smiled at him, "Why don't you sit down with me, Kyla?" She patted on the empty chair beside herself. Kyla stared at the chair and blinked a few times and then looked to Tristan and opened her mouth but no words came out.

"Don't you want to sit with me, Kyla?" Sasha asked, "I'm Dr. Jasper. I'm Sam's sister. I'm a friend."

Kyla's eyes slowly swung back to Sasha's direction.

"Tristan says..." she started, but closed her eyes and her teeth chattered and she had a full shiver. She swayed. Tristan put her in the chair.

"Sit down, princess; it's okay." He steered her, though, to the chair opposite him, putting him between Sasha and Kyla.

He'd told her to follow no one's directions other than his. It was good to see that *that* had gotten through.

Sasha rose, poured Kyla some orange juice, apologizing that she had no grape, and then left the room and headed to stairs to the basement at the back of the kitchen.

Sam picked up an apple from a big silver bowl of fruit on the centre of the table and took a bite.

Sasha was back with a medical bag.

"Can I take her vitals?"

Tristan nodded.

She leaned over, about to wrap her blood pressure monitor around Kyla's arm, but Kyla's palms came up and she gave Sasha a shove, sending her flying back into the refrigerator with a considerable amount of strength.

Tristan jumped to his feet, mentally pinning Sasha to the fridge.

"Why did you do that, baby?"

"No one touches me but you."

"It's okay. I'll allow it, Kyla. Let her take your vitals. Right now, with me here. Okay?" He caressed her cheek and gave Sasha a nod.

Sasha got to her feet, looking a little bit shocked. While she took vitals, Tristan explained the strange strength Kyla had started experiencing, talked about how she'd hit Celia and threw Liam out a window. It was odd that she still had it, despite being so weak.

Sasha took Kyla's blood pressure, listened to her heart, put the stethoscope to her back, put a thermometer in Kyla's ear, and then asked if she could examine inside her mouth. Tristan told Kyla to open her mouth. She did, Sasha checked Kyla's gums, while peering into her throat.

Sasha took the stethoscope off and dropped it into the bag,

"I need to do blood analysis to figure out if Kyle might be able to help."

Tristan cocked a brow. "Show me her brother first and your medical facilities and then we'll talk."

Kyla reached for the mug in front of Tristan and lifted it toward her lips.

"You don't wanna drink that love..." Sam said and that caught Tristan's attention just in time, so Tristan swiped it.

"Not that one, baby." He put it down and handed her the orange juice that was sitting beside it.

THE GROUND LEVEL BASEMENT was bright with windows facing the waterfront along a long corridor, but the rooms were all against the hill face. They all had blinds on glass doors, offering light or privacy. There were several rooms and it had the feel of a floor in a small hospital. They walked past a standard-looking exam room and a lab that, unlike Adrian's lab, didn't have a glass room attached for observation.

There were two rooms that Sasha had explained were for surgeries as well. There was also a door that led to inside the hill that the house was built into. Sasha explained there was an entrance to caves in that hill from behind a storage room in the hallway because the hill had a weapons and supplies cache, temporary lodgings for everyone on the island, and access into a dense forest.

They were not a violent group, she'd said, but they were equipped for if they ran into problems.

At the end of a long hallway was a set of white wooden double doors with a plaque marking the area private. She led them inside. Her office.

She walked around her desk to open a set of doors on a closet. She shoved a rack of hanging white coats aside, revealing a hidden door. She unlocked it with a key and used a fingerprint scanner at the same time. When the door opened, Tristan was expecting something clinical-looking but it was decorated like a bedroom. A double hospital bed was in the centre of the room and it was done with masculine denim coloured striped bedding. The room had light gray walls, a number of large houseplants, leather furniture in a seating area with a big wall-mounted television. Music played from the TV, which displayed nature photographs and a scroll on the bottom of the screen that read,

"Kyle, I'll be back shortly. Please relax and wait for me. There are beverages in the fridge outside the bathroom door. Dr. Jasper."

"In case he wakes spontaneously," she explained quietly, "This is my safe room."

Most royal vampires had a safe room, like Tristan had at his condo back home. His house was being repaired after the fire and he'd given specs for a safe room upstairs, too. There had been one in the basement, but after what'd happened with Kyla he had wanted another.

Tristan approached the bed with Kyla, who was holding his arm.

Kyle looked healthy, just asleep. Looks his mid-twenties age, his eyes closed, at rest, but it was immediately evident he and Kyla were family. They had similar facial features. He had a close-cropped dark hair, he looked like he was in decent physical condition. His skin looked healthy; his body didn't give the impression of being bedridden for any length of time. He looked athletic, had a runner's body like Kyla did but with some muscular bulk. He was connected to IVs and monitors and wore a hospital gown. It appeared that Sasha spent time here. Of course she did; she fed from him. But his throat looked untouched. No marks.

"Does he heal rapidly?"

"I beg your pardon?"

"His throat is clear. Does he heal quickly after you feed?"

"Oh, I uh..." she blushed, "I extract blood before I consume it. I don't have an intimate relationship with him. Feeding from him directly would be intimate. To me, that'd be wrong. I consider myself his doctor, I care for him, and I extract the blood I need. Only what I need. But he seems to heal at an average rate. Does Kyla heal quickly?"

"Almost instantly now since the turning attempt. So, you never feed directly from him?"

Tristan caught Sam roll his eyes. He cocked an eyebrow at him. Sam shrugged. Clearly there were things where Sasha and her brother were not on the same page with respect to feeding methods.

"No. Not anymore. I did at first but... it feels wrong."

"Well, you must not think a whole lot of us, then, because that's the way we've fed all our vamp lives. That's the way vampires have fed since the beginning of time."

She looked like she was weighing her words, "I grew up at Dr. Constantin's compound seeing that my whole life. Maybe that's why I feel the way I do about it. Knowing people were being fed on against their will. If you and Kyla are intimate consensually I think it's a beautiful thing." Her eyes got glazed. She was a romantic, clearly. "I wouldn't want to feed on anyone I wasn't intimate with in that way. When I fed on Kyle the first few times, it was out of a primal reaction. I had prepared when I was turned for being hungry but I underestimated the hunger. Despite draining several blood bags I was immediately moved to find the nearest feeder and I did. In my first three days as a vamp I murdered four people at the Constantin compound. I'm relieved I didn't find Kyle first because I know I'd have drained him and killed him. Dr. Constantin and I had a run-in, a physical one, and I escaped the compound but not for long and was put in a pit in the ground for weeks. When he released me he released me into the research lab and it took him and several elders a lot of effort to get me in line. I was resistant to their programming at first but they broke me.

He wanted me to keep helping him with his work, was willing to try to see if we could continue to work together, under threat, of course, if I didn't follow very specific directions. Then, once I was under control, he kept working at me to influence me to fall in line. I went about my business but I stumbled upon Kyle and he was in a coma. I'm not proud of my actions but he was unconscious and helpless and we all know how that affects a vamp. So I fed on him and that's when I discovered that his blood did things to improve my disposition and I hid that for a time. I decided to get out of there. I'd been engaged in email conversations with someone who used to work there who had escaped and who was joining this coalition so I worked my plan for a while and took the first opportunity to escape. I switched to test tubes because it felt like it was the right thing to do."

"Escaped?"

"Dr. Constantin didn't exactly give anyone with inside knowledge a whole lot of freedom to come and go, particularly those with connections to breeding Constantins and Kellys. It'd be even tighter security when there were Kovac/Walkers and Constantin/Kellys involved; security standards were high, especially after Kyla was taken," she gave him a knowing nod, "Can we take DNA and blood samples? I'd like to compare it to his. I need to do a cheek swab and a blood test for starters."

Tristan took a breath. Sasha put her hand on his arm and gave him what looked to be a sincere smile, "I want to help. Please believe me."

Kyla swayed and swatted at Sasha's hand, clearly not as strong as she'd been upstairs in the kitchen. Sasha moved away.

Kyla wobbled, and Tristan steadied her and pulled her behind him,

"Don't do that, Kyla. Sasha wasn't hurting me."

"Sorry. I'll keep my hands off him, Kyla."

Kyla didn't respond to Sasha. She was weak. Really weak.

"Tristan, this family has been torn apart from the start. Maybe Kyla can help her brother, once she's restored to herself, too. Never know. It could be completely symbiotic. He's very special to me. I want him conscious as well as breathing and I know that he wants his sister to be okay. He has felt her absence. I remember them as babies and later as toddlers. They were inseparable the few times we had them together at The Center. They'd fall asleep sucking one another's thumbs. Adorable and so close. They've both been orphaned, in essence. Their parents, as they knew them, no longer exist. It'd be wonderful if they had one another. I can't tell you how happy I am to have my own brother in my life again. The twin bond never goes away."

"What if he wakes and doesn't want to feed you any longer?" Tristan interrupted, expecting to see some truth in her eyes and he did. He didn't see a sneer or anything deceptive, only a sadness.

"If that's what he decides, I'd have to cope. But I know Kyle and he won't. He'll do whatever he can to help. I honestly believe that. He'd want to help Kyla and he'd want to help me." She shrugged but her posture slumped.

"And if he doesn't?" Sam asked, moving in to the room.

Her eyes filled with tears, "I'd rather be dead, Sammy. But I won't force him to feed me. I'll die first."

Sam's expression dropped, "A bit extreme, Sash..."

"I can't kill anyone else. I really can't." Her hands went into her hair and she looked mortified, "I took fourteen lives before I drank from Kyle and I dream of every one of their faces over and over." She removed her eyeglasses and wiped her now wet and red eyes.

Tristan was flabbergasted that this woman was actually a vamp. She was a woman. She was soft, emotional, sweet. Not hard, calculating, and callous.

Tristan looked to Kyla to see if she had any recognition looking at her brother. But she wasn't even looking at him. She was staring off at the television on the wall, eyes glassy. She looked like a shell of herself. Weak. Pale. Her scent was even muted, diluted. His chest got tight.

He sat her down at the sofa and tucked her hair behind her ear and looked over at Sasha and said, "I'll do the blood draw and the cheek swab. No one touches her."

Sasha perked up with a hopeful expression, "I'll be back with the supplies."

TRISTAN AND KYLA WERE in the room Sasha had given them. He was lying on his back and she was asleep with her cheek on his chest. She'd kept the sports drink and the juice down, thankfully. He'd told her to lie there and snuggle with him. He was deep in thought, sifting his fingers through her hair for a good long while, pondering all of it.

He would never trust easily again but he currently had no doubt that as long as Kyla's brother fed Sasha, she wasn't a threat to Kyla. It wouldn't stop him from taking an assessment every time he saw her, though. He'd cringed while letting her examine Kyla at the kitchen table. He hated anyone's hands on her.

Sam had gone off wandering to explore the island and meet up with a female vamp who he'd known a long time, after Sasha explaining how well the vampress was doing with micro-dosing of her 'special formula'. Sasha was in her lab working on the Kyla mystery.

As Tristan hadn't been sleeping much, he drifted off, but was woken by her having some sort of seizure. Her body was jerking and bucking to and fro and she wouldn't open her eyes despite him ordering her to wake up and stop.

"Kyla, baby; please. Stop shaking. Wake up. Talk to me. Talk to me."

She wasn't responding. She just kept trembling, her body jerking, and then she started to whimper, her face holding an expression of severe pain.

She uttered his name with her eyes closed, as if she was dreaming of him, and it felt like a blade sank into his heart. She said his name with so much agony in her voice. Tears sprang to his eyes and he just held onto her, rocking her.

"T-Tristan!" she cried out, louder this time, eyes bolting open, unfocused, the colour dull and the whites of her eyes still pink, and she tilted her head off to the side, exposing her throat. She wanted him to feed? She seemed far too weak. But she wouldn't stop trembling.

Maybe if he fed right now he'd get insight into why this was happening.

He lifted her hand and kissed the inside of her wrist and then his fangs pierced the skin. He watched her face as her blood trickled into his mouth, down his throat, and straight into his soul.

Her eyes opened and were on him, out of focus, but she'd stopped trembling.

Desperation was coming from her; absolute anguish came off in waves. More pain and anguish than even last time.

He kept drinking, feeling her blood nourish him, watching goosebumps rise on her arms. Her body went lax and her eyes rolled back and then her emotions shifted to desire and her other hand reached up and grabbed his hair with strength.

He smelled arousal coming from her. Her nipples were erect, poking through her t-shirt. His thumb grazed over one and she moaned and arched into his hand. He flipped her to her back, mouth still connected to her right wrist. He roughly pulled her tighter to him and ground his cock against her pelvis. Her legs opened and wrapped around him. His fingers found their way to her fly and he snapped her jeans button open.

He was overcome with the need to have her and she was all over him. Her back arched so that her pelvis was grinding into him; her hand still tangled in his hair. She yanked his hair hard, making his neck arch back. He looked at her face. Her eyes were closed but her mouth was open, ecstasy written all over her face.

He let her wrist go with a kiss and whipped her bottoms down her thighs, "Kick them off, princess," he whispered against her mouth and she got one leg out and then both of her hands were in his pants and she was pulling his dick out,

"Baby," she moaned and licked his lower lip.

He grabbed her panties with both hands and ripped them in half and then tossed the torn fabric aside and got the tip of his dick against her entrance. *Fuck*, her body was so wet and hot and ready that it was as if her pussy sucked the tip of him in. He followed. He thrust his hips forward and slammed as deep as he could go, getting goosebumps at the moan she let out in response.

There was no way that this was wrong.

She wanted this.

He *needed* this.

And right now, she had some renewed energy of some sort. She wasn't lucid, she was drunk with desire, though, and she was all over him.

"You feel so fucking good," he told her.

She moaned and pulled his head toward her mouth, nibbling on his earlobe and then nibbling on his chin. He kissed her with all the passion he felt for her, devouring her. Her tongue tangoed with his and although he couldn't feel her emotions, he could feel her hunger by her actions. She needed this. Completely, absolutely needed this.

"Yeah," she breathed.

"Come with me, baby," he flipped her, lifted her by the hips, continuing to plunge into her while he worked her clit with his fingers and she reared back into him, throwing her hair back. He gathered it over one shoulder as his teeth found her other shoulder and when he bit in, she started to come; he felt her pussy clench around him and her emotions rushed forward into him. More desperation and agony.

"Kyla, baby?"

He felt so fucking sour, regretting she'd been on her knees because he never got to see her eyes, see if she was lucid while she came like last time. He'd released her shoulder and flipped her, but it was too late. She'd already deflated.

She immediately started to convulse again. Her body was jerking like she was having an epileptic seizure. He jumped up, yanked his pants up while flipping her over to her side. Tears streamed down her cheeks and she started to bleed from her bottom lip, just a little; her teeth were dug in there.

Her eyes rolled back and all he could see were the whites of them. He hollered her name. But she just kept trembling, back arched, face contorted with agony.

There was a loud knock on the door.

She went lax, but was breathing shallowly. The jerking had stopped. He kissed her, tasting blood on her lip, holding her face and looking deep. "Rest, princess."

She shuddered a few times and then settled.

The banging on the door resumed.

"Hang on!" he shouted, agitated.

He covered her nakedness with the patchwork quilt on the end of the bed, zipped up his jeans, and then stared at the door and it swung open.

Sasha stood there, chewing her bottom lip. "Everything okay?"

"Do you have something you can sedate her with? She's had some sort of seizure."

"Have you just fed?" she asked, glancing over his shoulder. She looked disapproving and he could feel it coming off her.

"It was the only fuckin' thing I could do, goddamnit. She wouldn't stop shaking until I fed. But then it started again..."

Sasha raised her hands defensively, "Okay. Yes, I can sedate her."

Tristan blew out a breath of exasperation, "Alright. It's happening more and more often."

"She looks rough." He saw that Sasha's eyes were on the floor, looking at the torn underwear.

"Yeah, and yes we just had sex." He answered her unspoken question, "It felt like she was pleading for it."

"Have you been having a lot of sex since the turning?"

"No. This was the first time for *that*."

"Based on her temperature earlier, I'd say that was probably safe. I don't think she's ovulating."

Fuuuuck. That'd just take the fucking cake.

"Good," Tristan was relieved. He hated this *not* knowing. He'd taken his diagnostic skills for granted for all this time. The last thing that he needed to worry about was Kyla being weak like this, a zombie, as well as fucking pregnant.

"But to be safe perhaps you should refrain or use protect..."

"I'm not a fuckin' animal, fucking my comatose pet senseless while she can barely hold her fucking head up by herself!" He roared this and thrust his hands through his hair, "She needed me. I read her when I fed, which is the only time I can but I've got a split second to do it because she's so weak that I can't take a full feed, and she practically attacked me and she needed me to..." He stopped, not sure how to articulate it.

"I'm not judging. But condoms might be a good idea. I don't have any here, but I'll arrange to have my brother go to the mainland and get some. It'd be safer."

Bullshit. She *was* judging.

"She needed it," he defended, "When she climaxes, her eyes are lucid for a second. Or they were last time. I don't know about this time because I couldn't see them..." He stopped. He knew he was rambling, giving out too much info, "I know you probably heard of my reputation, my tendencies, and they were true, but with her..." he couldn't finish past the fucking pain in his chest. No one else he'd fucked since turning vamp had meant a thing. It'd all been empty until her.

"Tristan, I know you're just coping with the circumstances in front of you. I'm not here to judge. I'm only here to try to make some sense of this so I can try to help fix it. I've got some feelers out..."

"Feelers?" His rage was rising. He shrugged her off, she'd tried putting her hand on his forearm reassuringly.

"I'm only talking hypothetically to an elder. I've sent an encrypted message asking for information about anomalies regarding enchanted and bonded humans being turned. He's travelling so it might be a few days but this elder is someone who could be extremely helpful to us. He's the oldest vamp of my acquaintance who is part of our coalition. He'll be here next week but for now I'm just asking for general info."

"I haven't joined your coalition, Sasha, and I sure as fuck hope he doesn't figure out who you're talking about."

"I'm aware it's dangerous but we can trust him. I know I haven't won you over yet and I'm aware I could help you and you could take your pet *and* Kyle and head off with them both anyway, decimating what has been built here and then taking efforts to dismantle us, destroying me in the process.

But based on what my brother has said, the vouching for you he's done, and based on what I'm reading from you myself, I know I'm doing the right thing taking this big risk here but I'm doing it for Kyle, for Kyla, and for the cause I believe in.

So far you've said or done nothing to make me feel like I've made anything but the right choice. He's far older than most of the elders on your councils, older than Dr. Constantin, from Eastern Europe where there are a lot more vamps, a lot more recorded history, and he could be helpful."

"Right," he muttered and folded his arms. They were quiet a beat.

She finally broke the silence, "I want to set up to run Kyle's blood through her. I'll run it slow and we'll get data continuously while it runs, with you present, so that we can assess her. You said her blood returned after a few days from the attempt at turning so hopefully the worst that will happen is that if this does nothing, her blood regenerates within a few days. That's not a guarantee and it doesn't mean we're without risk. I've already tested and they have the same overall blood type, though there are nuances. She's got far more vampire markers than he does. Her markers read almost completely vampire but there's something there that isn't. It's really odd. I'd like to wait a day or two, if that's okay, to see if I hear back from this elder.

Would that be okay? If she's in discomfort I can give her sedatives to make her more comfortable."

Kyla's body jerked, arms going straight up, like that sleeping baby reflex and Sasha winced. Kyla's arms dropped listlessly and she took a deep breath and then whimpered through her exhale, brows drawn together tight.

Tristan blew out a breath. "She seems like she's getting worse. If she gets any worse tonight, just try it. I can't lose her. If she's stable through the night, wait for the morning for your return email. Tell me if you get any replies. Tell me if you find out anything."

She nodded, "It'll help if we move her downstairs, I think; all my equipment is there and I can set up another room, watch her stats, set up IV fluids, vitamins. Then she'll need to be next to Kyle for a few hours for the procedure."

"Just set her up in your safe room. Put a bed in the room with Kyle," Tristan said, "I'll stay down there with them. But don't try to lock me in. I can undo the locks hands-free but I'd rather not break your security system if I don't need to."

"I'll be there, too," she said "I sleep on that sofa most nights anyway. But tonight I'll be pulling an all-nighter in my lab so you can take the sofa if you want. Or sleep here. I'll keep an eye on her."

"Not leaving her. I'll stay with her there."

6

KYLA WAS SEDATED, ON a hospital bed with just a foot-wide gap between hers and her brother's bed. Tristan was watching from the nearby sofa.

Fuck, she was gonna freak when she found out that she had a brother. She'd almost lost her mind when she found out that her parents were alive. He and she hadn't even had a chance to talk about the fact that her junkie ex-boyfriend wasn't dead, either; that he'd been hauled to Adrian's compound brain dead and then turned into a vampire.

She had a twin and he had enchanted blood, too. She'd had no one, she was all alone with nothing but a chip on her shoulder for most of her life. And now it was all different.

She had vampire parents, two vampire sisters, a dead human sister, and a comatose twin human brother. There might be other relatives that came outta that breeding program, too. He didn't count Constantin as her family because that fucker didn't deserve the privilege.

And she had *him*, her vampire prince boyfriend, as she'd called him. He thought back to that moment when she flopped on the bed at his condo with her eyes bright and her hair fanned out, a huge slice of pizza in her hand, globs of cheese hanging off it, declaring with so much fucking light in her eyes:

"My vampire prince boyfriend is AWESOME!"

He smiled through his pain at the memory. He wanted to give her everything he could to make up for the fact that she'd had to endure all this so far.

He moved to her and leaned over to kiss her forehead, "I'm so in love with you princess. I'm gonna find a way to get you back."

He said a silent prayer that it'd work. He hadn't prayed in probably twenty-five years, not since he was a kid.

Except no... He'd prayed once, the night he'd been turned, and those prayers weren't answered.

Taryn used to kneel with him every night and say the Child's Prayer with him. She used to take him to Sunday School. She used to believe that faith could move mountains. Now she had zero beliefs beyond sating her own desires and fulfilling whatever agenda she had.

He hadn't prayed since the night he was turned when his prayers that what was happening to him was just a bad dream proved to be fruitless as he watched body after body fall limp after being drained without his hunger waning even a little bit.

He'd missed his mother so much in those first few months of being a vamp while wreaking carnage all around him. He'd left his mother alone, stayed away once he knew who he was, once he knew the truth about his roots, about Alexander Kovac, about who his father was, a man who'd also been murdered while Taryn was pregnant, but he'd never been told much about his father. He hadn't seen photographs and Taryn hadn't said much about him.

Growing up he'd been told his father had been killed while being mugged. After being turned he knew that there was more to it. His father was turned before his mother got pregnant but she'd had some sort of relationship with him before and after.

His mother had been adopted. She never sought out her biological parents. Her adoptive parents were older when they'd adopted her and had died before Tristan was born. After Tristan had been turned he'd been told that Alexander was beheaded by enemies and that his own father died protecting secrets. He was told that when the time was right he'd learn it all. He hadn't pushed back then.

He knew there were enemies to be wary of, but he'd had little involvement in those issues, dealing more with day to day issues in the quest to protect vampire secrets and prove his worth with Kovac Capital.

Taking over for Claudio, if that's what he did, would change that. He'd hit a new level, that final ladder rung, the pinnacle. And then what? All the truths? More responsibility with secrets, with what else? How much more truth could he handle? What else had been hidden from him?

He'd kept his distance from Taryn for a while after he'd first been turned, and it hadn't gone over well. He and his mother were close, so it didn't take long for Taryn to get tired of being dodged. She used the spare key he'd given her to let herself into his apartment about three months after he'd been turned. He hadn't been using the apartment much since turning, preferring to prowl at night for blood, or staying in a spare room at Andre's, but had happened to be staying at his place on a night where she'd come looking for him. But he wasn't alone.

She walked in on him feeding on a girl while another girl sucked him off. He didn't look her in the eye, just sent the two feeders into the other room while his mother proceeded to converse with his back, asking questions, demanding answers, in tears. He'd already penned her a letter and so instead of talking things out, he handed it to her, meeting her eyes and telling her to believe it, even though it was outlandish, but to read it at home and then to burn it as soon as she'd read it.

In the letter he'd told her what he was, what she was, how she could choose whether or not to be turned because it hadn't been offered to her at her coming of age because his grandfather had reportedly wanted him raised as a human, without knowledge of his true identity until it was time for him to be turned.

Taryn wrote back a careful cryptic letter asking him to turn her so that she could help him, be there for him, and told him that she'd burnt his letter as he wished. He sent Sam to erase her memory. Then he'd sent another vamp with strong programming skills ordering her to stay away from him because by that point he'd seen how Becky was adjusting to being turned. He stayed away a few months, but the emptiness was sinking in. It was getting old. The constant hunger, the gnawing feeling like something was missing.

He'd shown up at his childhood home on his 26th birthday and, in a fit of drunken despair while he'd been fasting out of self-loathing, and with a myriad of emotions churning inside of him, he turned her, while she slept. He'd leaned over her sleeping body and dripped blood from his opened hand into her mouth, thinking it'd help with the emptiness he felt after turning Becky and having it go wrong, thinking that he would have his mother, that she couldn't possibly be the same as Becky.

It didn't help. It made things worse. His selfishness ruined his mother. The truth showed him that his sweet, loving, golden-hearted mother was a scheming, nasty she-monster who cared only about feeding her own bloodlust and buying her son more power through her scheming. She wanted Tristan to have more power, so she could have more power as a result of being mother to a powerful royal vamp.

Taryn was cunning and powerful, being Alexander Kovac's daughter and being turned by Tristan's blood. She was hell on wheels times ten. She was the strongest female vamp he'd met. She also became the most deceptive and cruel vampress around, too. She took no time earning a reputation as someone no one wanted to cross.

He'd been wrong about Rebecca and his mother both. He'd turned Becky for Andre, seeing his mentor broken at the risk of losing his pet, a non-mesmerized pet who'd started out his prisoner and became his beloved treasured companion.

He started to wonder if Kyla had turned properly if Kyle's blood would work on her to turn off that bitch switch. Family members generally weren't able to feed one another, though. Even Adrian and Lyle hadn't been affected by the scent of Kyla's blood so that probably pointed to the fact that she wouldn't be affected by her brother's blood the way Sasha had.

He could suddenly see merits of a breeding program because someone like Kyle but unrelated to Kyla could be on tap, waiting to help. He could see how someone like Constantin would plan for various eventualities. He knew from conversations with Sam that there were other enchanted pets on site. There was a dormitory behind locked doors near the lab. Was there someone there who could help?

Tristan heard noise and saw lights from the corner of his eye, so he looked to Sasha, who was turning on monitors connected to Kyla, just the same as Kyle. She explained that she was watching Kyla's levels, providing her with IV fluids.

Before carrying Kyla down to the basement Tristan had dressed her in a bra, tee, and cotton panties with track pants that came just to her calf, and Sasha had braided Kyla's hair down one side to keep it contained. She'd been staring at Kyla with motherly concern as she did it. Tristan felt her maternal nature coming off her in waves, which was odd, since Sasha only looked ten or fifteen years older. But she was much older than that. Old enough to be Kyla's grandmother.

"Nice getting younger again after being turned?"

"Oh yeah," Sasha smiled brightly, "My crows' feet and saggy jowls vanished overnight. Better than any trip to the spa. An ache I was waking up with the last couple years? Gone. Believe me, I've struggled with the pros and cons of vampirism. Kyle's blood makes things even out. I look a little older than I would if I'd turned at 25 but I'll take looking forty and feeling twenty rather than like a senior citizen any day!"

He watched her extract blood from Kyle. He smelled it in the air and it didn't smell exactly like Kyla's blood. It smelled male, but it also smelled appetizing. He'd had to consume bagged blood occasionally and it never mattered the gender, but he'd never taken blood from a male at the source. He knew he was lucky for that; average vampires didn't have the luxury of being gender biased. Hungry turned vamps and true vamps of lower station couldn't be all that discerning at all, so they took what they could get.

He'd had it easy, because of who he was related to and because of the strength he'd displayed, he got given his preferred meals on a silver platter -—as much green eyed brunette blood and as much pussy as he wanted, like a king already crowned and on his throne.

And then he gets handed the sweetest fucking gift of his life and offered all the power he wants while he gets to keep his enchanted pet, a woman who was carved out of sunshine and fucking ambrosia completely for him. They'd lost her and went on a twenty- year quest to get her back for him. Then a team of people strive to make sure she can give him perfect and powerful children.

But because the timing had gone wrong Adrian took their child from them. And Tristan didn't know if it was a blessing or not because that child might've killed Kyla, but it sure didn't feel like any sort of blessing or relief when that loss happened.

Here was a different group striving to find a way to live differently. He didn't really understand it. There was more to them, more to their way of life. What had made a few vamps get together and decide to let their conscience guide them? How did they even get a conscience to begin with? Tristan was too worried about Kyla and too dog-tired to *go there* right now.

Sasha had gone down the hall to her lab. He kissed Kyla's forehead and went and stretched out on the couch, throwing his forearm over his eyes. He couldn't stop the pain in his heart and the nagging thoughts about how for so many years, ten of them, he wasn't even conscious of having a heart except on the anniversary of his turning, his birthday. The day everything changed. And the same day he'd, later on, get given the most beautiful gift he'd ever received. That gift that he was now at risk of losing.

HE WOKE WITH A START, feeling disoriented.

The lights were off in the room but there was a glow coming from the machines beside Kyla's bed and beside her brother's bed.

He got up and stretched while making his way toward her bed and what he saw floored him, froze him in mid-stretch. Kyla was on her side on the edge of the hospital bed, right against the rails closest to Kyle. Her hand was curled around Kyle's bicep.

He heard footsteps and knew it was Sasha and Sam approaching from behind.

"Wow," he heard Sasha whisper. She'd noticed it too.

"I told you how they were as babies. There was one time, I watched Dr. Constantin with them both when they were about three. We traveled to Swansea together to examine them. He put them facing one another on the carpet and gave them each those toys that have the grid full of holes where you put bulbs in to make designs. What was that called?"

"Uhhh, Light something. Lite Brite?" Sam put in.

"Yeah, that's it," Sasha nodded. "He told them to make him a picture of something. I think he was just trying to occupy them while he was doing something else, Katya and Lyle were being given workups in other exam rooms, but this was the start of other tests for Kyle and Kyla beyond blood workups because she made a grid design of a blue eye, Kyle has blue eyes, and he made one of her green eye. They were the exact same shape and size. Neither of them had peeked at what the other was doing, either. Kyle was focused but Kyla kept giggling, like she had a secret. Kyle looked so focused on his task; it was fascinating to watch this thing unfold. They had such a deep connection. Dr. Constantin was pretty certain Kyla could read Kyle's mind and copied his design but with his eye colour instead of hers. That's why I reached out to Sam a few times once I knew he had his eye on her for you. I'd hoped that she'd be able to pull him out of this coma. I sat with them during that same visit and he drew a horse, a stick figure on the Lite Brite, and told me that it was for his sister. That he wanted to give her a horse because she wanted one desperately. He would give her anything, everything. I packed those toys up to go home with them."

"No idea why he's in this coma?"

"Nope. Dr. Constantin played with him, with his chemistry, with his psyche. He must have played too much. Treated Kyle like a guinea pig. I don't even know what caused this because by the time this happened, I had recently become vampire and I was in the midst of my crash and burn phase instead of being in the lab. I wasn't paying attention until it was too late. I couldn't access Dr. Constantin's notes. I tried. But I couldn't so I couldn't figure out what he did."

Sam scratched his head, "I, uh, might be able to help with that."

"How?"

"Liam Donavan was a computer guru. He'd done a bunch of hacking to breach The Constantin Center's firewall. I found a backpack in the woods near the cottage where he'd parachuted in and it had his computer in it. I stashed it. Maybe he's got tools on there or information on there that'll help. He'd been downloading video and other internal files. We should get that info before Adrian gets woken, so you can have a looksee."

"I'd really like to see if anything in there is useful, either for Kyle or for our cause. I also wanted to ask you about the dagger you brought," Sasha looked to Tristan. "I want to examine it, try to isolate the substance it's made with. Our efforts could be considerably more successful with a tool such as that."

Tristan didn't bother stating he could get the information out of Adrian easily, just by staring into the asshole's eyes and forcing him to spill his guts. He wasn't pleased right now to find out Sam had been withholding that information.

"I'm going to have to say, Sasha, that I'll reserve making a decision on that until later," Tristan replied, "Let's see how things go. Sam, shut your fucking mouth about potentially classified information. And we'll soon be having a chat, so you can share what else you haven't told me."

Sam looked contrite.

"Understood," Sasha said, and she didn't seem too dejected. "I know that once your immediate concern, Kyla, is no longer of concern of this nature we'll have an opportunity to talk more, talk about what's next. At this time, we're in a coalition together to help the Kelly twins. And even if we part ways, you have my word that I will do what I can to keep things peaceful with us, with others who are involved."

Tristan nodded. "Have you heard from this elder? Can you tell me who he is?"

"I'd rather not say at this moment, in case it conflicts with things down the road, should we find ourselves on opposite teams but no, I haven't heard from him. I've worked all but two hours when I napped through the night on these samples, though, and I think it's time to taper her off the sedative and see how she's doing. I'm not liking what I see with her stats on screen. We may not want to wait. I don't know how long it'll take to get that reply. Why don't we get coffee and breakfast and then we can get started?"

Tristan knew he could get information out of Sasha, too. But for now, he'd reserve judgement on all of it. With some of what she'd known about Kyla and about him, he suspected there were double agents either within Kovac or councils he participated on.

A few months back he'd have ended her and blown up this island and every coalition member on it. Now, though, he wanted all the facts before he made any decisions.

IT WAS AFTERNOON AND Tristan was sitting beside Kyla's bed, holding her hand. He hadn't left the area at all, couldn't bear to have her out of his sight.

She was again sedated. As soon as her last sedative had been tapered off she'd spiked a high fever and started convulsing again before she'd even woke up. It'd scared the shit out of him; he'd never been so scared.

Now it'd been about four hours since Sasha had started drip-feeding Kyla her brother's blood and Tristan was getting antsy. There was a contraption between Kyla and her brother, she was now on her back, no longer touching Kyle, and the contraption was feeding Kyle's blood into the machine and then into the top of Kyla's hand at a slow drip. A screen on the machine was scrolling with numbers.

Sasha was asleep on the sofa and Sam had just gotten back after visiting with that old booty call. Apparently the new and improved version of this vampress was now worth more time than just a roll in the hay after having her bitch switch flipped to 'off'.

The computer scrolling the data started to beep and Sasha was practically airborne, rushing over from the sofa where she'd been sleeping.

She read the screen.

"What the fuck is wrong?" Tristan was on his feet now, hovering over Sasha, who was looking at numbers that didn't mean a fucking thing to him.

"Nothing, no; just an alert that the filtering has hit the levels that I set. We should stop now and wake her, see if there's a difference."

"It's done already?"

"Yes. So, I'm tapering off her sedative now." She pushed some buttons on a machine hooked to Kyla's IV, "And she should wake soon. We will see where she's at."

She pushed some buttons on Kyle's machine as well.

"Are you altering anything for him?"

"He's not on any sedatives. Only a feeding tube but he was exhibiting signs of pain last night so I'm just checking the dosage for the pain medication."

"Pain?" Tristan asked, "Why?"

"I don't know. It's never come up before. I'm wondering if he's having a sympathetic twin response."

Tristan frowned, "Corsican twins?" Was she some sort of fucking quack or something?

"It sounds odd, I know, but these things have been documented, they were documented with the Kelly triplets. I'm not saying that's why Kyle was experiencing pain, but his pain levels were very similar to Kyla's shortly after she was brought down last night."

Tristan sat back down.

"I've got to take care of Kyle; a few bio issues, so could you give me about five minutes?"

"Not unless I wheel Kyla outta here with me," Tristan folded his arms across his chest.

"Right." She didn't look aggravated.

He flicked channels aimlessly on the television while she dealt with catheters and whatever else she was doing for Kyle.

"I'm going to catch a quick shower and change," Sasha said. "I'll be back in ten minutes or so. If any alarms go off, can you or Sam come get me? I'll hurry."

TRISTAN WAITED WHAT felt like an eternity before Kyla's eyes opened. He watched. She was looking around, looking sleepy, disoriented, and like death warmed over. Sasha was checking numbers on the machine.

She looked glazed over, still, but he leaned over hopefully, "Hey baby."

She licked her lips and swallowed what looked like painfully and then grunted in pain and tried to sit up.

"Whoa, whoa. Stay put, baby. You need to lay here for a second. Are you thirsty?"

She nodded.

Tristan hit the controls on the side of the bed to move her into a more upright position and then gave her bottled water through a bendy straw.

"No change," he muttered to Sasha while looking at Kyla's eyes.

Fuck.

It didn't work. Fuck.

His chest felt hollow.

"I think we'll start things back up in about an hour. Give her more."

"Why an hour?"

"I need to run some tests on Kyle first. Make sure he can safely donate more blood."

"Right. Are her stats any different?"

"She's had a decent amount of nutrition with the IV I've given her. She's in some discomfort, though. Maybe you can take a feed from her and tell me what you get from her blood. Maybe you can also, uh...try to read her that other way, see if it changed things?"

Tristan snickered, "You're saying I should make her come?"

Sasha blushed, "We'll unhook her, and you can take her upstairs. That's your call. You said she regained lucidity last time so maybe you'll read more from her."

Sasha looked away. She was having a reaction of extreme arousal at that thought. Tristan tried to not let her see that he knew that but he and Sasha were both aware of one another's reading abilities, so she wasn't making eye contact while she disconnected Kyla from the machines.

Tristan scooped Kyla up in his arms and carried her back upstairs to that bedroom. She'd lost more weight. She was too thin. Her skin was too pale. She was frail. She was rapidly declining.

He gently put her on her back on the bed and looked down at her. He felt sick inside. He had no desire to taste her blood, knowing it was infused with her brother's, and he certainly didn't want to touch her sexually right now. She was a limp lifeless shell of the girl he fell in love with. He got into the bed and pulled her close and just breathed in her hair, breathed in the scent of her skin, which was a little different than even yesterday, due to the change in her blood composition and the fact that she was so ill. He felt his senses sharpen. He didn't have diagnostic skills with her, but they were stronger today than they had been with her and she smelled like she was fading away, fast. She was wilting like a dying flower.

"Come back to me, princess," he pleaded. "please."

"Yeah," she whispered. But he figured her word held no meaning.

He held her a while and then leaned over to her throat, "I've gotta taste you, baby."

"Uh huh."

Bile rose in his throat at the idea, but he forced himself. When he swallowed his first mouthful there was barely anything there. Not the desperation, and confusion he'd been feeling, not even the hunger that he'd gotten earlier as the primary emotion.

She was barely even there.

A pounding began, behind his eyes. The blood tasted similar to Kyla's with some nuances but feeling almost nothing coming at him? This wasn't like the night he'd turned her. This was as if she was just fading away into nothing. Kyle's blood wasn't helping her. It wasn't doing a goddamn thing!

She was gonna die. She was fucking fading away.

He got out of the bed, opened the door, and hollered, "Sam!"

Sam was there quickly; Tristan knew he'd been on the outer deck smoking a cigarette.

"Get your sister."

Sam and Sasha were both inside the doorway a moment later. Tristan was pacing.

"She's worse. She's fucking fading. I can barely even fucking feel a thing but what I *can* feel, it's not good."

"She might still have some sedative in her blood. Maybe try again in an hour? She's not convulsing. And we can give her more of Kyle's blood. He—-"

"She's catatonic!" Tristan snapped. "I can't hardly feel a fucking thing! She's dying! More blood isn't gonna help if what she's had so far hasn't done a damn thing!"

He didn't wanna say it but felt like an hour would just mean further decline.

"Did you try, uh..." Sasha started.

"No. Not doing... no." Tristan waved his arms. He was disgusted at the notion, even, because unlike the day before when she was all over him, he knew it'd be different. He just knew in his gut that she'd lie there like a limp noodle and he would feel like a fucking sicko for even touching her in a sexual way. He also knew that if he dared try and got no reaction from her he'd lose it. It was better not knowing. But he knew. He knew it would bring her nothing and him nothing but pain.

Touching her yesterday, her going wild for him, it might've been the last time. It might've been a parting gift. And fuck that he'd taken her on her knees from behind and not seen her beautiful eyes go lucid for a minute.

What a fucking mess.

My mess.

He'd forever be haunted by the ghost of her in his mind.

He wanted to go back and fix this mess by making different decisions, by not trusting anyone, ever, by not letting anyone influence his decisions. By never stepping foot on Adrian Constantin's property, by ripping the throats out of anyone who even glanced her way. He pushed back the rage that he was an inch away from unleashing on Sam for convincing him to go to Constantin's in the first place.

Not yet.

Sasha moved in front of Sam. She knew Tristan was holding on by a thread and out of her twin connection, she felt moved to protect her brother.

He read fear and protectiveness for her brother. He looked deep into her eyes, "You care for Kyla like she's your own. Like your very life depends on it. And it does. Do *not* let her die!"

Sasha nodded, "Absolutely. You have my promise that I'll do everything in my power to keep her safe for you. But why are you asking me this? Are you going somewhere?"

"I'll be back," Tristan dug through the duffle bag on the dresser and pulled his wallet and passport out and then grabbed the satellite phone.

"Where're ya goin', bro?" Sam put his hand on Tristan's shoulder.

Tristan spun and his fist swung out and knocked Sam back about ten feet, into the hallway. Sasha gasped.

Tristan clenched both fists at his sides, tried to take a calming breath, and closed his eyes, which he knew had changed. He took another breath. Calm wasn't even on the radar. He was in a cloud of cold fog; it was coming out of his mouth. He pushed the rage down, deep inside.

Tristan stopped in front of Sam who was on the floor, conscious, but rubbing his jaw and stared deep, "Guard Kyla and her brother with your life. Neither of you fuck with her. All you do is keep her alive and comfortable. Sasha, Sam, stay patched. Don't fucking touch her, unless it's to help her."

"You got it," Sam vowed and Tristan knew that he not only had no choice but to mean it but he actually *did* mean it.

He pushed buttons on the satellite phone to summon his ride.

"Tell whoever needs to know that there's a helicopter landing outside your door in a few minutes, not to attack."

Sasha nodded and rushed out to the kitchen where she had a walkie talkie on the counter.

Tristan leaned over Kyla and kissed her on the lips and then on each eyelid. Her eyes opened and fluttered and then shivered. He knew he was cold; it was the emotion.

He gently cradled her in his arms and took her back down to the bed beside her twin.

"I love you, princess. I'll be back in a little while. Be good. Wait for me. Don't go anywhere. I am ordering you to wait here for me. Don't leave; okay baby? Please?" He tucked her in with the big quilt on the end of the bed.

"Okay, Tristan." She closed her eyes and smiled. He was surprised she'd said even that, she seemed so far gone.

His heart split open and as he walked out, he pretty much left it on that bed with her. When he left that house, when he got onto the helicopter ten minutes later he had one focus, Adrian Constantin.

7

4.5 Hours Later, Arizona

HE'D HAD ADRIAN HAULED out of that pit by Jeff and Leonard. He was back in that cottage and he'd had the place swept for any cameras and had five of them removed. He was in the living room with Adrian. He pulled the dagger out and waited for him to wake.

He fired off a text to Rita, his PA at Kovac,

"Privately ask Rick to find me someone internal on the IT team with the same IT skills as Liam D and fly them to Phoenix, AZ ASAP. When they arrive at the Constantin Center, they should email me for directions. Send me details and I'll have them picked up. Tell Rick to instruct whoever he sends to tell no one where they're going. No one! You keep this to yourself, too."

She'd replied back saying she'd get back to him on that and then she asked when he'd be back. He told her he'd keep her posted and to continue to send all his calls to his associate, Rick as well as to tell Rick to email him with a progress report on everything happening.

Rick had tried to call him several times, but he'd replied with texts. The last reply to a text, sent two days prior, had said,

"Brandt wants to meet. Plus we need to discuss strategy re: filling Liam's position as well as other topics. Call me pls."

He didn't give two fucks about Kovac right now, but had to keep up appearances until he'd decided what to do next. He hadn't been keeping up appearances all that well since Kyla took off from his condo, but the occasional check-in and delegating of emails had been all he could do.

Rita was in a functional trance and had worked for him for 6 years. Most of Kovac was made up of vampires, the males, anyway. The few females working there were non-vamp because unless they had a disposition like Sasha, they'd be ruthless. And he'd never met a female vamp like Sasha. Ruthless worked in business sometimes but not a she-vamp's type of ruthless. It'd be a disaster.

His rage hadn't simmered in the least. He needed to bring it down a notch so that he could get everything he needed from Constantin before ending the fucker. But,he couldn't bring it down too far or he'd feel what was shadowing the rage: the despair, the worry that she was all but gone and that gone was ahead on the horizon.

Adrian's eyelids started to move, and he woke in a panic but didn't have the motor function yet to move the way he was trying. The longer a vamp was down the more time it took to get back to normal. As a result of his fear, he was frantic, trying to get off the floor but like a turtle that had been flipped onto its shell.

"Tr-Tristan, I.I..."

He was in absolute panic.

"You're dead," Tristan said calmly, a sneer on his face.

Adrian shook his head rapidly, "No, no. No. Please. I can help her."

"She isn't here."

"She's not? Oh God, she's not gone?" Adrian looked ravaged with despair.

"Not yet."

Adrian breathed relief.

"But she's dying. Your fault."

"I... I need a feed. Please. Let me get my bearings and we can talk."

"Fuck you."

"You'd have killed her yourself if I hadn't protected her during her cycle, Tristan! You turned her because she would've died!"

"After the cycle that only happened because of the drug you gave her to force a miscarriage? And turning happened after the safety you promised wasn't delivered."

Tristan's chest was rising and falling, his nostrils flaring, cold fog streaming out of his mouth.

Adrian's fear spiked higher.

"You know we couldn't take that chance. We had to make sure she could survive. You needed me. You needed... help. I helped. I can still help. There's so much I can help with. Please, let me—-"

Tristan looked right into Adrian's eyes "Do you have other enchanted pets on site? Besides Claudio's?"

"Yes. Twins. My own pets. But you can't feed from them."

"*My* bloodline?" He didn't want to feed from them. He wanted to know about royal pet blood sources on site.

"They are part Kovac. Your grandfather's twin brother sired them."

If Tristan cared a lick about his family, this might've bothered him. It didn't. Obviously, it was how things went, disgusting as this breeding plan was and he knew it made him evil to be willing to exploit innocents but when it came to saving Kyla, he didn't give a fuck what he had to do to succeed at saving her. If it was even possible. Constantin clearly went out of his way to breed pets for royals, to breed breeders for royals, to constantly do things for royal vampires, keeping them royal. This was the first he'd heard of Alexander having a twin. It was irrelevant right now.

"Non-related?"

"We probably still have Claudio's here unless you know otherwise but no other royal bloodlines on site right now. There are a few unturned true vamps in the dorm. Twelve enchanted pets. Two or three, I think, meet your preferred specs."

"But there are others? I want detailed information on your breeding program. I want all your information." He wanted to know if anyone else was there with blood like Kyle's.

"Take it. I'll log you in, give you hard copies of my records, whatever you need."

He threw a blood bag at Adrian, "Drink that and take me to the lab, your office, and to your feeder dorm."

Adrian finished the bag, "That wasn't enough. I need access to my girls. Take me to my suite?"

"Too fucking bad; up." Tristan stared in his eyes and then told him how to act around his staff, cool, collected, aloof. He instructed him to be completely at his command.

And then Tristan followed Adrian to his office, where Adrian gave Tristan access to all of his files and where Tristan packed up his computer. He had Adrian follow him to Sam's room where he'd grabbed Donavan's laptop bag that Sam told him through a text was stashed underneath a chest of drawers. Adrian then took him to his office where they collected a variety of numbered blood samples on ice and then the dorm off the hallway and was really fucking disgusted with what he saw.

The dorm housed dozens. Some were pregnant. Some were being experimented on medically. Some children were on site. Jackson Curtis was there, part of the security team for the dorm. He tried to approach Tristan and Tristan knew by his expression that he would say something that pissed him off, just like he'd done when they'd first met before everything went wrong.

He'd knocked on the door and asked about Kyla and said he wanted to talk to her and Sam had explained who Jackson Curtis was. Tristan had reacted by throwing him bodily across the room, wanting to end the fucker for what pain he'd caused Kyla, not to mention the fact that the sonofabitch had touched what was his, period.

He glared in the guy's eyes now and ordered, "Don't fucking talk to me. Keep your mouth shut until I leave."

He was also disgusted with what he'd seen on security cameras. The hedonism on the rehab floor was out of this world. He was beginning to see what Kyla and Sasha saw regarding vampirism and how fucking selfish it all was. He'd already started to feel that way after spending time with Kyla initially but now? Now it was even stronger.

Before her, he'd never thought twice about taking what he wanted in terms of blood and sex or anything else for that matter. There was a *live and let live* mentality among royals, though not among others. The royals watched those beneath them closely to make sure they stayed in line.

Today, his world looked a little different to him and it made him really fucking angry. He was losing Kyla and he was in a world that now made him sick to his stomach. That world was why he was losing her, but it was also why he had her in the first place.

He checked Adrian's private quarters and removed a laptop, ignoring Adrian's pets, three redheads who'd been asleep together in a big bed, two of them twins, obviously Tristan's own relatives. He felt Adrian's eyes on him as they were walking back to the cottage. Leonard stood outside, Jeff and one of Adrian's goons had been loading the helicopter.

He told them to guard the door and got Adrian back inside.

Adrian was radiating fea. "Please, Tristan. Take me to her. I can try to help."

"What can *you* do to help? What?"

"I...I..."

"I-nothing. You're scrambling to try to think of something to delay me from killing you."

"I can gather several vamps with programming skills and they can work on her. We can get her close. Maybe not completely lucid but above typical functional. We can..."

"Not good enough. I can program *you*. You think I haven't tried to talk her back to lucidity? You're done. I'm done. I am fucking done."

"The consequences of this—-"

"No. There won't be consequences of this. This is over."

Maybe he'd move Sasha here. Get her trying to undo some of the damage and then find a way to move forward with a different mindset. He'd meet with Brandt. He'd influence him if he had to.

He'd influence all of them, one vamp at a time. He felt like he had the power. It'd been rising in him, barely contained power, and he just had to figure out how to use it the best way, a way that he could live with, a way that would make Kyla proud.

Tristan felt the truth seep into his bones. If she died, he wouldn't be powerful. He'd shrivel up and die, too, but not before he unleashed wrath on everything in his sight. A beast inside of him would roar first in rage and in grief and bring his fist down on everything.

He reached forward and had Adrian's throat in his grasp.

"Tell me about Kyle Kelly. What did you do to him medically?"

"What do you mean?"

"I mean he's been unconscious since he was taken from here."

"The last I'd seen him, he was unconscious. Look at his files, you'll see. We did a blood transfusion and we also did some hypnotherapy and I medicated him with an experimental cocktail. He should've woken and recovered within a few weeks. I've used that cocktail to induce comas after severe strain on a person. It gives them a chance to heal. They generally wake up within 15-20 days."

"He didn't."

"I-I don't know. Take me to him and I'll..."

"Any parting words?"

"Fucking let me try to help her. You haven't let me try!"

"You don't touch her."

"If you try to blend her blood with her twin's blood..."

"It didn't help."

Adrian deflated, "I was so sure."

"You were wrong."

"I can pair you up with Kyla's sister's child. I saved the child even though the sister died in childbirth. She's in Switzerland at a boarding School in St. Gallen and her blood is exceptional. It's mixed with Jasper heritage as well as Voitenko two generations back. You'll have to wait for her to mature but..."

"I don't want her sister's child. Kyla is mine. And she's fucking dying because of you!"

And because of me. But someone has to pay.

Adrian was turning blue as Tristan's grip tightened. He loosened it. The bastard wasn't going to die an easy suffocating death. He needed to feel pain.

A phone was ringing from Tristan's back pocket. He pulled it out. He didn't know the number. It was a 206 area code.

Was it the satellite phone calling? He'd left it with Sam.

Gut rot.

Were they calling to say Kyla was gone? He didn't think he could cope with that news right now. He let it ring.

It stopped and started ringing again immediately. He stared at the screen, blood thundering in his veins, a chill rising in his chest.

"Please answer that," Adrian pleaded, wanting an extra minute, probably to think of another reason for Tristan to spare him.

He answered the phone, "Talk."

"Tristan!" It was Sasha and she sounded frantic.

The world stopped turning, everything went on pause except for his thundering heart, as he braced.

"I need you here as fast as you can get here. As fast as you possibly can, Tristan. We don't have much time."

"Much time for what? What's happening?"

"She's almost gone. Seriously. I think she's only waiting because you ordered her to but we don't have much time..."

Tristan's blood pressure hammered in his ears at the same time as it chilled.

"She's in a really *really* bad way but I heard from my contact. He knows of this scenario with Kyla. She needs your blood, Tristan. You need to get here and feed her *your* blood."

"What?"

"I'll explain when you get here after you feed her. Please hurry!"

"I can be there in a little over three hours. Do we have three hours?"

"Maybe. She's on life support, Tristan. She crashed. But I used a defibrillator, got her heart beating, and I've got her breathing on her own but she's really close to shutting down. Hurry."

TWENTY MINUTES LATER, he and a daggered Adrian on that helicopter, which had been on standby, were en route. He had Adrian's computer, Liam's computer, a pile of blood sample vials in a cooler, a suitcase filled with supplies to make more medical patches, and Adrian was daggered and unconscious."

Two hours, 56 minutes later

A SEA PLANE WAS SLOWING on its pontoons in front of the dock at Sasha's place.

Two minutes after that

TRISTAN WAS IN FRONT of Kyla's hospital bed opening his palm with his fangs and putting his blood into her mouth and he was praying. He was praying harder than he'd ever prayed, praying that it wasn't too late. The instant his feet touched ground he'd sped in, right to her.

All Sasha said was, "Hurry!"

For a split second, she wasn't moving. Wasn't swallowing. The blood from his palm was in her mouth, on her tongue, on her lower lip.

After a few seconds that felt like an eternity, Kyla swallowed and licked her lips and almost instantaneously Kyla's skin tone brightened from nearly grey to rosy and pink and her eyes opened.

They were lucid.

Lucid.

"Hey," she whispered, her voice sounding hoarse. "Holy crap; I had the weirdest dream..."

"Princess..." he choked out. Tears blurred his vision when it registered, when he saw her gorgeous green eyes and it penetrated that she was 100% there.

Part 2

Kyla

8

SHE HEARD TRISTAN'S heartbeat. She knew instinctually that it was his. It got louder and then louder still, like it was closing in on her. Her own heartbeat went stuttered, like it tripped over itself, and then it was righted -—it started to march to the tempo of his.

Everything went from hazy and weird to zooming 100% into focus. Her mouth tasted like grape Fanta. He was leaning over her, one of his eyes black as night, the other icy blue, his fangs showing and his face wasn't grey but it was hard, angry, tortured? Orange Dreamsicles, brownies, cookies, a myriad of desserty aromas all at assaulted her at once.

"Hey," she whispered, her voice hoarse, "Holy crap; I had the weirdest dream..."

His body locked, he blinked, and then tears spilled out of his eyes and one landed on her lip. She caught it with the tip of her tongue.

"Oh God," He crumpled onto the bed and let out a big stuttered breath into her chest.

She felt him. She felt his love, his relief, this immense and overpowering relief. It was gushing.

He was shaking, trembling hard.

Tears sprang to her own eyes at the sheer amount of raw emotion coming at her. It was in the air; it was on her. It was *in* her. There was just so much of it; more than had ever come at her before.

A pretty woman with wavy shoulder-length light brown hair, bright near-amber eyes, and glasses was in a doctor's coat and she was standing behind Tristan and she was crying and smiling: happy-crying. She smiled at Kyla and waved. Kyla gave her a little wave back. She looked familiar.

Sam was there, too, his hand on the doctor's shoulder, and he was smiling at Kyla, huge, smiling bigger than she had seen him smile so far. They moved out of the room and shut the door, leaving them alone.

Kyla put her arms around Tristan and squeezed. She saw tubes coming from her hand; she was hooked up to machines. There was a tube in her nose. It felt so invasive all of a sudden.

She looked off to the side, trying to take in her surroundings. No, they weren't alone after all. And she didn't know where they were.

She saw a bed with someone in it beside the bed she was in. Her eyes didn't linger; her attention turned back to the dark head of hair that was resting on her chest, the shoulders that were trembling.

He lifted his head and looked into her eyes. "Baby."

He was an emotional mess. She kissed his forehead, put her hands on his trembling shoulders, and rubbed her hands up and down his arms.

He started to pull tubes out of her hand, out of her arm, out of her nose and then he lifted her up out of bed. "Are you okay? Are you really *you*?" He started touching her face, feeling her hair, sniffing at her throat, kissing her lips.

"I'm fine," she chuckled. "What do you mean am I me? Are you *you?*"

She felt fine. In fact, she felt fantastic.

"You're you..."

He pinched her upper lip and lifted and then used his other thumb to press on her gums.

"What are you doing?" She shook her head in confusion.

He lifted her into his arms and then pulled out another tube and she felt an odd sensation down below. A catheter?

What the?

He carried her out of the room, through a doorway that was actually a weird coat closet, and then out of a big office, down a hallway of windows that she couldn't see out of because it was dark outside, and then up some stairs, then whooshed up and sideways and then into a bedroom.

He put her down on the edge of an unfamiliar unmade bed covered with a colourful patchwork quilt and then an instant later he was ripping clothes off her, pushing her back onto the bed and he was on top of her, unzipping his jeans as he kissed up her thigh to her magic spot, shredding the panties she had on.

He groaned, tasting her and making her back arch. He licked and nipped and sucked and she felt it with so much intensity, more than she could even process, and then she was on edge, all her nerves feeling...feeling so much. He started kissing the rest of the way up her body. She wove her fingers into his hair and tried to push his head back down, so he could finish what he'd started but he chuckled and kept moving up until his teeth connected with her throat. He drank ravenously.

She moaned, "I love you so much, baby" as she felt her blood enter him and it made her entire body tingle happily.

He moaned and squeezed tighter, kissed her throat and grabbed her ass cheeks with both hands and then he slammed inside, to the hilt. His right hand moved down to her clit and his fingers started circling. Her pelvis circled right along with him, feeling and smelling him, loving him, needing him, never wanting this moment to end.

"I love you so much, Kyla, you have no idea how much. Oh God, princess. Baby. Fuck."

"No, I do know, honey. I can feel it. I feel it more than ever." She touched his face, her eyes glistening. She felt so loved and cherished and felt so much love *for* him that her heart just might burst into fireworks.

"Our hearts are in danger of exploding all over this room," she told him as she wiped tears from her eyes and then kissed one from the corner of his.

What was all this emotion all about?

She felt a little bit foggy and *a lot* confused.

He gave her a huge dimpled smile, "I'm okay going out like that if you're with me. I can't live without you, my little cherry bomb. I've lived these last endless days, I don't even know how many, they all blended together, without having all of you and I can't do it ever again. I can't. I won't."

"My prince..." she whispered and kissed the cleft on his chin, "What happened, Tristan?"

His pace quickened, his penetration deepened, and then he came inside of her, his eyes shining with love and, strangely, with something that looked like fierce anger at the same time.

She whispered his name and then he rolled onto his back, taking her with him, pulling her close. He kissed her deeply, with so much freaking passion, passion she'd never even experienced from him before. Like he loved her more. Way more. And he loved her so much, before.

He tasted amazing. Sugar, spice, all kinds of nice.

She finally pulled back, needing air. His hands continued to roam her body, her hair; his lips travelled everywhere. He rained kisses all over her face and then started to nip with fangs all over her upper body and she squealed. She got up onto her knees, straddling him but he flipped her onto her back and moved down until his lips were on her inner thigh.

He bit in and started feeding again. Her eyes rolled back, taking in his emotions. His relief, his immense relief. Taking the sensations he was giving her. Amazing tingles, beautiful waves of euphoria inside her veins.

He moved back up; he was back inside her.

She giggled. "Wow, you're energetic!" She put her index finger in the cleft on his chin.

"You have no idea," he told her, and she felt all swoony...his gaze darkened carnally. He moved slowly, rotating his hips, and then his nose found its way to crook of her neck.

He was right; she had *no* idea. But whatever all this was, it felt huge.

"You smell so amazing." His fingers grazed her there and then his eyes gazed over her face warmly. "You feel so good. And I can feel you so much, baby..."

She wrapped her legs around him, "Hurry, honey. Finish and feed me. I'm so freaking starving it's not even funny."

He flipped so that she was on top and gripped the headboard behind him with one hand, his other hand on her clit.

"Ride me as hard as you can, princess. And then I'll feed you."

She did. She rode as hard as she could, and it was wild. Tristan looked astonished when he had his climax, the sound he made alone would make a stadium filled with women cream their pants.

News Alert! Pants creaming crisis -—nationwide!

THEY TOOK A SHOWER together in a bathroom down the hall from that bedroom.

"Where are we?" she asked him while he worked lather through her hair and she lathered up his abs. She knew something was up, of course, waking up to that drama and getting that kind of reaction from him and being in a weird place, but she'd just given herself over to the beauty of the moment.

"What's the last thing you remember?

"I'm not quite sure. It's hazy."

"I have a lot to tell you," he replied, pulling her close, "Tip your head back."

She did, and he began to rinse her hair out. His fingers felt so good on her head. She moaned at how good they felt. But then his lips, followed by his teeth were on her throat again, drinking.

"God, you're thirsty," she moaned.

He swallowed a few times and then let go, "You feel okay, right? I'm reading you right?"

"Yeah, fine."

"Because I'm feeling everything, thank god, and you don't feel depleted at all and yet I've fed so much. I've been a little starved but couldn't take much from you, couldn't risk depleting you too much."

"No, I feel fine. I need food soon but I'm good." She scrubbed soap over his chest and up over his shoulders, then trailed down toward his abs again. She would never get tired of rubbing her hands up and down those abs.

"Damn," he said and then drank more, this time from the other side of her throat and then he was inside her again, thrusting deep and lifting her off the shower floor, "You taste fucking amazing! Better than you've ever tasted."

"You always say that."

"And I always mean it."

She gave him a big smile and got her hands between his legs and started working him over.

He carried her back to the bed and was all over her.

'You're a machine," she groaned, "Take a break and make me an omelette before my vajayjay falls off!"

He laughed, "You've lost weight. I'll make you a ten-egg omelette with four pounds of cheese. As soon as I come."

She pulled away and pointed at his cock, "Down boy! You've come four times."

He laughed some more and rolled her onto her side and spooned against her, getting back inside from behind, his teeth piercing her shoulder as he growled. "I need one more. Now, baby."

TRISTAN PULLED HIS jeans back on and pulled her to the kitchen after his "one more."

Kyla had gotten up, put on some shorts and a t-shirt, and while Tristan made food, she looked out the window ahead of the long farm table that delineated the space in front of a massive window.

The landscape in front of her was hard to see as it was nighttime, but she could see that it was water beyond a beach. The sky was starry, giving her a bit of the promise of a fantastic view. There were two people on the beach, one carrying something over his shoulder. Was that a person being carried?

"Baby." He was behind her, bare chested, gray sweatpants sitting low on his hips, and he had plates of food, one in each of his hands. He kissed her shoulder and passed her a plate and they walked back to that bedroom. He climbed onto the bed beside her and they dug in to large cheesy omelettes with buttered toast.

He reached into one pocket and pulled out a bottle of water, put the plate on the bed and then reached into the other pocket and pulled out a purple juice box. He handed her the juice box.

She chuckled at it. "A juice box? Am I five?"

"Haven't got grape Fanta but you've been asking for grape. I found a few boxes of grape juice in the fridge, so Sasha must've found some."

"When did I ask for grape Fanta? Who's Sasha? Where are we?"

"Eat, then we'll talk."

"So bossy. Wait, I tasted grape when I woke up from that weird dream."

He showed dimples and leaned over and kissed her temple. Then he got a faraway look for a second and said,

"You have no idea how happy I am to have you telling me not to boss you. No fucking idea, princess."

She dug in to the omelette, freaking famished, "Uh...but yet you're still bossing me?"

He smiled big. No, huge.

"You tasted grape?"

"Mm hmm," she mumbled as she chewed a big bite of the food.

"Hmm."

"Hmm what?"

"Eat, princess. Then we'll talk."

"How 'bout some polite dinner conversation?" she suggested. "Where you enlighten me..."

He ate a bite, swallowed, then took another bite and swallowed a mouthful of water. She waited, watching him.

His expression darkened,

"Claudio and Liam both fed on you. They almost killed you. I had to turn you. I almost lost you. You almost died." A muscle jerked in his clenched jaw.

She put the fork down.

"Finish that?" He jerked his chin at her plate.

"I'm just taking a breather, Mr. Bossy Pants. Start at the beginning."

"You don't remember anything?"

"I remember like... I was dreaming. It was all... blurry and foggy and I kept hearing you talk to me, but your voice was far away. It was trippy. Like I was inside a kaleidoscope. And stoned."

"You were mesmerized. Or like that. But worse."

She frowned, ripped the plastic on the juice box straw with her teeth, removed the plastic and then jammed the straw in the hole and drank some. It was blah.

The omelette was awesome, though. Filled with cheese and sweet fried tomatoes with the perfect amount of black pepper. She forked up another bite.

"Claudio flooded the exam room with a gas that made me disoriented for a minute and I found him feeding on you. I stopped him. And then Liam was there, and *he* was fuckin' feeding on you. He gave me a dagger jab and when I came to, you'd daggered him but he'd been feeding and you were barely there, bleeding out, that bastard on top of you. Adrian and I got him off and I had to turn you. You were gonna die. If I didn't you wouldn't have survived. I thought you were gone, lost to me. A vampress who'd hate my fucking guts. But I couldn't let you die. I just couldn't."

She frowned, "I don't feel like a vampire."

"You're not. Not exactly. I don't know yet what your status is. When you woke up you were mesmerized, worse than mesmerized. You weren't a vamp. You don't have fangs. But you weren't you. You were a goddamn shell and it was bad, so fuckin' bad, princess. I couldn't feel you. Your blood didn't taste the same. You weren't vamp but you weren't you and I couldn't feel anything coming from you. I wanted to kill. Kill everything and everyone around me. Somehow I kept it together and tried to get my head straight so that I could figure out what to do. Fuck, I don't know if my head'll be straight ever again after all that.

At first you were just a shell but then after a couple days you started to get sick. You were having seizures and high fevers and they kept getting worse. I finally tried feeding again, thinkin' you were in withdrawals from my not feeding and you tasted like you, after not tasting like you. No, scratch that. You tasted like you, but you tasted even better, like your menstrual blood. Which was fucked because I couldn't feel you and you still weren't you and the strength I've been getting from your blood since then, baby, it's huge. It's like it's the nectar. Your blood, your menstrual blood, neither hold a candle to how your blood tastes now, how powerful it makes me feel. But unlike before, I have control now. I have new talents, I'm stronger. Than ever. I barely even had any before today and what little I did have, it was like a magic potion for me."

She took another bite of the food and put the plate on the long oak chest of drawers that was against the wall and climbed back into bed and snuggled into his shoulder, looking up at his face. He put his arm around her and cupped her shoulder.

"You started tasting better but you were still out of it and I could feel you but only while I was feeding and I felt like I couldn't even take much; you were so weak. There was something wrong, though. You were mesmerized, practically catatonic, and you were in pain, but my diagnostic skills weren't working. You were desperate for something. You kept getting worse and I couldn't help you. I've never been so frustrated, so lost in my life."

She kissed the hinge of his jaw and gave a squeeze.

"And then I just woke up?" she asked.

"No. There's more." His expression darkened again.

Yikes.

He took a big breath, "I found out some things. I found out some things about your family, your past. This is a lot to take in. Maybe we oughta get you some sleep and then talk some more after we sleep. It's like 3 o'clock in the morning."

"I'm not tired. I feel like I've been asleep for weeks. Are you tired?"

"Exhausted. Can't wait to sleep properly knowing you're here, really here."

"Oh."

He snuggled her close, "Here's the condensed version. But I'm knackered so will you save the who/what/when/why for tomorrow?"

"Can't promise that. But go..."

He smiled huge, with dimples.

"I found out you have family that might've been able to share their blood with you, hoped that blood in your veins'd help bring you back. So, we tried that and it didn't work. I found that family and brought you to him and Sasha, she's a doctor, Sam's sister, she tried it and it didn't work and you were getting worse, so I started to lose it. I had her and Sam watch over you and I went back to Arizona to find out if there was blood or some other mystery in Adrian's lab or on his compound that'd help. You were at death's door when Sasha told me she got a tip that I needed to get back here and feed you *my* blood. That you needed to consume my blood to save you. And it did. I opened my hand, fed it to you, and you opened your eyes almost immediately and you were you. You were at death's fuckin' door, baby. You crashed, and Sasha had to fucking put paddles to your chest. I hadn't had more than a split second of the real you in days that felt like years, and then here you are. I daggered Adrian and brought him with me with a pile of his lab shit. I have a whack of shit to figure out now. I have to talk to Sasha and find out about your needing my blood and what this all means. You're not vamp, but yet you needed my blood to bring you back from the brink of death. I don't know why yet."

Kyla was astonished. She didn't know how to react. This was a wild story.

Shit, my whole life is a wild story.

"Him?" she asked.

"Hmm?"

"Family?" she clarified, "You said you brought me to him. To who?"

"Your brother."

"I knew I had siblings. I just knew it! I knew from things Adrian said and things my father wouldn't say. Where is he? How much younger than me is he?"

Tristan blew out a long breath and took one of her hands in both of his and squeezed, "He's your twin, baby. You have other siblings besides. But your twin brother is downstairs in a hospital bed."

Kyla's jaw dropped, and she blinked a few times.

Tristan kissed her forehead and gave her hand another squeeze.

"Is he okay? Is he hurt because of me?"

"Because of you?"

"Because he gave me his blood?"

"No, princess. He's been in a coma for nearly two years. He's spent most of his life in that compound. Adrian did something medically to him and he hasn't woken up since. There's more but it can wait until tomorrow. I'll take you to him tomorrow and you can see him and talk to Sasha and hear the rest. Can we sleep?"

"Oh...kay..." she frowned.

"Be right back." He grabbed his plate, her plate, and left the room.

Kyla got up and stepped across the hall to the bathroom, used the facilities, and looked in the mirror. She stared, dumbfounded.

Turned to a vampire but failed. Almost died. Drank Tristan's blood and came back. Twin brother?

Whoa.

She wondered what his name was. What he looked like. What he was like. Dear in the headlights or what?

Panic spiked in her gut and chest simultaneously, but it wasn't her own panic; it was Tristan's. She heard him holler, "Kyla!"

Thrumming revved up inside her veins and her heart began to race.

She opened the bathroom door, "I'm here!"

He was there, looking relieved. He looked rough, like he'd seen a ghost.

"It's okay, I'm here." She put her hand on his chest. His heart was racing, giving her palpitations, too.

He leaned against the wall and took a big breath. The panic was still rolling off him in waves. He settled down and nodded. She pulled him close. He buried his face in her neck.

Suddenly Sam was there. Sasha was there, too.

"It's all okay," Kyla said, "We're good. Hi Sam."

"Welcome back, love." He smiled.

Tristan straightened but didn't let go of her.

"Thanks. Hi Sasha. Nice to meet you. Thank you for your help. Thank you so, *so* much."

"A pleasure, Kyla. We've already met. Several times. But I'm thinking that's a story for tomorrow."

"You'd be thinking right," Tristan said, "I've spent some time catching Kyla up some but there's a lot so the rest of it's for tomorrow."

"Right," Sasha smiled, "Sleep well."

"Where is he?" Tristan asked Sam.

"Boathouse; tied, gagged, and still daggered," Sam gave him a smirk. "And somehow he might've gotten a black eye and a split lip." Sam shrugged with a sheepish grin.

Tristan looked to Sasha. "You found all what I brought back?"

"I did. It's all refrigerated and / or down in the lab. We can go over it tomorrow. Why is he here, Tristan?" Her expression was grim.

"We'll talk tomorrow."

"Um...alright," Sasha was stressed.

"You don't have to worry about him going off and then making a plan to bulldoze in here and ruin what you've built. He's not leaving here alive."

Chills shot up Kyla's spine. Sasha winced.

"Night all," Sam said and headed down the hall.

"Thank you. Both of you," Tristan said softly.

"My pleasure. Truly," Sasha told him.

"Ditto," Sam called over his shoulder, "The least we could do."

"'Night," Kyla said.

Tristan led her back into the bedroom and they curled up together on the bed. He threw the blankets over them and let out a long breath and put his head on her chest on top of her heart. She put her hands in his hair and kissed the top of his head.

"Am I crushing you?" he asked, his voice a whisper.

"Not at all." She kept caressing his head with one hand and put her arm around his back.

"Hold me tight," he ordered.

She did.

"Tighter," he demanded.

"Mr. Bossy Pants," she said but complied.

It didn't take long until she heard his breath even out. Surprisingly, despite all the sleeping she'd been doing, she yawned, and it didn't take long for her to pass out, too.

9

CLAUDIO WAS WEARING goggles and his fangs were out. He was at her throat, ripping it with his teeth. And then Tristan hauled him off and ripped his head off. Literally. Tristan went black-eyed and gray hulk on him and separated his head from his shoulders as if it was nothing more than a piece of cotton. But then she saw Liam's face as his fangs got closer to her and she could feel her blood spilling out of her own throat, could smell it, could hear it dripping onto the floor. Drip, drip, drip... as Liam's huge fanged mouth closed in on her.

She jolted awake; gasping, sweating, shaking.

A dream.

God, thank God, it wasn't real. But it was real. It was just that it'd already happened.

Tristan had her. He was holding her close, kissing her, rocking her gently, "I've got you, baby. I've got you. It's okay. You're fine. Look at me."

She looked up into his gorgeous eyes.

"Thank fuck," he was relieved.

She clung to him desperately and choked on emotion. That felt so real; like she was in it again.

"Shhhh," he kept rocking, kept holding her.

She felt so lucky to have him to hold onto. She could feel how much he loved her; she felt protected. She rubbed her hands up and down the warm, smooth skin on his muscled back.

"Thank fuck what?" she asked, finally.

"That your eyes aren't vacant again."

He rubbed his palm lazily up and down her back, too, "What did you dream?" He kissed her forehead sweetly.

"I think I was re-living what happened in the lab. Claudio in those goggles coming at me, ripping my throat, then you ripping him apart. Then Liam... I'm soaked with sweat. I'm gonna go take a shower."

"Okay, baby; I'll come, too."

He threw the blankets back and reached to hold her hand. As they moved to the bathroom she saw the view and it was gorgeous.

It was blue as far as the eye could see, beyond a rocky-looking beach with a long and wide dock. A speed boat and two canoes were parked at a dock that was beside a large boathouse, the size of a four-car garage, at least. Sam was sitting on the dock in an Adirondack chair with a fishing rod in his hand, a cigar protruding from his teeth as he reeled something in.

"THIS SHOWER IS SUPPOSED to be for getting clean!" Kyla admonished Tristan, but doing it giggling as she'd been trying to get clean and her vampire clearly had intentions of a different nature for the shower. She'd been trying to scrub her skin, thinking that she seriously needed an alone shower with a razor, when she found herself with one leg hooked over Tristan's shoulder, Tristan on his knees, head buried in her kinda-in-need-of-a-shave girlie parts!

When they were done, Tristan having given her a spectacular orgasm plus having fed from her inner thigh, and back in the bedroom getting dressed, Kyla putting on jeans since she hadn't gotten time to shave her legs, she took in their surroundings.

The room was large and sort of plain, white walls, no artwork, older-looking utilitarian furniture, but comfortable and that view was absolutely spectacular. She could stare at that view every morning for the rest of her days and not grow weary of it.

"Wanna go eat?" He kissed her shoulder and wrapped his arms around her. She nuzzled in.

"I missed you so fucking much, baby," he told her, "I can't even..." he trailed off.

She put her palms on his forearms and squeezed.

"I wanna keep you all to myself, but we have to talk, find out what's goin' on."

She nodded, "I'm hungry, anyway."

"Let's go feed you."

"'Kay."

Sasha and Sam were at the kitchen table, huddled close. Both of their heads popped up when Tristan and Kyla walked into the room hand in hand.

Sam got up and poured coffees from a coffee pot for them and then motioned toward the cream and sugar sitting on the table.

"Good morning. Feeling good?" Sasha smiled.

Kyla nodded, "Feelin' fantastic."

Tristan put her at the empty seat at the foot of the long table, what felt like miles away from Sam and his sister, and then he took her cup and doctored it with sugar, grabbed milk from the fridge and gave it a splash and then stirred, sipped it, and passed it to her.

She smiled at him and took a sip.

"Nectar of the freakin' gods," she moaned, noting he was still being a royal taster.

They all laughed at the irony.

"Speaking of nectar of the gods ..." Sasha said, "We've got to chat."

Tristan sat beside Kyla and lifted his chin.

"Things were pretty touch and go there for a while. I really was worried that you wouldn't make it." She was looking at Kyla.

Kyla winced, not sure how to feel. She knew Tristan had been stressed, but it was all hard to relate to because she hadn't, essentially, seen or felt any of what'd happened.

"Thank you for helping us," Kyla said.

"My pleasure. Maybe you can help, too." She offered.

"How's that?" Kyla inquired.

"I don't know yet *how* but Kyle..."

"Careful," Tristan warned. Kyla wasn't sure what he meant. She looked at him quizzically.

"Nothing puts Kyla at risk. Don't ask her to do anything that would."

Sasha looked at him and then forged on.

"Of course. I need you to know that when I got that call back from my contact, the Ukrainian elder who is coming to see me in a few days, he'd read my message and, Tristan, he knew immediately that I was talking about you."

Tristan's jaw clenched.

"Please don't worry. It's only because it's common knowledge who you are and how those things are handled in terms of enchanted pets. Anyone in a high-level position would have an idea based on timing alone. He keeps his eye on things. He didn't know specifics, not about what'd transpired of the union of you both, but any elders with ties to North America would know that you were paired with someone chosen for you specifically and because of your bloodline, they'd know it'd be anticipated. Anyway, he's also aware of Dr. Constantin's work. Well aware. He's not a fan, obviously. He'd like to know if you could meet with him. If he cannot convince you to join us he's willing to be outed. He feels the time has come. I hope you'll consider it, all of what we have to say. You are welcome to stay here and relax. He will arrive in a few days. He says he has a lot of information to share about your bond with Kyla."

"Keep talkin'," Tristan urged.

"The gist of what he's told me is that by you feeding her your blood, you've altered the course of your connection. Because she was already bonded to you, you doing that cemented a completely symbiotic relationship. A marriage, if you will. Essentially, the bond between you two has strengthened her as it strengthens you, because of the amount of vampire DNA she has. This isn't possible unless there's a high amount of vamp DNA on both ends. Wouldn't work if one of you was simply turned, for instance. And while new talents are evolving in you, she's also evolving. We know she started evolving even before the turning, but now it'll escalate. She now relies on you. You two are firmly symbiotic. If she'd been turned vampress by a family member, by a true vamp, or even a turned vamp the results would've been different. She would've gone straight to royal vamp. But because she was turned by the vamp she had already been bonded with, it generated these results, a symbiosis. She feeds you. You feed her. She's a bit like a fangless vamp who feeds only on her mate. She didn't have enough blood at the turning and then going without put her into that state."

Shit.

Kyla shivered. This was huge.

"You and Kyla personify the term soulmates. Some animals mate for life. Vamps are among such animal, but few of them know this. It's a choice, a choice *you* made, even if you didn't know it. You can now only exist together. There's push and pull, where you each continually give one another what the other needs. You continually evolve for one another. But it's not always easy to do that when you don't know what the other needs. If this was generations ago and you were in an established coven, you'd be told that this was an option among royals and enchanted blooded unturned royals, but one that requires a complete level of commitment. Nowadays, that doesn't happen much. Not only because it's not widely known about, but also because it's only possible with a very high level of vampire DNA.

There's more dilution in the race nowadays than generations ago when this was more likely. A lot of things about our race are changing because of evolution. This isn't widely known about. For some good reasons. But yeah, soulmates." Sasha got a dreamy expression and Kyla suspected Sasha was a romantic at heart.

"Kyla, if you were completely turned to vamp you'd no longer be able to feed him but due to the fact that you'd bonded," she turned to Tristan, "The turn she took, while she was down, gave you even more of what you needed. It was a sacrifice she was making for you. Being a symbiotic relationship, because you turned her to vamp, she needs to feed on you as well. In the early days she needs a lot of it. It's a choice the vampire makes, and it shouldn't be made lightly because you need one another to survive. You feeding her was the start of the symbiosis. She didn't have a constant supply of your blood to continue to change. You needed to feed her again to continue with it. But you didn't, because you had no idea, so she became ill. Now you should also know that if you lost Kyla, you'd get sick as well; you'd die, eventually, and it'd probably be a long and painful death. For her, it would be painful, but likely a lot quicker. The longer you're together, the longer that would take. You need one another like never before. You have a bond that will continually deepen. You don't have fangs for feeding, obviously, but his blood is *your* nectar and he'll have to provide it for you when you need it. The elder is extremely powerful and he's very familiar with this. He is a child of parents who had a symbiotic bond just like yours. He says there's more, but he'd like to meet you."

"How much? How often?" Tristan asked.

My blood is his nectar. His blood is mine. Wow.

Kyla let out a big breath. Tristan's gaze met hers and his eyes communicated emotion, love for her. She smiled.

"Not sure. The practice isn't widely known about. Sergey, the elder, is happy to discuss it with you."

"Sergey? Not Sergey Voitenko?" Tristan asked.

"Yes."

"Fuck me." Tristan shook his head. Kyla looked at him. He gave his head a shake. "I'm surprised he's part of this coalition."

"You'd actually be very surprised just how many vampires are ready for change, Tristan," Sasha said, "And if you opted to be part of that change there's no telling what could happen."

Tristan gave her a blank look, revealing nothing. Kyla was a little confused. She was about to start firing questions. Tristan cut off her thoughts by saying, "So for now, we let Kyla dictate the pace for feeding?"

"Yes, I think so. Keep an eye on her. Look for signs of discomfort or lethargy. If you'd stay until he arrives, Sergey will have more information. We have other things to review as well. Would anyone like some breakfast? I can toast a bagel like a champ."

"Sergey knows all this, but Adrian didn't?" Kyla asked.

"No. Dr. Constantin is well-versed in many areas but as for the old ways, Sergey makes him look like a fresh-faced teenager in contrast. And Sergey isn't a fan so isn't very forthcoming. I know Dr. Constantin has tried to strike a friendship with him in order to gain information in a few areas, but Sergey was never receptive. There haven't been a lot of pure blooded vampires in the last few hundred years. The race became very diluted with turned vamps. That's why Dr. Constantin's breeding program was implemented here. But as much as he knew, he evidently didn't know about this. That's all I know. We'll learn more when Sergey arrives. Breakfast?" She moved toward the counter.

"Tristan makes the world's greatest omelette," Kyla offered with a smile and took a sip of her coffee.

"Not in the mood to cook," he told her and she could feel tension from him as well as see it as he pondered some of this new information.

She shrugged. "Then I could eat a bagel." She rose to get up.

"I'll get it," Tristan motioned to both her and Sasha to sit back down.

"Sasha, do me a favour and give Kyla the lowdown on who you are, how you've been involved in her life? About Kyle?"

She nodded and sipped her coffee and then began,

"I'm Sam's twin and couple years ago, I became vampire. I should've been turned half a century ago, when my brother was turned. But Dr. Constantin, he stopped that from happening. He controlled my life. Beyond what he does with his breeding program for blue blooded vamps he's a renowned medical professional in the vampire community. He helps with vampire illnesses, medical, mental..."

"I'm aware," Kyla said, sipping the coffee, watching Tristan move around the kitchen, getting a bagel into a toaster and fetching a tomato from a basket on the countertop. He rinsed the tomato and then grabbed a knife from a big knife block and sliced it super-fast. Then he lifted an avocado from the basket and held it up and looked to her She gave him an enthusiastic nod.

"It took me a long time to successfully grow those. I bet that's the best avocado you've ever tasted," Sasha beamed.

"Yum," Kyla replied and started wringing her hands together in anticipation. She was fricking starved.

"So anyway, about two years ago I had to look after a vampire who'd recently been turned. He'd been turned while brain dead so required some close examinations, extra care. I was in a functional trance otherwise. You see, Dr. Constantin knew me as a child, I grew up around him, and so we had a relationship before I began to be mesmerized. Children are immune to most types of mesmerisation but after puberty, tend to go into a state of mesmerisation whether the vampire wants it or not.

Dr. Constantin and several high-level vampires all programmed me. They worked with me for a number of sessions to try to help me keep my faculties more than the average entranced human. I knew what was happening around me but I was very pliable. I followed directions. I felt like I was on autopilot most of the time. My brother was turned at age 25 and he became vampire. I was not turned. Our bloodline is such that Sam would have an important advisor and service job with royal vampires. I was intended to be a breeder and to remain human until those obligations were finished, but I wasn't able to conceive. Dr. Constantin wanted to turn me but didn't want me to lose myself, become a typical vampress. We've nicknamed it the bitch switch. It's tongue in cheek and it's really much more serious than bitch.

If you've met any female vampires so far, and I'm sure Tristan has enlightened you a little, vampresses tend to be very cold, very unfeeling. Extraordinarily selfish and without empathy. The overwhelming majority, anyway. Some more than others. Our cousin is vamp and his turned vamp wife is tolerable. She only shows her bitch side in extreme circumstances. The thing is that Jet gives her a very privileged existence. She rarely has reason to go off. But many females are far worse."

"Rebecca Jamieson," Sam interjected. "She has met Becca. She's also briefly met Dawn Jones, not to mention had quite an interesting run-in with Celia Wickson. And then there's Taryn Walker."

Kyla nodded with big eyes.

Sasha gave her a small and understanding smile and then continued.

"Royal and turned vampresses alike are feral. But I was sure I could be different. I had to look after a newly turned vamp and I desperately wanted to be vampire. I'd long since given up trying to convince Dr. Constantin of this, but I was aching for it and I'd been concocting serums in an effort to try to combat the bitch effect. I wasn't getting much of an opportunity to try them out. But I did get a chance to try one with a visiting vampress and it seemed to have helped so I had hope. Dr. Constantin sloughed me off. I got upset. He didn't want to take a chance and have me unruly, on his hands and not able to continue with our work. I had a lot of responsibility. Anyway, I saw an opening. I went quiet with him on the topic for a few years but finally saw that opening with Jackson Curtis."

Kyla's eyes bugged out. She'd thought about Jax many times since seeing him pressed against that window staring longingly at her but there hadn't been an opportunity to find out more.

Until now.

"My brother brought Jackson Curtis to us and long story short, he, freshly turned, wound up in my care and I wasn't mesmerized by him due to the fact that he was so new. Royal vampires freshly turned have more acute strengths than a turned vamp and that turned vamp takes time to develop skills, so it worked in my favour. I had a brief window and used it and convinced Jackson to turn me. I was wrong about the serum I'd developed, and I was wrong in thinking I had control over my emotions, my urges. It was bad. I did bad things. Really bad things."

Tristan put a plate in front of her. Toasted bagel with avocado, cream cheese, and tomato and warmed her coffee up, too.

"Anyone else hungry?" Tristan asked.

Sam and Sasha both said *Not me, thanks* in unison and then Sasha continued.

Kyla was trying to process all she'd been told. Thinking about how Jax looked so much healthier.

"So, to backtrack a bit, we've met, you and I. When you were a child. I was heavily involved in the breeding program, so I've spent time with you and with your brother, Kyle. Your parents, too. We performed a variety of periodic tests before you were taken away."

Kyla's heart began racing. Kyle. Her brother. Her *twin* brother. She took a big sip of coffee. Too big. But it didn't burn going down, surprisingly.

"Kyle and I were close. Before I was turned, while he was awake. We were good friends. I'm sure I was a parental figure for him. He lived at The Constantin Center in Arizona from the time he was nearly four. You were taken, and things went wrong and Kyle was brought in. Your parents' memories were wiped. Kyle had a sheltered upbringing there. Dr. Constantin tried to make it as normal as possible for him, spent quite a bit of time doting on him, but that was until he hit his teens and then the experiments really started. But, one thing that wasn't done was that female vampires were not ever fed Kyle's blood. I took it in small doses for several weeks, sneaking to steal it.

I started to see a change. I started to become me again, only vampire. Yet me. It was a dream come true. But I had to get away from Dr. Constantin. I escaped The Center and took Kyle with me. But he was in a coma. He's still in that coma. I know that taking his blood without his consent was wrong, Kyla. But I also believe that knowing your brother as I do, he would be okay with it knowing how it helped me and knowing how it saved me from hurting others. I really do believe he would be okay with it. But it's been two years and I haven't figured out how to wake him. I *want* to wake him."

Kyla was silent a moment, listening to Sasha, thinking that she seemed very sincere. She seemed so different from the other female vamps Kyla had been exposed to so far.

"What if he doesn't want to stay here? What if he wants to go and you can't feed any longer?" Kyla asked.

"That's his choice."

"Is he in a trance?"

"He was. Before. With others. But with me, before I was vamp we spent a lot of time together, so we had a lot of conversations, lucid ones. He remembered you. He worried about you. He wanted you to be okay. He was hoping you were far away, away from anything to do with this life and that somehow you'd be able to live a normal existence with no exposure to vampires."

"Why can't I remember him? I remember my parents a little, but I don't remember him."

"I don't know why," Sasha answered, "Perhaps due to being traumatized with being taken? I'm not sure."

"She might've been wiped," Sam said.

"She's immune to programming," Tristan reminded him.

"But she's not immune to wiping. I've done it myself."

Kyla stared at Sam, "You have?"

A dangerous vibe was coming off Tristan.

She didn't remember being taken. Her earliest memory was sitting on a park bench with an older lady who told her that she'd be found new parents.

Kyla looked at Tristan. He was leaning against the kitchen counter, arms folded across his chest, watching her.

And she could feel him. She gave him a sad smile. She felt pain sweep through the room coming from him. He regretted all she'd been through so far. He was deeply affected by all of it. Kyla looked deep into his beautiful blue eyes and smiled. She loved him so much.

"I'll explain," Sam said, after you've finished talking to Sasha."

She ate the last bite of the first half of that delicious sandwich he'd made and got up, wiping the corner of her mouth and dropping a serviette on the table and moved to Tristan. He enveloped her into his arms. She tipped her chin up to look at him. He was looking down at her, arms tight around her.

She kissed the cleft on his chin and turned back to Sasha,

"Can I meet him?"

Sasha got to her feet, "Give me ten minutes and then come down?"

"See you in ten," Tristan replied and motioned back to the table. "Gonna finish your breakfast, baby? Sam?"

"Mmm hmmm. This is delicious." She sat down and lifted the remaining half and took a bite. Sam was still seated on the other end of the table and his eyes were on her.

Sam winced and looked to Tristan. Tristan jerked his chin, urging Sam to answer.

"Why did you save Jax?" she asked point blank after swallowing, "And what do you mean you've wiped me?"

"I told myself I thought maybe we could use him. If we couldn't use him, he could be used to lure you somehow, perhaps. I was having trouble getting you to Toronto. You weren't following my directions. The only thing I was capable of with you was wiping your memory of me after each attempt. So I'd try to influence you but it wouldn't work and then I'd wipe your memory. But I, uh, had an attack of conscience after his accident, which occasionally happens to me where things with you are concerned, and then thought I'd just bring him to Adrian and put him there temporarily in case we needed him. Adrian found use for him."

"An attack of conscience?" Tristan asked.

Sam nodded, "I felt responsible for the death of his brain. It was odd. I shouldn't have felt bad after what he'd done but after I saw how Kyla reacted, I did."

"How were *you* responsible for his death? He jumped off a bridge."

Because I told him to take a flying fuck.

"Because I told him to do as the lady said. You being that lady."

"Wh-what?"

"I heard the argument. Heard why you were pissed and I was pissed for you. I was tasked with looking after you until you could be delivered to Tristan and he'd put you in danger. You stormed out and then he went to follow you and he was tweaked and I didn't want him getting near you in that state, so I stopped him. I caught him in the hallway and encouraged him to do what you'd said."

The bridge was a two-minute walk from their apartment. Jackson must've left the apartment and went straight to the bridge.

"Oh my god," Kyla's hand covered her mouth.

"I, uh," Sam looked down, "I regret the pain that caused you. When I saw your emotion, read it from you at that hospital, that's when I had a conscience attack and after you left, I dealt with things, revived him, brought him to Adrian's."

"The emotion *that* caused me?"

Tristan straightened up

"Yeah," Sam winced.

Kyla felt a laugh bubble up from her gut. It turned to pain and then she shrieked, "Do you have any motherfucking idea how it felt to tell a guy to kill himself and then he goes and kills himself? I thought he did! I thought they pulled the plug and that he was dead because I destroyed him. Oh my fucking..."

Sam stood up, "I—-"

He didn't get a chance to finish because suddenly Kyla was making her way to him, feeling the cold fury rise up in her and she took a swing but before it connected, he flew backwards without her making contact, landing against the refrigerator, causing things that were on top, cereal, a basket of drying herbs, a bunch of odds and ends, to all spill over him.

He got to his feet quickly and she was still advancing, ready to go for his face with her fingernails. She was *that* enraged.

"You asshole," she hissed.

Before she made contact, Tristan hooked Kyla around the waist with his arm and hauled her back, "Stop."

"You motherfucking fucker!" she screeched at Sam.

Sam looked to Tristan, "I'll go." He looked to Kyla, "I'm sorry to have put you through that. He was a loser. He wouldn't have killed himself, he would just have continued to deal drugs and make your life miserable. Make others' lives miserable. I got him out of the way. The way I did that was wrong. And I regret the impact it had on you, love. But it also got you closer to home, near Tris, so I could keep a closer eye on you."

Kyla let out a big guffaw of astonishment.

All that time thinking that she was responsible for what Jackson had done and he'd been hypnotized by a freaking vampire. All those hours of torturing herself. She went limp in Tristan's arms. He pulled her tight against him and put his lips to her temple,

"I've got you. It's okay, baby."

She felt his strength seep into her bones and nuzzled in.

Sam exited via a door near the kitchen that led out to a deck and staircase, which he descended.

Kyla stared out the window and watched him walk toward the boathouse. She walked to the window.

"My god..." she moaned and thrust her hands into her hair. Then her forehead was against the glass.

He turned her by her shoulders toward him and put his hands into her hair and kissed her forehead, "I'm sorry, baby. I didn't know all that. I knew that guy was there. He approached me, and Sam told me who he was to you. We were in the middle of everything, you ovulating, you know. I couldn't take the time. I didn't even care, there was so much goin' on. I'm sorry."

She sniffled, "That was just...fuck. I can't even wrap my head around it. Everything I've known for how long now has been a lie?"

"Babe, don't do that again."

"Do what?"

"Attack a vamp. I pushed him back and then mentally pinned him so he couldn't fight back. But if he'd laid a finger on you even in defense, I'd have ended him."

"Mentally pinned?"

"It's new. I can pin people. Read minds. Influence stronger. Move objects hands-free, barely trying."

"Phew. Was I out that long?"

"Not that long but yet an eternity, you know? A lot happened. Days blended into nights. It was one long dark night for me."

She squeezed him and kissed his soft lips.

"Sam is going through an identity crisis. I never knew anything about attacks of conscience or anything like that before, but these patches Constantin put on him to keep your scent from fucking with his urges, it's fucked with his humanity levels. He's acting ready to jump ship and join this coalition."

"What *is* this coalition?"

"The vampire militia that took you from your parents. They want to make vampires more humane, eliminate the royalty mindset, level the playing field, take the power-hungry ones out of their positions of power."

"So they do that by stealing kids from their parents?"

"Well, it sounds like things went wrong. Everyone who knew your whereabouts got dead or imprisoned. It sounds like it wasn't supposed to go that way. They wanted to get you and your brother out of the breeding program. Maybe to stop you from being given to me later on. They got you but failed getting Kyle. They're on a quest to stop royals. Stop all the elitism. Explains why I was tailed, watched for so many years before I was turned. I was told they had something to do with my grandfather's death, with my father's death, but at this stage, who knows."

"Does it sound like this is a worthy militia to join? It sounds like it might be. I mean, not knowing about your father and grandfather."

"Dunno. Not going to be too hasty at deciding anything. I have a lotta shit to figure out."

She raised her hands. "I'm just reacting to what I'm seeing and hearing. A female vampire who helped bring me back to you from the brink of death? Sam with a conscience? Heck, a female vampire that isn't evil?"

"Yeah. I know." He let out a breath. "Let's go meet your brother."

"Okay." She took another bite of her sandwich, which had regrettably gone cold, and a sip of her now tepid coffee, and then followed Tristan down some stairs, down a hall, and into an office. She still felt hungry, ravenous, actually. Was she craving Tristan's blood? She had no frame of reference to compare this to. At the back of the office was another door. He opened it. This was the closet they'd come through the night before.

Inside the room, Sasha was drinking from a small test tube filled with blood. She put it back into a stand on a table near the two hospital beds. She saw three more test tubes there, filled with blood. Her eyes moved to the form on the non-empty hospital bed. She moved out of Tristan's arms, closer to the bed.

She looked down at the guy laying there with his eyes closed. He had dark short hair. His body looked muscular, like he worked out. He was attractive, resembled Adrian a little bit.

"You two were very close when you were babies." Sasha moved closer. Tristan moved to get between them. He was being very protective.

"The only way you could be told apart in the face was that his eyes were blue, yours green. Until you grew a bit and you started to look like individuals."

Sasha put her hand on the side rail of the hospital bed.

"The twin bond was strong with you both. Maybe even stronger than with Sam and me and we have a pretty thick bond. We were pretty sure you could read one another's minds. You were also exceptionally bright, even as a baby; so intuitive. You stacked blocks, did puzzles, everything ahead of your age. You were very strong willed, stubborn, and feisty."

She heard Tristan chuckle. She shot him a pretend indignant and evil eye but then smirked at him and winked.

"The first time I met you, you were about eight months old and when your parents took you both to leave, you were in your mother's arms and I waved goodbye to you. You waved back. Then I saw you again when you were two years old. You saw me and smiled and waved at me instantly and when I asked them if that was typical they said it wasn't. I knew you remembered me. At three, I saw you reading your brother's mind during a game of Go Fish, that I'd taught you both. He would get frustrated at how you could guess every card in his hand. It was like you read his eyes, knew what he had. Have you continued to have those traits?"

"No," Kyla answered softly, "I don't think so. I've always been intuitive about people, I guess. Not long ago, after meeting Tristan, I started to have dreams and some of them came true. Or sort of. Sometimes they were a little different. But I don't think I can read anyone's mind."

"Sasha?" Sam poked his head in and motioned for her to come to him.

"I read to him sometimes." She grabbed a book from a shelf filled with what looked like mostly medical and homeopathy books, and passed it to Kyla, "This was a book I used to read to you both when you'd come to The Constantin Center. I brought it with me when I left. Maybe you'd like to read it to him? Sam, Tristan, and I can talk? Maybe the sound of your voice will work miracles for him."

She passed Kyla a colourful hardcover book called *Garbage Delight.* Kyla began to flip through it, skimming short nursery rhymes. She smiled. Something nagged at her memory, but she couldn't pinpoint it.

She sat on the empty hospital bed beside his and crossed her legs and began reading aloud, glancing at him periodically.

After reading several pages of nursery rhymes, she put the book down and looked at him.

"They tell me I'm your sister. I always wanted a brother. It'd be great if you'd wake up, so I can get to know you."

Nothing.

She put her hand on his hand. He was warm. Maybe a little too warm.

She decided to wander out of the room via the closet and found Sasha, Tristan, and Sam talking in the office that the closet had led to.

Tristan's eyes warmed when he saw her but conversation halted. It felt awkward.

"Can we get a walk on the beach? I'd love some fresh air," she said to him.

Her eyes landed on Sam for a beat. He gave her a small smile and he looked guilty.

She gave him a half smile. She didn't have it in her to hold a grudge, especially knowing he'd helped so much so far. She was glad he seemed to feel the same.

"Which of us was born first?" She asked Sasha.

"He was."

A big brother. Just like she'd always wanted.

"I think he has a bit of a fever," Kyla said.

"I'll check him. Thanks."

Tristan's eyes were on her. She grabbed his hand and tugged.

"SO, WHAT NOW?" KYLA asked as she and Tristan were sitting on an Adirondack chair on the dock. Tristan was sitting; she was on his lap, legs thrown over the side.

"What now?" he parroted.

"Where do we go from here?"

"There's a lot to figure out," he replied.

"List it," she invited.

"List it?"

"List what we need to figure out. We'll prioritize that shit together and then decide what to do."

He gave her a little smile. But there were no dimples.

"Don't humour me. I'll tell you right here, right now Mr. Vampire Bossy Pants, I am now actively involved in all of what goes on. You aren't going to keep hiding stuff from me."

He squeezed her thigh. "I just want you safe. That's all I have ever wanted. Despite the fact that I failed repeatedly at that. You're in my head now; couldn't hide stuff if I tried. And I don't want to."

She felt a twinge at his demeanour about failing at protecting her. She let it slide, "Good. And exactly. So don't try. We're a team. For forever. List."

It started to penetrate then, that she'd have to drink his blood. She felt a little green.

"What is it?" he asked, "You're stressed."

"Just processing. List?"

"Alright. Well, Adrian's in that boat house, daggered. I have to deal with him. Your brother's unconscious. We have to figure out what to do about that. I have to figure out what to do if you ovulate or start your period again. I have to figure out how to keep you fed and whole. I have to decide what to do about this coalition, about Kovac, which right now consists of several VPs and board members who are actively trying to get my attention. Where we'll live. What to do about my mother, she's dangerous, I need to shut that shit down. Whether I want to talk to Sergey and the danger that lurks with him. The list goes on."

"Let's break it down. Adrian?"

"He's dead."

"Dead?"

"Not yet. But I'm gonna kill him."

"Tr—-"

"He's dead." The cold look in his eyes chilled her belly deep inside, "He's taken so fucking much from us. He played games, took your parents from you, took your brother from you. Took a baby from you and me. Fucked with me repeatedly. He's got to pay. He's gonna."

Kyla took a deep breath, feeling pain in her heart, in her womb, seeing a blue-eyed dimpled baby boy in her mind.

"Sasha wants me to meet Sergey Voitenko but I don't know yet about that. I feel like we need to go home and take a time out, give me time to look into and figure shit out without undue pressure. I don't know much about him, know he's an elder. Met him once or twice briefly when I worked with Andre. I got the impression he was very strong, that he was reading me like an open book. I do *not* want him fucking with me. I feel powerful. Stronger than ever. I can program Sasha, Sam, Adrian even. But I don't know what sort of powers Sergey has. I'm not putting you at risk so we're leaving tomorrow. Heading home. I'm doing more research to learn more about this militia, more about Sergey, before I make any decisions. I'm going to feel things out with some council members. I got an email that they want a meeting soon to discuss Claudio's position. We get home, take it easy and spend some time together, catch our breath, and then I attend that meeting and we go from there. I am sending an IT specialist to The Constantin Center to work on decoding some tech stuff. I've brought a lot of shit here to Sasha but again, can't trust her completely, I'm too jaded, so I've got duplicates of a lot of things back in Adrian's office that'll be looked over by someone else, too. I'm thinking about sending Sasha there, too, but that's still to be decided. So far does it all sound good to you?"

"Sounds good," she replied quietly, and he gave her a squeeze.

"We'll go to the condo. We can make use of the panic room if need be. I told the contractors repairing the house to add one there in the master bedroom but I think I like the idea of the condo for now. If I have to step out to meetings or whatever the office is 2 minutes from there rather than half an hour from the house."

"Good plan," she said softly, "Why might we need the panic room?"

"I don't know if you'll bleed, if you'll ovulate. How that'll impact us. I've asked Sasha to ask Sergey, about that and about how to make sure we keep you *you*. We'll have some answers, hopefully, before we leave."

"Okay," she said quietly.

"What's on your mind?" he asked.

"I feel your power," Kyla told him.

He shook his head, not understanding.

"There's this feeling that I'm getting from you and it's a little scary."

He cupped her at the jaw, "Once bitten, twice shy. I'm ready for anything when it comes to protecting you. I won't let anything happen to you again. I don't blame you if you have trouble believing that. I've let you down so many times already. I won't let you down again." He stared deep into her eyes.

"If you feel like I don't trust you or that I blame you for anything then your radar is broken."

"My radar isn't broken. It's keener than ever. And I'm wide awake, eyes wide open, watching for any threat and I'm protecting you from *any* potential threat. I want you to breathe easy. That's my goal."

She snuggled in, burying her face into the crook of his neck.

She felt weird, looking at his throat.

"How's this whole feeding thing gonna work? The idea of drinking your blood makes me more than a little bit queasy. And I don't have the right teeth for it."

"We'll have to figure that out."

"Yeah," she had a sour face, "When you became a vampire did the idea of biting people or drinking their blood gross you out?"

"Nope. I instantly craved it the way you crave sugar."

She wrinkled her nose. "I'm not a vampire. I don't know what I am."

"You're my princess," he whispered and kissed her sweetly. She wrapped her arms tighter around him.

They were silent a moment. Kyla watched a bird gliding over the water, swoop down, catch a fish, and then take flight.

"I wish we could stay here a while," she said.

"It doesn't feel safe. I've only met Sasha, there are other people in their coalition on this island and until I know more, I'm not feeling it."

"Okay," she said.

Suddenly he went tense and alert. She looked over her shoulder, seeing a woman with long flowing wavy ash blonde hair and incredibly long legs approaching.

"Oh, hiya," she waved, calling out. "Sam around?"

Tristan instantly rose, pulling Kyla behind him and his fangs were out.

The woman froze in her tracks, looking like she was paralyzed.

"Go back where you came from," he hissed, "You never saw us."

She immediately turned on her heel and walked away.

"Faster!" Tristan called and then she whooshed and blurred away.

"What, why?" Kyla started, his hand wrapped around the small of her back, plastering her to his back.

"She was vamp." Tristan watched until she rounded the house and was out of sight.

"Sasha is micro dosing the female vamps here with Kyle's blood, but I don't feel safe enough to trust it."

"Oh."

"They don't know it's Kyle's blood."

"Oh."

He spun around to face her.

"I was going to ask if we could bring him with us."

Tristan's brows snapped up.

"I don't want to leave him here. I want to try to help him. I don't want him with people just bleeding him dry."

She could feel tension emanating off him.

"He's key to the coalition right now. He's what's keeping Sasha even. She's trying to synthesize his blood so that she can stay even without feeding from him, but she says she's not close to that yet. She also needs his blood so that female vampires who want that switch flipped to off can have it."

"That's...that's understandable but, Tristan, he's just lying there in a bed being bled."

"Okay, how's this? We go home, figure some things out and then go from there."

"What does that mean?"

"I influence her to make sure she doesn't remove him from here so that we can get back to him. She's taken good care of him the last almost two years. She thinks of him as a son, but she needs his blood, those other females on that island need it, too. They don't even know where it comes from, but it helps them. Listen, how about if we make a decision soon? Let me do some research. Either I decide to join up with them and we go from there or we extricate him at the point we decide I'm not joining."

"Is joining a possibility? It must be if you're saying that but... but really?"

She wanted to talk about this, explore the idea together.

He was conflicted. She felt it. He pulled her close and she inhaled his sugary sweetness, felt the strength of his arms, the heat coming off him. She lifted her chin and looked him in the eyes. His hair blew back in the breeze and she chewed her bottom lip. His eyes sparkled.

"I don't know enough yet. But maybe. Let's talk about it later. For now, let's go have a nap," he whispered the last part seductively, an even more dazzling sparkle in his eyes.

Mm hmm.

She found herself thrown over his shoulder. She squee'd in delight as he walked back toward the house.

She dangled. But she was anxious, so she didn't want to wait.

"Whoosh, babe," she told him.

"Whoosh?" he chuckled.

"Fast. Go fast. Whoosh!"

"Sounds a little like I'm your dog on the end of a sled."

"No, that's mush. But whatever works. Mush. Whoosh. Just hurry!"

He slowed his pace even more.

She spanked his sexy ass and he gave her ass a squeeze in response.

They got up the stairs and inside the door and she heard Tristan say, "Brandy was on the beach lookin' for you. I sent her away, made her forget she saw me."

"Thanks, bro, sorry about that." she heard Sam reply. She was still upside down over his shoulder. A few seconds later they were back inside that bedroom they'd slept in the night before and she bounced when she landed in the bed.

She gave him a big smile. His gaze was dark and heated. She felt it right between the legs.

He leaned over and kissed her stomach, where her t-shirt had ridden up.

"I fucking missed that smile and the fire in those eyes so much," he muttered this against her belly and she squirmed.

"That tickles."

"Does it?" he looked up with a devilish smile and then ran the back of his hand very gently over her belly and then went into a full-on tickle.

Kyla screeched, "No t-tickling! No tick-tickling!"

"Okay, fine." He stopped and then invited, "Tell me what you *do* want?"

She got up onto her knees on the bed. He sat, feet dangling over the side, beside her.

"Maybe try feeding me? Food hasn't been doing it for me, I don't think. I'm like...starving."

"You only got a mouthful to wake you so that makes sense. Let's see." He bared his fangs and bit down into the heel of his hand. Kyla's eyes widened.

"Wait, no. Eww. Ick."

"Too late," he replied and held his hand out.

She hesitated. He hooked around the back of her neck with his free hand and drew her closer. She looked down at the blood pooling on his palm and took a big breath, leaned over, feeling her stomach rumble as if she'd been staring at a full buffet table, and she tentatively darted her tongue out and leaned forward, dipping the tip of her tongue into the blood that pooled there.

It tasted like sweet grape. Like grape pop but more. Way more. Kids' grape cough syrup, grape Fanta, purple Crush, and Welch's grape jelly all fused together? She closed her eyes, pulled her tongue back, licked her lips, looked up into his eyes, something moved between them, something sweet and caring, and protective. She closed her eyes again and dove in, getting suction going on the wound on his hand and feeling it hit her throat was like feeling a gush of sweetness, not tooth-achy sweetness, either. The most blissful taste she'd ever had in her mouth. And this peaceful euphoric feeling swept over her.

His fingers from the other hand dove into her hair, bringing her closer, then cradling her tight against him. She felt his body heat, felt her eyes roll back, her nipples tingle, and flood with warmth. Warmth everywhere.

"Stop, baby," he said softly.

"Did I take too much?" she asked.

"Naw, but that right there went straight to my fucking cock."

She released his hand and sank onto the bed, eyes on the ceiling, something that she could only think of as sweet ambrosia in her mouth and she felt giddy.

Tristan's lips were on hers, his tongue was in her mouth, one of his hands in her hair. Her hands rose up his back under his t-shirt and she pulled it up and off him and then she flipped him and she was on top.

He chuckled, eyes sparkling. Her mouth was back on his hand, but the wound had already sealed. She groaned in dismay. He brought it to his mouth, bared fangs, and pierced it again and she dove for it, latching her mouth around the wound. He grabbed the back of her head and then his mouth was in the crook of her throat and he pierced her skin and that's when everything went insane.

She was drinking from him, he was drinking from her, and she felt like she was fucking flying. Soaring through the clouds toward heaven.

He fumbled to get his pants undone with one hand, letting go of her throat, and then she stopped sucking on his hand and was helping get his cock out and then they wrestled, and she was on top, impaled on him. Groaning, grabbing for his hand again and then she was on her back as he pounded over and over and over.

"Harder!" she demanded.

"I'll hurt you..."

"No. Harder. Fuck me harder!"

He complied and then she felt like she was falling as a crash pierced the air and they slid. The bed was broken and now they were on the floor, tangled up. Arms legs, his cock, her pussy, his fingers raking her ass cheeks, her fingernails raking his back. Her cries and his grunts piercing the air. She giggled and then saw his face. His gorgeous fucking face.

"I fucking love you," she moaned as they rolled.

"Mm, I fucking love you." He said.

"I love fucking you," she cried out, hitting that beautiful peak, feeling the build at her crotch and in her chest and then an explosion of sensations, beautiful sensations, a kaleidoscope of beautiful feelings and colours inside and outside of her.

How can I be feeling colour? I don't know but somehow, I am.

Tristan buried his teeth in her throat again and thrust hard once, twice, she pulled him closer by his hair and then he stilled.

He trailed sweet soft kisses along her throat.

She lifted his hand and looked at his palm, which had zero signs of being opened up.

"That was beautiful," she told him, tears in her eyes, and then she tenderly kissed his palm.

"*So* beautiful," he agreed, caressed her cheek, and pulled her up off the floor. He looked at the bed, surveying the damage.

"We cracked the bedframe. But should be an easy fix."

She giggled, "Aren't we the rudest houseguests? Breaking furniture with our fucking..."

He snickered.

She started to get her pants back on and fixed her bra and tank.

She looked around and felt giddy. He got his pants done up and she jumped up and threw her arms around him, her legs around his waist, "That was fanfuckingtastic, Tristan. Oh my God!"

He smiled huge.

"I mean like seriously! Does my blood taste like that? Does it make you feel like this? Holy fucking moly!"

He gave her a squeeze on the bottom and kissed her lips, "Probably. I feel how much you like it and I gotta say, I like how much you like it."

She let out a little growl and playfully bit his throat, not breaking skin, "God I wish I had fangs, too." She sucked on his throat hard. He walked to the long chest of drawers and sat her on it.

"Lemme get Sam in here and fix this bed. Then I gotta make a couple calls."

"Okay, I wanna take a bath. Shave my legs and my hoo-ha. Maybe visit with Kyle for a bit again. When are we leaving?"

"I'll arrange for tomorrow morning."

She was full of energy. She was having trouble sitting still. She didn't know what to do with all the energy. She wanted to do cartwheels and backflips. She felt like she could climb Mount Everest, walk on water. She swung her legs, heels bouncing against the chest of drawers. She felt joy bubble up as she had a thought,

Now he's my all-I-can-eat-and-fuck buffet. And next time I'm going to rip his clothes to shreds, too.

She giggled.

Tristan opened the door and called down the hall for Sam and then looked back over his shoulder at her and smirked, seeming quite amused with her behaviour.

"Sam? Grab a toolbox and gimme a hand?"

"What'd ya do?" she heard Sam.

"Bed frame cracked," Tristan mumbled.

"Ha!" Sam laughed loud and poked his head in. He arched one brow high up and gave her a smirk.

Kyla felt the heat rise in her face and knew her face was red. Sam's eyes landed on her. "Ha!" he repeated and then backed out.

She hopped off the dresser and stood aside while Tristan and Sam took a look at the bed frame. Then she grabbed some clean clothes and toiletries and signaled to the hallway as she passed Tristan. He stopped her by catching her elbow. "Kiss me."

She did, with a big smile, spotting a hickie on his neck. She chuckled and kind of skipped along to the bathroom.

SHE SPENT MORE TIME at Kyle's bedside that day, reading to him. Tristan stayed nearby, talking to Sasha and Sam in Sasha's office. She and Tristan later took a canoe out together and rowed out a ways away from the shore and they had a nice afternoon, a quiet one out on the water, just relaxing with the peaceful scenery, barely talking, just enjoying the day and being together.

When they got back, Sam announced he'd caught enough fish for dinner and said they'd be having a campfire with some others from the island that night. Kyla was interested in that, but Tristan gave her a firm shake of his head, meaning *no*.

"I haven't met anyone else in this coalition yet. The fewer people that know we're here, the better. For now. While I investigate all of this."

"But getting to know them might give you some more insight?" she suggested.

He shook his head, "Not ready to have you around other vampires right now. Not remotely."

She understood and more than that, she felt the absolute utter *no* emanating from him at that idea. She felt like his eyes alone were a protective shroud around her.

She thought maybe it'd be a bit different here, if they were all 'good guy' vampires but Tristan wasn't convinced yet, was still sussing things out, and said that he didn't want to have to patch them all and then program them to ensure that they were all capable of being around her.

Programming might be enough on its own but programming plus patching was the only way that he felt safe enough but that would only solve the problem as long as the patches lasted. Sasha was going to get supplies to make more; Tristan had gotten her information about Adrian's recipe for them.

But she knew he was concerned that programming might not be enough to keep her 100% safe with a larger group. Others could arrive; news would travel. For now, only Sasha and Sam were aware he was there. And now Sergey Voitenko. Tristan said he wanted to leave first thing in the morning in case Voitenko had any designs on arriving early or having someone else arrive.

Instead of joining the community fish fry, which was being done at that vampress Brandy's place on the opposite end of the island, Kyla shopped in Sasha's greenhouse and then chopped some fresh picked vegetables for a salad that she made for them while Tristan made them some chicken quesadillas while multitasking on his computer sending some emails and texts as well as making a few calls at the kitchen table.

But he'd walked to the greenhouse and watched. He'd followed her to the bedroom when she went in to change after getting salsa all over the front of her top, and seemed to be unwilling to be more than ten feet from her.

KYLA WAS BEING GENTLY jiggled.

"Wake up, princess. Time to go."

"Arrrgh. But it's nighttime."

"Yeah, but our ride is here." He lifted her up and planted her on his lap. She nuzzled into his throat and kissed his jaw. He was dressed.

She didn't even remember falling asleep. They'd eaten dinner in the bedroom and then she'd wanted a nap afterwards. They'd been in bed, Kyla snoozing and Tristan on his computer doing work stuff, and it wasn't even dark yet. Now he was jiggling her.

"What time is it?"

"Just past three o'clock."

"Why are we leaving in the middle of the night? Did something happen?"

"I don't want Sergey coming early and catching me off guard. I don't wanna chance someone stopping over like Brandy did yesterday. I just want distance, so we can figure shit out. I don't want to be caught off guard at all."

"Mmkay. I have to pee and brush my teeth and pack."

"I packed. Get dressed and ready quick." He passed her a bundle of clothes and her toiletries bag.

When she emerged from the bathroom in yoga clothes, a ponytail, no make-up, and unsure if she wanted to have coffee or to simply curl up and sleep on the ride home, sShe found Tristan in the kitchen with Sasha and Sam. Both Jaspers were half asleep-looking.

"I'll call you when I have those answers. Just be careful in the meantime. Watch how she's adjusting," Sasha said and then gave Kyla a smile.

"Take good care of Kyle, please," Kyla said.

"Always," Sasha smiled.

"Thank you for everything," Kyla said, "Sincerely."

Sasha smiled bigger, "Hope to see you back here soon. I was telling Tristan we have a beautiful log home available next door. We have about half a dozen empty homes on the island here, ready for occupants. I think the one next door is the best of the bunch. Beautiful beach. It would be lovely if you two took it over, if we became neighbours. I'm going to make sure it's reserved, just in case."

Kyla smiled noncommittally, but was thinking she'd love to see that home and would love to be here, close to her brother. Life on a small island with very few threats compared to being in a big city? It was something that really appealed to her. For now, at least.

Tristan took her bundle of sleeping clothes from her as well as her makeup bag and tucked them into the gym bag on the table and then zipped it up.

"Okay, we're off."

"What about Adrian?" Kyla muttered as they descended the stairs, "Did you already...uh..." She didn't want to say the rest. Didn't want to acknowledge that Tristan may have committed a murder. Well, another murder.

Even if the monster deserved it.

"He's comin', too," Tristan replied.

"He is?" Kyla was startled.

"I'm not letting him far out of my sight. I'm just keepin' him for now until we get all the shit sorted out from his lab."

Sam followed them to the seaplane parked at the dock and then he went into the boathouse. Tristan put Kyla on the plane, sat her in the seat and buckled her in and then stepped back out to talk to Sam and deal with that "cargo". He got on the plane alone.

"No Sam?" Kyla asked.

"No. He's scoping things out here, watching things for me. And he's getting reacquainted with his sister and acquainted with himself. Something's shifting in him. He forgot to change the patch and was cool around you. Completely cool. I don't know how or why. It could be just my influence, ordering him not to want you, not to hurt you. But that doesn't always take for a hungry vamp and there are no non-vamps on this island, so he's been living on blood bags. It's working now but we'll see what happens."

"What'll you do without your right-hand man back home?"

"I've got other guys who can help me."

"More minions? Endless minions to cater to the whims of the prince?" she teased.

"Yeah." He looked deep in thought, contemplating something. He looked a million miles away.

It didn't take long after the plane took off for Kyla to fall back to sleep, head on Tristan's shoulder. Tristan snuggling her close.

She didn't know what was next, but she felt cautiously optimistic. The fact that this coalition had high level elders on it was good news, wasn't it? This coalition had a *live and let live* attitude and that didn't sound *at all* terrible. When compared to the world of elitism, hedonism, and carnage Tristan had described, some of which she'd witnessed, it sounded awesome.

There was a lot to figure out, sure, but they'd come through things okay so far, despite some seriously big challenges.

10

TRISTAN WAS STANDING over Liam Donavan. Or, what was left of him. She could make out his features on a face, blood streaked long blond hair, but the rest of Liam was on the floor in the great room of the cottage back at Adrian's compound. Kyla was looking down at Tristan, eyes black, his skin grey, and his fangs were out, Liam's head in his hand, mouth open, teeth broken, toothpaste commercial smile long gone. The rage rolling off Tristan was petrifying.

She jerked awake, startled. But she was in the safety of a cocoon made of Tristan. He wrapped his arms tighter around her and pulled her closer, "S'okay, just a dream," he muttered, half asleep, eyes still closed. He kissed her forehead.

"Did you see it?" she asked.

Could he see inside her dreams?

"No," he opened his eyes. "What was it?"

They were still on the plane. She was on Tristan, curled up in a ball on his lap, head on his chest and he was reclined in his plane seat. She sat up straighter and looked out the window.

Dawn was kissing the sky. Dark blue with a line of orange and yellow and crimson, almost like a horizontal rainbow, with the sun, a ball of yellow fire. She wiped her eyes with her fingertips and yawned. It was surreal beauty in front of her, but she couldn't help but still be affected by the ugliness from the dream.

"Liam Donavan, in pieces. You..." She stopped. She didn't want to describe it.

He gave her a squeeze and was about to speak but a man's head poked out the cockpit door, "Can you buckle up, please? We land soon."

Tristan jerked fully awake and his arms instantly went tighter around her for a quick squeeze and then he stood, lifting her up and then putting her in the seat beside him. He buckled her seatbelt, stretched with a loud yawn, and then sat back in his seat, pulled it back to fully upright, and then buckled his belt.

"A horrible dream," she muttered, "So gross."

"A memory," Tristan whispered darkly.

"Memory? That happened?" she hadn't yet asked what'd happened with Liam.

"You saw me kill him, or saw the end of that. I don't know. You were out of it but afterwards I saw you at the top of the stairs, watching me. Did this dream take place back in that cottage at the compound?"

Kyla shivered and decided to push it away, "Yeah. Uh, I have to pee," she said with a yawn, trying to be casual, trying to *feel* casual.

"Hey!" Tristan called, and the door opened to the cockpit.

"Does she have time for the bathroom?"

"Yes sir, if she's quick about it."

Kyla unbuckled and dashed to the tiny bathroom. She pushed the dream away by not looking at her reflection, not wanting to see what she knew would be a freaked-out expression. When she was back, she buckled in beside him and put her hand on his thigh.

He took her hand and brought it to his lips and as he kissed it, he stared deep into her eyes and she knew he didn't want her to be affected by that memory. She felt chills run up her body and she wasn't sure if they were from the dream, from the intense look on his face, or maybe a bit of both.

"Love you," she whispered.

"Love you, princess." He gave her hand a squeeze and his body loosened, as if he was relieved that she wasn't holding the memory against him.

How could she?

Liam could've killed her, almost did, and he could've even killed Tristan. And he'd sexually violated her, too. From what she knew of Tristan and what she'd remembered when he tore Claudio apart she certainly didn't expect Tristan to just give Liam a black eye for his transgressions.

She looked out the window and could see Toronto below. So much had happened since she'd left for Vancouver Island. So many things. Everything kept changing. Would it ever settle down and resemble normal?

On that thought, she decided she couldn't think about it right now. Right now, she really needed coffee. And she was about to have some seriously good coffee because they were home and she knew that Tristan had stocked her favourite coffee back at his condo.

THEY TOOK A TAXI BACK to the condo and Tristan immediately called a locksmith while Kyla set up the coffee maker. He explained that Sam had had some guys bust in to get some of their things and since changed the locks. Tristan was having them changed again. Immediately.

Knowing others had been in his place didn't sit well; he'd told her the condo was his oasis, his completely private space, so he spent a lot of time looking over everything. He had Kyla wait upstairs while the locksmith was there. And then he'd passed Kyla a pen and pad of paper and asked her to make a shopping list for the concierge to have groceries delivered for the upcoming week. This task kept her busy while Tristan prowled around checking everything out.

It was sort of eerie being back there with the huge amount of emotion she'd felt last time she was in the space. The apartment was clean, sterile, cold. It didn't feel like home. The feeling of airiness she'd felt the night they arrived here from the villa, after the fire, wasn't what she felt now. She suspected it was because she'd last been here when she left him.

But it was home for now. Essentially, it was going to be a prison, though, she suspected, because Tristan had stuff to figure out and he was going to be crazy protective. He'd barely let her out of arm's reach other than to go to the bathroom, since waking her back up from that state of mesmerization. She was dreading the idea of being cooped up.

He ended a phone call and she approached and took his hand and walked him to the sofa. He sat, and she climbed onto his lap and curled up, head on his chest, straddling him, her knees by his hips. His arms went around her, and she inhaled him deeply.

"Things gonna be okay?" she asked.

"Absolutely. Nothing is gonna hurt you again. Ever."

"Nothing will hurt you?"

"Nope."

"Better not," she said, "I couldn't bear it."

"You won't have to."

He bit into his hand and presented it to her. She took his palm gently into both hands and flipped her hair over to one shoulder to present her throat to him and laid her head on his shoulder. They both went for what they needed, holding each other close, listening to the other's heart beat in perfect time with their own, and then Kyla shifted to grind her crotch into his as she started to undo his shirt gently. Gentle didn't last. He reached over and shredded her t-shirt and threw it aside.

She smiled and then grabbed his shirt and pulled as hard as she could and shredded it, too.

His eyes sparkled with surprise and amusement.

Drinking his blood while fucking was starting to feel as natural to her as his drinking *her* blood while fucking now did. What a switch from the start when she thought he was gorgeous and great in bed but was all, "Fangs? Not so much..."

His blood was sweet, the connection was deepened during the act, like they were braided together as one. She adored this feeling of oneness.

She released his hand and started to shimmy out of her pants and panties but he couldn't wait. He pulled her back to him by her hips so that their groins were together and ripped the crotch out instead and then she rode him, giving him a shake of her head in exasperation at yet more of her clothing being destroyed.

His eyes flickered with amusement; his hands were on her hips and then his eyes went dark with carnal intensity. She rocked, gasped, and raked her fingers through his hair as she planted kisses on his mouth and then nipped his lower lip, hard, drawing blood, making his eyes go wide with surprise.

Then she sucked on his lower lip, moaning. He flipped her onto her back and started powering so hard and so deep that she felt like she was being drilled into the ground. She tried to flip to get back on top, but he fought it and so it turned to wrestling. Kyla put all her strength into it and this meant that the sofa they were on flipped onto its back and they rolled onto the floor. Tristan groaned and rolled them again and then he was pinning her, feasting on her throat, while her heels dug into his lower back and she grounded against him.

"How the fuck did fucking you get better when it couldn't get any better?"

"Mm, I was gonna ask you the same thing," she moaned, grabbing his hair with both hands and dragging his mouth to hers.

TRISTAN WAS SMILING and bouncing a gorgeous baby with curly dark hair on his knee. He held out the baby in offering. "Take her, Kyla; she wants her Mommy." The green-eyed baby reached her arms up in the air toward Kyla, wanting to be lifted.

Kyla's eyes bolted open wide. She was sitting up. She was more affected by that dream than the dream of Liam Donavan in pieces.

Was that dream a premonition? Or was it just wishful thinking?

She deflated.

She wished she'd gotten to the part where she held the little baby close, where she could feel the soft curls between her fingers, bury her nose against that baby's skin and inhale her scent. Cuddle her close. She felt longing deep inside her chest. It fucking hurt.

But, was this a baby that would be or that'd died because of what Kyla's 'grandfather' had fed her? Maybe he'd killed twins in her. A blue eyed boy and a green-eyed girl.

She'd only slept a little while, since she'd had a nap on the flight as well as slept half the night before heading back.

She went to get up out of bed, but Tristan hooked an arm around her waist and yanked her back so that she landed on top of him, her back to his front.

"Hey!" she cried out on a bit of a giggle.

"Mm, get back here. Another bad dream?"

"A weird dream."

"Talk to me."

"Naw, it's alright."

"You're gutted. You were happy and now you're upset. Why?"

"I just was thinking about what happened, after I ovulated and...you know... My dream was... there was a baby."

She felt something from him that was beyond frightening. His eyes started to darken in colour.

"Tristan, don't go there."

His lip curled.

"That's why I didn't wanna say anything." She put her hand on his face. "Let's just snuggle a little? Please put that anger aside and just hold me? You're scaring me."

"Don't be scared of me. Don't ever be fucking scared of me."

"No, not scared of you like you'll hurt me. Scared of your emotions. They make me feel so much, too."

"I need to spend this energy. It's either anger or something else." He was trying to push it aside; she could feel it.

"Then fuck me, my prince."

His eyes flickered with heat, but he held back a minute.

"Please?" she batted her eyelashes at him.

He flipped her onto her back and they started making out. But it wasn't sweet. It was desperate. She dug her nails into his back, he was roughly kissing her, grinding against her. The making out rapidly descended into some very fast but hot and heavy missionary position sex that transcended to Kyla's legs hooked over Tristan's shoulders while he spectacularly pummeled her, his eyes on hers and exuding ownership, hunger, and intensity.

It was blood-free, or so she thought, but then Tristan got out of bed and she saw that her nails had ripped his back open.

She winced at the sight of it, "Babe!"

He stopped and turned around to look at her, naked Adonis body on display.

"I cut your back."

"Hmm?" he reached a palm over the opposite shoulder and touched and then saw blood on his hand.

"You'd better clean up your mess, little tigress..." He still wasn't smiling but his expression had softened a little.

She pounced. He caught her in his arms and then took two steps back to the foot of the bed and put her on her back, then flopped beside her on his belly and she leaned over and started to follow the diagonal trail of bloody scratch marks across his back with her tongue.

He let out a sexy growl and she felt it between her legs. By the time she got to the last score mark on his back it was already healed underneath the red drying blood. It hadn't been a lot of blood, but it was enough to get her motor seriously running.

"More," she whispered against his earlobe, climbing over to his right side, staying on her knees. He turned over onto his back and grabbed her knee and repositioned her so that she was straddling him fully. He guided his cock back inside her, "Mm, you feel so damn good."

"More," she whispered, leaned over, and playfully nipped at his earlobe.

"In a minute," He pushed her back gently by the shoulders, so she was upright. He began kneading her breasts and then sat up and got a nipple into his mouth and sucked, hard.

Her head rolled back, "Mm, more, baby."

He chuckled, "Greedy little girl," then he planted another kiss on her lips.

She nipped at his lower lip, "Yes, so greedy. And I need more. Now, baby. Please. I'm not joking."

"Uh uh; not yet. Good things come to good girls who wait," he teased and rolled her onto her back, her head at the foot of the bed, lifted her ankles, and drove deep inside as she wrapped her legs around him.

He was balancing on a palm, the other palm reached up to cup her jaw, and she twisted to bite down on the heel of his hand. He pulled it away.

She whimpered, "Tristttttannnnnn. Please."

He chuckled, "I like it when you beg, princess, but biting me like a naughty minx while you beg? Tsk tsk."

"Don't make me beg," she said, zero humour in her voice or on her face.

He threw his head back and laughed at her. She felt anger rising.

She tried to buck him off. His expression dropped, and he pinned her harder.

"Ooh, we gonna fight? It's been a while since we've done this."

She slapped his shoulder, "Get off me."

"Hey?"

"Grrr," she growled, "Don't tease. That's not nice."

"Easy..." he warned.

"Get off me."

"Princess, calm down."

"Fuck that!" She shot the dirtiest look she could muster.

"Kyla, chill out. We're just playing. I want you to beg. Then I'll give you what you want." He leaned closer to kiss her.

But she was done.

"Get off!" she pushed and turned her head to the side, denying the kiss.

He chuckled a little, "Okay, settle down, gorgeous girl. Do you know how gorgeous your eyes are when you're angry?"

"NO!" Cold shot up the veins in her arms and she shoved and knocked him back, "Don't fucking tease!"

He went backwards, braced with his hand to catch himself, but cracked his head on the headboard. She tried to scoot away, he grabbed her and threw her back down on the bed on her back and pinned her.

Underneath her anger she felt emotion coming from him. But it wasn't anger. The only anger she was feeling was her own. From him she felt other emotions.

Concern.

Shock.

"Kyla! What the fuck?"

"Get off!" she ordered.

"No. Fuck that; chill out first."

She started to struggle, wiggle out of his grasp. He held tight and pinned her wrists above her head.

"Get the fuck off me!" she spat, really fucking pissed off.

He stared into her eyes, teeth gritted, his jaw working.

She tried to squirm again.

He wasn't budging.

She gave up the struggle but went into stare down with him, shooting daggers out of her eyes at him.

Seconds ticked by. Neither of them was relenting in the stare down.

Kyla's chest was rising and falling fast with her anger. She couldn't seem to reign it in.

Finally, he leaned forward, until his nose was about an inch from hers. He stared harder.

"Lemme go, Tristan," she requested bitchily.

"You gonna be nice?"

He kept staring.

"Let. Me. Up."

He hesitated but then he backed off her and as soon as she had the opportunity, she rolled off the bed and stormed into the bathroom and slammed the door.

She was in front of the mirror, hands gripping the edge of the counter, white knuckled. She stared in the mirror at her reflection. Her hair was wild, her eyes were hard and angry. Her mouth was set in a tight line. She took a big breath and then her heart started to race, and regret started to flood through every vein in her body.

What on earth was that all about?

She covered her eyes with her palms and then her shoulders started to shake at the same time as the tears started to flow. Hard.

What the fuck was that?

The door opened, and she lifted her hands away and saw him in the reflection, behind her, his expression cold, mouth in a tight line, too.

She spun around and immediately did a face plant, buried her face in his chest and started sobbing. His body was 100% tense.

"What the hell was that? God, I'm so sorry. What the fuck is wrong with me?"

I was like a fucking she-hulk!

The tension in his muscles loosened and he wrapped his arms around her, pulled her close, and his hand massaged the back of her neck.

"Shhh," he said and then dipped to grab her thighs hoisted her up. She wrapped her legs around his waist and put her head on his shoulder. He carried her back to the bed and pulled the covers up over them both. They were on their sides, face to face, and her arm was thrown around him, his around her. Her face in his chest.

"I'm sorry. I don't know why..." she didn't know how to finish.

"Shh, it's okay. Here." He leaned back and dropped his fangs, bit into his wrist and she latched on immediately, tears streaming as she sucked on his wrist. The blood flowed fast and she gulped it down, feeling relief surge through her at the same time as a rush of shame.

He rolled so he was on his back, her head on his chest, his other hand against the back of her head, stroking her hair while she continued to drink and cry.

"That's enough, baby," he whispered against her head with a kiss and she stopped.

"I don't know what that was," she said softly, licking her lips.

"We'll figure it out," he said but she could hear and feel his concern.

"I didn't like it," she told him, "Why did I—-"

"It's okay, princess. Shh. I've got you."

Whenever he said those words to her, they churned up so much feeling inside, so much relief.

As long as he's got me, I'll be okay. Somehow...

They cuddled a little while quietly, but both their brains were working overtime and both were well aware of the other's tension levels. When he broke away, it didn't feel good. She felt like there was a new weight on them.

FOUR DAYS LATER

Tristan was busy. Kyla was bored.

This apartment was killing her. This *life* was killing her slowly, tortuously. The cause: Boredom.

Bored.

Bored, bored, bored.

She was being a selfish brat, she knew it. But she was having trouble stopping it.

He was figuring things out. Doing his research. He was still at the information gathering phase, according to him. She could feel his tension, but also his focus and concentration. He had to be careful, poke around without arousing suspicions.

He spoke to Sam and Sasha daily. They were both providing information, too. He also spent a lot of time on the phone with someone named Rick, who he said worked for Kovac as well as someone who was on site at Adrian's compound, investigating some IT stuff.

Adrian was daggered and stashed in the trunk of one of Tristan's cars in the underground there at the building. There was an infrared nanny cam in there with an app on his phone, so he could check Adrian periodically and she knew he checked on him in person, occasionally, too, whenever he left the condo.

He had only left a few times so far to go to his office during the first two days home but was mostly working from the apartment, focused on phone calls, on emails, on figuring things out while also overseeing things at Kovac Capital.

So, he was busy.

And she was bored. She wasn't accustomed to boredom. Well, not before meeting Tristan. She felt powerless. And she hated it.

They were together nearly 24/7 and he was attentive and sweet. He was giving her plenty of attention, so it wasn't like she had any reason to feel neglected. They were having a lot of sex. A LOT. At least four or five times a day they fed on one another and fucked one another. They were both insatiable. And the sex was wild. And her vag never got sore.

Sometimes she'd look at him and just pounce. The reverse was true, too. And it got physical and rough sometimes as they struggled for power.

He always won, of course, unless he relented and let her have her way; she couldn't help but want to dominate the sex sometimes, hold him down, try to bite him. She never broke the skin and it turned him on like crazy when she'd bite his shoulder or dig her teeth into his throat and he would fuck really hard when she pulled his hair. He seemed to get off on it when she tried to take control. But he didn't actually let her take full control and sometimes she found that frustrating.

If Kyla had her way, that's all they'd do. Fuck and feed. But that might've been because there was precious little else *for* her to do.

He hadn't withheld or teased her about feeding from him again since she'd had that stupid tantrum. And they hadn't really talked any further about her tantrum or the dream about the baby.

They ate, drank, fucked, showered, slept, watched movies, and she did yoga and Pilates, read, or surfed the web while he worked on his computer or made his calls.

They pretended that her irrational tantrum had never happened.

She hoped it was a one off. She suspected it wasn't, though. She didn't know where it'd come from, it had concerned them both, but there were so many things on their plate right now and it wasn't as if they could decode that mystery, knowing so little about this new and improved bond they had.

With the way she was feeling, it felt like another tantrum was on its way in.

She felt like she was PMS'ing without cramps or pimples, just with her mood, and that was a little bit scary, because she had no idea at all what another period would bring. Had they not noticed ovulation? Had that just not happened? She found that thought weirdly depressing, which made absolutely no sense and having her emotions all over the place made her angrier.

She wanted out of the apartment on the day after the incident with the tantrum. He didn't want that. He told her it wasn't safe and that he'd feel better if she was at the condo. Then he left to run to the office, so she did as he asked and stayed put but pouted about it.

The next morning she'd suggested they go out together for a walk, get some air, a Frappuccino, something outside the apartment.

"Go for a Frappuccino?" He looked at her like she was insane.

"Don't do that," she snapped at him, slamming her coffee cup on the counter and storming toward the stairs to head back up to the loft bedroom.

"Don't do what?" he asked.

She kept going but he caught her by the hand and pulled her back to the sofa.

"Don't say 'Go for a Frappuccino' like I'm crazy the way you said 'call you a cab?' to me after the first night we met."

"I'm only slightly less likely to go for a Frappuccino with you now than I was to call you a cab that day."

"Don't be an asshole," she clipped and got up and headed up the stairs.

He followed.

"Aren't you glad I didn't call you a cab?" he whispered behind her ear as she reached over to make the bed.

She felt a twinge.

"Of course I am." Regret surged through her at her attitude.

"Baby...please understand. I don't want you out there, vulnerable."

He proceeded to reiterate that he was busy and unnecessarily repeated that he wanted her safe and he could better ensure that if she stayed in.

She nodded, saying nothing, then moved to rummage through a basket of clean laundry she'd just done in order to match up socks. She knew he was right. Deep down, she knew. But she couldn't help but feel like she was going a little stir-crazy.

He worked from the condo all that day but went out for two hours in the evening. And while he was gone, Kyla paced like a caged tiger.

When he was back, she tried to act normal. They had ordered in pizza and they cuddled up in front of the TV in the bedroom and watched three episodes of the first season of Game of Thrones.

And she fell asleep cuddled up to him.

A good night's sleep did nothing to improve her claustrophobia. So, stupidly, the next morning, she snuck out right after he left to go to the office for a meeting.

Stupidly.

Yep, Kyla knew it was stupid. It was stupid-dangerous. But, she took her Taser, her purse, and her cell phone, lifted her dagger out from under the pillow, and she snuck out, thinking it was logical to do it that way and she'd only dash out for ten minutes. Her right hand was in her jean jacket pocket and she'd held the hidden dagger the whole way to the store.

Ten minutes to get some steaks for dinner and then back. And she wouldn't keep it from him. She'd told herself she'd tell him, and he'd know it went okay, and then he'd chill out a little bit regarding her being out of the condo.

She'd rationalized that she'd just be zipping to the small gourmet supermarket less than two blocks away, she'd buy some steaks to cook him a nice dinner, and then get back in. No biggie.

It'd get her some air. It'd make her feel normal for a half an hour. She knew it was a bad idea, but she did it anyway. It was almost as if it was a compulsion that she had no control over.

So, the trip there was fine. Uneventful. It was great to be out, alone, breathing fresh air like a normal person. And she was alert, but felt completely safe.

But, on her way back from the market, with nothing strange happening, everything totally ordinary, just as she'd stepped outside the door of the store, her cell phone went off and it'd been him calling.

She was fumbling with her wallet and the bag, and it only rang three times and stopped before she was able to answer it. She was about to call him back but then she felt the thrumming of him tracking her inside herself and an intense emotion inside. Panic and anger.

Uh oh.

The panic was hers. But the anger?

The anger was his.

She hurried back toward the condo building, eyes darting to and fro, to ensure no one was tailing her.

He was on his way out of the elevator as she approached it. His eyes went big and dark and he grabbed her wrist and ducked back into the elevator. In her fumbling she heard a clatter. The wrist he'd grabbed was on the dagger and she'd dropped it. She looked down it was on the floor between their feet and very close to the elevator door, where there was a gap that was big enough to swallow it up and where it would've happened had it skidded just a few more inches. She winced, crouched, nabbed it, and then got it back into her pocket.

He was about to speak, and she could feel that whatever was about to come out would do so in an animalistic roar because he had an "Are you fucking kidding me?" expression on his face but a hand stopped the elevator door from closing and then a couple, about their age, stepped in. Tristan's mouth snapped shut and he glared at her. She winced, chewed her cheek, and leaned over and pressed the button for their floor and then leaned back against the mirrored wall.

As the elevator climbed, she could feel the tension emanating off him like a living and breathing monster. He'd moved in front of her protectively and she just stared at the back of him, chewing her lip nervously.

They got off the elevator first and the rip-roaring fight started the minute they got back into the apartment.

"What the hell were you thinking?" he demanded, and she knew he was hanging onto his temper by a thread.

"I had to get outta these four walls, Tristan. I feel like I'm in a cage. Since we've been together do you realize how much time I've spent cooped up? It's making me nutso! I just got some steaks for dinner. See?"

"Are you fucking insane?" he hollered so loud and so angrily that she felt herself cower a little.

He advanced, and she backed up right into the back of the sofa.

"Is your need to get fresh air that much more important than your need to fucking breathe and survive?"

She opened her mouth to speak, but he kept going.

"Do you have any fucking idea what it was like to get here and see that you were gone?"

"I was gone not even fifteen minutes," she whispered.

He looked at her like she was an idiot.

She *was* an idiot. She knew it. But she defended herself anyway.

"There's a note on the fridge."

There was. It said "Gone to the store. Back in 10." And she had hoped he wouldn't get back before she did and see that note. He shouldn't have been back. He'd left not that long before she did, to go to some meeting. She hoped she could just chuck it in the trash and go about her day, making him a nice dinner, feeling better after having got outside like a normal fucking person for ten minutes. Then she'd tell him about it and he'd hopefully realize that things could get normal for them.

"Do you think I made it to the goddamn fucking fridge? I opened the door and knew that you weren't here immediately. I couldn't smell you, I couldn't feel your presence here, but I'd felt it in that fucking hallway so even though I ran through the apartment to see if you were here, I knew you weren't. The only thing that kept me from flying through the glass and out the fucking window to find you fifty odd stories down instead of going down in the elevator is that I could feel that you were out there, not a fucking care in the world, traipsing down the street. The note on the fridge doesn't mean squat. What matters is how absolutely stupid that was! Looks like chaining you to the bed is the only way to keep you from—-"

"Don't you fucking dare!" She cut him off and got right in his face, "You do that to me ever again and you'll fucking lose me. Grrr!"

She felt the cold jet out of her fingertips and she gave him a shove, hands flat against his pecks. He didn't budge but his face got angrier. He caught her by the wrists and his eyes narrowed. She yanked her hands away and stormed away from him, dropped the bag with the steaks on the island, pulled out the dagger, and then stormed upstairs and put it back under the pillow and then she paced. And paced.

She was still feeling claustrophobic. Even more claustrophobic than she'd felt before she'd gone outside.

Maybe the villa would've been better. Then there was at least the courtyard where she could get air while still being safe. Yeah, in a pit. In a prison.

No, she doubted it. She knew she'd be fidgety there, too. She felt like she was coming out of her skin half the time since they got back here. All she had was the open concept level with the kitchen and laundry room and living area plus the upper loft bedroom. Unless you counted the walk-in closet and the panic room and bathrooms.

Yes, there was a view. It wasn't small. It was bright, airy, and luxurious. But so what? A prison was still a prison, whether it was a panic room without windows or an open concept condo in the sky.

Tristan's fuck room. Tristan's bedroom. Tristan's condo. Tristan's panic room. Hotel rooms. The room and then the cottage at Adrian's compound. One prison after another after another.

So he can keep me safe.

She felt a big pang of guilt. She let out a long slow breath and sat on the bed, scooted up to the pillows, and pulled her knees up to her chest.

Damn it! What's wrong with me?

She knew he had a load of things on his plate and she was putting more stress on him with her attitude. She also knew he was going it alone and wasn't taking her up on offers of help. If she could help, maybe she wouldn't be so bored. But regardless, she was being a brat, a liability. They'd been through so much already and she was making it worse.

He was at the top of the stairs, eyes on her, jaw working with tension, arms folded across his chest.

"I have been caged-up crazy. I was sure I'd feel 100% better if I could just go down to the butcher shop, grab some steaks like a normal person, come back and cook you a nice dinner. It was a block away and I had the dagger—-"

"Kyla, seriously!" He was pissed. She could see it. She could feel it. "Do I need to remind you that there's a lot fucking going on here? Do I actually need to go over that with you? Cause you can't have forgotten..."

"Tristan, I'm just feeling caged. I..." she stopped talking. There was nothing else to say. She knew her argument held no water whatsoever. The fact that she was even trying to defend herself was idiotic.

"Fuck!" he bit off.

His eyes went darker. Not black, but definitely darker.

"Kyla, I was so fucking tweaked on the way here from the airport it wasn't remotely funny. I can't shake anxiety about your safety after all we've been through so far. I need you to please find a way, baby, to dig deep and respect my protectiveness and my need to know you're okay. I don't think that's too much to ask. After everything that's happened, you know I'm not overreacting about there being very real threats out there."

"I'm sorry." She looked down at the blanket.

Silence. Loaded silence.

"You fucking should be," he finally clipped, "After all that, I can't believe I have to even say these things to you!" He turned and went downstairs, leaving her sitting there with her mouth hanging open.

She moved forward, looked over the banister and saw him sitting at the kitchen island.

She descended the stairs and then approached, "Did your meeting get cancelled?"

He didn't answer her, didn't acknowledge her presence in the room, just kept clicking away at his laptop.

She put the steaks in the fridge while waiting for him to answer. His vibe was seriously pissed.

She stood there, staring, waiting, refusing to be ignored.

"I'm Skyping instead," he finally answered.

"Why?"

"Because I can't fucking trust you right now to stay put."

"You can trust me," she said softly.

"Oh, yeah?" He shot her a look of disbelief.

"I'm sorry, Tristan. But you've gotta understand..."

He shot to his feet, the barstool he'd been sitting on falling over.

"It's not a sincere apology if it ends with a 'but', Kyla. I felt you moving further from me, that's why I'm back here instead of at the office."

"I'm sorry. But let me help with all this. Give me something to do. I'm going crazy."

"Do you hear yourself? Apologizing for being a brat and then doing something else that's even worse? Threatening me with losing you, then asking to help me?"

The computer started ringing with an incoming Skype call. The screen said, 'Rick @ Kovac'.

"Give me the room for this, I have to do it on video," he told her, and his eyes moved to the staircase, telling her he wanted her to go back upstairs.

She huffed and stormed up the stairs.

When she got to the bed she threw herself on it and then chastised herself for being a brat again.

What's wrong with me?

She heard him answer the call. She didn't stay to eavesdrop. She went into the bathroom and started the tub.

She spent a good forty-five minutes in the bathroom. Loofahing, deep conditioning her hair, shaving her underarms, legs, and her hoo-ha, and staring at the ceiling in deep thought.

She had to find a way to chill out and be there for him instead of being a pain in his ass. Why was she being so irrationally stupid?

Her stupid behaviour had to have something to do with this deepening bond. But if it was symbiotic then why was she not being very giving? She was acting like a spoiled princess. She sincerely hoped she wasn't about to get her period.

Many times over the years she'd had irrational moments and then an 'Aha!' moment when she'd seen that it was indeed Shark Week starting.

After her bath, she plucked her eyebrows, blow-dried her hair and then got dressed in jean shorts and a t-shirt and gave herself a manicure and a pedicure while watching some daytime TV gameshows.

After a while, she looked down over the loft's half wall and saw that Tristan was on the sofa, rather than at the bar, and he had his stocking feet up on the coffee table, his tie still on but loosened, top few shirt buttons undone, blazer off, and the neck of a bottle of beer in his grip while he watched a soccer game on the big screen TV. Even pissed off and casual like that, he exemplified the term "suit porn" sitting there like that.

She hesitantly went down the stairs and as she passed him heading to the kitchen area, she caressed the hand that was dangling, holding the beer, with her fingertips. He didn't flinch. Annoyance and frustration were emanating from him.

She started working on dinner and hoped she wouldn't fuck it up. She felt so sad while she did it. She felt immensely guilty.

As she was frying mushrooms and sautéing onions to go on top of the steaks, which she had soaking in a marinade, waiting to go into the oven under the broiler with some baby potatoes, she felt his presence behind her. He moved her hair back with his chin and kissed her throat.

She turned the burner off, chucked an unwashed pile of raw green beans into the colander in the sink, and turned around into his arms and kissed him on the chest where his button-down shirt was undone a few buttons.

He kissed the top of her head and then tipped her chin up with his hand so that he could kiss her.

He kissed her softly, gently, reverently.

"I love you," she whispered against his lips.

"Love you," he whispered and dipped his tongue in and grabbed the back of her head so he could go deeper.

"I'm gonna try really hard to not be a brat," she whispered, after he broke the kiss.

He hiked her legs up so that they surrounded his waist and walked her to the sofa and put her on her back and then was on top of her, grinding into her. She hooked her legs around his waist and started grinding right along with him. She pulled his shirt out of his suit pants and ran her nails up from the dimples at the base of his spine up to his big hard shoulders.

"Good," he whispered.

"Just sayin', I'm not usually a good cook but I've been known to do a steak okay. Hopefully it'll be worth that argument."

"Just give me mine bloody and I'm good," he kissed her, "But nothing is worth an argument."

"You're right. I'm sorry. And if I'm bratty again, you have my permission to spank me," she told him.

"I fucking will," he said back and it rumbled up from his throat. She felt that rumble in her clit.

"And cut the talk about leaving me. Not only would I stop you, but you know it's not even an option. And it's an asshole thing to say. Do you want out? Do you not love me?"

"I'll never leave you, baby. Even if I could survive without you, I wouldn't survive without you. I won't say that kind of thing anymore. I didn't mean it." Tears were in her eyes.

"How would it feel if I said that to you?" he challenged.

Devastated. Utterly gutted.

Devastating would be an understatement. Her heart would shatter like glass at that kind of threat.

"I'm so sorry. I didn't mean it, Tristan. I love you. I love only you. You're the only person on the earth I love, so you get all of my love and I'm an asshole, and I'm so sorry."

Then she felt him smile against her cheek as he planted a kiss on her cheekbone.

"Okay. Love you, too, princess."

"I'm sorry," she repeated.

"Okay, baby."

He grabbed her bottom with both hands and rotated his hips so that his hard cock was rubbing right against her clit.

"Here or upstairs?" he asked.

"Here, but quick. I got in a whole lot of trouble with my awesome vampire prince boyfriend buying those steaks so I wanna make sure they don't get ruined."

"He's awesome, is he?"

"He *so* is. He's been running himself ragged to take care of us while I've been a rotten little brat and he deserves a really nice dinner, as a start. Then maybe a whole bunch of consecutive blowjobs. But after the dinner. I don't got that much time right now."

He stood them up, undid her shorts and yanked them down. She stepped out of them while he undid his pants to free his cock and then guided himself into her, a seriously hot look on his face, his eyes warm and filled with love. Kyla arched her back and reveled in the feel of every inch going in. They toppled back onto the sofa.

It was a quickie, but it was a good one. There hadn't been any feeding. She had been about to whine about that and caught herself. Regardless, she knew he felt it.

Afterwards, she finished cooking dinner, which turned out surprisingly great, and they ate quietly at the island, Tristan watching a sports news show, Kyla tolerating it for him. After the meal, they loaded the dishwasher together,

"I think we oughta go to the island," Tristan said.

"Yeah?" she put the dish towel down and gave him her full attention. She agreed. She suspected she'd get outdoors, have a bit more freedom there. And she'd be near Kyle. Maybe she could help figure out how to wake him up.

"Yeah. Sergey Voitenko is arriving there tomorrow. I think it'd be good to have a conversation with him, learn more about this bond you and I have. Especially with how things have gone since we've been back here. Maybe there's other stuff we need to know."

She nodded, "So we can find out why I'm being a bitch?"

He caressed her face and smiled. What he didn't do was disagree with her statement.

"Are you worried about him?" she asked.

"Not really. I've dug around. He has a good rep. Highly respected. Blood that's bluer than blue. He's rumoured to be over 400 years old but no confirmation on that. No red flags coming up. He's stepped back from a few councils in recent years. He was really active in Europe for decision-making but has been quiet the last 30-35 years."

"What about his strengths?"

"Very little known about that, but he's rumoured to be extremely strong. Telepathic. Has Telekinesis."

"You've got those, too."

"Uh huh."

"But you're not an elder."

"Nope."

"Hmm. Wonder what you'll be like in 400 years."

He made a funny face and she felt something coming off him that wasn't pleasant.

He cleared his broody expression and said, "So, I'm thinkin' that Sam bought some redemption helping me out with you. Maybe I take a little leap of faith with him and his sister, have a conversation or two, at least. Contingency plans, of course."

"Of course."

"Sasha promised us privacy, house next door to hers, quiet part of the island where no other vamps visit. We stay there a few days over this weekend, feel things out. And then you and me come back, I have a big meeting mid-week next week back here. We have a chat when we get home about how we feel."

"That sounds good." It felt good to be involved in the decision-making process, not simply being told what'd happen.

"Alright."

"So, we'll head out tomorrow. I have a few meetings and then we'll go. Can you pack for us?"

"Okay," she gave him a squeeze, "Um...do you think I'm gonna get my period?"

He shook his head, "I'm not sure but you haven't ovulated again. At least not that I've noticed."

"I don't know if all that's changed now," she said, "But these mood swings feel like PMS."

He let out a big breath, "I don't know, baby. We'll get to the island and see what Sergey says. I feel you again, so I can only hope I still have the ability to detect ovulation. Your first period with me came without warning, though, other than those cramps, but you were on all that birth control. Do you have cramps?"

"No."

He shrugged, "We have the panic room. We'll use it if things get scary. You have that dagger. Use it on me if you need to, jab me and get locked in the panic room. If you have to leave the apartment because I can get into the room then you jab me, go, get in my Escalade and drive to the Four Seasons down the road and check in there into the Kovac corporate suite. I set that up when we had the banquet so it's open for us whenever we need it. I'll add your name to the list. Then I know where you are. Okay? Maybe you oughta wear that dagger. We'll get you a belt sheath on our way to the island and a leg holster for it, too. I'll also get you an untraceable credit card for emergencies. That way you've got the means to be safe without anyone knowing your movements. The concierge for this building will have information about you, will know to let you in if you *ever* need to get in. I'll get you a card and we'll leave a double here, in the panic room."

"Okay."

This was good. She felt relief. Strategy and forward motion was good. Hopefully things wouldn't go wrong again.

His phone rang. It was sitting on the coffee table. She glanced at the screen.

It said "Taryn calling."

Tristan glared at the phone and then rejected the call.

"What's up with her?" Kyla muttered, feeling a chill.

"I sent her home after things went bad. I haven't talked to her."

"You don't call her mother, mom?"

He looked at her blankly.

"It says Taryn on the phone, not Mom."

"Not since I turned her, and she ceased to be that person."

Kyla gave him a squeeze, "Wanna talk about what she was like before?"

"No, she's gone. I fucked that up."

"But what if Sasha can..."

"Don't."

"Don't?"

"I can't hope. Not right now. I have too much to do, to keep you safe, figure out how to handle things for us. She's not on radar other than keeping her away from us. She makes me lose focus, makes me irrational. I can't..."

"Okay."

Maybe he couldn't hope but Kyla could. She'd hope *for* him. Kyla hoped that somehow Sasha could synthesize whatever in Kyle's blood turned off the evil in female vampires and that Tristan could have his mother again.

11

THEY WERE BACK ON THE island.

And it was beautiful, traveling to it on a boat with Tristan, after another chartered flight, of course.

Kyla loved the ride, loved the idea that good things could be coming. She hoped her instincts were right. Her instincts told her something good was on the horizon and that maybe someday soon they could have some adventure. Adventure that didn't come with looking over their shoulders all the time.

Tristan was keeping an aircraft and a boat on standby and showed her how to use the satellite phone to summon either, should she need to leave the island without him.

The idea of that made her heart hurt, but she sucked it up and listened to his directions.

SASHA, TRISTAN, AND Kyla were in the house that was next door to Sasha's house, getting a tour. And Kyla loved the place.

There wasn't a close neighbour on the other side and the place was secluded, similar to Sasha's, a charcoal-coloured log home with red cedar shake shingles on the deep pitched roof. The house was two storeys with four bedrooms and a big open concept main floor that was essentially a big great room with a large Hollywood style kitchen and a utility room and powder room. The place was very bright with plenty of windows, had an attached small green house and a dock and boathouse as well. It was just two storeys and wasn't built into the hill as Sasha's was but still backed up close and Sasha said that like all the other homes on the island, there was hill access from the basement into a cave system, for emergencies. She assured them that no one could simply access the homes from the cave. There was no way into the homes from the cave as there were no doorknobs and the locks were strong but there were exits from the cave system, including an entrance deep into a forest on the island.

The home was sparsely furnished, the previous occupant had left a few things and Sasha augmented that, equipping it enough for them to be comfortable for the few days they'd planned to stay. An older TV, three-seater brown leather sofa, and half a dozen chairs, some mismatched, around a round kitchen table were all the furnishings on the main floor but the kitchen had a newish three door fridge and a propane stainless steel chef's stove with six burners. There were non-fancy but totally usable cooking implements and dishes stocked there.

As for communication, there was satellite line-of-sight internet and minimal but still existent satellite television. The living room had an older large screen rear projection TV. On the front porch, which had a big covered veranda, was a red wooden swing and a side deck with screened in gazebo area that held an octagonal patio table with seating for six. Directly across from that was a tire swing hanging from a big old tree with a branch as wide as a standard tree trunk in the perfect spot for holding that tire swing or for sitting on, getting lost in a book, or for maybe building a tree house that could hold a bunch of kids.

Upstairs, the only furnished bedroom was the master and it had a big beautiful oak canopy bed with red drapes pinned back on the canopy. Small night tables that didn't match and a big pine armoire that also didn't match were all that was there but there was a stationary bike in the corner of the room as well as an elliptical machine.

The room had a wall of large windows covered with thinish off-white drapes.

Sasha had explained that Sam had talked of her love for running but they didn't have a treadmill. She had gotten Sam to bring this exercise equipment in from her clinic. The same patchwork quilt from Sasha's guest bedroom was on the bed. Kyla fingered it.

"Your mother made that. After your parents were brought in, some of their belongings were fetched by my brother. I saved that for you. I meant to tell you so if you leave again, you can take it with you."

Kyla felt a pang in her chest. She had very few memories of her mother. She remembered her parents being lovey dovey. She remembered her mother's gentle touch. But, she didn't remember much else and didn't really allow herself to feel much about her lost parents over the years.

She'd been too young when they'd supposedly died to have full memories but what memories she did have, she suspected she'd just kept in a secret place that was only hers but that she hadn't allowed herself to unlock, really.

She'd never wanted to let the memories out of wherever they'd been locked because that'd leave the door open to let the pain in, too.

She smiled at Sasha, "Thank you for that."

"I saved some books and a few things for Kyle, too. He appreciated it but wanted the quilt for you. And he said you loved to lie on that quilt with him to watch cartoons when you were small. It was made from your and Kyle's baby clothes and baby blankets. He said that he wanted it saved, just in case, but hoped you'd never be found, that you'd never have to know the truth about who you are."

She still didn't remember Kyle, only her parents.

Why was that?

Tristan seemed less than interested in the tour, knowing Sasha had been trying to sell them on settling there on the island, after Tristan joined this coalition, but had been patient through this part of the conversation.

Kyla knew it was because he was anxious to sit down and meet Sergey.

"Sasha, where is Sergey?" he asked, almost as if cued by her brain.

"He's on a hike with my brother and giving Sam a tour of the cave and tunnel system. They'll be back soon. An hour, I think. You two are here a few hours ahead of schedule otherwise I know they'd be here. How about if you two settle in and then come by in about an hour, hour and a half, and we'll do dinner?"

"Fine," Tristan said.

Kyla suspected he'd purposely wanted to catch them off guard with his arrival time. He was obviously still being cautious, and this was good.

"I've stocked you up with some refreshments," Sasha added, "breakfast stuff, beverages, grape juice, avocados and tomatoes, etcetera. We can do big meals at my place if you like or if you don't want to, I can send more food over."

"We've brought some, too. But thank you," Kyla said. She'd stocked a cooler that they'd brought.

Sasha nodded and was about to leave them alone in the bedroom.

"How's Kyle?" Kyla asked.

"Sasha leaned her shoulder against the frame. "I've had to have him on some pain meds. Since having you here he's been showing signs of pain. It's manageable with the meds, but it's odd that it started then and hasn't subsided. He's been running a low-grade fever and he's had some hives on his arms and legs."

Kyla didn't like the sound of that. Sasha looked concerned, too. She said goodbye to Sasha and then they were alone, so Kyla put her toiletry bag into the nice big master bathroom. It was huge with a big soaker tub, a skylight, his and her sinks, the whole bathroom done in brown and taupe with copper accents, pale and dark brown marbled tile, and pearl white bathroom fixtures. It seemed like someone had started to fancy up this place but hadn't finished. She loved the idea of being able to do that for them.

"Hey?" she asked as she wandered back out to the bedroom. He was staring out the window toward the shoreline, deep in thought. She could feel his confliction, how far away he was.

"Hey," he snapped back and looked at her.

"What's the matter?"

"Nothin'. I'm not looking forward to having this dinner. I'd leave you hidden but I can't stomach the idea of leaving you here by yourself so I have to have you around a vamp who's older than me, knows more about our bond than I do, and who might be a threat."

"You'll keep me safe," she told him with a smile.

"If I even smell a threat in that room I'll rip him to shreds. I give no fucks, Kyla. I'm not playing these political games anymore. I know you've been having nightmares about some of the violence I've shown you, but you need to know that's nothing compared to what I'll do if anyone looks at you the wrong way again. I have you back and nothing, but *nothing* is gonna fuck with that."

Kyla swallowed back the twinge of apprehension at that comment and moved to him. She fingered his chin cleft and then sifted her fingers through his soft hair, cupped the back of his head and pulled him toward her mouth. He melted into her and then the kiss went desperate and he backed her against the bathroom door, twisting his tongue up with hers, taking her breath away. His mouth moved to her throat and he sank in there, drinking, one hand on her hip, the other on her jaw. She kissed his wrist. He released her throat, used his bared fangs to pierce his palm, and then his palm was over her mouth.

Kyla's eyes rolled back as her tongue flicked over the wound on his hand. They wound up in a tangle on the floor. Arms, legs, mouths, and other very tingly parts.

THEY WALKED HAND IN hand to Sasha's next door, which wasn't visible from the house they were in but by following the shoreline past a small wooded area, they were there in ten minutes.

Sam was outside, bent at the knees, rifling through a large tackle box. When they were close he closed the lid and waited, eyes on Tristan.

Tristan's grip tightened on Kyla's hand and she felt like he was on high alert.

"Bro," Sam held out his hand, loose-gripped and Tristan reached out and they did a biker-like handshake, catching one another's thumbs as they cupped around the side of the other's palm.

Sam gave Kyla a cautious nod.

"You're not patched," Tristan noted.

"I am not." Sam confirmed.

"And? Still?" Tristan was tense, ready to strike.

"I'm good. Completely. More on that during our conversation with Sergey. I only left it off because of some things he's said. You're not going to have to worry about her setting me off. Things have changed because of what you two now have. The patch wasn't giving me empathy. Well, maybe it did initially but I don't need it to keep that. I feel the same, bro."

"Hm," was Tristan's non-committal response. "You moved that trunk??"

"I did."

"Where?"

"Boat house."

The large trunk they'd brought with them contained a daggered Adrian Constantin.

The headed up the stairs.

"So, Sergey?" Tristan inquired.

Sam nodded, "Solid."

"Yeah?" Tristan's eyebrows furrowed. He almost seemed disappointed.

"Definitely," Sam said firmly, still nodding. Sam's eyebrows rose, "I really think you should consider this coalition, bro. I'm not kidding. It's been enlightening. He hasn't said much about what's happened with you two, after you turned her, but what little he has said to me sounds all good. Your call man, but I suggest we do this dinner, talk, and you and I meet later or maybe tomorrow after you've had a chance to think on it. I see this for us and I'd be happy to be part of it, you leading the way."

"Let's see how this first meeting goes," Tristan said, "then we'll talk."

"Alright. Don't judge anything based on the food, though, man. Sasha's cooking, so the meal part of the evening could be a disaster."

Kyla smiled and followed them into Sasha's entrance on the middle level of the house. Sasha was in the kitchen. It was a disaster zone and she looked completely frazzled. There was a burnt scent in the air as well as something spicy and yet cinnamony and that combination did not smell *at all* appetizing.

"Oh hi. I, uh... sit down. Beverage?"

"I can get one. How can I help?" Kyla asked.

Sasha definitely needed help. She appeared to be making a stir fry.

She had noodles in a bubbling pot, a frying pan of assorted vegetables cooking, and another pan with chicken in a brown sauce but that was what smelled both burnt and strange. Cinnamon mixed with teriyaki and a whole lot of garlic permeated the air. Kyla loved all those smells individually but together? She usually loved the scent of cooking garlic. She knew Tristan did, too, but this wasn't a good garlic smell. At all. It smelled like burnt garlic.

A vampire who overdid it on the garlic. Ha!

"Nope, I'm uh... I'm good," Sasha said.

She really wasn't.

Kyla opened the fridge and grabbed an opened bottle of wine from the top shelf and topped up Sasha's wine glass, which had been sitting, half empty, on the counter smack dab in the midst of a mess of carrot peelings, pepper ends and seeds, onion skin, and broccoli and cauliflower stalk clippings.

"Thanks!" Sasha said brightly, adding a whole lot of salt to the pan with the chicken.

Kyla looked to Tristan and Sam who were sitting at the table, but Tristan was sitting sideways at the chair closest to Kyla, in arm's reach. Kyla poured herself some wine.

"Beer?" Sam asked.

"Water," Tristan replied.

Kyla passed Tristan a bottle of water and went to pass Sam the beer bottle, but Tristan intercepted it and he passed it to Sam himself.

Kyla started picking up peelings and put them in a small bucket that was on the other end of the counter, that had some apple and orange peels in it, looking like it was dedicated to food waste for composting. Sasha started frantically scraping at the chicken, which appeared to be sticking to the bottom of the frying pan, intensifying the burnt teriyaki and cinnamon smell.

Sam wrinkled his nose and shook his head at her, silently communicating his feelings about his sister's cooking.

Sasha caught the expression and pointed her finger at him.

"Want me to set the table?" Kyla asked.

"Sure. I, uh, have my hands kinda full. Placemats and dishes are all right where you are. Drawers, cupboards."

"Where is he?" Tristan asked.

"Shower. He'll be down any minute. He's staying in the room you two used when you were here."

"How many vamps with him?"

"Nope," Sam answered pointedly.

"No? Pets?"

"None," Sam said.

"None?" Tristan asked, but then Tristan bolted to his feet and blocked Kyla against the counter by the sink by standing directly in front of her, against her, his hand wrapped around the back of her, pinning her front to his back. She felt his skin's temperature drop. She jolted and tried to prepare for the worst.

Please, not more worse...They'd had enough worse to last a lifetime!

"I've got you," he said over his shoulder and he'd turned his head in that direction, so she saw his eyes briefly. His pupils were black, and he'd dropped his fangs.

"No, Tristan, I don't travel with pets." A guy appeared in the kitchen, having come down the stairs. Kyla peeked around Tristan's bicep and took him in.

He was absolutely beautiful. He looked younger than Tristan. He looked a bit younger than Kyla. He was very fit and had a dark crewcut and olive skin with eyes that were somewhere between silver and amber. They were luminescent. He was tall and wore dark wash jeans and a black t-shirt that stretched across his broad chest. His feet were bare. He looked casual, at home.

He smiled at Kyla, one dimple on display on the left side of his smile, and then his gaze was back on Tristan. He was on the other side of the long wooden table. He stopped when his thighs were against the table. He reached his hand out in greeting toward Tristan.

Tristan waited a beat and then accepted the handshake.

Something electric passed between the two men and Kyla felt it in her chest. It was an odd sensation. She wondered what it felt like to Tristan.

"I'm no threat to either of you. Please relax." Sergey said and he sat down at the table on the other side.

"Shit!" Sasha cried out as she jumped back. The bubbling pot was spitting at her and it looked like there were far too many noodles in the medium-sized pot.

"Excuse me, I need to drain this," she said.

Kyla went to move but Tristan hadn't yet let go of her.

"Babe," she whispered and tried to scoot them away from the sink. They got about three feet from it when Sasha, the pot in both hands, was dumping the pot's contents into the sink, but then she cussed again.

"Damnit!"

Kyla glanced over and saw that there was no colander in the sink. Sasha had poured a big pot filled with rice noodles into the sink. Not that they'd be edible. They were a large congealed mass.

"I thought I put that strainer in there," Sasha muttered.

"You don't travel with a pet and you're royal," Tristan observed quietly, ignoring Sasha muttering about having thought she'd put a colander in the sink.

"No. I'm a widower," Sergey answered, "No one knows this and usually I keep a decoy with me, but knew it'd be unnecessary here."

"Let's just make some more," Sasha mumbled, "Oh damn. I'm out. I know! I have some rice."

Kyla tried to shift out of Tristan's hold to head over and shut the stove off, but he grabbed her and pinned her behind him tightly.

"Could you turn that off?" Kyla asked Sam. The stove was red hot and Sasha wasn't paying any mind to it as she had her head in her pantry, looking for rice. The veggies were overcooked. The chicken was burning.

"You're not—-" Tristan started but didn't finish.

"No. I'm not affected by her. Not to worry. No one is. Thanks to you binding her to you."

"What?" Tristan asked.

"I take it you haven't been in touch with anyone in the know."

"No."

"Then sit. I'll elaborate."

"I'll just help Sasha," Kyla said to his back.

"No. Sit," Tristan ordered and sat and pulled Kyla onto his lap. His arm went around her belly.

She was a little bit frazzled at this but said nothing. She knew it was proprietary as well as protective, but Sasha was in chaos with the food and Kyla just wanted to help get things under control. It wasn't a priority to Tristan right now. She wanted the news, too, but didn't want the kitchen to go up in flames in the middle of their conversation and it seemed like it was highly possible that Sasha could burn the place down. The place felt chaotic.

Sam stepped over to aid his sister. Tristan was tense. All this activity behind them and a potential threat in front of them and information coming out that was needed made him tweaked and he would very likely stay that way.

Tristan stiffened as Sam placed Kyla's wineglass on the table beside her. Then Sam put a stack of placemats and plates on the table and moved to help his sister some more.

She felt Tristan in a big way; he was very agitated with all the movement.

"Could everyone just sit fucking down?" Tristan snapped.

Everything went super quiet. You'd hear a pin drop.

"How about we give them two secs to get the food on the table, babe?" Kyla suggested softly, her hand on Tristan's cheek.

She could feel his jaw muscles working against the palm of her hand. Sergey's eyes were on her. Tristan's fingers dug into her hip a little, but he waited. She knew that he was very frustrated. An eternity later, (just a minute or two, really), she heard beeping and shuffling behind them.

Kyla sipped her wine and put her free hand on Tristan's, which was on her hip. She stroked his fingers soothingly and felt him relax marginally.

Sergey was watching Sasha and Sam with a look of amusement on his face.

A gigantic steaming bowl of the mixture of meat and vegetables was placed in the middle of the table. A bunch of chopsticks were then plopped down, then the microwave beeped and a moment later two packets of instant microwaveable rice were dumped onto the big bowl of chicken and veggies.

Sam and Sasha sat. Sasha blew her hair out of her eyes, looking exasperated.

The vegetables were looking overcooked. The rice was Spanish style instant rice, since the rice noodles had been a bust, so it didn't really go with the Asian theme. The chicken was apparently trying to be teriyaki but the amount of cinnamon scent in the air did *not* say good things.

Sam gave Kyla a horrified look as he started to pass the big bowl around, scooping a very tiny portion onto his plate. Kyla's lips tipped up in a slight smirk but at sight of Sasha looking so completely frazzled Kyla managed to clear her expression.

"This is why I don't cook," she explained, "And I apologize for this in advance. Apparently I mistook the ginger for garlic and I also knocked a bunch of spices into my marinating bowl of chicken and one of them opened. You can likely guess which one by the smell in here. I wanted to just take something out of the freezer, but lost track of time so figured I'd wing this."

Kyla smiled and chuckled a little nervously, thinking that if the sautéed veggies, chicken and rice hadn't been mixed together she could've tried the veggies and rice combo but as it stood, it was a one-dish disaster.

Tristan was stiff as a board, expressionless, but his impatience rolled through her as well as off him.

"Can I move to a chair beside you, babe?" Kyla tapped his hand. He released her, but he hadn't released his jaw from the tight clench. She moved to sit between Tristan and Sasha, but Tristan took her by both hips and swung around to redirect her to the empty chair on his other side, where she'd be beside no one. Sergey was across from Tristan and Sam was beside Sergey, diagonally across from Sasha.

Sasha, and Kyla served themselves. Sergey and Tristan had eyes on one another. Tristan looked impatient. Sergey looked absolutely composed. Sam was sitting, not eating.

"So, please, allow me to enlighten you as to what I think you should know and then if you have questions, you can ask them. Regarding your binding, of course. And then Tristan, whenever you want questions answered about my role here and my hopes with respect to an allegiance between us, we can discuss that. If that needs to wait, I'm fine with it."

"Fine."

Kyla moved the veggies around on her plate. Sasha took a bite and made a face and put her chopsticks down, got up and got her head into the freezer section of the fridge and pulled out a frozen boxed pizza and looked at Sam. He nodded enthusiastically. Sasha looked at Kyla, who smiled and shrugged.

"I'll do it," Sam mouthed.

"I can cook a frozen pizza, Samuel," Sasha defended.

"That's debatable," Sam grumbled.

"Seriously guys? For fuck sakes. Would ya *can* the comedy show?" Tristan snapped.

Sasha winced and put the pizza on the counter and sat back down.

Sergey smiled and sipped from a bottle of beer. Tristan jerked his chin up and Sergey started to talk.

"In the last few hundred years the vampire lines got very diluted due to the advance in transportation modes, spreading round the world, breeding happening outside vampire circles, the sheer number of turned vamps increasing, and so forth. Because of that, many of the old ways and traditions are becoming a thing of lore or becoming less and less known. Some councils have popped up over recent years striving to ensure that our bloodlines don't get so diluted that we eventually cease to exist as we do. I have more than 75% pure vampire in my family line, Tristan. About the same amount as you. But your family lines are stronger than mine, slightly. I feel it. I'm older than you but you're already more powerful than I am. And this is astonishing considering the fact that I was born vampire, never turned. I might be more knowledgeable than you are but that's the only advantage I have. We have some common strengths. You'll develop more as the years go by. I can only imagine what you'll have when you get to my age. That said, I mean you no harm; you're not a threat to me and I'll explain why. I think you and I can help one another achieve some common goals, at least I suspect they're common. I can certainly help you understand what's happened between you and Kyla. Her bloodline and your bloodline together were pure enough for this union. It's not often an option nowadays and because you two didn't know it was an option, I can see how this happened. Serendipitously.

My parents had the same relationship. They are still going strong."

"They're like us?" Kyla asked.

He nodded.

"Still alive?"

"And well."

"Both of them?

"Yes."

"Wow," Kyla breathed She put her hand on Tristan's thigh. He covered her hand with his and she could feel his mood shift. His face gave nothing away.

"In a scenario such as yours with a person that you've bonded with who has extremely rare blood, when you feed that mate your own blood, you bind that mate to yourself. That's what you've done. If any other vampire had turned her, she'd have just turned and with that, it could've destroyed the bond you had. Because you'd bonded and because of how royal she is, you've bound her to you and this bond is only breakable by death. If one of you dies, the other will wither. This relationship takes a serious commitment, vampires mate for life. It's just that very few know this."

Wow.

Sergey sipped his drink and smiled, then continued. "You benefit because her blood becomes yours only. Other vampires won't be attracted to it, which I'm sure is a relief to you. If another vampire does try to consume it, they'll become very ill and she'll most likely murder them for their efforts. You'll also have a better chance of successful procreation. It's not guaranteed; bound couples can still have trouble conceiving, but if she does, she doesn't face the typical human risk of dying giving birth to a vampire infant. Your children probably won't need to be turned. I was born vampire. I didn't need to be turned. I grew, as a normal child, but stopped aging after reaching full maturity."

Tristan's hand squeezed hers. She wanted to cry out with joy. But she held it together.

"You'll share a strong bond, be able to read one another, be able to feel one another. Feeding one another will deepen your bond and make you both stronger." He stopped and sipped his beer again.

It all sounded like good news. It all sounded like great freaking news. No one chasing them to steal her away or drain her? The chance of a baby together without Kyla dying? A life that long? Together?

"This is great!" Kyla couldn't help but blurt.

Tristan looked at her with apprehension and then looked back to Sergey. His heart was beating faster. It was making hers palpitate.

"There are some side effects." Sergey went on.

"And those are?" Tristan asked.

"Women turned in this way can be a little bit unruly. Not like she'd be if she were turned by someone else but still a bit unruly."

"Hah!" Burst out of Kyla.

Tristan looked at her narrow-eyed. The blue was coming back into his eyes.

Sam and Sasha both looked amused.

"She's a bit like a baby vamp in her temperament. Thankfully it should be short-lived."

"How short?" Tristan asked.

"Hey," Kyla whispered, "I haven't been *that* bad."

Tristan rolled his eyes. Sasha giggled.

"It's not easy to say. That's individual. And she will be desperate to procreate. If it doesn't work out, it could get...." Sergey winced, "Hairy. That temper can be directly tied to ovulation, menstruation even after she adjusts to her new status."

"How hairy?" Tristan asked.

"Tantrums, irrational behavior, depression. It could go a variety of ways, depending on her personality and how strong she is. Most female vampires today don't realize it's difficult to conceive because they're not bound to a strong and compatible male and that's a big reason why many are as unruly as they are. Vampires were meant to mate for life. This is a marriage and the female relies 100% on her mate and he relies on her as well, although not in the same way. It's believed that she doesn't have fangs because it could make her very dangerous if she becomes unruly and because her mate provides for her needs, she doesn't need them. You can feed elsewhere, it won't be as nourishing, but you can, if you need to or if you desire. She cannot. Another vampire's blood would make her violently ill."

Kyla's eyes rolled. Clearly vampires were unevolved in terms of feminism.

"I was diagnosed as infertile in my early 20's and when I was turned I was a nightmare," Sasha pointed out, "Until Kyle."

Sergey nodded, "We need to circle back to that, Sasha. Hang tight. And Tristan, your mother, who I am very familiar with, was turned when she was post-menopausal and while she experienced reverse aging, it was too late for her to conceive again. The inability to conceive added to her poor disposition. Being royal with that poor disposition was a recipe for... well, Taryn, to be blunt. We royals innately want to procreate. Turned vamps, too, but royals in particular. Males and females alike. Beyond drinking blood, that's what we are motivated to do. The dilution of the bloodline has made that difficult. Males find their enchanted human females and want to feed from them. If they don't become pregnant, many go into a rage and kill them without even realizing they're weeding them out so that they can move on. Not until it's too late. But the nature of our world today, that's not widely known and there aren't that many suitable females available, not that many suitable males either. The bloodline dilution has taken a toll, has affected our natural urges."

"Hence some of these breeding programs out there," Sasha mumbled.

"Exactly. Vampires won't voluntarily be seen as vulnerable, especially royal don't want to show that to turned vampires. But populations were dwindling. Councils and committees were formed. You all know the gist."

Tristan leaned back in his chair, shaking his head.

"So, you're suggesting that the breeding programs are important. But yet your coalition is trying to dismantle them?" Kyla asked.

"We don't want to dismantle them. We want them in the right hands. We want royal vampires to have the choice to be put into the breeding program, the choice to meet and potentially mate with another compatible vampire. Not be put into these programs against their will, not be watched their whole life and turned at a royal council's will and with that royal council determining who they'll breed with. The North American breeding councils are out of control."

"So it should kinda be like a vampire match.com?" Kyla asked and everyone but Tristan laughed.

"What about you? You're here alone. How do you feed?" Kyla asked.

Sergey smiled, "I searched the world for a hundred years until I found her, the one I wanted to be mated with. I had over 250 years with her. But she was murdered. We couldn't have children and had a rough time of it but had many beautiful years together despite that. They killed her 36 years ago and I'm withering. I'll start rapidly aging very soon. I might have five to ten years left at most. Because of my age and my lineage I won't start to age and desecrate for another 2-3 years. I have no desire to drink blood from anyone else and I won't thrive without her blood."

Kyla looked at Tristan and knew he'd feel the same.

"Dirty water," Kyla whispered.

Tristan squeezed her hand.

"I don't share this information freely as I'll continue to weaken. As you know, vampires prey on weakness. That's another reason this type of bond is kept quiet. If you want to kill a powerful vampire you could do it in a roundabout way by killing his mate. When the time comes that I begin to weaken, I want to end my life rather than live through the agony of slow withering and decaying," he said, "The last few decades have been difficult enough. But in the meantime,

I would like to partner with you, Tristan, to right some wrongs in the world for vampires. We'll never be in a position to live out in the open, that's not what I want, but I want to bring together work of some of our greatest minds and strongest vampires to pave the way for a better future. One where vampires can have children without putting their mates at risk, perhaps. One where vampires who cannot breed won't self-destruct. One where female vampires can choose to breed, mate, or perhaps be medicated so that they can be even-tempered instead of at the whim of their overactive hormones. One where control freaks such as Adrian Constantin are not allowed to have the power to treat younger vamps or vamps with less vamp DNA like puppets. There are few vampires as strong as we are and very few mated with an enchanted person with a vampire marriage and I cannot tell you how to live your life, but I recommend the bond with you and Kyla stays secret. Maybe once things are different, there will be vampires like us who can choose to come out of the shadows. But it's dangerous."

"I agree," Sasha chimed in.

Tristan pinched the bridge of his nose.

"Wow," Kyla whispered. So, before this, she was bound to Tristan. But now he was bound to her, too. And she was unbreakably bound to him and needed his blood to survive. But the thing was, she *could* survive, could be around a whole heckuva long time!

Tristan looked at her. She couldn't help but think outloud, "So a bunch of threats that have been plaguing us have been taken away by Tristan binding himself to me but then before we even get a chance to get excited about it, immediately we realize we're still under threat."

Sergey gave her a nod, "Basically. But work with us and you have me, my parents, and our network of vampires in the Ukraine, Romania, Greece, and several other countries who all want the same things."

Tristan was filled with anxious energy all of a sudden.

"I need sustenance. And not this," Sam pointed at the table after a long beat of silence.

He got up to go to the fridge and pulled out a blood bag.

"I'll make pizza," Sasha mumbled and started fiddling with the oven.

"I'll do it," Sam intercepted, "Sit."

"Any questions so far?" Sergey asked Tristan.

Tristan looked thoughtful.

"I'm sure you'll want to think on all this."

Tristan gave him a short nod.

Sergey's voice lowered as Sam and Sasha moved back to the oven, but Kyla could hear him clearly as he leaned forward toward Tristan.

"Tristan, you'll have to be patient with your bride, here. My mother and my wife both were fiercely independent and stubborn. It was a point of contention in my parent's marriage as well as mine. You need to feed her regularly and you need to feed from her regularly. She's still gaining strength so needs a daily feed for the next few months, at least. This has to happen even if you're in a squabble. It might not be easy if you're in a squabble but it's necessary. I tell you this because the squabbles happen often in the early days."

"How often? Feeding?"

"At least daily, if possible, but she could last three, four, or five days, maybe before feeling withdrawals. In six months, try skipping a week, if you like, to see if she has any tolerance for that. But don't go longer than a week for at least ten years or you could both begin to feel effects of withdrawal and you now know how she'll react to withdrawal. Years from now you'll have longer tolerances, a month or longer if needed, if there's a reason for you to be apart that length of time. How often are you feeding now?"

"Four to seven times a day," Kyla answered.

Sergey chuckled, "Honeymooners."

Kyla giggled. Tristan was still being wary but then he smiled with dimples.

"Have at it. It won't hurt either of you. Sasha?" Sergey redirected his attention, "Today your brother gave me some of your backstory with respect to Kyla's brother. When you fed from him the first several times, did you augment those feedings with other blood?"

"No," Sasha replied hesitantly.

"Then you should know that since you only consumed his blood and did it consecutively over that time, Kyle Kelly is bonded to you. Not the same depth of bond of Tristan and Kyla but your brother filled me in on our walk today, said you fed on him consecutively at his throat for a few weeks while he was unconscious. Since you fed on only him, that tells me he's bound to you."

"Yes. It was before, before I could stop myself and then I started using a test tube as I started to feel less, you know, driven by urges."

"It's quite possible he'll wake if you feed direct again."

"What? Really?" Kyla asked.

"Sasha, as you've only just recently informed me of the power of Kyla's brother's blood, I didn't know, or I would've imparted this information. He was unconscious when the process began but he became your bonded enchanted liege, but he was unconscious so would've gone into withdrawals without direct feeding. If your liege is in withdrawal too long, a comatose-like state is possible. It doesn't always happen, but it has been known to occur. It's as if they're putting themselves on ice awaiting their vamp. They might expire without the proper care, but you've been caring for him. If you feed at the source rather than bleeding him into a tube, it's possible he'll wake."

The room went wired. It made sense.

"How do you not know this?" Kyla accused, "Sam told Tristan about *our* bond, didn't you, Sam?"

Sasha shook her head innocently. "I'm not well-versed on the whole enchanted human / vampire bond. Dr. Constantin didn't enlighten me. I led a very sheltered life before I escaped."

"I didn't know all of what'd happened with her and Kyle before she left," Sam defended, "Only bits and pieces. We've been getting reacquainted, but I've been walking on eggshells because of my being in the middle here. None of this occurred to me."

"C'mon, man. You're smarter than that," Tristan accused.

"Sadly, it appears I am not." Sam looked stricken, "Sorry, Sash. I only knew a little about the enchanted bond. I didn't keep anything from you on purpose."

"So, if she feeds from his throat, my brother could wake?" Kyla turned back to Sergey.

"It's not a given. I don't know why he was unconscious when she fed on him initially but it's possible that her lack of contact feeding is what is keeping him asleep."

"Oh my God. I've bonded him to me. What does that mean?" Sasha looked like she'd been given a terminal illness diagnosis.

"Absolutely. It means that he'll want to feed you. He'll fight anyone else who tries to feed on him. If anything happens to him, you'll mourn him greatly. You might go rogue unless you find a suitable replacement."

"Is it crazy that I want to wake up Dr. Constantin right now to tell him this?" Sasha asked, "I pored over notes that Sam got me. It makes sense. He should've woken up within a short time after the last experiment, apparently."

"You're not waking Adrian up," Sam informed.

"He's here?" Sergey asked.

"He's daggered and in the boathouse. Tristan brought him here," Sam answered.

Sergey got a sadistic look on his face that chilled Kyla's blood.

"You're not waking him," Tristan told Sergey.

"We'll talk later. I'll explain our history. But no, I'm not waking him without your permission."

"The next time he wakes, it'll be because I wake him, so I can end him," Tristan said.

"He and I have a long history. One with plenty of reason for me to want to watch you kill him. I hope you'll allow me to observe." Sergey's eyes got a sickening glint in them. Tristan got a similar expression on his face.

Kyla shuddered.

The oven dinged, and she watched Sam remove cellophane and then slide the pizza in.

"See that? The cellophane come off first, Sasha."

Sasha balled up a serviette and tossed it at him.

"She learned that the hard way the other day."

Kyla giggled.

"Kyla and I need to go," said Tristan.

She knew he wanted away from this madness.

"Meet for breakfast?" Sasha invited, "And then we can see about Kyle?"

"Wait, what? Shouldn't we do it now? Maybe that's why he's in pain. Maybe we can stop the pain?"

"We should wait. Talk things out first. There's a lot here to contend with. Sasha needs to make this decision." Tristan tried to lead her toward the door.

She stopped and put her hand on his chest. "But he's been asleep for two years. He's hurting. He—-"

"Baby, one more day. Let's go." He was saying 'let's go' aloud but he was also communicating non-verbally that he needed the heck outta there right then, so she agreed.

"Fine. Tristan and I will cook at the house you lent us. Meet us there at nine?"

“I hope it’s not a lend,” Sasha said, “And he’s okay. I’ve got his pain under control. I think Tristan’s right. We should sleep on this, talk more in the morning.”

I hope he’s okay.

And she hoped it wasn’t a lend, as well.

She thought this but didn’t say it. She knew Tristan read that. He gave her a look and was giving off emotion she couldn’t quite translate.

“But you *are* going to wake him tomorrow?” Kyla asked Sasha.

“I’m going to try. I have a lot of mixed emotions about this though, Kyla. I didn’t know I did that to him. I didn’t know or... I can’t say I wouldn’t have done it. I was a nightmare after I was turned. But I mean—-I didn’t mean to inadvertently make him my enchanted pet. I really didn’t. I knew about the matching up process for the breeding program for bloodlines, but I was on a ‘need to know’ basis and I didn’t know all this. Never did I think I’d done that to Kyle.”

“I’m sure he’ll understand,” Kyla said, “I mean, based on what you’ve said about him.”

“I’m not sure he will,” Sasha’s expression dropped.

“Are the effects the same on a male enchanted pet as a female?” Kyla asked Sergey.

“He’s bonded so he’ll want to feed her, though he won’t be very cognizant of the want. The bond isn’t as strong when a female vampire bonds a male to her as when a male vampire bonds with a female human, but there is a connection. It’s not the same as the mutual binding but the connection is there.”

“Will he be mesmerized? Because I wasn’t. I was still very driven to feed Tristan. I had withdrawals. I started to feel things more sharply but I wasn’t catatonic.”

“I heard that you were lucid and that lucidity is likely what made Tristan bond with you in the way that he did. If you’d been mesmerized it might’ve played out differently. But your brother will be mesmerized. He was mesmerized with vampires before Sasha fed from him, so I suspect that'll be the same. The only way around that is if he's turned. If he's turned, their bond breaks but then his blood also changes. If she turns him, he'll be mated to her the way you are with Tristan so that's not recommended unless you two have that sort of relationship, Sasha, one where you want to mate for life. Kyla, it appears, from the research with Adrian's notes that Sasha shared with me, that you've got the lion's share of the vamp DNA and that's probably why you were lucid. A vampire marriage results in lucidity as well. It's rare for it to be the case beforehand. My mother wasn't lucid until she fed on my father's blood. It altered the nature of their relationship, obviously. The same happened with me and my wife."

Kyla blinked and her mouth dropped, "So, it was just him who made the decision for them to have that kind of bond?"

"Yes."

"And you with your wife?"

"The same. I saw what I wanted in her and decided I wanted her lucid, wanted her to be only mine. She had enough vampire in her bloodline for it to work."

"So you chose her. She didn't have a say."

"Correct."

"So I guess you're not as evolved as I initially thought. You saw what you wanted and just took it."

Sergey chuckled, "I'm an alpha male royal vampire. Through and through. But I wanted her, specifically."

"I know the type," she grumbled, swirled the rest of her wine around in her glass, and then downed it.

"On that note, let's go. Now." Tristan got to his feet, even more anxious to go, "Thanks for the insight. You a nighthawk?"

Sergey nodded, "Completely."

"Come down for a nightcap around 1:am, after I get Kyla to bed?"

Sergey smiled, "I look forward to it."

"You wanna wait fifteen minutes and take pizza with you?" Sasha asked.

"No, that's okay. We can get a sandwich. Thanks."

"Goodnight," Tristan said and let Kyla lead the way with his hand to the small of her back.

"But thanks for dinner, Sasha." Kyla called back, and Sam laughed a big belly laugh at Sasha's expense. Sasha stuck her tongue out.

"Want me there for this nightcap at one?" Sam followed and asked Tristan.

"No; you're good."

Sam nodded and stopped at the door.

When they got outside, Kyla whispered, "How do you know I'm gonna be sleeping at 1? What if I'm not tired?"

"You'll be tired," he gave her a carnal look and she felt it between her legs.

"Should you program them to leave Kyle until the morning?"

"Why?" Tristan asked.

"I kinda wanna be there. And if he's mesmerized, he'll probably need me to tell him what's happening. And she might not wait."

"It's not our problem."

"But...huh?"

"He's bonded with Sasha. He's her responsibility."

"Wait, what?" She felt her anger rising.

"I'm not trying to be flippant, princess; I know that he's a concern to you, but we have bigger fish to fry right now."

"Wait a fucking minute!"

They were now at the bottom of the steps outside.

"No. Quiet. Let's get back before we talk further."

She folded her arms across her chest, absolutely pissed, and ignoring some intensity coming from him both at her and *in* her. But he didn't seem to care that she was pissed. He grabbed her and lifted her into his arms and then they were whooshing down the beach.

He put her on her feet inside the door and then locked it, took her hand, and climbed the stairs to the bedroom.

He pushed her onto the bed and started tearing at her clothes.

"Tristan, wait. What're you doing? We have a heckuva lot to talk about!"

"I need you. Right now."

In a blur, her jean skirt was shimmied off and then her underwear were torn, his jeans were off, and he said, right against her mouth, "Please be wet, baby," and instantly, her body complied. She moaned as slammed his hips forward and was planted to the root inside her.

His head slowly moved down toward her throat.

"Wait," she blocked him with her shoulder against her ear, "Wait."

"Fuck that," He used her hair, a little roughly, to access her throat and then bit into her shoulder and then her throat and started to drink.

She felt a hint of frustration but as he started to drink, that hint dissipated, and she grabbed his arms and moaned.

He released her throat and their eyes met. He shook his head in astonishment, "I worried so fucking much that I'd lose you, then that I'd ruined you, followed by thinking I'd never have you truly back. I worried that we'd never stop worrying about your period, about your getting pregnant. It's all different. You're mine. You're mine for fucking ever. We could live 400 years or longer. Four hundred years together, with you. Not just the next few decades. The rest of my life." His mouth was on hers and his hands were in her hair.

Joy bubbled up inside of her. It felt like champagne bubbles in her veins as he drank more. She'd been so shocked by the news of

Kyle that it'd temporarily overshadowed all the amazing news they'd gotten at Sasha's table.

"We're vampire married," she giggled. "I didn't say *I do*. I didn't even get my wedding."

He released her throat, kissed her, and laughed into her mouth, "Want one?"

"That'd better not be a proposal, Mr. Vampire, because laughing into my mouth while your cock is inside me, asking if I want *one* when talking about a wedding, isn't an acceptable marriage proposal. At all."

He laughed a big belly laugh, "What d'ya know? The tough chick with the attitude wants me on bended knee with a diamond ring."

"It doesn't have to be that..." she mumbled, embarrassed. She turned her head away. He took her chin and directed her back so she was looking at him.

"I'll find a better way to ask," he said, "though just sayin', I think it's a foregone conclusion. No escaping me now, princess. Or should I call you *Mrs.* Vampire? Mrs. Bossy Pants Vampire?"

"I don't want to escape. Even if I could. I don't want to. I love you." Her eyes roved his face and then she gripped the back of his neck, "I love you so much it hurts but it's the sweetest pain I've ever had, my prince."

"Me, too." He kissed the tip of her nose.

"So. Are you, uh, gonna join this coalition, you think?"

"Yes," he whispered.

"Yes?"

"You think I should?"

"Yes. Yes, I really *really* do." She nodded enthusiastically.

"I know you do. I could feel it from you from the start of explaining what little I knew. Now, after all of this? Absolutely. This is the way forward."

"Yessss," she squeezed him and kissed his jaw, "Now that that's sorted, with the finer details to be sorted later, how 'bout you feed me something that's actually edible, so I can pass out and you can go have your nightcap and talk strategy with Sergey?"

"What do you want me to feed you? Food? Me?"

"Both. I want a tomato avocado grilled cheese with a Tristan nectar chaser. An orgasm or two for dessert."

He kissed her closed mouth and hard, then it transitioned to wet and deep, his fingers tangled in her hair, their hearts tangled together. They had dessert first, then he made her that sandwich.

12

BIRDS WERE SINGING. Loud. Lots of them.

Kyla's eyes opened, and she saw that all the windows in the bedroom were open, the light off-white drapes billowing with a breeze, and the breeze caressed her face. She smiled big.

She could live another 375 years or more. She could see and do a whole lot in her life. She'd have Tristan by her side. She might get to actually meet her twin brother today.

Someday, and maybe even someday soon, she could have Tristan's baby. And survive childbirth to actually meet that baby. And maybe it'd be a little baby girl with curly hair and green eyes. Or a dimpled baby boy with blue eyes. Or a dimpled boy with green eyes or a dimpled girl with blue eyes.

God I hope our baby gets his dimples.

And then another and another. They could make babies every year for the next few hundred years, couldn't they? Would she look older while he stayed young or would she stay youthful? Would she experience menopause at some point or be fertile as long as she lived?

How crazy that so much of what'd happened was related to a vampire's innate urge to breed? She was now bound to Tristan, he was bound to her, mated for life, and driven to feed him and give him babies. They needed to feed off one another to survive but they could survive for hundreds of years.

How crazy was all of this?

She had time to find things out. She didn't need to know everything right this minute, so she let herself feel the breeze, feel all these emotions. She didn't want to hide from emotion. She wanted to allow herself to embrace it without overthinking everything.

Joy bubbled up and it felt like it smashed the remaining ruins of the wall she'd spent so long building up around herself.

The ocean looked active, busy, with rolling waves. The sky was busy with birds. It was a gorgeous view. It was a view she'd be very interested in waking up to every day for the next however many days it was that they'd live here. This place could be home. This was the first place she'd been to where it felt like it could become home.

She didn't *have* to spend the rest of her life here, but she wanted to stay a while.

She also wanted to experience life. Live it. Feel it. Roll around in it and soak up every bit of it. Make friends, experience new things, dance around in circles laughing with uninhibited joy.

She hopped out of the bed and twirled and giggled. Then she felt silly. But she was alone so there was nothing to feel silly about, so she twirled again and laughed at herself.

She didn't know where Tristan was, but she could feel him nearby. She somehow knew, instinctively, that he was near and that he was okay.

She made the bed and wandered to the window and stretched, enjoying the scenery for a minute while the rest of the sleepy cobwebs cleared.

After coming out of the bathroom, she caught the aroma of coffee. She followed her nose and found a steaming hot cup on the small table beside the bed.

She lifted it, took a sip, reached under the pillow for the dagger, which was in a holder with a clip on the back. She attached it to the waistband of her shorts, better safe than sorry while things were still revealing themselves, and she decided to go find Tristan.

He was outside, doing pull-ups from a low hanging tree branch just outside the door. He let go of the branch and stood, smiling, arms open for her.

She approached, after putting her coffee down on the small wooden side table beside the swing on the front porch. He had a cup there, too.

"Hi." She got up on her toes, put her arms around his throat, and kissed him on the mouth. His eyes sparkled and his dimples came out.

"Hop on and hang on," he invited and squeezed her bottom with both hands.

She linked her fingers behind his neck and hopped up, throwing her legs around his waist and he then continued doing the pull ups, Kyla attached to him like a koala bear. She nuzzled his throat, taking in his sweet scent.

"Good morning," she said.

"Good morning, to you, too, Sunshine. You're very bright and cheerful today."

"So are you. I like it. But I have a question."

"Shoot..."

"Why are you out here and not in bed waking me up with your tongue?"

"I didn't realize that was a requirement," he teased, still doing pull ups, effortlessly holding her weight, not even sweating.

She clamped her legs tighter to hang on but let one arm go so that she could stroke his flexing bicep with it.

Yum.

"Well, it's not, but maybe it should be..." she said.

She felt good about the fact that he wasn't hovering this morning, that she'd woken up with him feeling good enough to be outside, rather than within arm's reach. "Maybe it should go in our prenup."

"Our prenup?" Tristan chuckled.

"Well, yeah. We're gonna need one."

"We won't ever get a divorce, princess. Even if we wanted one, which we won't."

"Yeah, but it's my chance to make my demands. Demands that you'll agree to. In writing."

He let go of the branch and grabbed her bottom and squeezed, "If you get to make demands, so do I."

"Well, we'll both have to think on that and then let the negotiations begin."

He jumped back up and did a few more pull-ups.

"How was your chat with Sergey last night?"

"Very good." He smiled and let go of the branch and wrapped one hand around her bottom, to support her, the other hand went into her hair. He kissed her on the mouth as he walked them over to the swing and sat, keeping Kyla straddling him.

"Yeah? Enlighten me."

"Well..." he smiled, swinging them back and forth, "You'll keep gaining strength from my blood and I'll keep gaining it from yours. That growing physical strength you're exhibiting will keep growing. You'll be a formidable opponent, apparently. We'll keep strengthening each other. A truly symbiotic relationship. We'll have about the next 20 to 25 years where we can have babies. Sometimes it can be longer but that's the average among the few other pairs Sergey knows. You won't ovulate every month, but it'll be frequent. The temper tantrums might get rough if we miss, but I won't want to kill you during your period. That blood'll be good for me, so I'll probably make use of it. And I think I can handle you."

"Oh, you think so?" she dared, trying not to think of him making use of that blood.

Her first instinct was to think 'ewe, yuck' but that thought didn't sink in because blood was what they both needed and if it helped him... *have at it.*

He put his hands to her hips and squeezed, eyes sparkling. "I know so."

"Apparently your libido will be difficult to keep up with when you ovulate, but I think I am equipped to handle that, too."

"Mm. You definitely have the equipment for that," Kyla said against his lips and then nipped at his lower lip, catching it between her teeth and tugging on it, pressing her crotch into his.

He sucked his lip back in, rose, threw her over his shoulder, and carried her inside, straight to the bedroom, where he put her on her back and got his lips about an inch from her mouth.

"I'm so in love with you, delicious girl," he said.

"I'm so in love with you, delicious man," she replied.

"I feel really good about all this," he said.

"Me, too," she agreed.

"If it sounds strange that I agreed so readily, it *is* strange, but I know he's being transparent. I know it in my gut. And just because I seemed to come to this conclusion easily doesn't mean it'll be an easy road. It could get ugly."

She swallowed hard and nodded.

"Adrian has to pay. The shit Sergey told me about him? Guy's a joke. It's a wonder he wasn't exterminated years ago by councils on other continents. He didn't have a lot of the info Sergey gave us because elders in the know didn't respect him, didn't trust him."

She nodded, unsurprised.

"The breeding program they're dismantling in Europe? They were using stem cells very creatively. There's a lot we can do to make changes, big changes, help Sasha with her research and she's got information that can help European doctors with theirs. But despite that, there will be people who really don't want me making changes. But I have the power to do it. Between influencing others to some of the formulas Adrian had developed that we now have our hands on, to having you, knowing you're not going to be under threat constantly from me with ovulating or your period? I feel good. But I still have to keep you safe. Above all, above everything else, you are my number one priority."

"I know," she replied, and she felt it coming at her, all his love and concern and protectiveness. She knew he'd do anything to keep her safe.

"Sergey had to keep his wife hidden; they lived reclusively. He couldn't let others see that she wasn't aging. I don't want that for us, for you. I know how you feel about it. But I don't know how we'll play that down the road. Anything can happen. I need to protect you, especially as I make some key moves to shift things. But she was killed. Their home was discovered and she was killed to punish him when he showed some interest in becoming involved in this coalition. Those responsible didn't know that they were mated for life, just thought she was his enchanted pet. Those responsible for Sergey's wife's murder were reportedly also responsible for the death of...are you ready for this?"

Kyla nodded.

"My father."

Tristan rolled over onto his back.

Kyla turned toward him, leaning on an elbow,

"What! What?"

"But there's a strong suspicion Adrian was part of that, too. And my grandfather, Alexander. My father was supposedly entertaining the idea of moving in the coalition direction. There were several royal vamps being courted by the same people that started this and my father was one of them. As a kid I was told he was mugged and murdered while my mother was pregnant with me. When I was turned I was told he was murdered by those responsible for the murder of my grandfather, as well. It's known for a fact that Alexander Kovac is dead. It was a fight to the death not long before I was turned and both he and the man that killed him died in that fight and there were credible witnesses, including Sam, Jet Jasper, and Andre Tsakos. But

Jonathan Walker, my father, went missing 35 and a half years ago. He was never found. Sergey and he were friendly. Sergey was already an elder, my father was only thirty-one, vamp for six years, when he got Taryn pregnant with me. But they knew one another and Sergey tells me that he was being courted, that my mother being pregnant with me and my father's knowledge of what my birth could mean for the power for the North American royals made him a prime target for the coalition to win over. Alexander Kovac got wind of that and didn't like it. He'd chosen my father to mate with Taryn. They were married, but supposedly my father loved her. There was a lot to love back then. She was put into a functional trance when they got married and she was to be turned after my birth. Jonathan Walker didn't make it to meet his son. Sergey thinks my grandfather was part of the crew that arranged to off my father. He doesn't have proof of that but it's a hunch, despite some rumours about specific vamps. He knows who killed Alexander and believes that those same vampires did not kill my father, despite the rumours. He believes Adrian Constantin was involved as well. Constantin and my grandfather were thick as thieves; Sergey's words. I believe every word that comes out of his mouth. He's not deceiving me."

"No, I don't think he is, either."

"So, today we have a busy day, princess. We're talking to Sasha about waking Kyle and then I'm waking Adrian Constantin and finding out the truth about whether or not he was involved with my father's death. And today is the day that Adrian Constantin dies."

Kyla was in shock. Not that Adrian was going to die, all the other stuff.

"That's the most important stuff. Sergey said he considered trickle feeding me information but it's all on the table now. He and I are very much on the same page. He knows the challenges I have ahead of me. He has the knowledge I need about key players; he understands what you and I have. He's given me a lot to chew on but I'm feeling confident that I know the way forward. I can't predict what'll happen, but I know what I need to do next. He's got a lot of fire power behind him. Me joining this coalition will mean a real fighting chance here in North America. What do you think?"

"I think it'd be a whole lot easier for you and I to ride off into the sunset and live a happily ever after, just the two of us."

Tristan stared.

"But," Kyla took a big breath, "That's not who you are. You have an opportunity to lead. It is your birthright and it's kind of your responsibility because now you can do something amazing with that privilege. Your royal blood, your strengths, your connections, the gift we've been given. And all the science we have from Adrian and Sasha's efforts plus the other stuff? I am not sure how things will play out but babe I am so *so* lucky that I'll get to see you accomplish so many great things. I will help you any way that I can. You tell me what you need and I'm there for you, my prince."

"The gift we've been given?" He studied her.

"Each other. For forever."

His gaze went heated and she felt emotion wash right through and then his mouth was on hers and they tangled up in one another, both feeling intense emotions about all they'd found out, about all that could be ahead of them.

"THIS...IS...PHENOMENAL!" That was Sam's reaction at the big breakfast Kyla and Tristan had cooked together. Well, Tristan had done most of the cooking, but Kyla had helped.

Sasha, Sam, and Sergey were all at the six-seater round dining table in the great room of the home Tristan and Kyla were staying in and the table had dishes of a variety of breakfast foods.

Sergey had eaten only a little, saying he didn't have a big appetite, hadn't had one since he'd lost his wife.

Hearing that, Kyla didn't feel all that hungry any longer. Imagining losing Tristan really would feel like losing part of her own soul. And now she knew their souls were linked. She felt him. She felt his emotions and felt his love both inside and outside when he looked at or touched her physically. Losing that after having it only this long would be devastating. Losing that after having it for hundreds of years? She couldn't imagine.

She found herself thinking about that while looking at Sergey sitting there. He gave her a small, sad smile and she suspected he'd read her mind or deduced what she was thinking about. She wasn't sure which though, if it was just written on her face or if was that he was using his telepathic powers.

Sasha was quiet through the meal and Kyla suspected she was contemplating things regarding Kyle.

"You okay?" Kyla asked her, as they did the dishes together.

She sipped some juice from her glass that was still on the table and nodded. "I'm nervous. I don't know if I can wake him and if I do, I don't know how I'll deal. He wouldn't know anything about anything unless we told him. But we have to tell him. He needs to meet you and he needs to know what's happened. I'm so nervous that he'll hate me. I stayed up half the night last night worrying. I wrote him a letter, explaining, in a condensed version, all that's gone on. If he does wake, I'm thinking perhaps you can have time with him and give it to him?" She reached into her cardigan pocket and passed Kyla an envelope.

Kyla smiled and nodded.

"Maybe we should go do this," Tristan suggested, coming in from outside where he'd gone with Sam and Sergey, while Sam smoked a cigarette. But she'd noticed she was in his sight at all times. He still wasn't comfortable enough to leave her alone in a room with a vampire.

Sasha winced and put the tea towel down on the counter and then nodded. "Yes, we should see if this does it."

Sasha and Kyla followed him out the door. Sergey, Sam, and Sasha all whooshed in an instant, startling Kyla.

Tristan smiled, kissed her nose, and then said, "Hop on," and turned his back to her and crouched.

She hopped on for a piggyback and seconds later, they were in front of the stairs at Sasha's house.

They went up, inside, and then down to the basement to where Kyle was.

Sam and Sergey were standing back.

Sasha took what looked like a cleansing deep breath. Kyla stood back, her back against Tristan's front, his arms around her collarbone and stomach.

Kyla said a silent prayer that this would wake Kyle and sent positivity forward in her mind, pushed with all her might, whether it'd do anything or not she figured it couldn't hurt.

Sasha glanced at Sam. "I haven't even intentionally dropped my fangs in almost two years."

"You'll be fine. It'll be alright," he told her and gave her a smile and Kyla decided that despite the Jackson thing, which she sort of understood now, she liked Sam a whole lot.

Tristan gave her a little squeeze so she suspected that because he felt all of what she was feeling right now he was lending strength. She felt incredibly lucky, for once.

Sasha took off her eyeglasses and said, "Here goes everything," and dropped her fangs. Instead of Kyla feeling startled at that, she felt her gums tingle, thinking about the possibility that if it hadn't been Tristan that'd turned her, but someone else, she'd have fangs, too. She'd have the ability to feed on anyone. As it stood, she had 100%

reliance on her vampire to feed her, but she was, in essence, some sort of sub-species of vamp now. Goosebumps rose on her body. Tristan stroked her arm and kissed her ear.

Sasha leaned over Kyle and her hair fell to lay across Kyle's chest as she went for his throat.

A beat later she heard Sasha moan as she drank, and it felt like they were all witnessing something that was very intimate and probably should've been done in private. Sasha used one arm to hold the bedrail for balance and her other hand was fisting Kyle's blanket.

Kyla's arms broke out in goosebumps. After going against her urges of sinking her teeth into Kyle for so long, Sasha got to do what vampires naturally did and the room went electric with Sasha's hunger. Kyla could actually feel it, probably through Tristan's emotions. She looked back at Tristan and cocked her head.

No, that wasn't through Tristan.

Her gaze moved to Kyle and felt her knees go weak. She had a strong sense of déjà vu, looking at him. Was this emotion, the feeling of hunger, was it coming from him?

A few seconds ticked by, and then Sasha let go. Kyla saw her lick the wound. And then Sasha straightened her back and took a step back, pulled her fangs back in, put her eyeglasses back on, and composed herself, straightening her pale pink hooded cardigan. She stood and gazed down at Kyle lovingly. And then Sasha's head rolled back in a way that seemed like ecstasy. It must've felt very poignant to her to do what she was driven, innately, to do, but had been fighting against for so long now.

Sasha re-gained composure and put her arms around herself and shivered. Sam moved to her and put his arm around his sister. Sasha leaned into him.

The room went quiet as everyone looked at the hospital bed. Kyla felt like she was willing his eyes to open. They all stood, quietly, and for what felt like the longest time.

Kyla felt her shoulders slumping as she felt defeat start to penetrate. Sasha looked like she had mixed emotions. Kyla was sure it was mixed emotions because Sasha had a conscience, a maternal connection with Kyle, but yet had no choice but to use his blood.

Sasha needed Kyle's blood. And Kyle needed Sasha to feed. And several other women on the island were being fed some, too, in order to keep them from being psycho bitches from hell.

Things started to change on the screen beside Kyle's bed.

"His pain. It's gone," Sasha breathed.

Kyla's knees suddenly went weak again. Kyle bolted upright into a sitting position, with a gasp, his eyes wide open. He looked bewildered. His eyes moved first to Kyla, then to Sasha, and then through the room's occupants and then straight back to Kyla. He gave his head a shake.

Kyla stared directly at him and their eyes met. A flood of memories hit her like a harsh slap.

Childhood memories, foggy ones, but small snippets sailed quickly through her consciousness. Playing, reading, building Legos, playing Lite Brite together.

Lite Brite!?!

Grid pictures of blue eyes, green eyes. Running around a park. She flew down the slide into her father's arms with a squeal and then her father plucked her up in the air, tossed her up, and caught her and they watched Kyle slide down the same slide.

"I'll catch him, Daddy!" Kyla heard her little girl self say as she struggled to get out of Lyle's arms, so she could catch Kyle.

Then she saw the woman on the park bench in that same park telling her that her parents were gone, that there was an accident, and that it'd be better if she didn't remember her brother, only that her parents were dead.

"If you remember your brother, you'll try to find him. And finding him would be finding big trouble, sweetie... So it's better if you forget. But if you do happen to meet again, as soon as you lay eyes on one another, you'll remember."

Kyla felt sick. Bile rose in her throat. Kyle's blue eyes were still on her.

"Clear the room," Tristan said.

Tristan, Sam, Sergey, and Sasha moved out.

"I'm just outside the door, princess," Tristan said, "But be careful."

Kyla nodded, not taking her eyes off her brother. Tristan kissed her temple and she heard the door shut.

"It's you," Kyle said.

"I don't know about any of that medical stuff you got goin' on there so careful, kay?"

He looked down at his hands, looked down to a tube hanging out of the blanket, made a face, looked to the medical monitors beside his bed, and gazed around.

"Do you want something to drink? Maybe something small?"

Kyla moved to the refrigerator in the corner and got a bottle of water and walked over and passed it to him. Her heart was racing.

He grabbed the water bottle but dropped it on the bed and grabbed for her hand.

"It's you. How? Who were those people?"

"You know who I am?" Kyla asked.

"Of course I do."

"How?"

"He showed me pictures of you after they found you. And I know you. Are you okay? What's going on? Where are we?"

"He?"

"Adrian."

"I uh, I have a letter for you from Sasha," Kyla reached into her jeans pocket and passed the envelope to him. He let go of her hand to accept it.

"Who's Sasha?"

"Um, the doctor. If you read that, I'm sure it'll help. It explains everything. I'll just go tell them you're okay while you read that. I'll be right back."

Kyle opened the envelope, pulled out the folded up letter.

Kyla stepped out the door through the closet in Sasha's office and saw that everyone was there. Sergey was speaking but stopped talking when Kyla stepped out.

"He seems okay; he's reading the letter."

"When he's done, let me know and I'll come in and disconnect all the machines, okay?" Sasha looked very concerned, very pale. Nervous.

"Okay."

Tristan kissed her quick on the mouth and she went back in, got another bottle of water, sat on the sofa, and then opened and downed it. Kyle was still reading the letter.

After an eternity, he put the paper down. She'd been trying to avoid watching him read, but couldn't help but look at him periodically.

I have a brother. A twin. And I'm remembering.

He let out a big breath.

"How are you?" he asked.

"I'm, uh, good. Better now that you're awake."

"But you're with him? Is he good to you? Or aren't you sure?"

"He is. I love him."

"So, you know him. You remember time with him?"

"Yes. I seem to be immune to mesmerizing. And yeah, I love him."

"I was sick about it when I found out they had found you and were planning on giving you to him. I tried to escape so I could help. I failed. Adrian wasn't happy."

"I bet not."

"You've met him. Adrian?"

Kyla nodded, "I kind of hate his guts."

Kyle smiled, "I kind of get why. Without you even telling me."

Kyla smiled and then her expression dropped, "Long story, but yeah. Um, whoever stole me made me forget you. I'm sorry that they did that."

He shrugged. "You remember me now. That's good."

She nodded, "As soon as you opened your eyes it lifted that spell or whatever. It's still kind of setting in for me."

He nodded, "So, you love him?"

"I do. I never loved anyone before. I guess since I was stolen. I didn't know how. But he... he's amazing." Kyla's eyes filled up.

Kyle smiled.

"He's gonna help change things. A lot has happened but he's going to help. And so is Sasha."

"Who's Sasha?"

"The letter. That's from Sasha." Kyla was confused.

"Dr. Jasper?"

Kyla nodded.

"I thought her first name was Samantha."

Kyla shrugged, "I know her as Sasha."

"She's been like a mother to me," Kyle mumbled, and she wasn't sure what the mumble meant in terms of how Kyle felt about the contents of the letter. "But I always called her Doc."

"I should go get her. She'll get all that equipment off. She'll want to check you out, make sure you're okay."

"But I won't remember any of it. Because she's now a vamp."

"I don't know if that's how it works."

"That's how it works."

"Oh."

"Alright. Well, see ya later?"

"Yeah. I guess there's stuff to figure out but I'll come back as soon as she's done. Or as soon as I can. Okay?"

He nodded, a faraway look in his eyes.

"Um, bye for now." Kyla moved to the door.

Awkward!

"Kyla?"

She turned back to him.

"I'm glad I have you back."

She smiled, "I'm glad I have you at all. I didn't know I had a big brother. I always wanted one."

"I'm six minutes older," he announced. "And I'm definitely still taller than you."

"I can't wait to get to know you," she said and laughed and then she had a memory of them standing against the growth chart in their apartment together and her being upset that he was always taller.

"I know you already," he told her, "I've known you all along. You're happy. You're smiling. It's good you're not sad all the time anymore."

"Did you feel my feelings, Kyle? While we were apart?"

He nodded, "Yeah. Often."

"That must've sucked."

He smiled, "At least I knew you were out there. I wanted to get to you. But, I couldn't."

They stared at one another for a beat and then Kyla shook off the sadness she felt at all this information, at all Kyle had never experienced being imprisoned his whole life. At the fact that he'd been a guinea pig for Adrian. She started to get angry.

"I wanna kill him myself. Motherfucking asshole."

He shook his head and smiled, "*Now* you actually seem like the sister from my brain."

The door opened, and Tristan poked his head in, looking concerned.

"You okay, princess?"

"Yeah. Let's go. See ya in a while, Kyle?"

Kyle laughed, "Yeah, after a wyla, Kyla."

See ya later, Alligator. After a while Croco-Kyle.

After a Wyla, sister Kyla.

Suzy grew a mustache, a mustache, a mustache...

She heard her little girl voice with his little boy voice chanting this together. They were both on their bellies on that quilt, reading a book of nursery rhymes together and making up their own.

"Suzy's face is smooth again!

"Polly's face is gone!"

Peals of little kid laughter.

"You two are supposed to be asleep." That was their mother. She was beautiful.

Kyla's heart hurt and then the cold anger started to rise in her.

"I'm gonna fucking kill him myself, Tristan. Let me do it. Take me to the goddamn boathouse!"

"C'mon, baby. Let's let Sasha do her thing."

"She's really special," Kyle said aloud but he was looking away, not looking at Tristan but addressing him.

"Please know how special she is. She deserves a life. A real life. Happiness."

"I know she does. And I promise you, she'll get that," Tristan said, with an edge to his voice, emotion in it that made Kyla's anger evaporate but that also made her heart swell. He moved Kyla back out of the room, shutting the door.

Tears flowed down Kyla's face.

She moved out of the room, ignoring Sasha, Sergey, and Sam. Tristan was behind her.

They went upstairs and outside and then he lifted her and zoomed back to the house next door, straight to bed, where he got her under the blankets and held her close while she cried for a really long time, but doing it knowing that going forward, life would be a heckuva lot different than it had been, and in a very good way.

She had family. She had Tristan.

And the outlook was looking good. So, they were emotional tears but beyond thinking about all that she'd had taken away, it was mostly just a good cry that she needed to have.

"I LIKE IT HERE," KYLA said to Tristan. They were still in bed snuggled up together, but her eyes were now dry and he'd made her some lunch.

"Yeah," he replied with a squeeze.

"It feels like home."

"Does it?"

"Mm hm. Can we stay a while?"

"I have a meeting in a few days back home. That's the start of big changes, baby."

"Oh," she deflated.

"But if all goes well and you want, we'll come back here as much as we can. I still have shit to figure out with this coalition but yeah, we'll tell Sasha we'll take this place."

She brightened, "Yay."

13

KYLA HAD SPENT A COUPLE of hours with Kyle later that day. This was while Tristan had a meeting in Sasha's kitchen with most of the other vampires on the island. A few had gone to the mainland for supplies.

Kyla and Kyle were camped out on the sofa in his room watching the latest Star Wars movie on Blu-Ray and eating popcorn that she'd brought in. Sasha had a big movie collection in her living room upstairs and was apparently a bit of a Star Wars junkie and told Kyla that it was something she and Kyle had in common.

Kyle hadn't had much popcorn and Kyla apologized for bringing it in, in the first place. She'd been told by Sasha that his digestive system might be a bit off after being on feeding tubes for so long.

She'd come in with the popcorn and the movie plus the quilt their mother had made because she'd remembered family movie night.

They'd sit on the quilt on the floor and watch from the family's extensive VHS collection of Disney movies with a big bowl of popcorn or Goldfish crackers or Teddy Grahams while their parents cuddled on the couch and occasionally, now that Kyla thought about it, disappeared to their bedroom while the twins were occupied.

Neither talked much. Kyle was out of his hospital gown and now dressed in jeans and a t-shirt. He was a handsome guy. He was about six feet tall and built like a bodybuilder. He'd commented that he had a lot of time on his hands so spent a lot of it in the gym back at The Constantin Center. Kyla figured that 2 years bedridden didn't do much for muscle mass, but he hadn't looked like he'd suffered. Perhaps that was a supernatural blood bond thing.

"Did you see Sasha? Do you remember her coming in?"

He shook his head, "I remember her face. She doesn't look the same. But that's all I remember. She came in and said hello to me and then she told me she had to take care of a few things for me and that's the last thing I recall. And then the next thing I remember I was alone in here and there was a meal on this coffee table with a note to eat just a little and to buzz her if I had any problems or questions." He motioned to the cordless phone on the table, "She said in the note that she has a camera in here, to ensure I'm okay, not to spy on me. Whatever." He rolled his eyes. He was annoyed.

"You're annoyed with that."

"Nothing's changed in my life so far after almost 2 years asleep. I get it; I know why she needs me here. And yeah, I'm fine with it for now. For you, especially. I can help, so I'll help. Her letter said she's close to synthesizing my blood and that she wants to help me have a semi-regular life somehow, but that it's not quite yet possible with the threats out there. She worries my being out in the open here could change things with the other vampires on the island. Once she's done and finds the way to replicate whatever in my blood helps her, I'm gonna ask to be turned."

"Uh...what?"

"That's how I'm feeling now. I don't think I'll change my mind."

"But..." Kyla didn't know how to finish that thought. She had to think on it. Maybe it *was* the most logical explanation.

"Hopefully it'll be within the next year. I'm ready for my life to start. And 25 is the optimal age to be turned. I replied on her note and said Okay."

"Okay?"

"She asked if I was okay with her plan...to try to find a way to get me free but to be able to use my blood for now. I said *okay*."

He didn't look okay with it. At all. He looked bitter. They watched the rest of the movie in silence and then Tristan came in to get her.

THEY WERE ALL INSIDE the boathouse. Sam, Sasha, Sergey, Tristan, Kyle, and Kyla.

Tristan initially tried to tell her she should stay with Kyle in the safe room, but Kyla wasn't having it.

"I need to face him. I need to, Tristan."

He'd shook his head, "No."

"Yes."

"No, princess. I..."

She screeched and stomped a foot, "Tristan! I am telling you right now, I'm there. If you won't let me do it myself, you at least need to let me be there!"

"No. It's not gonna be neat and tidy, baby. That fucking motherfucker is going to feel my goddamn wrath. I don't want you anywhere near that wrath."

She gave him a pleading look and directed as much emotion at him as she could.

He took her face into his hands and pulled it close, "Princess. Brat switch?"

Her expression softened more. "Please?"

"Why would you want to see that?" He looked concerned.

She shook her head, "I don't know. It's not that I wanna see that, but I need to be there. I just do."

Maybe she just didn't want to be in the dark, waiting behind closed doors while their lives happened.

He gave her a nod, understanding seemed to pass through them.

"Alright. You can confront him but you're not staying for the party," he'd finally relented.

"I'm stayin' for the party," she insisted, hardly able to believe that she was referring to murdering her grandfather as a party, "and my brother needs to be there, too."

"AW, FUCK ME."

Those were spoken words from Kyla and Kyle's maternal grandfather when his eyes opened, and he saw that he was tied to a chair that was propped against a wall in the boathouse in the middle of a semi-circle that included Sam, Sasha, Tristan, and Sergey. There was also Kyla and Kyle, a little further back (Kyle who wasn't *with* them but who Kyla had wanted present for the symbolism. He was sitting beside her looking like the classic mesmerized deer-in-the-headlights).

Adrian's eyes went huge as he took in the faces of those around him.

Sam cracked open a blood bag and held it out to Adrian's mouth. Adrian gulped some back.

"That's disgusting," Adrian spat.

"Sasha created it. It's several small animals plus a vitamin infusion. Very nutritionally complete." Sam looked very pleased.

"Samantha," Adrian greeted.

She folded her arms across her chest and said nothing. But the look on her face said it all. She was facing her tormenter. That was very evident.

Adrian's eyes moved to Sergey.

"Voitenko, what an unpleasant surprise. You're part of their militia. Shocker." Adrian wasn't shocked. "Samuel, I expected you'd consider joining your sister but I'm disappointed. Figured you'd know how fruitless that'd be. Now, with Voitenko a part of it, I can see the sudden allure. And Tristan? You, too? Your grandfather is turning in his fucking grave."

"What about my father, Constantin? Is he turning in his *fucking* grave?" Tristan leaned close to Adrian.

Adrian's eyes went huge.

"Is my father turning in his grave, Constantin?" Tristan demanded.

Adrian's lip curled, "No."

"Why?" Tristan demanded.

"He's not dead."

Kyla's heart skipped a beat.

"You know where he is," Tristan sneered.

"Yes."

"Tell me where he is," Tristan ordered.

Adrian let out a big breath, "In a covered pit on my property. Daggered." Adrian's face contorted, probably at the fact that he had to impart this information on Tristan's demand.

"But you don't wanna let him and the other one in there with him out, Tristan. It's a recipe for disaster. If you trust nothing else that I say to you, trust me on that."

"Oh my God," Kyla blurted, her hand coming up to cover her mouth.

Adrian's eyes moved to her and he smiled and it looked genuine, "Nice to see you're back."

Kyla's body locked tight.

"And you've met your brother. How have you brought her back?" he looked to Tristan.

"You'll never know," Tristan said, and he was seething.

Kyla felt a twinge in her gut and a chill swept over her at the cold and calculating emotion on his face.

"Samuel, break Sergey's neck," Adrian ordered, looking directly at Sam.

"Nice try, Adrian. But Tristan's already taken steps to ensure you can't influence me."

Tristan's grip went to Adrian's throat.

"Get her out of here!" Tristan hissed toward where Sam stood. Tristan's skin was grey, and his eyes were black.

Sam moved into Kyla's space and reached for her hand.

Kyla swatted at his hand, "No... I need to—-"

"Now!" Tristan roared.

"Kyle, follow Sam and Kyla. Go to the safe room at the back of my office closet downstairs. Go right there. Quickly," Sasha told Kyle and Kyle got to his feet.

Before Kyla could finish her protest, Sam had her over his shoulder and her surroundings were blurring. She tried to reach for her belt, so she could grab the dagger and stop Sam from whatever he was doing but he caught her wrist mid-run and a moment later she found herself inside Sasha's house, inside the safe room downstairs.

She felt the cold rise in her, she was pissed. She was about to strike out at Sam, but he cut her off.

"Sorry, Love. He needed you out of there."

"What? I needed to be there, Sam. Shit!"

"No, Kyla. You don't need those images haunting you. It's gonna be a long night. Trust me. You don't want to be there."

"Why did he tell you to go after Sergey? Isn't Sergey so much older and therefore stronger than you? How stupid was that?"

"Not stupid at all. That's Adrian, though. He gets me to go after Sergey so that Sergey kills me in defense. That punishes me, and it punishes my sister. It also punishes Tristan and then puts Tristan and Sergey on the outs. That's how Adrian's mind works."

Kyle was there. Sam was quickly out of the room, without a goodbye, and the door was shut.

Kyla reached for the knob, but it was locked.

"Shit. Shit, fuck!"

She paced a minute and then was aware of movement behind her. Kyle was reaching into the refrigerator, pulling out drinks,

"Coke?"

"Pepsi, if there's any. Or ginger ale." she muttered, "Fuck! They locked us in!"

"Who?"

"We were in the boathouse, Tristan woke Adrian and then when Tristan started to lose it, Sam brought me back here and Sasha told you to follow. I wanted to be *there*. That man has stolen so much from us! I wanted you there, too. If ever you *do* become a vampire you'll remember, I think. You'll probably remember all the times you were mesmerized."

He winced, "Not sure I want that."

Kyla shrugged, "But wouldn't you want to see Adrian punished?"

Kyle shrugged, "I'm mostly a pacifist. I think I'd rather see him mesmerized and forced to right all his wrongs."

Suddenly, Kyla wanted Tristan to stop and reconsider. Tristan could likely do that! Kyle was right. Why couldn't they use Adrian to help them with their cause?

She reached out for Tristan in her mind, pleading for him to stop and talk to her before continuing. But she felt something really horrible hit her gut. She felt his rage, she felt something so sinister slithering around in her veins that it reminded her of the sensation from the night she'd tried to run away when Tristan had bit her and unleashed punishment into her veins. But this was multiplied. By a lot. Bile rose in her throat.

She was pretty sure that the inside of that boathouse was a bloodbath.

She ran to the bathroom and barely reached the toilet before she projectile vomited. She was in that bathroom on her knees first vomiting and then dry heaving for at least the following hour. And it was extremely reminiscent of the night with the spider and snake sensation in her veins.

TRISTAN WAS THERE, in front of her. She'd fallen asleep on the sofa. Kyle was sitting beside her, staring at the television. She'd been sleeping, her head on the arm of the sofa, her feet were on Kyle's lap. Kyle had lifted her off the bathroom floor at one point, when she'd finally stopped with the dry heaves. He'd put her on the couch and covered her up with their mother's quilt.

"Let's go," Tristan reached for her hand.

She couldn't really read him. His face was serious. His mouth was tight.

She took his hand.

"Goodnight, Kyle."

"'Night," Kyle muttered, still staring straight ahead.

She and Tristan walked the walk back to the house next door in silence, in the dark, at a normal, maybe even a slow pace. She spotted no one else, but lights were on in Sasha's main floor and she saw shadows moving up there.

Back inside the other house, she went right to the bathroom and brushed her teeth and then took a shower. He didn't join her. Maybe he'd already had one. She shivered.

She wasn't getting much emotion from him, so she didn't know what to make of that. Back when she'd first been locked up in the safe room with Kyle she'd gotten loads of emotions, ugly, nasty ones, but now he seemed completely calm.

When her shower was done, and she was rifling through their bags for something to wear to bed, she heard him come in and felt his presence as he walked past her back, then she heard the bathroom door close, followed by the water in the bathroom turn on.

She waited in bed, under the covers, after having turned on a lamp, arms folded over her chest.

He came in, dressed in track pants and nothing else, flicked the ceiling light off, and got into bed with her.

"So?" She asked.

His eyes met hers. They were hard, steel-blue.

"Is he dead?" Kyla asked.

Tristan nodded, expression softening, his eyes roving hers searchingly.

Kyla felt hollow. She closed her eyes and let out a long slow breath.

Tristan turned the bedside table's lamp off.

"You sent me away."

"I know."

"Why?"

"You would've tried to stop me."

"You don't know that."

"You would've. That's who you are. That's not who I am."

She shivered. She probably *would* try to make him stop. The second Kyle's suggestion had come out about making Adrian help Kyla wanted to ask Tristan to reconsider.

"And I don't want you seeing any more violence. You've seen enough. It's my job to make you happy, to look after you, not to be the source of nightmares for you."

She scooted down in bed and turned her back to him and closed her eyes, a tear trickling down her cheek.

He leaned over and caught it with his soft lips, "Can I hold you?" he asked against her wet cheek, his breath warming her skin.

She nodded, lower lip trembling.

He spun her to face him and wrapped her up in his arms,

"No fucking one will ever come between you and me again. I will inflict endless violence on anyone that tries to fuck with what we have. Do you hear me? This is non-negotiable, Kyla."

She nodded, eyes shut tight, cheek against his chest.

"Sleep, princess. I love you."

She nodded, unable to speak.

After what felt like an eternity, she fell asleep. He was still awake.

TRISTAN PLUNGED A DAGGER into Adrian's gut and Adrian's beat up face fell forward.

Was he dead?

Tristan lifted an axe, his lip was curled, his skin was grey, and his eyes were coal black. The axe came down, chopping off Adrian's right arm at the shoulder. It fell to the ground with a thud and the blood that spurted out was as graphic as in a Tarantino movie. Tristan grabbed the dagger and dragged it upwards to Adrian's upper gut, below the chest and then yanked it out. Blood spilled from his gut as Tristan watched, chest heaving up and down.

Adrian woke and saw his arm on the ground beside him and started to scream. Tristan punched him in the face over and over and over while Adrian bled out. Adrian's face had already been punched, a lot by the looks of it, and now it was like his face was caved in. Tristan was covered in blood and he was shouting words that Kyla couldn't make out at Adrian in a chilling guttural voice. Adrian was crying in agony.

Sam and Sergey were laughing, both behind Tristan. And then Tristan started to laugh.

The laugh died, and Tristan's expression went dark again and then he plunged the dagger back in, making Adrian's head roll forward until his chin rested on his chest, and then Tristan brought the axe down to cut off his other arm and then pulled the dagger out and Adrian woke again, screaming in pain.

Tristan lifted the axe high over his head and she understood him this time when he said, "Now you can watch me cut off your leg. But before you pass out I'll dagger you so that you won't, so that you'll be frozen and fully lucid, aware of that pain." and then the axe came down.

Kyla was screaming. And screaming. Tristan was shaking her.

"Kyla, wake up! Wake up, baby! It's okay..."

She woke, and she was off and running out of the room. She was fighting with the lock on the door, and then she was out of the house, running toward the water, frantic.

She stopped when she got to the shore and fell to her knees, out of breath.

The water was warm. It lapped at her knees. She took breath after breath after breath, her fingers dug into the wet dirt in front of her.

Tristan touched her shoulder, "Baby?"

She was sobbing.

"Kyla what was it? Tell me."

"You cut off his arms. His leg. With an axe. You kept punching him and his head was caved in. And he was screaming. And you tore the knife up his middle and ...God. I could barf."

"C'mon." He took her wrists and dipped her hands in the water to rinse off the mud and then lifted her up by the waist and put her on her feet, took her hand, and they walked back to the house.

She shivered a little, "I'm gonna get into dry clothes."

"I'll put coffee on," he said quietly.

She washed her hands and face and brushed her teeth and then changed her clothes. When she went back out she found him sitting in the gazebo outside, in track pants, bare-chested, with two cups of coffee on the table. He was staring out at the water.

She climbed into his lap and put her head on his chest. His arms wound around her. It was breezy out there. His chest was cold.

"You should put a shirt on," she rubbed her hands over the skin of his arms.

He shrugged.

She gave him a squeeze and absorbed the feel of him for a minute, then scooted up to reach for the mug of coffee at the other end of the table.

"Mm."

It was good. She stared out at the water, watching the waves, shaking off the remnants of that dream.

Tristan was quiet, also staring out at that water.

"See, I bet the real event wasn't nearly as bad as that. If you'd just let me stay I wouldn't have had to conjure up the worst possible scenario in my warped brain."

He closed his eyes and his face looked pained.

She felt pain coming at her.

She straightened up in his lap.

'What's wrong?" she asked.

"Nothing," he lied.

"Tristan?"

He let out a long breath and his eyes opened, stormy gray.

"What?" she choked out, feeling impending doom settle on her like a shadow.

"You saw exactly what happened, by the sounds of it. I tried to shield you from that ugliness, *my ugliness*, but you dreamt it, anyway."

Bile rose in her throat.

Oh god.

He lifted her up, put her on her feet, and backed away from her.

"You probably want some space," he said quietly.

She stared, astounded.

"I can't go far, can't stomach the idea of leaving you unprotected but if you wanna go inside, I'll hang out here. If you wanna see your brother, I'll get you there, you can spend some time and I'll stay out of the room. You don't have to go hide in the bathroom, Kyla."

The wind picked up and she shivered. She stared at him.

"What do you prefer? Tell me what you want? I'll do it. As long as I'm not leaving you unprotected."

She glared and then grumbled, "I prefer that you sit back down and let me crawl back into your lap, so we can drink our fucking coffee and then maybe we can feed one another, if that's okay with you. But maybe you should put a shirt on first, so you don't freeze to death."

His look of surprise was actually cute.

He swallowed and sat back in the chair. She stormed inside, grabbed Tristan's Oregon Walmart hoodie from the bag, and handed it to him.

He put it on.

She climbed onto his lap and put her arms around him, her head against his chest.

He let out a long slow breath. He was relieved. And surprised.

THINGS WEREN'T EXACTLY normal the rest of the day. Things were quiet between them. But, that was okay. Things had been rough so far and a bit of a whirlwind since they'd gotten back to the island, so it was totally fine with her to be able to catch her breath.

She spent the morning in the gazebo drinking coffee and enjoying the scenery. He gave her space anyway. Or maybe he needed space. She wasn't sure. When she moved outside, he was outside but not in her personal space. When she went in, he followed, but wasn't in arm's reach.

He made them some eggs and toast and then Sergey and Sam were there, so she said good morning and then went inside and left them alone out there.

She came back out with a pot of coffee, two more mugs, and the milk and sugar, and then she went back inside and left them alone while she made the bed and did some Pilates and then took a bath.

By the time she was dressed, Tristan was packing up their belongings.

"What's up?" she asked.

"Road trip. Constantin Center."

"Yeah? Who?"

"All of us."

"All of us?"

"Yep."

"What's the plan?" she asked.

"Well, I hate to tell you this but that looks like home base for a bit. I know... you'd rather stay here, but there's some stuff that needs to happen and that's the best place we figure it *can* happen."

She made a scrunchy face, but nodded.

Tristan continued.

"We pull my father from that crypt. The other one in there is reportedly my great uncle, my grandfather's twin brother; Lucian Kovac. This is the first I've heard of him but apparently in the good vs. evil twin line-up, Lucian was the good one. Says Sergey, anyway. But Adrian Constantin disagreed, and he wasn't lying to me so I'm not sure if the truth lies somewhere in the middle or what. Alexander and Constantin put them there and we'll have to see what's what."

"Wow. Why didn't he just kill them instead of putting them in the ground for decades??"

"Fuckin' Adrian. He never killed anyone on purpose. He needed all the meat he could get for his fuckin' experiments."

Kyla shivered.

"We'll all head there. Sasha is gonna work with whatever is there in the lab, continue her work with Adrian's research as well as her own for Kyle's blood, those patches, that steel for the daggers. The Constantin Center is now home base for the coalition. Makes sense. There's equipment, lodgings, security. A few coalition members from Europe are heading there in a few days, too, to join efforts in the lab with Sasha."

She nodded.

"We'll go for a while. Come back here later when we can. I'm rescheduling my meeting with the Kovac board to happen there. This is the beginning of change."

She nodded.

"Hey?" his hand cupped her jaw.

"Yeah?"

"You and me. We okay?"

She nodded, "Of course we are."

"You shaken, still?"

She nodded, "A little. I'll be okay."

He pulled her close.

"I'm sorry you feel this way. I'm sorry you saw."

"I know. I'll be okay."

"Kyla?"

"Hm?"

"What can I do?"

"Nothing, Tristan. I just need time. That's all."

He made a face.

She sighed, "I don't know how to do this eternal blood bound relationship all that well, babe, it's new to both of us. But I'm gonna guess that there might be times in the next few hundred years when one of us just needs a little time to deal with something. It's not anything the other can rush."

"Don't put distance between us."

"I'm not. It hasn't been 24 hours, Tristan. Seriously. Chill."

"I love you."

She nodded, "I know. And I love you, too." She put her arms around his waist and squeezed tight.

"You're mine forever, baby," he said against her temple, "And I want it to be a good forever."

She nodded, "It will be. We deserve our happily ever after."

14

"PLEASE, LET'S NOT GO back there," Kyla pleaded. She was talking about that cottage on the grounds of The Constantin Center.

"I don't wanna be in those four walls, either, trust me. We'll take space in the main house for now."

She chewed her bottom lip while the car was pulling up to the gates of The Constantin Center. She and Tristan were in a rented car and there was a van with Sergey, Sam, Sasha, and Kyle following behind them. In a few days a few of the others from the island would be arriving to stay at the compound as well, leaving only two vampires on the island to keep an eye on things there.

The two guys that she remembered from the night Tristan's villa had the fire were at the gates of the compound. One motioned to the gate house and the gate opened.

"WHAT'S THE PLAN?" SHE asked.

"I'm flying Esther here. I'm having her turned." Tristan said this distractedly.

"What? Your housekeeper?"

"As soon as she's turned she'll be able to access memories about everything she's seen while under her functional trance and as Alexander's pet, she'll be helpful in piecing some events together. She's gonna be unruly for a few days but that's happening. She'll be here tonight. Adrian's version of events with Lucian Kovac aren't sitting right. He made the guy sound like evil incarnate. Sergey says he was a friend, so it's surprising. Adrian says he's responsible for Sergey's wife's death, a rampage of murders of other enchanted pets around the same time and Adrian believes that. Events Adrian spoke of could be corroborated by Esther if she was around, which timing wise, she probably was."

"But to make her a vampire?"

"She's part of things already, Kyla. She'll be better off vamp versus being a functionally entranced housekeeper until she dies. Being vamp will give her a longer life, more quality of life."

He was impatient.

"Yeah, if being a bitchy evil vamp is quality, sure..." Kyla muttered.

"Maybe only for a little while, though," Tristan said.

So obviously he had hope about Sasha's formula, too.

They'd had no feedings and no sex so far and she wondered if it was making him edgy. She felt edgy, too. They'd be in their room, alone, very soon and then she'd see about fixing his mood. Maybe it'd help with hers, too. She was always euphoric after feeding.

She didn't enjoy the feeling of walking the halls, and then up that staircase to the rooms, from that big open common area, though. It felt eerie. The place was emptied out, but she thought back to their time there and it was far from pleasant.

"We've spread word that The Center is closed for thirty days for renovations. That'll give us some time to figure some shit out, stop the dropinskies who show up periodically. We've kept a few staff members here, but just a few. Cleaning, kitchen, security."

"Where are all the patients?" she asked.

"Discharged or transferred. There's a small rehab facility in Nova Scotia. I know the doctor there. He's not at Adrian's caliber of experience but he's also not a mad scientist, either. Vamps who truly needed to be here for something will be taken care of. The dorms are still filled with feeders and people involved in his breeding program. We have to decide how to handle that."

"What'll you do?" her eyes were wide.

"Not sure," he lied.

She glared, "Don't lie to me."

He rolled his eyes and clenched his jaw. They'd walked down a hall and climbed another set of stairs to the floor that had held the banquet room where she'd pushed that female vamp, Celia. They then climbed another flight she hadn't been on last time. Now they were on the top floor at a set of double doors. Tristan produced a key from his jeans pocket and let them in.

"What's this?" Kyla stepped in. It was a large sumptuous apartment. High ceilings, exquisite décor done in mostly black and white with mostly red and silver accessories, expensive architectural details. Everything was gleaming, rich, and, gorgeous.

"This was Adrian's apartment. I've had it cleaned for us. We'll stay here. We'll stay in the second bedroom, not his room." He made a face.

"Why here? It feels eerie." It was like a palace, but she felt like her skin was staticky.

"Because in this building it's the largest living space so you hopefully won't feel closed in. All the cottages feel similar to the one we stayed in. Here feels different, doesn't it? There's only a small kitchenette as he had things served from down in the main kitchen, but it'll do for snacks and coffee. There's a big terrace out there. Lots of flowers. Pool. It's nice. Go look."

She wandered down a long hallway furnished with a long oriental rug down the centre, marble tile underneath, and opened two arched glass doors to a huge private roof terrace filled with greenery and flowers in every colour of the rainbow.

Tristan was behind her.

His lips touched the top of her head.

"I've got to meet with everyone. Here's your phone. Keep it with you. Go ahead and get comfortable. I've asked them to send Kyle in, in half an hour."

"So, about you lying to me..." she started.

He pulled her back inside and into a bedroom. She barely got a chance to look around when the sundress she was wearing was ripped down her body.

She was about to protest, about to tell him that he was doing a good job of keeping their laundry easy to keep up with, because half of what she wore ended up in the trash due to being decimated, but first she felt the wet flood her panties and then she felt his tongue behind her ear so she decided to save that talking-to.

"Need you." His teeth were elongating against her throat.

"Need me to be distracted so you can avoid an argument, you mean?" She pulled away and his fangs retracted.

"Is it working?"

"Yeah," she tugged at his jeans, "But don't lie to me."

"Okay. And good." He helped with his jeans. She put her hands on his shoulders and shoved him backwards. He fell onto his back onto the bed.

He gave her a hot look, catching his bottom lip with his teeth.

She pounced, holding his hands over his head.

He smiled, "Oh no! You've got me now, little cherry bomb. What're you gonna do?"

"I'm gonna detonate all over you," she warned, "Don't patronize me. And no lies."

"No lies." He looked her right in the eye.

"I mean it."

"I know you do."

"Good. Don't forget."

"Not possible," he smiled, "Everything about you is unforgettable."

She flopped on top of him, her face buried in the pillow beside his head. His arms wound around her and then he flipped them, so she was on the bottom.

She gave him a half a pathetic smile.

"You okay, baby?" he asked.

She shook her head, "No. Not really. I don't wanna be here."

He let out a big breath. "I know. If I could help it, I would."

She nodded, "I know. I'm trying really hard to keep my brat switch turned to off."

"You're doing good," he said, "I have better things to do than spank your sassy ass."

She gave him an indignant look and then slapped his bum,

"Maybe you've got the sassy ass," she muttered.

He balanced on his palms, hovering over her, "We've got about ten minutes until I need to be downstairs. You wanna do this now or save it till I can get back."

"Do what?" She glared.

"Get your blood tasted. Then fuck."

She scrunched her nose up at him, "A ten-minute fuck. Hmm, let me see?"

She narrowed her eyes and then said, "Fuck yeah."

He was good at the quickie.

"You're crazy," he told her and then he bit into his hand.

His phone rang. He answered with his right hand while her mouth attached to the left.

"Yeah?

There was silence. She ran her hand up the ridges of his cock, which was straining against his sexy Calvin Klein underwear.

"Fuck!" he snapped.

She released his hand and his cock.

"Fuck. Be right there."

Radiating from him was absolute fury.

Kyla's eyes widened, "What?"

"I'll be back. Taryn's at the gate throwing a holy fit because they won't let her in."

"Oh shit."

He got up and did up his jeans.

"Sam and Sasha are on speed dial for you, too. If I'm not back soon, text one of them to get you dinner. Someone will bring Kyle. I'll be back soon."

"Tristan, be careful!"

"Will do, baby. Dagger on your belt or under your pillow if I'm not back by bedtime, okay?"

"Okay."

She kissed him.

She sat on the bed, dazed for a few minutes, trying to reconcile that there was the nightmare-Tristan in the boathouse, and the Tristan she'd just had. They didn't seem like the same person. But they were. And she had to find a way to be okay with that. She knew she'd find a way. It wasn't just that she had no choice, but she really wanted to find a way to understand. She knew their experiences were shaping them and with a long life together they would both continue to evolve.

"WHERE'VE YA BEEN?" Kyle asked her.

Sasha had brought him up herself, saying that Tristan and her had a conversation and decided they didn't want any outsiders, even functionally entranced people, to have access to Kyla right now. There were staff members accustomed to Kyle, so Kyle would spend time with Kyla when Tristan wasn't there, keeping her company, dealing with any housekeeping staff, etcetera.

After Sasha had dropped the vacant Kyle off, she said she didn't have news on Tristan, other than that no one was at the front gate that she knew of. Sasha left.

Either Taryn had left, or Tristan had let her in.

Kyla wouldn't hesitate to jab that witch with her dagger!

"What do you mean where have I been?" she asked Kyle. Only a moment had passed before Kyle seemed to be back to himself from his glazed-over look.

"You were gone. And I didn't know what happened. And now we're here. In this hellhole. Why? What happened with Adrian?"

She winced. She'd been dreading this. She felt terrible.

"They've made this the base for the coalition for now, while they work on a few things. Security, lots of accommodations for everyone, centrally located. Equipped labs, you know."

"Yeah, makes sense." His face was sour. "What about Adrian?"

"Can you read my mind, Kyle? Cuz if you could and I didn't have to talk about it, it'd make my life suck a whole lot less."

Kyla sat on the big soft white sofa thinking it was gorgeous and lush to sit in but how could a vampire think it was practical to have a white sofa?

"Nope, can't read your mind, sis. When I focused hard at night alone I could reach out and feel your general state of mind. That was pretty much it."

"Oh. Dang. Well, I'll just say it then. Adrian's dead."

Kyle snickered. That was an interesting and surprising reaction.

"Are you happy, sad, what?" she asked.

"How'd he die?"

"From what I can gather, the love of my life tortured him while demanding information and even though Adrian didn't deny the information because he can't, Tristan has this super vampire hypnosis thing where he can make people talk, then he, uh, methodically dismembered him, making sure Adrian didn't pass out so he could feel everything."

Kyle looked a little bit disgusted.

"This is why I wasn't looking forward to this. Pacifist twin brother vs. maniacal bent-on-vengeance vampire soulmate."

"Adrian deserved it," Kyle said.

"He probably did. But I kind of liked the idea you had of making him right his wrongs."

Kyle shook his head," I thought on it and no, it wouldn't have worked. Tristan's probably better off being able to move forward with that checklist item ticked. If he was bent on vengeance it would've just clouded his judgement to have to work with Adrian day in, day out."

"Yeah, maybe. No, probably." Kyla thought on it, chewing her thumb nail.

"So, this is Adrian's apartment. You guys staying here?"

"For now, yeah. I have some bad memories associated with the cottage we used here last time. He's had you up here?"

"Yeah, plenty. I wasn't always locked up in the dorm. Sometimes I'd be aware of conversations with him, too. He used me as a guinea pig for some cocktails for this level he could get me, said it was above functional trance. It was always temporary with me but it worked. I figure Dr. Jasper was a few steps above that, before she got turned, but I know the cocktail he used on her had some bad side-effects. Mine, too, but not as bad as her. None of the non-vamps here had their full faculties but sometimes I felt close. So I've got memories with Adrian. Plenty of them. And Dr. Jasper and I talked a lot and she knew a lot of what was happening with some of the experiments, so I know a lot of what was done to me."

"Horrible?"

"Yeah. He was an egomaniac. And cruel. He fucked with people for kicks. Called it medical research but he was mostly a sick freak.

So, anyway, enough about that. I know he's got an Xbox in here. Wanna play GTA?"

"Shut up!"

"Shut up?" He looked stricken.

"GTA?" Kyla asked, jumping to her feet.

"Grand Theft Auto."

"Shut. Up!"

"Why? It's a video game."

"I know what that is, silly! I can't believe you're asking me that."

"Why not? Because I've led such a sheltered life?"

"No, because I flove that game! I rock at it."

"Flove?"

"Fucking love. Flove."

Kyle laughed and got up and opened doors to a double-sized wooden armoire in front of the sofa. Inside was a largish television and an Xbox but there were dozens and dozens of video games plus headsets, all the gear.

Three hours later, Kyla texted Sam,

"Kyle says the cook here makes good burgers."

Sam replied straight away,

"I can find out about that."

K: "Please do, if you would, kind sir. He says to ask for the KK special. And some junk food. Lots of junk food."

S: "And grape soda pop?"
K: "No. Pepsi pls."

S: "Roger."
K: "And cream soda."
S: "Ok."
K: M&M's if you can find them.

K: Peanut, not just chocolate. And something white chocolate too.

S: "Anything else?"

She didn't know if that was impatience or amusement.

K: "Don't think so but I'll let you know.

K: Maybe some chips & onion dip, too."

He didn't answer after that.

But about a half an hour later there was a knock on the door.

Kyle jumped up and said,

"You go in the bedroom. Shut the door."

Sheesh. Brother Bossy Pants.

But she was smiling, a lot, liking this business of having someone else around who cared to keep her safe.

She got a text.

It was Tristan.

T: "Everything okay?"

K: "Yes, fine. Kyle and I are playing XBOX. Sam is getting us dinner. I think Kyle is at the door getting said dinner. I'm in the bedroom, hidden until said dinner is delivered and door is safely closed and locked. What's up with you? Mommie dearest gone?"

T: "Not yet. Long story. I'll be late. Kyle will be picked up at midnight. Don't wait up."

K: "Oh, ok. Wake me when you come in. xo."

T: "I will. Love you."

K: <3 u2. Xxoo

"SHE'S IN THE DORM, under guard. *And* daggered."

Tristan was telling her about Taryn. He'd come into bed, curled into her, and kissed her. Kyla had sat up and asked for an update.

"She was at the gate throwing a holy fit, demanding to be let in. I had a guy on her and didn't realize he hadn't reported in for over twenty-four hours because we were on the move from the island. She probably killed him."

"What does she want?"

"I let her in because she threatened to go on a rampage to the gate guys if they didn't get me to the gate. When I got there, she turned on the waterworks and spewed all sorts of garbage about being upset that I was upset after things went wrong with you. Said that despite how horrible of a person she now is she felt my pain due to the mother-child bond and she wanted to know I was okay. I've been dodging her since things went wrong. She heard I was here somehow, I'll be finding out how, and so she showed up. I daggered her and she's out of my hair for now."

"So there's only my dagger under the pillow and the other in Taryn and that means you're unarmed. I don't like that."

"I don't need it. And tomorrow we're pulling Jonathan and Lucian out of that pit and they're daggered so that gives me two more, if I leave them undaggered. But we also have the lowdown on that steel he's using. A shipment is due in three days and according to the purchase order there's two dozen of them but we can get another shipment in about two-three weeks. They come from a Japanese knife company. It's not some secret steel, it's just their specific mix. Their mix of alloys works perfectly. He pimps them out with those crystals. That's the shit that puts a vamp down. Can you believe it? I'm having the place combed, too, in case he's got more hidden. His father got into a fight with a Japanese vamp years back and that vamp ruled Japan's vamp society because of his knife. Adrian's father, your great grandfather, took him out when he was sleeping, stole his knife, sourced the knife, bought the knife company. Looks like you and your brother might be the heirs to that particular fortune."

"Shit. I grew up with nothing. I'm Japanese knife heiress?"

"Yup. Well, Japanese knives. You don't look like a Japanese heiress."

"Too funny. I'd like to announce myself that way and see how people react when they see I'm not Japanese. And we have sisters. And a mother. Maybe the family fortune has to be split five ways."

"Yeah, well let's hold that thought. We need to determine whether your mother and sisters are worthy or not. Not to mention this place and his other assets. You're heiress to all of that, too."

"What do you know about them?" she asked him, "My sisters?"

"Not much. Yet. That's on the to-do list. After about 400 other things. He's never placed an order that big so that tells me there might've been something up his sleeve. We need to be on our toes. My IT guy is still going through phone records, emails, shit like that from the last six months."

"Yikes," she said, not liking the sound of that.

"So, did you have a good night with your brother?"

"I did. We had a laugh. We ate a pile of junk food and some double decker bacon burgers with three kinds of cheese and fricking huge onion rings on them, the Kyle Kelly special, apparently. And he wiped the floor with me with video games. Adrian had quite a collection of Xbox games. It's like a bloody video game store in that cabinet!"

"Glad you had a good night, princess." He cuddled closer.

"Sorry you didn't." She twirled her finger around his chin cleft.

"I can handle anything if I've got you to come home to."

My heart.

"You do. I'm all yours."

"I don't want you to have nightmares tonight, baby. All day I kept thinking about you dreaming that last night. And it fuckin' kills me. I talked to Sergey and he told me his mother would dream shit when his Dad was tweaked, too. His dad found a way to keep her blocked from the ugly. I don't wanna lie to you, but I also don't want you to face that shit. So, I'm gonna learn how to do that. And I won't burden you with details you don't need to know so when I ask you not to push on a topic, you need to give me that, alright? Some people down in the dorm will be turned, some will be relocated after being wiped. We have to see about that, but I don't want you pushing when I ask you not to push. Okay?"

"No," she said firmly, "Absolutely not."

He let out a sigh.

"Tristan, I'm not gonna be the mousey little lady here. You might as well get used to it. We're in things together."

"Fuck," he grumbled. "I don't want you to be the mousey little lady, Kyla. I didn't fall in love with a Stepford wife. I fell in love with you. But shit is ugly right now and I'm giving you fucking nightmares!"

"I'll deal."

"You shouldn't have to..."

"But I will. Don't compartmentalize your life with me, Tristan. That's not okay. Would it be okay if I did that to you?"

"No. It wouldn't." he answered quietly.

"Yeah. It wouldn't. So forget that idea. I'm tired. Goodnight." She turned away.

He hauled her back, "Snuggle."

"You've pissed me off! I don't feel very snuggly right now."

"Well I do, so suck it up." He held her tight.

A long while passed. She knew he was awake. She had her cheek against his chest and he had her wrapped up with both arms.

She was starting to drift but fought it, "Wait. We haven't had sex today. You haven't fed. And I only got a little."

"I know," he muttered.

"I'm pissed at you."

"I know that."

"But we can still do that," she said.

He laughed a big belly laugh and rolled her onto her back and then blew a big raspberry on her belly.

KYLA WOKE UP HEARING a groan, Tristan's groan. She felt sensation below. A joltingly beautiful sensation.

She opened her eyes and saw sparkling dark blue eyes.

Dark blue?

His mouth was between her legs.

"Kyla, baby, you're bleeding."

"Hmm?" she tried to shake off the sleepiness.

He groaned, and his tongue went deep, making her back bow.

"Bleeding?" she breathed.

"Yeah. Fuuuuck..." His eyes rolled back, and he fisted the sheets next to her hips. He was white knuckled, devouring her, and she was rocketing into fucking outer space with a massive orgasm washing over her.

She let out a loud gasp when she came.

He leaned up and licked his lips and then was on her and in her before the orgasm had even ended.

"That's fucking amazing..." he said, "So fucking good."

He rammed hard, to the hilt. But he didn't just ram. He got a slow but powerfully hard rhythm going and every time he hit that hilt he rotated his hips, making Kyla whimper like a puppy.

Lost in sensation, she threw her arms over her head and he leaned forward and sank his teeth into the inside of her bicep, making her whimper louder. He let go of her bicep, bit into his own, and then covered her mouth with the bleeding bicep and she latched on while he kept slamming, gyrating, and groaning.

She hit another peak, his blood in her mouth, his mouth drinking her blood, and his cock hitting her g-spot.

He slammed and slammed until he exploded inside of her and then collapsed on top of her.

Her hands went into his hair and she yanked it back and went for his mouth, kissing him hard.

"I fucking love you," she said, feeling kind of drunk, and then it dawned on her that she'd kissed his mouth after he'd gone down on her while she was having her period.

Her period.

She burst into tears.

He moved back and cupped her face with his hand, "What's wrong?"

"My period." She started to sob.

It felt like her world was ending. She was sobbing uncontrollably. Tristan rolled them, so he was on his back and pulled her close. She felt wet between her legs and knew that blood with his semen was coating the inside of her legs.

"That's so fucking gross. I need to brush my teeth, and a...a sh-shower," she mumbled, choking on a sob.

"Okay, baby. You okay?"

"No! I got my period."

He nodded, "But I'm me. I'm not hurting you. I'm not dangerous. That blood is amazing. And you're not in danger." He caressed her face, "I feel whole, princess. I'm not the grey hulk."

"But I got my period!"

He looked at her blankly and then it dawned on him.

"I'm not pregnant," she mumbled, absolutely fucking crushed. The tears fell faster, and he moved to her and kissed them away.

"Maybe you ovulated while you were catatonic. I didn't know, princess. But maybe I'll know next time. And we'll make love every day, every single day, so we won't miss next time. Okay?" He caressed her cheeks with both thumbs, his fingers woven into her hair.

She nodded and buried her face in his chest, hiccoughing.

He caressed her back and then tapped her bottom, "Let's go get cleaned up and then we'll change the bed."

She nodded and sniffled.

As irrational as she knew it was, she felt like her world was on the verge of ending.

SHE WAS A MISERABLE bitch all day. She wanted to swim in the pool on the terrace and she had wicked cramps and her flow had gotten so heavy she didn't think the tampons would even help for swimming, so she pouted.

Kyle came over and they had lunch and played video games for a while but she was being a sore loser because he whooped her ass at everything, so she made an excuse that she wasn't feeling well and went for a nap.

She ate dinner alone, delivered by Sam. Kyle left with him.

The dinner had grape pop and she didn't want it. She was miserable about not having the ability to choose her beverage. Miserable about absolutely everything.

She found the pop had tasted off ever since tasting Tristan's blood. Her favourite beverage now tasted dirty.

His blood, though, it tasted like the grape she craved.

So, she drank water, begrudgingly.

Then, Tristan came in that night after she was asleep, and she yelled at him for being all up in her bloody business like a fucking bloodhound. He woke her up by going down on her.

"That's disgusting. Stop!"

She had clamped her knees shut on his head and was pretty sure her kneecaps had hurt him because his head came up and she'd cracked them again, his head right in the middle and the motion so forceful that her knees were radiating pain.

"It's not disgusting," he told her, "It's amazing. Be a good girl or I'll give you a spanking." It was an empty threat, or just an erotic one, because he didn't look angry. He looked like he was super- duper horny.

"Ew. Yuck. Get away from me!" She scampered out of the bed, pulling up her underwear, and went into the bathroom to take a shower.

He was in there with her a minute later. Naked.

She saw him throw a tampon into the toilet. He flushed it.

Gross. He must've yanked it out while she'd been sleeping.

She pointed at him, still soaping up her vajayjay, "No. Out!"

He chuckled and shook his head, ignoring her request for him to leave. He got in, reached up to grab the detachable shower head, then dropped to his knees with it and grabbed the soapy sponge out of her hand and chucked it aside. He twisted it and put the now pulsing shower head right against her clit.

"Holy fuck!" she gasped and grabbed a handful of hair at the top of his head, going weak in the knees.

He rinsed all the soap off and then his tongue went deep. He kept the pulsing showerhead angled upwards, right on her clit, and she went absolutely mental with sensation. Her legs gave out on her, but he caught her and then carried her back to the bed and she didn't say a thing when he lifted her legs to put a towel under her bottom, and then went to town on her with his tongue.

She didn't say anything as she fisted the blankets with her mouth open in a big O but she also didn't look down because ... ewwww.

When he was done, she stuffed a big overnight pad in her undies before going to sleep.

KYLA WOKE UP ALONE, but it was still night. She could hear voices, so she got up and listened at the bedroom door. She could hear Tristan and Sam's voices.

"We caught her breaking past security at the dormitory. She didn't kill Hunter, she put him under her orders. He came in and debriefed me but left out those details. Because he didn't remember them. I didn't know she'd influenced him, so he was in the dorm, talking to Leonard, and then he got to her and pulled the dagger. He was carrying her out, she wasn't yet conscious, so I stopped them, locked Hunter down, but think he's oblivious since he was just following her orders. But bad news is that the dagger is missing and so is Jackson. Jackson was on duty in the dorm. I've dropped Taryn here, so you can deal with her and I'm gonna go help Jeff, Leonard, and the others find him and shut this shit down."

Kyla winced. She reached under the pillow for her dagger, put her robe on, tucked her dagger into the pocket and walked out to the living area.

Tristan's mother was sitting on the sofa, looking directly at Kyla walking in. She was disheveled-looking but still beautiful. Her long wavy dark hair was loose and she was in jeans, boots, a blue blouse the same colour as her eyes (and Tristan's eyes) and a navy blue blazer. But her eyes were bloodshot. She had a blood bag in her hand.

Tristan was instantly in front of Kyla, backing her up. Sam had already gone.

"Get back in the bedroom, Kyla," said Tristan.

"Here," she handed him the dagger from her pocket.

He accepted it, "Thank you. Back to bed."

She looked over at Taryn who was staring at her,

"She's better. She's better, Tristan? Is she vampire?"

"No, Taryn. Nevermind."

"Nevermind?" Taryn was clearly offended, "Nevermind?"

"None of your business."

"My son. My son and it's none of my business? What's happening here, Tristan? I need to know what on earth is happening!"

He took two steps back, Kyla pressed behind him with his palm against the small of Kyla's back. It was his signature protective pose.

"What's happening here is that I have Kyla back. It doesn't matter how. But I'm here because I'm in an alliance with the Voitenko family and several other European elders to shut down the bullshit happening here with the royals. Oh, and I'm here because I also found out that Constantin and your father put my father in a pit with a dagger. So he's in the ground, beside your Uncle Lucian. We're waking them tomorrow."

Taryn looked stricken, "What?"

"Yeah, that's right. Your husband isn't dead. But now Constantin is," Tristan replied, then muttered, "Go back to bed, baby. I'll be there soon."

Kyla wasn't moving. She was watching Taryn come completely undone.

Taryn's hand moved up and covered her mouth and she started to tremble. "Jonathan?" she started to shake as tears started falling.

Tristan went completely stiff.

"Yeah, your husband isn't dead. Although I don't know what the fuck he'll think when he meets you and sees what you've become. And stop it. That's twice you've turned on the waterworks for me, Taryn, and that's twice too much."

"Stop calling me by my name, Tristan. I am your mother!"

"You know you're not my mother. You used to be my mother. But you are not her."

"And whose fault is that?" she hissed.

"Mine," He said coldly.

Kyla's reached forward and put her cheek against his back, her arm around his stomach and squeezed as pain lanced through her. That pain was both hers and his.

"Please go to bed, princess. I can't stomach the idea of her breathing your air." He let go of her.

She nodded and got up on her toes and kissed the hinge of his jaw and then backed into the bedroom, seeing Taryn's wet eyes on her, looking filled with pained emotion. She shut the door.

Things were quiet for a few minutes, but Kyla didn't fall back to sleep. There was no way in the world she would be able to.

Tristan finally came in, it might've been an hour later, maybe more.

"Where is she?" Kyla sat up.

"I took her downstairs, locked her in a bedroom in the dorm. She wants to be there when we open the crypt. She's a wreck. Never seen her like this."

Kyla cuddled close.

"Not like her typical vampress hissy fits, either. I don't know what this is."

"Thinking her husband has been dead for 35 years and finding out he isn't? That's gotta be... rough."

"Yeah. She never met her father, doesn't know Lucian."

"Did Sam find Jackson?" Kyla asked.

Tristan nodded, "Yeah. He's locked down, too."

"What was he up to?"

Tristan laughed, "Planning his murder of me so he could have you back."

"Wh-what?"

"Carrying a torch, apparently. Either stumbled onto the dagger in the empty room or was helping Hunter. Either way, he knew what it was by watching Hunter remove it. Was gonna hunker down for the night with it and figure out how to get to me and take me out."

"What an idiot. Vampirism hasn't changed him."

"So, tomorrow oughta be an interesting day," Tristan said.

"Yeah. Can I be there?"

"Where?"

"At the crypt. The pit, whatever. When you open it."

"No. No goddamn way!"

"But..."

"Kyla?" He was astounded that she'd even suggest such a thing.

"Let me be there for you."

"It could be dangerous. No way. My mother, two desecrated and starving vampires, uh uh. Fuck that shit. Besides, rumour is that Lucian killed Sergey's wife. If that's what happened, it might not go well. Sergey's said he can deal but he could go rogue. Rumour has it that Lucian wasn't on board with the coalition, but my father was. But Lucian wasn't on board with the breeding program either. Adrian said he had a screw loose, was jealous of Alexander so was constantly stirring shit up, undermining things. So those two in that pit together, I don't even know if they'll go after one another. We are gonna separate them into the two pits and leave them there with feeders and a week's worth of blood bags for a few hours and see what happens. We figure out which one, if either, we let out, interrogate, then go from there."

"Feeders? They'll drain them!"

"Don't you worry about that. Not your problem."

"Wh-what?"

He sighed, "Don't you worry. We've got access to a population of pieces of shit people for that purpose. Don't ask. Just know that the feeders won't be missed."

"Oh my God. Are you fucking kidding me?"

"Don't go there, Kyla."

"Well, what'll you do with Jackson?"

"He's gotta die, princess."

"What?"

"He's a liability. He's a threat to us."

"Can't you just..."

"Program him? No. I'm not programming someone to *not* hate me, *not* want my girl. Fuck that. That's not something I'm willing to chance. He's done."

"God," she sobbed, covering her eyes. But then she felt her anger rising. She was about to speak, but Tristan beat her to the punch.

"What? He was dead to you two years ago. That's not Jackson down there. That's a cold-blooded vampire who heard you're special, who's had Taryn in his ear, telling him that you used to be his, you've got special blood, but I took you. Yeah, he's the one who told Taryn I'm here. She found out who he was from Constantin and before she left here last time she ordered him to get word to her when I came back. And now God knows what he's got in his mostly brain-dead skull."

"I don't want you to kill him."

"And I don't want you to even worry about this. That's why it'd be better if you were cut off from this shit. I'm not doing it. I'll give the order, though. So, you won't have to dream it."

She didn't like this dark side of him. Didn't like it one bit. But it was who he was. Whether that was who he always was or who their circumstances had turned him into, she didn't know. Maybe a bit of both. He'd said things would get ugly. But this ugly?

"I wanna talk to him first. See if I can convince him to—-"

"No. Fuck that. You're getting nowhere near him. He doesn't exist. He's not the same. He was brought back from being brain dead, Kyla. He's so far from the same he might as well be a different guy completely. A vampire in Jackson Curtis's body. That's all. Some of us retain some of our humanity when we're turned, but his brain was dead when he was turned so he's got nothing in there that remotely resembles his old self. Talking to him is pointless."

"How do you know this?"

"I discussed it with Sasha."

"Fine, goodnight."

"Kyla?"

"Whatever, Tristan. You're in charge. Obviously. So I'm gonna go to sleep. If that's okay with you?"

He let out a big breath.

"You're giving me a fucking headache, you know that?" Tristan muttered, "Haven't had a goddamn headache in 10 years. Now I get them constantly."

"Go fuck yourself!" She got out of the bed and stormed out, stormed across the hall to the master bedroom and slammed the door.

It was a beautiful bedroom. But she didn't want to get into the bed. Adrian's bed. It was the size of two king-sized beds side by side. She sat on the floor against the closed door and put her head in her hands.

The doorknob turned, and the door pushed against her back.

"Don't," she called out.

"Move away," he told her.

"No. Leave me alone."

"What're you doing?"

"Leave me alone!"

"Move away from the fuckin' door and let me in."

She shifted to get up to move and he burst in. He was huffing and pissed off looking and moving toward her with purpose. She tripped and started to do a pathetic backwards crab crawl to get away from that intensity, but he leaned down and scooped her up and then turned around and carried her back to the other bedroom and put her in bed and got in and yanked her roughly against him.

He was huffing, pissed right off. He got his mouth an inch away from her face,

"I'll put him in a prison. I won't have him killed."

Kyla blinked.

"We should have prisons for vampires. Not make every serious misstep reason for an execution. So that'll start. Okay?"

She nodded.

"Go to sleep," he growled.

"'Kay," she squeaked.

"We won't use feeders in those pits. We'll use extra blood bags."

"M'kay," she said softly.

His body was tense and tight, but he was still holding onto her.

"But you're not there. You're not even here. I've decided I'm sending you, Sasha, and Kyle back to the island before I do this. You stay with her. You stay safe. I am not fucking around. This is non-negotiable."

"Okay, babe." She leaned forward and kissed his chest and then closed her eyes.

The tension in his body lifted away. Kyla fell asleep.

15

KYLA AND SASHA WERE watching a chick flick and they were both laughing and crying at the same time. They were crying at the sweet romance but laughing at one another and themselves because of that crying.

Kyle was asleep. Kyla spent most of her time with him but spent time with Sasha in the evenings after Kyle had gone to bed because she felt bad about leaving Sasha alone, without company, but didn't want to do it with Kyle because obviously he'd glaze over if all three of them were in the same room. Plus, she was lonely herself, not wanting to face an empty bed.

She missed her vampire prince.

It'd been three days since she'd been back on the island. She and Tristan hadn't spoken at all since she'd arrived and that was leaving a huge hole in her heart right now.

Because he was busy, maybe, but more likely because they'd argued. The morning after their argument he'd put them on a plane, not even talking to her about it, much.

He was growly,

"Time to go," he'd said, putting a cup of coffee beside her. She'd been in bed, but awake and lazing.

"Go?"

He glared, "Pack. Fifteen minutes. You don't need much." And then he'd left the bedroom. She knew by his expression he was thwarting an argument with his attitude and normally she'd have been all up in his face about that attitude but she'd gotten a lot of concessions from him the previous night, so she bit her tongue, did as she was told, and then met him in the living area.

He was standing there, arms folded, looking out the window, exuding authority. He walked her out to the terrace, past a gate she hadn't noticed before, to a landing pad where a helicopter was sitting, running.

Holy crap.

He wasn't messing around.

He reached for her and kissed her passionately, with tongue and a grope on her bottom, catching her completely off guard based on his attitude up until that point, and then he swatted her bottom and pointed to the stairs.

"Love you. See you in a few days," he said, "Satellite phone is in your bag if there's an emergency. I'm programmed and I programmed a few services. Sasha has a cocktail made with my blood. Drink some every day. Wear that dagger. Got me?"

She nodded. "Got you. Love you, too," she said, "Please be safe." and then climbed the stairs, her heart sitting in her stomach.

Sasha and Kyle were in the plane.

Kyla had buckled up beside Sasha and looked out the window, watching Tristan stand there, as the plane took off.

Now it was three days later, and she didn't know much of what was happening, really. Sasha had been in touch with Sam and Tristan as well and had told Kyla that both Jonathan and Lucian had been successfully woken and that Jonathan and Taryn were currently holed up, together, in a cottage on the property.

Together. Yup. Kyla found that to be some interesting and juicy information.

Lucian was in a holding cell. Re-daggered. Bad guy. No one knew much yet, but they were sure that more investigation needed to happen to figure out why he was in that pit as well as what should be done about him.

Sasha said that Sergey, Tristan, and Sam were due back to the island the following day.

She'd been sleeping in Sasha's guest room and she'd been sad. She'd played the events of the previous few days over and over in her mind and part of her was worried not just that he was going to the dark side but that he'd stay there.

What they'd been through had a profound impact on them both, but particularly him, since she'd been catatonic for days after what'd happened in Adrian's lab.

But even with what'd happened before that, the miscarriage, being separated, all the fears and uncertainties, all of it... she knew she loved him with all of her heart and felt so lucky to have this man to share her life with.

My prince.

She missed him from the minute she'd gotten on the plane. And she knew that bond or no bond, light or dark, blue or black, she wanted to be in this for the long haul, completely present, being everything he wanted in a woman. Wanting to give him babies. Wanting to make the house on the island a home. Wanting nothing but that right now, wanting it so badly she was aching for it.

She could give him babies for the next few decades, lots of babies, and then maybe she could get her degree, open a business, build houses and dig wells in Kenya, do an eco-tour, do something else, knowing they had a big beautiful family together to enrich their lives together.

On a positive note, her period had stopped. It'd only lasted until the day she'd gotten there. She was looking forward to baby-making. She knew that this was partly due to the bond they had but in her mind, she didn't care if it was hormone-driven, couldn't wait to see the fruit of their togetherness, of their love.

On a not-so-positive note, on the third evening she started to get itchy. Withdrawals.

Tristan had given Sasha a blood sample before they'd left, and Sasha had mixed it the way she generally did for the women on the island that were being fed small doses of Kyle's blood. She called it micro-dosing and said it was a small amount that was added to grape juice but that she'd hoped that it'd buy them the few days until Tristan was back. She hadn't been feeding from him long enough to have any sort of stamina for blood fasting yet.

The beverage she was drinking didn't taste great. It tasted like watery grape juice, and evidently it wasn't concentrated enough to keep the withdrawals from starting but Tristan would be there the following day.

She went to bed ignoring the itching, anxious to have him back.

"KYLA! WAKE UP!"

"Sasha?"

"We have to get into the safe room. Now, quick!"

Kyla jumped out of bed.

"What happened?"

"Hurry!"

Kyla grabbed her robe and put it on and got the dagger into her pocket. She fumbled into her bag for the satellite phone.

"We don't have time!"

"I need this!" Kyla grabbed the phone and put it in her pocket with the dagger.

Sasha grabbed her hand and they ran downstairs together. There were lights outside, big lights on the beach. Two or three watercraft were almost to the shore.

Sasha and Kyla got to the basement, in through the office closet, where Kyle was asleep in the bed in the safe room. Sasha woke him and took them both through a doorway into a long dark hallway lit only by her flashlight. Kyla didn't feel good. In fact, she started to feel a strong sense of impending doom.

Sasha had a flashlight lit and then another door opened, and Kyla's heart nearly stopped when she realized they were inside a cave. A cave! It had stone walls like the tunnel in her dream.

The alleyway with the stone walls and her bloody hands outside the hotel in Phoenix wasn't the tunnel from her dreams.

Was this?

"Oh God, no! We have to get out of here!"

"It's okay. This leads to our true safe room. There's a weapons cache, food, and a way out into the deep part of the forest so we can get out of here."

"My phone can summon a plane for us, a boat. I can call Tristan."

"Good," Sasha said, "Call him first."

"Who's here? Who is that?"

"I don't know but I know it's not good. Almost no one is here but those who are on watch haven't reported anything odd. They're either taken out or they're part of this."

"Shit."

They were in a big open room with tables and chairs and a hallway leading off.

"There are bathroom facilities, food and medical supplies, sleeping areas that way. There's also a cave exit that's not too far." Sasha pointed to the left hall, "Kitchen, weapons cache, meeting rooms, and a longer way out that way," she pointed to the right.

"Kyle," Sasha said, while pulling navy blue sweatshirts and sweatpants out of the cupboard as well as white running shoes; there was a shelf of them.

Kyle's attention snapped to Sasha's face.

"Get into these," She told them, "If anything happens to me, you take care of your sister, okay? Get her to Tristan. And if Tristan can't get you to me afterwards, please track down Dr. Levi in Dartmouth, Nova Scotia. He will carry on with my work, okay?"

"Yes," Kyle answered blankly.

"Why would anything happen to you?" Kyla asked.

"Because you two are going out there and getting on a plane. I'm staying here. I'm going back to my place to see who they are, find out what they want. Figure out if there's someone on my team dead or if someone's double-crossed us."

"Why won't you come with us? Figure that out later."

"Sorry, Kyla. I need to do this. Follow me," She headed into a room filled with shelves that held guns. She passed two to Kyla.

"Keep those until he's lucid and give him one. Point and shoot if you need to. A vamp needs a lethal shot or he won't be down too long. Depending on how old he is will dictate how long before he can heal. A vampire that's royal and an elder can handle bullet wounds unless they're right to the heart or the brain or big enough to blow out a vital organ. Shoot to kill, if you have to shoot. Make it count, Kyla."

"But..." Kyla started.

Sasha shook her head firmly, "Tristan needs you to be safe. So do I. Because I care, Kyla, and frankly because without you Tristan will be nothing and we need him. I'm going to go out the short way and figure out who they are. If we separate, you both have a chance to get off this island safely. Go the long way. Go; quick."

"But without you, Kyle will go back into a coma. You can't separate."

She shook her head, "No. I talked to some experts. Kyle felt my presence; that's why that happened. If I wasn't around him, he'd have gotten over it after a few weeks. We don't have the same bond you two have."

Kyla believed that. She'd started getting better after withdrawal in Victoria after a few days.

"He would've woke up from that coma. He doesn't need me. Hurry. Go that way," she pointed to the hallway, "Kyle, take your sister. Keep her safe. Go fast." Sasha passed him the flashlight and two bottles of water, which Kyle put into his jacket pockets, "Don't stop until you are at the end of the tunnel and then be careful. It's dense, but there's a path from the mouth of the tunnel that leads to a dock at the water down a ways.

"Are they definitely bad guys?" Kyla asked. Kyle took her hand and started moving.

"I don't know, Kyla. I'm about to find out, though."

Kyla suspected the answer was yes.

Kyle was pulling her toward the right.

She felt a sense of impending doom as she followed him. They began to jog.

She looked back over her shoulder and gave Sasha a hopeful look, chewing her lip. "I hope you're okay."

Sasha waved at her with a sad look on her face, grabbed two guns, and turned around and went down the other hallway.

Kyla fished the satellite phone out of her pocket. She found Tristan's cell in the directory. They were out of the main area and now the drywall was transitioning to stone. A stone tunnel.

A stone freaking tunnel. Kyla's blood ran cold.

She was about to hit dial but the phone started to ring.

It said, 'Tristan - cell' on the screen.

"Tristan!"

"Kyla?" he answered, "What the fuck? I can feel you. What the fuck is happening there?"

"Tristan, I.. shit," she tripped and almost fell.

Kyle was jogging too fast.

"Slow down, Kyle!"

"What's going on?" Tristan demanded.

"There were a bunch of lights on the shore. Boats. Three of them, I think. Sasha put us in the secret hideaway in the hill. She went back to be a distraction, so Kyle and I could get out. Kyle and I are making our way through a tunnel. Holy fucking fuck!" Her voice went panicked.

"What is it?"

"A snake, a snake!" She saw a black snake slithering up ahead in the lit part of the ground that the flashlight shone on.

They were in a cave and there was a fucking black snake.

"Who am I gonna have to run from, Tristan?" In her dream she'd been running from Tristan in the stone tunnel.

"Kyla, slow down. Stop. Take a breath. Talk to me."

"Kyle is on a mission. Sasha told him to get me out of the cave through this long tunnel and he's freaking pulling me by the arm and he's not lucid. He's running. He doesn't understand he needs to fucking stop. Stop, Kyle! Snap out of it, damn it! How the fuck are you running so fast after being asleep for two years?"

"Kyla and Kyle are in the hill, in a tunnel Sasha's sent them down." Tristan was talking to someone.

"Where does it go?" He was asking someone with him.

"She said it goes deep in the forest," Kyla said but she was out of breath. The snake was out of sight, but Kyle was still pulling her forward through the tunnel and she was a fast runner but hadn't been running much and Kyle was evidently a fast runner, too, and somehow didn't seem to have lost muscle mass, like you'd expect someone to do after being in bed for two years, so she couldn't fricking keep up.

She heard Tristan talking to someone, then his voice got louder, "Kyla, Sergey knows where you're heading. Get to the mouth of it and stay hidden in there. We're coming. Please tell me you have a dagger."

"I have a dagger. And two loaded guns."

"Good. Good, princess." He sounded relieved.

"We're just about three hours out, but we're getting there as fast as we possibly can. I love you, baby. I love you."

"Love you. Who is this here, Tristan?"

"No clue, baby. I'll be there as soon as I can be. Don't be afraid to use those guns, princess. Aim for the head. Double fucking tap. Okay? Don't let anyone fucking hurt you. Promise me." His voice was thick with emotion.

"Promise, baby." Hers was, too.

"Gotta go. I'm on my way to you. Turn the ringer off. In case you have to hide. But before you do, look at it. Familiarize yourself with the phone in case you have to use it in the dark. There's an SOS button. It has a tracker. I can track you myself but in case someone else here needs to track you, like a chopper. Okay?"

"'Kay." It'd be hard to do this while running but she'd try.

She ended the call, "Gimme the flashlight!" she demanded and Kyle gave it to her but kept running. She pulled out of his grip and tried to use the light to find the ringer setting, flashed the light all over the phone and noticed the SOS button on the top. She shoved the phone in her jeans pocket as he caught her wrist again and sped up.

They kept running, they ran for a lot longer, it felt like it was an hour before Kyla saw a bit of light.

And the whole time, she felt Tristan's pure fury. He was stewing while he tried to get to her. She knew his blood was boiling. They could feel one another a three-hour plane ride apart.

Light was ahead. It was reflecting, coming from some reflectors at the mouth of the tunnel.

Kyle tripped and fell and because he had her wrist, she went down with him.

She took the opportunity to try to catch her breath. But it was gonna take a while.

"Okay, alright, we're here. Kyle. Talk to me."

Kyle was completely winded, gasping for air.

"There's water in your pocket. Drink some. Give me the other."

He reached for his pocket but was frenzied. She knew he'd been running on pure adrenalin, Sasha's directions, and little else. She knew how powerful a vamp's directions could be on someone. She could see how affected Kyle was from that long sprint and knew that he'd have kept going if they hadn't gotten to the mouth. He'd have kept going until he dropped.

They both drank their water and caught their breath.

"Wh-what n-now?" Kyle breathed, "Another adventure with you this soon?" He looked amused. His smile died when he took in her expression.

Kyla let out a winded huff, unable to see the humour. He had no idea why they were at the mouth of a tunnel, no idea why he probably felt like he was gonna die from exhaustion.

She explained their predicament, heart beating wildly, struggling to regain normal breath.

"I gotta whiz, sis. Hang on." He stepped outside the tunnel and around the corner.

And then she heard noise. The area they were in was fairly thick, but she was pretty sure that there were people close by. That wasn't Tristan already. It couldn't be.

She heard a noise that couldn't be all that far away. Men talking?

"Get back in here, Kyle!" she whisper-shouted.

He was back.

"Shh!" She pulled his arm back inside, grabbed the flash light off the ground and turned it off, and then passed him a gun and they backed up a few feet.

"Do you know how to use that?" she whispered.

"Totally. I'm a gamer," he said.

She rolled her eyes at that but hopefully it was the truth. They stayed in the dark, a few feet back in the tunnel, but Kyla watched.

She heard footsteps. At least two people, maybe more.

Oh God, what? What now?

"I smell it; do you smell it?" she heard a man's voice.

She didn't know what he was talking about. She only hoped he couldn't smell *them*. Kyle put his arm around her in a comforting way. She leaned in.

"I'm bleeding," he whispered, "my leg's bleeding."

Oh shit.

"Point the gun at the tunnel entrance," she whispered, "They get close, we shoot. Aim for their heads."

Kyla had never shot a real gun in her life. Those elephant tranquilizer guns at close range didn't seem like they'd count.

Light flashed directly in her face. She squinted.

"They're here! Both of them."

She heard a male voice and knew she didn't know it, so Kyla aimed high and pulled the trigger.

Kyle pulled his, too.

They both clearly missed doing anything significant because she heard a cuss and then the light got bigger as one of them whooshed into her space, grabbing her by the throat.

Kyla reached into her pocket, got her dagger, and jabbed him in the side. He went down. Kyla turned the flashlight on. Another one was there, flashlight in their faces and Kyle pulled the trigger and shot him in the face. He went down.

She heard a whole bunch of shouts. There were a bunch of people outside.

"Oh shit,"

She grabbed her dagger out of the guy on the ground. They were blocked in.

"Let's run back," Kyle said, grabbing her wrist, it was the hand she was holding the gun with.

"We ran for forever. It's one straight path. They'll catch us. Better to run out shooting and have more than one direction to run."

The mouth of the tunnel had been closed in on. They had no choice. He started to sprint for the way they'd come and Kyla felt sick inside because she knew that there was no way in hell that they would be able to run faster than vampires and get anywhere.

"Stop!" she told him and pulled out of his grasp. He grabbed for her arm again. He had no idea what that tunnel had been like, being on autopilot running through it. She had to make him listen.

Cold shot out of her and she struggled free and shoved him.

Kyle went flying back and landed on his ass, dropping the flashlight, which made it light the way toward the mouth of the tunnel that was now filled with at least half a dozen men.

Kyla blocked Kyle, held the dagger in one hand, the gun in the other.

Two big lights flashed on them and then pointed at the ground, lighting the space. A man stood there smiling.

Kyla didn't know who he was.

"The Kelly twins, I assume? I'm Brandt Brooks. Not sure if you've heard of me."

"No," Kyla said, knowing he was vampire.

He'd be a beautiful vampire, too, if he wasn't so fucking weasly. She knew he was a sick-headed individual just by looking at him.

"I'm on the board of directors for Kovac Capital."

"Oh," Kyla said. Her heart thumped wildly.

"Come with me and this will go simply." He stepped forward and looked her right in the eyes.

She stared, blankly, intentionally. He was a tall, fair, and handsome man dressed in combat gear. She didn't know what Brandt Brooks knew about her. She did know that her brother would be mesmerized by these vampires, so she was on her own. She'd have to figure things out for the both of them.

The guy on the ground that she'd stabbed with the dagger started to stir.

"Watch out, sir. She's got one of those daggers," The guy on the ground said.

"So, it's true. You're lucid. I thought maybe my men had just fallen because it was too dark for you to be entranced. Guess it's true. I saw you at the Kovac sales conference a while back. You probably don't remember me."

"What's true?" Kyla hissed.

"That you're Tristan's enchanted pet and that you're immune to a vampire's charms."

Kyla didn't answer.

"Your sweet smelling brother doesn't seem to have that same immunity."

Kyla looked at her brother and he was standing there, dazed, blood trickling down his shin.

The vamp on the ground lunged forward and got his tongue to Kyle's leg and groaned.

Brandt kicked him before the guy could clamp on with teeth.

The guy yelped, "Sorry, sir. He just smells so..."

"I know. I'm not nose blind," Brandt said, "Let's go. Give me that dagger."

"I'll give it to you alright," Kyla threatened.

He snickered, "Please. You have a dagger and I know what that dagger does. But there are eight of us. You really think it'll help you?

"What do you want?"

"I want your blood, of course. Your brother's, too. There's a very anxious female vamp who's waiting for it. Let's go."

Cold shot out of Kyla at Brandt and she sent him flying into two guys behind him, the force knocking all three of them over. The guy on the ground grabbed for her and she kicked him in the face and then fired the gun twice, in front of her. Brandt was up and at her, reaching for her throat, fangs out. She went to jab him but he caught her wrist and the dagger fell, clanging as it landied on the stone ground.

"Get the brother," Brandt ordered and hauled Kyla out of there.

She struggled and dug deep for that icy cold strength, but it didn't come and he was too strong for her.

THEY WERE ON A BOAT. She, Kyle, Brandt Brooks, and one of his guys. The other remaining guys were on another boat. She didn't see a third boat.

Kyla had engaged the SOS button on the phone in her jeans pocket. But she'd gotten caught doing it so Brandt hauled her onto her stomach and frisked her and confiscated the phone. He threw it into the ocean.

They were leaving the island.

She'd have jumped overboard and taken her chances if it wasn't for Kyle, who was just sitting there, staring off at nothing.

She shook her head in dismay and prayed Tristan would find her.

2 Hours Later

THEY WERE INSIDE A motel room. She was sitting on a bed, knees cocked, back against the wall, hands tied behind her back. She'd gotten feisty and punched him in the mouth, drawing blood, trying to stop him from bringing her in here so Brandt had tied her hands, getting right up to her ear.

"Can't wait to taste you." He licked the side of her face and she wanted to puke.

He'd been so much stronger than Liam when she'd hit Liam back in that cottage. This guy must be a stronger vampire. And Kyla hadn't fed in four days, not properly, so maybe that was weakening her.

Damn it.

Kyle was somewhere else, she didn't know where, but suspected the motel was housing this group with a few rooms.

"I don't know you but I'm telling you right now, I *do* know that Tristan is going to turn you into mincemeat with his bare hands."

Brandt locked the door, seeing his goon out, and turned to her.

"I've got this dagger, though. Maybe I'll put it in him and then while he's down I'll turn him into mincemeat instead. And then you'll be my pet. My unending source of strength. I heard he's got the strength of a 300 plus year old vamp from having you just the last few months."

"How do you know all this?" Kyla asked.

He snickered, "I have a sister. She's on the island. Pretending to be part of that coalition and fucking Sam Jasper, plus there are some other bits and pieces through associates, I've got a pretty good idea of the picture with that island as well as with you and Tristan. I'm somewhat familiar with Adrian Constantin's breeding program, as a product of it myself, and as a royal who's been given his share of enchanted secret pets. Plus, he offered to equip me with those daggers for a price a few weeks ago so I know what they can do. I'm not getting stronger from the blood of my enchanted pets. I'm 122 and Tristan isn't going to rule over me. He's a kid, compared to me. Brandy gets Kyle and I get you."

"Sam's a double agent? That's a surprise."

"He's not."

"Pillow talk? That's unprofessional."

Brandt cocked his head, "Never said Sam told her a thing. But she's got eyes and ears all over that island. That big house that's all windows? We've been investigating and knew plenty about Dr.

Samantha Jasper. Brandy wanted Kyle and she was reporting to me on the coalition's plans. I know Tristan is in Phoenix and heard you three were back at the island."

If Kyle's blood made Brandy even-out, why did she want Kyle? Maybe even with the bitch switch turned off, she was still just a greedy bitch.

Kyla felt thrumming start up inside of her body.

Oh God. He's tracking me! Please let him be close.

When this had happened in Victoria, he'd been close. She prayed that'd be the case again now.

But Brandt had a dagger. What if he hurt Tristan? Kyla's head started to pound with the tension.

Then it occurred to her.

If Brandt drank her blood he'd become very ill. Sergey had said that and told her she'd probably murder a vamp who tried to drink her blood for his efforts.

"You probably won't even like the way I taste. Don't vampires have a preferred type?"

"How do you know you're not my preferred type?" he asked.

"I'm just saying. You might not even like the way I taste."

"Rumour has it that Liam Donavan is dead because he tasted you. Although I'm not sure why, other than that you're supposed to be enchanted. You don't smell enchanted to me. You smell good, but you just smell like a woman. Nothing special. Your brother, though... he smells enchanted."

"Well, Tristan did kill Liam because he couldn't stop himself from tasting me. The same for Claudio."

Brandt looked startled.

"Tristan killed Claudio for tasting you?"

"For tasting me, yes."

"I heard Claudio committed suicide."

"Nope. Tristan ripped his head off for drinking my highly-enchanted blood. I've been told it's like mixing baking soda with vinegar once it's in a vampire's system." She shrugged.

His eyes widened. "So, why don't you smell enchanted to me? I'm very attuned to these things."

"I'm not bleeding."

"It doesn't matter. I have an acute sense of smell. I know what enchanted smells like."

Kyla shrugged, "Maybe I'm an anomaly. Or maybe your sniffer isn't working properly."

He put a knee to the end of the bed and crawled up toward her. She gulped.

"You're not real bright, are you?" Brandt asked her.

The thrumming inside of her was getting very loud.

She was glad it seemed that Brandt was the one who wasn't too bright. He couldn't stop thinking about her blood. He couldn't wait to try it.

She wanted to send Tristan a warning, that there was a dagger in the room, but she didn't know how. All she knew was that if she could get this guy to drink from her, he could get sick and that could give her, and maybe Tristan if he got here really soon, an advantage.

She also knew that vampires loved to prey on the weak, so she whimpered, "Please don't hurt me."

But inside, she was feeling the cold fury rise. She had to keep it down for now, so he'd bite her and hopefully become violently ill.

His nose was in the crook of her neck.

"Let me be the judge of whether it's extraordinary or not."

Kyla braced and fought the overpowering urge to fight him. It wasn't easy.

His teeth sank into her throat and the sound that came out of him made her blood feel like it was curdling. He leaned back and said, "Holy hell! How the... you taste like fucking heaven! I've never tasted anything like that in my life!"

Oh no. Oh god, no. Kyla felt doomed. Would she now get drained? Was Sergey wrong? Those words were very similar to what Tristan had said the first time he tasted her blood. But these words didn't make her skin rise with goosebumps. These words now terrified her.

All of a sudden Brandt leaned back and rolled over onto his side and began retching off the side of the bed.

A horribly putrid odour filled the air. His face was black like coal and he was puking blood. Her thrumming halted.

The door burst open and Tristan, Sam, and Sergey were there.

Tristan's eyes were black. He whooshed straight to Brandt, who looked like he was rotting with that black skin, blood gushing from his mouth.

"He has the dagger!" Kyla screeched but it didn't matter. Brandt hadn't stopped throwing up blood when Tristan got to him, leaned over, and ripped his heart clean out of his chest. He whipped it against the wall and then Tristan's black eyes were on Kyla's throat, which was bleeding.

She leaned forward, showing him that her hands were tied and he looked to Sam and Sergey.

"Untie her," He went to the bathroom and turned the water on.

Ouch.

Sam rushed over and started untying Kyla's hands.

"Sam! Sasha? Is Sasha okay? She's in trouble. And Kyle! Where's Kyle? Brandy..."

"She's okay, love. She got into it with Brandy, who tried to detain her, but Sasha tore her apart and got hidden in the safe room in another house down the way until we arrived. Your brother's blood made her strong enough; Brandy didn't stand a chance."

"Thank God. Kyle is here, in another room with some of this guy's goons."

"No, we got him. He's okay. Goons: not okay."

"Phew. Where is he?"

"He's in the truck with Jonathan."

"Phew."

"Let's roll," Tristan said, coming out of the bathroom, drying his hands.

"Let me and Sergey take care of clean-up. You two head back. We'll find our way."

Tristan nodded and grabbed Kyla's hand and walked her into the bathroom and then hefted her up by the waist onto the vanity.

She looked at his face. His angry face.

He hadn't looked her in the eye yet.

He lifted a washcloth from the towel rack, ran water and liquid soap over it and started wiping her throat.

She winced.

He shook his head, "It's blistered where he had his teeth on you. Hang on." He soaped it, rinsed the soap off, and then he put his mouth on the sore spot and it brought instant soothing.

"Tristan?"

"What?"

Her lip trembled.

"Why won't you look at me?"

His eyes met hers. They were still black.

"I'm trying to get my head together, Kyla. I'm a little bit fucked up right now."

"Fucked up?"

"I'm about to rip everything in sight apart. I'm about to tear my own heart out."

"What?"

His eyes met hers again, returning to blue, and he was absolutely wrecked, ravaged.

She sobbed and put her arms around him and pulled him close. "Don't do that."

He nodded and let out a long breath.

"You're supposed to comfort me after rescuing me, not refuse to look at me and then threaten to take yourself away from me."

"I'm sorry, princess. I can't even... I can't take this shit anymore. I wanna take you and go live in a fucking mountain cave and keep everyone the fuck away from you. I would never ever have sent you to that island if I thought... fuck. Brandt made an excuse to avoid coming for the meeting we had today. I didn't know it was because he was planning to go to the island. Didn't know Brandy was his twin. How did I miss that? Fuck."

"Oh Tristan," she kissed his forehead, "It's not your fault."

"I keep failing, princess. Why?"

"You're here. I'm safe. You didn't fail."

He wrapped her up tight in his arms and carried her out of the hotel room. Sergey and Sam were bent over Brandt, rolling him in plastic.

He put her onto her feet when they got outside and then Kyla and Tristan kept going, hand-in-hand, down the parking lot to the end, where there was a big dark SUV with the engine running.

The passenger door opened, and a tall, dark, and beautiful man stepped out. He looked like he could be Tristan's brother.

"Kyla, Jonathan Walker. Your future father-in-law."

It was dim, but Kyla was astonished at the resemblance. No wonder Tristan was so beautiful. Between Taryn and this man, holy moly.

"Hi," Kyla said to Jonathan, and then glanced at Tristan and said, "That better not have been my proposal, either."

Jonathan smiled with dimples.

Holy shit.

Her heart skipped a beat.

"Nice to meet the princess, finally." He winked and got into the back seat. Tristan put her in the front passenger seat.

Kyle was sitting in the back seat, looking glazed over but otherwise fine.

Tristan got into the driver's seat and backed out.

His hand went to her thigh. Her hand rested on top of his.

Two Hours Later

THEY WERE BACK AT THE house next door to Sasha's. Jonathan and Kyle were at Sasha's house. She expected that all was well, and that Sergey and Sam would soon follow.

She and Tristan were in bed.

They'd just gotten there and she knew he was still 'off'.

"Guess you have a lot to tell me," she said.

He nodded, "Later. Right now, there's nothing but us. Is that okay?"

"It *so* is. Now, please feed me my prince, I'm starving!"

Epilogue

One Month Later

SASHA HAD FOUND A WAY to synthesize Kyle's blood. Working with some other vampire doctors and combining their research gave Sasha the ability to offer a supplement for vampire females as well as herself, in order to regulate their hormones. This could make a lot of vampresses a whole lot less bitchy. It wasn't going to be rolled out immediately to the general vampire public; there were a few test cases to try it out on first.

Tristan nominated his mother.

And of course, Sasha was also taking it. She said she'd no longer feed from Kyle.

Taryn had now been taking it for a week and although he'd kept her away from Kyla, he said it seemed like it was actually working. Taryn and Jonathan were trying to continue their relationship from where it left off. Kyla didn't know how it was going, really, but Tristan was feeling cautiously positive about all of it. Tristan and his father were getting to know one another. And that was going very well.

Tristan got a lot of insight about the past from Sergey's father, Dmytro Voitenko. He'd found out his father had been put in that pit in time-out by Alexander due to the fact that he was ready to take off with his pregnant wife and join the coalition. Alexander found out and stopped it. He got caught up in a war with the coalition that took up so much of his time that he opted to keep Taryn and Tristan safe and secret. He had them guarded from a distance while she raised Tristan alone. He had a plan B. He was trying to raise an alternate, so he could choose which prince might become king, but that didn't work out. Tristan told Kyla that when he was a kid his mother had always joked how she never knew how she stretched a dollar so well. Taryn got periodic infusions into her bank account and was mesmerized into thinking nothing of it.

Some coalition members took out that plan B Kovac family. Violently. Some reorganization had to happen within the coalition and possibly with Lucian's involvement. That was still being investigated. Some of them were exterminated.

Now the coalition was getting stronger. Key members were going public. Adrian was gone. The European breeding program was on the verge of being shut down, too.

The remaining human pets at The Constantin Center were being relocated. Some were being given new identities, some were being turned. Some were being moved overseas. Some were so far gone from what they'd been through that a task force was being put together to figure out what to do for them.

There was still hedonism in vampirism. There were still women being taken from their lives and fed on, sexually interfered with, and then returned to their lives none the wiser, but things were on the right path and there was now a democracy going into place to deal with things in a way that didn't come from a place of elitism.

Tristan decided to contact Andre Tsakos. He had to talk to Andre about some Kovac business. He asked Andre to relocate from Cyprus and step in for the USA, taking over Brandt Brooks' position with Kovac Capital. Tristan said that Andre and Rebecca were going to travel to The Constantin Center and that was where Tristan had planned to approach Rebecca, make her the offer of trying out Sasha's formula. He was planning to keep Kyla far away from her, though.

Kyla had asked Tristan to recommend that The Center be renamed. Perhaps to The Jasper Voitenko Center. Sergey's mother Anya was also a doctor and she'd been instrumental in helping Sasha.

One of the European doctors worked with Adrian's serum to block mesmerization and decoded the recipe easily. It worked on Kyle. Kyle was still pondering whether or not he wanted to be vampire. He and Sasha had a conversation about it and he told Kyla he was still thinking things over. It was nice that he was lucid all the time. He and Tristan even got along pretty well. He still had his issues with vampires after all he'd been through, but he was coming around, thinking about his future. She wasn't sure where things were at with him and Sasha, really, but he told Kyla he wanted to find their mother and sisters and talk to them. He knew Lyle and Katya from occasional visits to the compound and he'd known the sisters before they were turned; they lived at The Constantin Center with him for a while. He wanted to approach them about the serum as well, but agreed to wait until Taryn and possibly one or two others had seen some results. There was a niece, as well. She was okay for the time being at boarding school, but Kyla and Kyle were interested in learning more about her.

Sam took a stock of that anti-mesmerization serum for himself and had planned to start dating. He wanted to connect with someone, he'd said. He was planning to play the field a little bit and see how that went. He said he'd sworn off female vamps for the foreseeable future, after what'd happened with Brandy, who Kyla suspected he was actually falling for, before things went wrong.

There was a lot happening with the dismantling of the breeding program at The Constantin Center. A lot happening with some of the medications and formulas to help vampires with their urges, their hormones. It was still early days.

Despite Brandt, Claudio, and Adrian now out of the way, there were a few unhappy elitist council and board members to deal with. Tristan, Sergey, Sergey's father Dmytro, and a few other elders all met with the top North American vampire council to discuss proposed changes, including an elected council government of sorts, and either royal, true vamp, or turned vamp could run for office. A court would be appointed as well. Lucian Kovac would go on trial for multiple murders. He was involved with the coalition against the breeding program but had been twisted, apparently mostly due to jealousy of Alexander. Adrian claimed Lucian had taken out dozens of people housed at The Constantin Center almost thirty-six years earlier in order to stop the breeding program. He'd allegedly murdered pets or wives of several senior council members as well as elders. One of those women was Sergey's wife, Anastasia Voitenko. No one could seem to read Lucian for the truth. He was quite demented, which might have been why.

Sergey wanted to kill Lucian when he was pulled out of the ground, but Tristan had convinced him to put him on trial instead. To do things the democratic way. It was a bone of contention since Tristan had already killed Adrian Constantin for fucking with his life, so Sergey and Tristan had gotten heated about it. In the end, Sergey had agreed, the day before they opened the crypt, to see about doing things in a just and fair way. And that was part of why Tristan had relented with Kyla about Jackson and about not putting people, as much as they might deserve it, into the pits with two hungry vampires who hadn't eaten in decades.

Esther, the housekeeper, was now a vampire, and had also started on Sasha's serum. She'd experienced reverse aging and was working to help run the housekeeping and management of The Constantin Center. She'd filled in a lot of the blanks about her twenty odd years of service to Alexander Kovac. She'd be testifying in court to some of those events, including events related to Lucian Kovac, when that time came.

Tristan and Kyla started renovating the home next to Sasha's home on the island. They also travelled back and forth to Toronto for meetings related to Kovac, as well as to Arizona where things were happening. They were busy. Kovac had been reorganized somewhat.

Tristan had recruited some turned vampires with excellent resumes. Things were looking good.

Two Months Later

Kyla got her period again. She'd skipped it the previous month but hadn't got a positive on a pregnancy test and she was, to put it mildly, ***Hell. On. Wheels***.

Tristan was still working hard at helping to establish the new world of vampire councils.

He was also working hard to deal with Kyla, tolerate her temper tantrums as well as deal with her insatiable sex drive. He'd told her that he hadn't sensed ovulation so she didn't know if his senses regarding that bodily function hadn't come back, or if she wasn't ovulating for some reason. She was worried about it, obsessive about it. But she was biologically driven to feed and have sex.

Tristan thought life was pretty damn good.

Three Months Later

"We're gonna be late, princess!" Tristan had called.

"I'm done, I'm done!" Kyla got to the bottom of the stairs, thinking they were leaving hella early to go to dinner. It was just past lunch time!

They were going for a boat ride. She had been excited about it. They were at their place on the island, which was starting to look and seriously *feel* like home, but Tristan had told her to dress up for this date, that they were taking a boat ride and going out for dinner.

Dinner. In a public place. She was stoked.

Tristan was still very protective, but the fact that she was seriously strong helped. Feeding several times, a day helped her become very strong, as was evidenced in a recent argument where she lost it on him, he'd hauled her over his knee, spanked her and told her that he was gonna spank her until he flipped her brat switch off. Kyla had gotten very angry and held her own during a wrestling match with him, and then pissed off turned to very horny, with Kyla fighting her way to be on top during sex and they'd both gotten off on that so much that she knew he knew she was badass enough to handle a lot thrown at her. It definitely helped that in addition to knowing she was gaining strength as the days went by that any vamp who dared to try to drink her blood would become violently ill and ill enough to give Kyla an advantage to end the vamp or get away.

She wore a red chiffon swing style dress that she'd bought on a shopping trip a few days back with Sasha. It was feminine and sassy, and Tristan's favourite colour.

Tristan had gone on the trip, too, but had gone into Seattle for a meeting while Kyla and Sasha shopped. Her vampress escort, the dagger in the holster under her sundress, and her emerging bad assedness had given him the confidence necessary to be apart in public. It was a huge step in getting over what she figured was a bit like posttraumatic stress disorder that made him extremely protective. But he probably always would be, despite her emerging bad-assedness.

She'd gone for a trim and had taken about 12 inches off her hair. That was something Tristan hadn't been too happy about.

She still had oodles of hair; it was still past her shoulders, but he had a little bit of a prick switch flipped about it. He got over it in about a day. The three blowjobs probably helped.

He was dressed up, too. He looked delicious in a black suit with a dark blue dress shirt, no tie, his eyes standing out like always, piercing, beautiful.

"Hello gorgeous!" He helped her into the boat and kissed behind her ear, "You look delicious enough to eat."

"Thank you; you do too."

He really did!

WHEN THEY GOT TO THE mainland there was a car waiting for them. They were driving to Portland. The restaurant was called Venetia and Tristan said that every vamp he knew ate there when they were in Portland; the food was reportedly to die for.

It was a romantic little Italian place. Dim. Red and white checked table cloths. Candles on the table.

The man who seated them was in a tuxedo and spoke in English with a thick Italian accent, complimenting Tristan on how beautiful Kyla was.

The food was amazing; Kyla loved the pizza. The place was quiet. There was just one other couple, sitting at a table way on the other side. She had gorgeous long red curly hair with eyes that were so striking, like blue sapphires, that they were reminiscent of a royal vamp. Perhaps she had vamp DNA, maybe enchanted blood.

Her guy was tall, blond, and looked like a male model. They were totally into one another and paid no mind to Tristan and Kyla at all.

Tristan reached for her hand when they were served dessert, which was the most delectable-looking sky-high piece of tiramisu she'd ever seen. It had at least 8 layers and on top of a mountain of swirly frosting sat a big plump chocolate-dipped cherry that had a knot in the stem.

"I think we're gonna have to get this packed up to go, babe," Kyla rubbed her belly, "I'm stuffed."

Tristan shook his head and squeezed her hand. "You don't want your dessert with coffee in it? Who are you and what have you done with my fiancée?"

She laughed, "Uh, no. Calling me your fiancée and skipping the actual proposal won't cut it, either."

"Okay, then how's this?" he asked and stood up, lifted the cherry, which was carefully camouflaging a beautiful diamond engagement ring, and put it aside.

He lifted the ring, sucked the frosting off in a very seductive way, (*that mouth!*) and got on bended knee.

She heard a happy-sounding gasp from the redhead at the other table.

"I want to spend my life giving you your happily ever after. Being one another's all-we'll-ever-need buffets. Hundreds of years, thousands of them, if we're really lucky. Which we are. We are so lucky. I want you to be my wife. Will you marry me, Kyla?"

She burst into happy tears and nodded.

Holy Swoon, Batman!

He kissed her, and it tasted like Tiramisu. The best Tiramisu ever.

"DON'T YOU DARE RIP my dress!" she breathed against his lips as he backed her into the seriously swanky hotel room in Portland, where they were spending the night.

"Get it off quick then, baby. I don't know if I can stop myself."

She was preserving that dress. It was the dress she got engaged in.

It was also the dress she wore the night she got pregnant with their daughter, a beautiful curly-haired cherub-faced princess with her daddy's blue eyes and dimples.

But Tristan didn't call their daughter princess, even though Kyla thought of her that way. He still called Kyla his princess on a daily basis.

He affectionately nicknamed their daughter his little Pixie. She was indeed little, she was sugary sweet in personality, but occasionally, she was also extremely mischievous.

When Tristan and Kyla made love in that hotel room the night of their engagement, they knew that conception happened because once again, Kyla's womb felt like it was set on fire when Tristan climaxed and both of their eyes glowed when they got that sugary-sweet release.

She cried through that orgasm, tears of uninhibited joy.

"Did you know I was ovulating?" she asked later that night, snuggled into him in bed, feeling joy leak out of her eyes and emanate from her pores knowing that they'd made a baby and that she would actually survive the birth.

"Not until we got here," he snuggled her close, "It was like you spontaneously ovulated. I guess all I had to do to get that to happen was propose."

He was smiling huge, with dimples.

"You did good." Kyla wrapped one arm around Tristan and kissed his chin cleft and then a dimple.

His eyes sparkled and then he flipped her to her back and moved down her body until his fangs sank beautifully into the inside of her thigh.

The End

(For now...)

From the Author:

SO, IT TOOK A LITTLE over a year to get all three books out and I'm sorry for those who waited between installments, but I didn't want to say Goodbye to these characters, I guess.

So, no cliffhanger, but the door is intentionally left slightly ajar (Who am I kidding? Wide open! Why? Because I'm thinking we need stories for some of these other characters and as things progress, you might want to see where things are at with Tristan and Kyla, right? I hope so!).

I hope you enjoyed this series!

When I first started thinking about this book I had very dark and graphic scenes in my brain involving the "nectar". I'd started to wonder what'd happen if a vampire was addicted to it, being that it's so taboo. I had daydreams about the plot and how horrifying it'd be for the heroine to see him getting off on something that she'd typically deem disgusting and unfathomable. I also read some interesting things about beliefs and rituals associated with supernatural things associated with that blood. I was very intrigued!

I shied away from my original dark vision in some of these scenes in the first two books because I thought I'd get severe reactions to the plot line for the book. Maybe I still went too dark for some of you. Maybe others would've liked to have seen it get a whole lot darker. In the end, I hope I managed to strike a decent balance between the two extremes to give you an interesting story that was fun to read and get lost in.

I plan to finish the Black & Blue novella that I started writing for Tristan's POV (I didn't know Essence would give you some of that so I haven't gone back to it yet) and there may be some extra dark scenes written so I can purge the words yet to be realized on paper that are trapped somewhere in *my* kaleidoscope of a brain.

I hope you enjoyed this story. At this point in time I'm considering adding books to my 'to-write' list for:

- Sam
- Kyle
- Rebecca (I'm fascinated by the evil vampress murderess character who started out as a sick sweet girl. I bet hers is a story that'll be interesting to tell!)

And maybe more. We'll see what happens and who else we meet on the journey and see how their lives are progressing as well as get an opportunity to learn more about some of the other characters in the books. ☺

No ETA for those yet.

Acknowledgements:

Thanks to Pauline, Susan, Jennifer, and Divya for beta reading Essence for me!

And big thanks to Kass for your feedback and even bigger thanks for putting the cherry on top for me. Cheers for that, babes! ;)

Thanks for coming along with me for this ride and for those who bought the first book in April of 2015 when I released it, thanks very VERY much for waiting a year to get to book 3. I'm sorry it took this long but I truly hope it was worth it!

HUGS!

Book One Acknowledgements:

Thanks to those who offered to quickly read and provide feedback before Nectar went live (Nicola, Pauline, Rachel, Tiffany, Elaine, Tonya, Mariah).

Playlist:

Love Bites, Def Leppard

Lips of an Angel, Hinder

Bring me to Life, Evanescence

Note & Acknowledgements

Thank you to my Facebook & Goodreads & Twitter friends. I LOVE YOU GUYS!

Big thanks to the members of my Nectar Spoiler group on Facebook who cheered me on through writer's block!

Thank* you*, dear reader, for helping me live my dream! I write not for fans or for praise nearly as much as writing because I need to.

My fans make living this dream even better than I ever dreamed it could be!

Thanks ***so*** much for supporting indie authors! If you enjoy this book, please consider leaving a review on where you got this book as well as on Goodreads and social media. Reviews, social follows, and shares all help me get found by readers like yourself who like these sorts of stories.

Want to connect with me on social media? Links are below!

Like DD's Facebook page at http://www.facebook.com/ddprincebooks to be informed about the timelines for upcoming books. Subscribe to The Scoop, DD's newsletter for book news, teasers, beta reading opportunities, and contests: http://ddprince.com/neswletter-signup/

Follow me on Twitter[1].

Check out my website: http://ddprince.com

I'm on Pinterest[2].

And follow me on Goodreads[3]! I'd love to know what you're reading

1. http://twitter.com/ddprincebooks
2. https://www.pinterest.com/ddprincebooks/
3. https://www.goodreads.com/author/show/13177248.D_D_Prince

What else can you read from DD Prince?

The Dominator, by DD Prince was her first release and is a dark romance involving a family with ties to organized crime. This book has a flesh payment plot, an arranged marriage, and a dominating / damaged alpha male who falls in love with a naïve girl who believes in love and family.

The Dominator has also become a series, without cliffhangers, but should be read in order. After reading The Dominator, Tommy & Tia's story consider reading Truth or Dare; The Dominator II, for Dario Ferrano's story. The Dominator III; Fete is expected to be released in early to mid 2016.

About DD Prince

DD Prince is an indie author who has been writing ever since she learned she could put pen to paper and create with words. She has a passion for faith, family, friends, food, and words. She lives in Niagara Falls, Canada with her own alpha, who she fell in love with at 17 years old and they're still going strong. She has two wonderful messy boys, 2 cats, and a talking Pacific Parrotlet (who probably thinks of her as his girlfriend). She's a Smut Muffin who loves to read and write dark, contemporary, and paranormal love stories, especially when love -—whether dark, sweet, or co-dependent is the anecdote.

DD's favorite author, 1-click, no questions asked, is Kristen Ashley. If you haven't read a KA book you are missing out!

Other favourites include: Judy Blume, Rohinton Mistry, Stephen King, Anne Rice, CJ Roberts, Pepper Winters, SC Stephens, JA Huss, Tiffany Reisz, and so many others! Some of her favourite books were written by indie authors and some of the listed indie authors above gave her the courage to put her work out there.

She has many characters to introduce, stories to tell, and looks forward to sharing them.

Sample from The Dominator, by DD Prince

SAMPLE OF THE DOMINATOR:

Buy a copy of this dark romance – learn more at ddprince.com.

This is a story about Tia and Tommy, a couple thrown together through an arranged marriage. She's young, naïve, and wants to believe in love and family despite growing up in foster care. He's a broody and controlling alpha male who stands to inherit a business with extensive ties to organized crime. He doesn't have any use for women beyond having them sate his depraved carnal desires until the two are matched by their fathers, two men with secrets.

The Dominator does not have a cliff-hanger.

The Dominator, by DD Prince

Tia

In a few weeks it'll be my nineteenth birthday. Some say it should be my ninetieth as I'm what they call an old soul. A few weeks after my birthday I'll be striking out on my own. Well, sort of. I'll be transitioning out of the foster care system and into my first apartment.

My foster parents, Rose and Cal, who have been wonderful to me for the past 5 and a half years have arranged for me to rent the apartment above the garage at Rose's parents' home. So it'll be my place but I'll still be close to people who are like family; the only family I've had for a very long time.

Because I've been a ward of the court for the past few years, the "system" will supplement my income through college and pay for tuition, too. The foster grandparents' home would be the perfect blend of being on my own and having someone around in case I need help.

Nona and Nonno Caruso have been like I'd expect real grandparents would be to me and the half a dozen girls that live with Rose and Cal Crenshaw at the moment. I'll be the 5th girl to move into the garage apartment; the family has been fostering for years and they've helped over 100 teen girls have a home and a stable family for at least a little while.

I could've opted to move out and finish my victory lap of high school from my own place on my 18th birthday but they invited me to stay and being an only child who embraced this busy, hectic, and crazy house full of laughter and love and great food, I was happy they invited me to stay the extra year.

I've been in care since I was 9 and was moved around quite a bit before finding home here with the Crenshaws. My Mom committed suicide and that led to my already troubled father falling completely off the rails, landing me into the foster care system.

His partying and gambling got progressively worse and he'd always had trouble holding a job which was amplified without my

Mom around. My Dad tried to move me in with his sister, my Aunt Carol, one night after he got beat up pretty bad right in front of me by loan sharks, but she'd said *Not a chance*. She actually said that right in front of me. Shame on her. And shame on Dad for asking her in front of me.

Not only did she refuse but she then called social services after coming to the apartment to argue with him because of seeing the way Dad and I were living. They took custody of me so that he could get his life together but he never actually did manage to do that for long enough to get me back. I was better off in care anyway. I thrived in it, especially once I got to the Crenshaw home.

Dad seemed like he *wanted* to try a few times -—he'd go long periods of time without seeing me and then he'd turn up for a visit, tell me he was doing better, then he'd sometimes even do a monthly visit two months in a row but inevitably over the past 9+ years, the more common pattern was for him to get my hopes up and then let me down and disappear for many months at a time. I stopped having expectations of him a long time ago. Becoming a ward of the court made it simpler. They stopped trying to make him try.

I've been through a few different foster homes but Rose and Cal's has been, by far, the most nurturing of all. I moved here when I was 13 and not only do they go out of their way to make their home a real home but whatever isn't provided that me or the other girls need through the "system" they take out of their own pockets. Three years ago they bought all us girls bicycles out of their own pockets for Christmas. The year after we got to go to Disney World together, on their dime. They're amazing people and they've helped so many girls get their lives together. I hope to repay them someday.

Rose, a sweet round woman with a heart of gold, tells me all the payment she wants is my happiness and success. And for me to continue to be a part of their family. Come for Christmas, come for special dinners on my birthday whenever I don't have other plans, have them at my wedding someday, think of them as my family. I've been so lucky with them.

Cal is an architect and Rose is a homemaker. They have one son and one daughter. Their son is autistic and one of my favorite people in the world. Their daughter Ruby is amazing too, with all the foster girls and with her little brother. Ruby has become my closest friend, like a sister, really. She's a year younger than me otherwise we'd just get a place together.

I'm lucky to be moving to the Carusos'. It's a cute bachelorette apartment above the garage in a great neighborhood and the grand-parents go to Florida for the winter so a few months after I arrive, I'll have the place totally to myself. Ruby says she'll stay over on the weekends.

I'm starting in school in the fall for social work so I can make a difference in the lives of other kids who might otherwise fall between the cracks. So many kids do and many blame the system. I've had a great social worker all along who has always cared about my safety and happiness. I aim to follow in her footsteps and strive to do the same for other kids.

I wouldn't say I'm a model student or model foster child. I've gotten caught sneaking out to go to parties. I've skipped school a few times. I've gotten drunk and high and I'm not a virgin. But I'm not a slut and I'm not a bad person. I know what I want from life and I'm grateful for the blessings I have.

I miss my Mom. I still don't know why she killed herself. I wouldn't say she was a happy person, and maybe her unhappiness ran deeper than I knew. I also don't know why my Dad couldn't seem to pull his life together. Even though he was never together before she died, he was really really messed up afterwards.

I don't know how often he checks it but I've sent him a Facebook message to tell him about high school grad. I'm not counting on him making it. He's never made it to any school plays, birthday parties, or anything else that I've asked him to come to. When Dad shows up it's generally very random. I don't know why I sent him an invite but I guess I've never totally given up on him. I've always tried to believe that people are redeemable.

Tommy

"Her name is Athena. They call her Tia. She's yours if you want her."

"Mine?"

"Yeah, yours." Pop waved his hand dismissively, "For whatever."

I was sitting in my father's office absorbing this news, news that a nineteen year old girl was coming to me as a gift from my father, that she comes to him as payment for unpaid gambling debts. Pop said he was about to have the news of the payment arrangement conveyed to her father and then I could do what I wanted with her. "Whatever" meant I could put her on the streets under one of the pimps on my down line. I could also sell her off overseas into the slave trade and pocket the profits myself. Yeah, we had contacts in a variety of industries, including those of the seedy underworld. Looking at her photo, she'd fetch way more on the black market than the debt her Daddy owed. Way more.

Or, I could keep her for myself. My cock twitched, looking at her. Silky straight long chestnut brown hair, big jade green eyes, beautiful skin, full lips, fit yet curvy, soft-looking. She sure didn't look like she was just about to graduate high school.

Re the down line, our family business has somewhat of an MLM set up. We receive commissions based on a variety of pursuits. Some call us mafia. I don't really use that word. You might say I say tomato, you say tom-atto and while it's all the same fruit, of course, there are many varieties of tomatoes. We're businessmen. Yeah, not all of what we do is legal but it's not all shady business deals and gambling debts, either. The way it's set up creates multiple layers and plenty of income streams and the money flows up to the family coffers from a variety of areas, like security, construction, and a variety of retail and whole-sale businesses. There's also a grayer type of security, loan sharking, prostitution, and drugs. We deal in herb, not in chemicals, and it's a very small part of our business.

Yeah, organized crime exists in the 21st century. No, it's not always as glamorous as it's portrayed on screens and it's not always seedy, either. It's a living. Some days are fairly ordinary. Some days are awesome. Some days we have to make tough decisions. I'd had to make many tough decisions so far and I was sure there would be many more.

My father was a working guy who was connected around town and he wanted to start his own business. So he and his best friend, a guy also connected, started a construction company. The company did well; they were smart businessmen. Over time, they saw the need for a number of other services and they had the capital to begin expansions so they could better provide for their family without paying 50% of their earnings in tax. The company has grown by leaps and bounds in the past 30 years. After the construction company, he opened a coffee shop. He now has six of those coffee shops and it's moving to a franchising model in the next 5-7 months. He's silent partner in some restaurants, in some hotels, a few nightclubs, too. Some of those night clubs have back room card games; some that deal in big money.

Drugs and druggies, alcohol and alcoholics, hookers, nymphos, bookies, gamblers, loan sharks... they're always gonna be out there. Why shouldn't we profit from it? We have the brains and the brawn and the green. And because of that we've got the cars, the houses, the fat bank accounts and the high tax brackets so we look above board to the tax man and have the fat rainy day funds in our mattresses, attics, basements, whatever. And this isn't all we do; it's just a way of supplementing things.

Why bust our chops for a bit better than minimum wage and work like a dog our whole life to put money into a retirement plan we may never get to spend? Successful men get between what men want and the source. That's what we do. You want to bet on the races? We can help. You want to get your rocks off, find someone to cater to your fetishes? We'll hook you up. You need money to pay off your gambling debts or start up a new venture? Guess, what? We can help there, too. It all fits like a puzzle together nicely. People need protection. People need money. People need help from builders to build those businesses they want us investing in so we do the investing and we do the building. And people need vices so that the end of a hard day they've had a little fun. People need to pay up, too, though.

And because men can have too much of a good thing and get caught up in the sins of the flesh and the thrill of the bet it can get dirty. Some people don't pay their debts. Some people need to be dealt with. Sometimes people get greedy and try to take from us. We have to make hard decisions sometimes. People come to play; they must be prepared to pay.

I'm 29, Pop's namesake, I'm inches away from taking over the family business and we feed ourselves and look after our family this way so we take it seriously. If people borrow money, they have to pay their debts. We prefer cash as our currency of choice, of course, but sometimes creative financing comes into play when someone can't pay.

My family may be wealthy but I've earned my stripes, too. Pop didn't believe in sticking a silver spoon in my mouth. He clawed his way up and believe me, he made sure I had to do the same. He called it character-building. I called him a hard ass.

I started at the bottom and worked my way up. I bought my first place, a downtown condo, with cash, no mortgage, cash I earned from age 14 to 19. No one could ever say that I didn't deserve to sit in my father's chair when that day came.

Sitting in my father's office and getting told he was handing over a flesh payment on a debt to me was intriguing, to say the least. I'd never seen him take this kind of payment before.

"Why are you letting the guy pay like this? This isn't our style. There's more to it. Spill."

Pop shrugged, "This was my choice, not his. Too many questions, Tommy. Just think of it as a gift. A bonus for all your hard work. Look at her."

He pushed the picture closer. I'd already seen it. My Pop didn't like questions, that was for damn sure. I guess I sort of inherited that quality from him. But I needed to know the whole story, particularly because he was probably only a few key decisions away from retiring. He didn't look ready to retire, he's only in his 50's and looks like he's in his 40's. But my Pop has worked hard to build his empire and he says he wants to enjoy the fruits of that labor before he's too old to really enjoy it.

"What kind of guy gives his daughter up for debts? The debt is measly," I said. He looked reflective and a long moment passed. "Pop..."

"I bought his debt. There's history. Long family history. This guy! He..." he waved his hand, "He was like one of those, what do you call... fan girls. He tried to crawl up all our asses and worm his way into the business. But he was always a liability so he didn't get the time of day. He disrespected me many years ago. Took something from me. He paid a price. But I don't know that his price was enough," he tapped on his temple with his index finger, "and some nights I still lay awake thinking about what he took from me. This daughter; she's all he's got of any value. And look at her. I'm thinking she's young, she's beautiful, you could make her yours. Marry her, maybe. Your call, I know, but that's what I think. It'd be a shame to put her to work or sell her off. I saw opportunity. I acted. Two birds with one stone. Pay this guy back by taking his last thing of value. Take her to pay his paltry debt and help our family move forward." He shrugged like it was no biggie but was looking at me studiously. I could see that it *was* a biggie.

I shook my head. This was Pop's way. He was telling me this Tia was mine to do what I wanted with but dropping his suggestion of 'marry her, maybe' was his way of saying, "Marry her" without outright demanding it. If I didn't, he'd be disappointed. People know better than to disappoint my father. I also know that bonuses aren't in his vocabulary so he isn't giving her to me as a bonus, he's got plans. But my father knows me. He knows better than to tell me what to do outright. When he really wants me to do something, he does this.

"Married, Pop? Who says I'm ready to get married?"

"Tommy, my boy, you're almost 30! When I was thirty I already had 4 kids. You don't become a man until you start a family of your own and need to be a family man to take over the company. You decide who you marry, of course, and this young girl, she's part Irish, half Italian. She's beautiful, she's young so she can be molded into what you need her to be, and that doesn't mean you can't still have your fun. It's your decision, of course, my boy..."

"I'll think it over."

This was the best way to handle my father. He'd been pushing me to get married since I was about 23 but never this bluntly. As his eldest son, it was expected, before I took over the company. I'd been prepped and primed to take over this company ever since I could remember. He'd drilled a lot into my head over the years and I'd jumped through hoops to prove I was worthy. Not just to him, to myself.

To him, settling down showed a commitment to family, showed I was ready to be a man, so to speak. I was sure I'd already proven I was a man many times to my father with tests I'd passed, decisions I'd made, problems I'd taken care of, opportunities and profit I'd brought the business -—he knew I had what it took. My father was a demanding prick and I'd paid the price of being his son many many times. I was all but in charge as it was already. In his mind he wanted me to do this to show everyone, his associates, his enemies...that I was ready to take the helm. It was an old school way of thinking but that was how it was with Pop.

He'd put me at the bottom of the ladder when I was 14 and made me work my way up like any other soldier that worked for him. I knew what it took to take over for him and I knew I was ready. Evidently he thought I needed to take one more step on this journey before he was willing to hand over the keys to the kingdom.

But married? He'd talked about me being married in a "someday when you're married," or "someday when you're a father," "someday when you run this business," way for years but I'd never given getting married much thought. Pop certainly enjoyed being married, he got married often, but despite his love for walking down the aisle he wasn't a man who believed in any sort of marriage sanctity.

Me? Women were a means to an end for me. They satisfied my desires. I had a healthy appetite and an active sex life with as much action as I wanted. I didn't do relationships -—didn't want to, didn't need to. I never had the desire to get serious, to be monogamous. I knew women liked the way I looked and they liked the money, the power, but I hadn't met anyone I cared enough about to take things to any level other than physical. Thomas Ferrano Jr. was a force to be reckoned with in and out of the boardroom, the boxing ring, the bedroom, and more and I'd been busy my whole life, proving myself, focused on the business.

I liked control in and out of the bedroom and was very partial to rough sex. I had my pick of playthings to suit whatever my fancy was on any given day. Blonde, brunette, redhead, African American, Asian, whatever. I'd certainly never met someone I'd wanted to marry or even date seriously. Dating someone? Getting serious? That'd feel too much like giving up control to me. Not interested.

Never desired having the same woman in my bed night after night, rarely was I interested in even having the same woman twice. Who needed a woman nagging me, thinking she could tell me what she didn't want me doing, asking me inane questions that I couldn't be bothered to answer? I had no desire niggling at me yet for kids, either. I had nieces and nephews through my two sisters and the kids were fantastic but they weren't my problem on a daily basis. Being Uncle Tommy was just fine by me.

Married? Sheesh. I knew how Pop's brain worked and to him, it was necessary and I'd need to do it to get what I wanted. Full control. I wanted control, control in all areas of my life. Pop was slipping just left of his prime; it was time. Pop was missing the boat on some great opportunities that could make us a lot of money and get us out of the small time game in a few areas. I could take the company to greater heights, areas that made more money and lowered our risk. If I had to get married to get him to give me the keys to the kingdom and for me to not have to run business decisions by him, maybe that's what I'd have to do.

He and I butted heads a lot; I guess what everyone says is true; we're a lot alike. And if I was head of the business I'd want to think about an heir to take over for me some day, rather than promoting one of my nephews.

My buddy and business associate John was married and had kids and he also had power. He and I got hammered one night at the sex club I belonged to and a conversation came up about my lack of desire to hook up with one girl night after night. He'd talked about how fucking amazing it was to have a submissive, a woman who would bow down and do anything he wanted to please him. I had that whenever I wanted. It wasn't the same girl each time but there was no shortage of women in the club who'd pant in heat when I approached them. Johnny said I didn't get it, didn't understand what I was missing, how amazing it was to have her submission, her trust, her commitment. He played at the club. His wife was cool with it. His wife liked threesomes, even. And his wife didn't tell him what to do; she yielded to him in everything. He told me there were relationship parameters and he knew what her limits were and said he had loads of room to play.

I'd laughed and slapped him on the shoulder and said, "See Johnny, that's where you and I are different. The only way in the world that'd go down for me is if there were no limits, no safe words."

Control. Full control. I looked at the picture sitting in front of me again and the way she looked... I thought about control. I thought about controlling the business, being in full control of my own destiny, and I couldn't help but think about controlling her.

Pop was watching me mull things over. *Fuck*. I looked at him, conceding, "I'll meet her. We'll see."

My father got that look on his face that he gets when everything is falling into place. That look was one of the very few things that could chill me to the bone.

Tia

Graduation day. How exciting! Two other girls from Rose and Cal's were also graduating so today was a big day at the house. We were all "all dolled" up. My hair was up in a sleek up do that everyone said makes me look a little bit Katy Perry pin-upish. Bright red lips, smoky eyes. Rose told me I looked 25 instead of 19. I feel like I'm older, anyway. Always have. This was probably because of losing my Mom so young.

It was probably also due to being almost on my own for the better part of a year at 9. After Mom died Dad would leave me alone for hours at a time, sometimes overnight, while he nipped out to run "errands". I learned how to make simple meals at that age, to cook and clean up after myself. At 9 I even paid the electric bill once when

I noticed that there was a disconnection notice taped to our door. It was a rare occasion that my Dad's wallet had been full of cash so while he slept off a bender I took the bill and took the money and walked the 3 blocks to the bank and paid it.

Social services hadn't looked too kindly on it, though, when I told them about it in my interview when they'd come over to check on me after my aunt had called. I'd been proud of myself when I told them I could get myself off to school, make my own breakfast and pack my own lunch, and that I'd even paid bills at the bank with money from Daddy's card games.

Yeah, that had gone over *so* well that they hauled me into care. They'd come and found me at home alone with almost no food in the fridge other than some dried out old Chinese take-out but a case of 24 beer in the fridge and nothing but some saltines and beer nuts in the cupboard. The green mat had still been on the dining room table from a poker game Dad had hosted two nights before and it was filled with crushed beer cans and overflowing ashtrays. He'd always told me to stay in my locked room during those games.

Dad turned up drunk in the middle of the meeting and blubbered like a baby in front of the social worker. He was ruined after Mom died. I felt like I had to take care of him back then. Lord knew he couldn't take care of me. I guessed that was what made me an old soul, the fact that I had to be.

Anyway, here I was all ready to graduate high school, wishing my parents were there to see me get handed my diploma, graduating on the honor roll. I didn't know if Dad would make it. I doubted he would. I knew that Rose, Cal, and Susie, my social worker would all be there for me and that was okay.

After the ceremony we had a family celebration planned at Rose & Cal's and tonight there was a big dance and after party planned, too. My ex-boyfriend Nick had been sniffing around me all week and I wasn't looking forward to seeing him tonight.

I'd dumped him a month ago because I found out he was selling pot on the side from his gas station job. Some people would buy gas and when they came in to pay, He'd slip them dope. I wanted no part of that. Yeah, sure, I smoked up once in a while but I had no desire to build my future with a guy who would put his future in jeopardy. He was a loser. I didn't like to think of my Dad as a loser but in reality, that's what he was. I wasn't about to get tied down with a loser of a boyfriend, too.

Nick was trying to win me back. I wanted no part of it. Nick was 22, he was gorgeous, long hair and leather jacket, tattoos, and he was a bad boy. I was attracted to the look and the swagger of bad boys for some reason, but when it all came down to it they'd get dumped as soon as they showed me their true bad boy colors. It sounded dumb, of course, because while I was attracted to them, I didn't want to waste my time on someone going nowhere but downhill.

As I got dressed for grad I thought about the guy that had come into the ice cream parlor I worked at the other day. He'd come in while I was working my last shift and he was well-dressed, as sexy as a movie star, and carried himself with confidence. He was so tall and strong-looking. He was 100% grown-up male and so very different from Nick. Older. Somewhere near 30, I figured, and he gave me tummy flutters like I'd never had before. What would it be to date a guy like that? A guy that oozed sex appeal and power? He seemed so together. A man.

As me and my foster sisters got ready for our big day they were giggly but I was deep in thought about the guy, the ice cream parlor hottie. I hadn't stopped thinking about him the past 2 days and the past 2 nights. But that had been my last day at that job so the chances of seeing him again were small. He'd flirted with me but I'd been like a deer in the headlights. I wished I was older, more confident, and that I'd given him my phone number. I was *so* over Nick, so over guys that were like Nick.

I had a sneaking suspicion Nick was trying to get my attention because he knew that tomorrow I'd be moving into my own apartment. He wanted alone time with me. He and I had done the alone thing plenty of times and I didn't need to go down that road again. It wasn't exactly symbiotic.

Nick texted that he wanted to attend the graduation ceremony but I had only a limited number of tickets to give out for family members and friends and since I had no one but Dad I'd given my extra tickets to the other girls who had other guests. I'd only sent one to my father at his last known address along with the Facebook inbox message and a note to pick his ticket up at the school office if he did get a chance to come.

I was ready for new things. A new place, college in the fall, and new opportunities. Maybe a new guy, too. One who was ready to be a man, not a boy living in 1 bedroom apartment shared with 2 other guys who rotated using the bedroom when they had girls over with the never-innovative sock on the doorknob as the clue that the room was "in use." Gross. I told Nick I wasn't using that room for sex. We'd done it in there once and never again. We'd done it a few times in his car but it was certainly not very fulfilling! Neither the car nor the bedroom had been cleaned in months. He undoubtedly saw my upcoming apartment as an 'in'. No thanks! He'd already texted me three times today, trying to get me to agree to 'talk' later on tonight.

As I walked up on the podium to receive my diploma I had the surprise of my life. My Dad, in the audience, smiling at me. He sat beside Rose, who was chatting softly to him while snapping pictures of me. Nick was sitting behind my Dad, dressed up and smiling at me, too. I avoided his gaze, tried not to think about how handsome he looked. Looks weren't everything! Why was he even here? I bet Ruby gave him a ticket; she'd been trying to get us back together.

After the ceremony was over we were all in the school's courtyard for photos. Dad rushed to me. He looked good. I'd only ever seen him in a suit once, at my Mom's funeral. This was that same suit. He had his dirty blonde hair gelled back and he smelled like expensive cologne. He looked together-looking. Seeing him like this reminded me of how he was before Mom died. His green eyes sparkled. He was good-looking for his age. Everyone said I had his eyes. He'd never been perfect but we did things together. He taught me to cook, I'd hang out with him while he tinkered with his car, he'd hold me high in the air with an airplane ride to bed every night that he was home at bedtime, read me bedtime stories with such effort and emotion, doing different voices for every character. He wasn't the perfect father or husband before she died but after she died, he was like a shell of a man who tried to drink and gamble away his pain.

He swung me around in a giant hug, making me squeal. "Athena! I'm so proud. You look all grown up. Look at you. Someone take our picture!" He called out to the rest of our group and Rose hurried over with her camera. Susie, my social worker, eyed my dad warily.

I knew she'd lost patience with him over the years. Getting me to agree to be a ward of the courts made her life so much easier because she didn't have to continually try to reach him to find out what was what with him, to get him involved in decisions that needed to be made, and so forth. When it'd finally happened and he lost his parental rights it had been 11 months since he'd made contact. He always managed to miss birthdays.

It hurt that he could go that length of time without checking on me, leaving others to raise me. It hurt but I wasn't the sort to start laying blame aloud. I always just thought of him as broken.

He'd found her dead in the bathtub with slit wrists one day. It was a day when I was supposed to have been picked up from school late after a field trip that required parents to pick up the kids because it got us back after 7:00 at night. That night was a long one and I'd sat in the principal's office for hours and hours while they tried to find someone to pick me up. The principal had been huffy and snippy, too, clearly with plans for the evening that had to be cancelled due to this poor little neglected girl who hadn't been picked up from school.

Finally my Aunt Carol had come along and brought me to her home. She hadn't told me about my Mom. She let me overhear her on the phone telling someone else that she was stuck watching me for the evening because my father was a wreck, mourning his dead wife who'd killed herself. What a way for me to find out. She was a witch, my Dad's sister.

She hadn't bothered with me for all these years, just wrote me off. Mom hadn't had any family step up either. I heard she had an older brother but it seemed she was a bit of a black sheep with her family or something, too. I really had no idea. No one sought me out after she died.

I may not have had siblings by blood but there were many foster kids I'd shared homes and rooms with that I thought of as family and would've gladly been an auntie to their kids if I was needed.

So, here Dad was, all smiles for the camera, looking well-fed, well-groomed, and yet there was a weird aura about him, something in his eyes, a nervousness in his laugh. He seemed off, like there was something shifty going on. He kept checking his phone and looking around suspiciously. When everyone had gotten their fill of camera flashes in their eyes Rose tried to corral everyone so we could go back to her house where a big buffet and gifts were waiting.

"Please join us, Gregory," she said to my Dad.

"I'd love to!" he beamed, "Tia, ride with me. We can catch up on the way back."

I nodded, feeling like something was way off. Did he have something to tell me? I was happy to see him. It'd been ages since I'd seen him, but something was off, I could just feel it.

He had a decent enough car, surprisingly. We drove through a coffee shop drive-thru for Dad to get a coffee and me to get an iced cappuccino on our way and then we parked so Dad could get out and have a cigarette first, knowing I wouldn't want him smoking in the car with me.

"Thanks so much for coming, Dad."

"Like I'd miss it!" He gave me an 'Are you kidding' look. As if he hadn't missed other milestones, like my first communion, my confirmation, school plays, every single birthday since my 10th, and so forth.

"What's new, then? You working?" I asked.

He nodded, "Yeah, I've been working at an auto parts place over on Dufferin Street for about 7 months. I do parts counter, a few minor repairs. Got a nice apartment. Got myself a nice girlfriend, too. You'll like her. Sadie. She's a schoolteacher. Teaches kindergarten. This is her car."

"Really? That's awesome." It'd been the longest he'd held down a job for ages and this was the first relationship he'd ever told me about. He knew what was going on with me already; I'd filled him in with my Facebook message where I'd invited him to come to the grad ceremony.

"Something off, though, Dad? You seem stressed."

He nodded quickly and lifted the lid off his coffee and took a sip, "Yeah, we need to talk."

I frowned, "Okay?"

He sat down on a picnic table outside the coffee shop and picked at an imaginary thread on his suit pants, "I'm in some trouble. Chickens coming home to roost, sorta thing."

My heart lurched, "What kind of trouble?"

He let out a heavy sigh, "I have old debts from when I was gambling. I haven't gambled in a long time, Tia. I go to a support group. The debt was sold to someone high up in organized crime, someone who hates my guts and has a vendetta from years back. He's decided to make life -—difficult."

I nodded, urging him to continue, feeling dread spread through my gut.

"I need to figure this out, find a way to get them paid. They've already given me an extension but they want a marker. I just need a few days to sort this out. I was hoping you could help me."

"How? How could I help you?" I didn't have any money. Well, $248 in my savings account from my job at the ice cream parlor but that was it.

"You need to be my marker." He said, resigned.

"Your what?"

"Yeah. I know it's not ideal but I have a plan to clear it up and then there won't be anything else. This is the last loose end from my old life, Tia. I'm really sorry to drag you into this but I have no choice."

"Dad..." I began.

I noticed a black SUV pull in beside us. The passenger window rolled down and a shady-looking guy in the passenger side wearing dark sunglasses was eyeing us.

"Tia, it's just for a few days. I have a plan, I..." He glanced over his shoulder and then his shoulders slumped.

"Dad, you can't expect me to...who are these people? What on earth have you gotten yourself into?"

Dad's face took on a look of desperation, "Sweet pea, I'm sorry. I've been such a fuck up."

He hadn't called me that since I was little, since before Mom died.

"You need to go with these guys. Trust me. I'll make this better. It'll be better."

"It's my high school fucking graduation!" I shrieked, looking over to the SUV. Was this them?

Dad blanched. I've never before sworn at him, never raised my voice at him. I've always treated him like he's fragile. The front passenger and rear passenger doors of the black SUV opened and two big burly guys in suits looked out.

"Problem, O'Connor?" the burly guy from the back seat asked in a gravelly voice.

"Naw, no. Not at all. Not at all. We just need one minute." Dad was like a stuttering fool, "Tia, please." His eyes plead with me.

"Dad..." I folded my arms. I could not believe he came to my grad to set me up to be his marker. That it was the only reason he came!

Burly guy from the front seat lifted his shades off, "We need to go, O'Connor."

I took a step back as the two of them got out, leaving their doors opened, revealing a big scary looking black dude in the back and a younger blond pissed-off looking but hot guy in a suit in the driver's seat.

Dad leaned forward and took my hands in his and his face had a look of desperation that made my scalp prickle, "They'll kill me," he whispered.

What the—-? What would make him use me as a marker? Did he think they wouldn't kill *me*? Did he think they wouldn't hurt me? How much money did he owe these guys and how would he even pay them off?

He'd let me down countless times. In the early days of foster care he'd promise that his life was almost together enough to gain custody back. He'd promise to take me places, buy me things -—I never needed or wanted things but he always tossed promises around and he never ever kept them. Why would I believe him now? Why would he put me at risk, make this even an option?

"Just hang tight. They'll keep you comfortably in a luxury hotel suite or something like that. You'll be fine. Look at it like a little getaway."

I tilted my head at my dad, dumbfounded. This couldn't be real. Back at Rose and Cal's, they were waiting for me. There was a big beautiful cake congratulating me, Mia, and Bethany for all graduating. Ruby, her brother Connor, the other girls, and everyone's friends and relatives were all there. There was a table filled with everyone's favorite foods. There were graduation gifts. Tonight there was a dance and all my friends would be there. He was ruining this, a pivotal day that I'd worked so hard for. I was a nearly straight A student. I was on the motherfucking honor roll. I'd beaten the odds despite my screwed up childhood with a loser father and a mom lost to suicide. I didn't deserve this. Something like a combination of pain and rage rose in me.

"Athena, sweet pea; trust me." His eyes implored me.

"How much do you owe? Do you even have a way to pay them back?"

He nodded, "It's not out of my reach, and I have a plan."

"It must be pretty bad for them to want human collateral, Dad! What'll they do to me if you don't pay?"

He put his hands on my shoulders and said, "I just need you to trust me."

I held my breath. Burly man #1 and burly man #2 seemed like they were staring me down from behind their Men-In-Black sunglasses.

I was about to open my mouth to say No, no way but then the hot blond guy came out of the vehicle and rounded it. He strode to the passenger side where this standoff was happening and took my elbow and ushered me into the SUV, his mouth in a tight line. Burly guy #2 opened the back door. It happened so fast that I was in the vehicle before I had a chance to protest.

"In!" Blond hot guy was dressed like Mr. GQ and he was angry. He blurted at the goons, "For fuck sakes," then he gave Dad a chilling death stare. Before I had a chance to react, angry hot guy got back in the driver's seat. Then we were pulling away from my Dad who was standing there with his hands in his pockets watching the SUV pull away.

I was sandwiched in between backseat burly guy #2 and the big scary-looking black dude. I glanced over my shoulder out the window to see my Dad take a sip of his coffee and dial a number on his phone. Backseat burly guy passed the big black burly guy on the other side of me my seatbelt and he fastened it for me.

I frowned. Dad had looked so flippant, so nonchalant as he dialed that number and sipped his coffee. What on earth? I was so flabbergasted I couldn't even think straight. Half an hour ago I was graduating from high school. Now I was some kind of marker for my father's gambling debt. Now I was in an SUV with a bunch of scary looking men heading, where? I was trembling.

No one was saying anything. No one was even looking at me. The blond guy was driving and radiating this pissed off vibe and there was some kind of sports event on the radio. I gulped hard and just stared straight ahead, saying a silent prayer.

Tommy

It'd been a couple of weeks since Pop had told me about Tia O'Connor. A long couple of weeks. I'd given the matter thought, like I'd promised him. In fact, I thought about it more than I'd care to admit because the more thought I gave it, the more it made sense. Getting married meant getting handed the keys to all of it. It meant I wouldn't be second guessed, it meant I'd be in total control.

The idea of owning a woman did things to me. I couldn't deny the fact that I'd been thinking about the fact that in addition to being in control of the business, I'd be in control of her. Owning this girl, having her available for my every whim, it was stirring something in me. And did I have whims.

Something about the idea of a girl who was mine, a girl who probably hadn't already had dozens of sexual partners... it appealed to me on a deep level, a level so deep I was having trouble shaking what felt like cravings; the things I was imagining doing to her. Naw, I wasn't deprived but I certainly *was* depraved.

I'd dreamt about her almost every night since seeing her picture. Filthy dreams. I woke up every night a few times as a rule, anyway, but since seeing her picture I'd woken up sweaty, with a hard-on, after delicious dreams of her across my knee getting spanked and fingered, dreams of her tied to my headboard, dreams of her on her knees in front of me, taking my cock into that gorgeous mouth with her hands tied behind her back with one of my belts.

It got even worse after I managed to gather intel about her because in addition to the way she looked, she had other qualities I liked. I decided to check out the goods myself, in person, because I put one of my men on detail to watch her and report her activities and after a week he came to me with a report and some photos and I was ready to get this going.

I'd probably never before defined what my 'type' was but I now knew. She had a smokin' hot body and though she was younger than I'd normally go for she didn't look 19. I knew where she lived, where she worked, where she spent her time, who her friends were, and I knew what sort of person she was.

My man had taken candid photos of her at school, at play, in the pool in her foster parents' back yard, in a barely there string bikini. He'd been watching her, how she interacted with others. She wasn't hard to read at all. She was quite the open book.

My cock twitched at the thought of her in that tiny bikini. Her silky chestnut shampoo commercial hair fell ¾ of the way down her back with bangs that swept gently across her forehead and I could imagine wrapping the long length of her hair around my fist and pulling her head toward my cock. I imagined taking handfuls of it while I did her from behind.

She had the sort of lips women paid to upgrade to. For a second, while looking at her file, my jaw tightened at the fact that my man had taken this photo of her, looked at her in those scraps of material. I felt like a possessive prick, wanting to knock him out for even looking at her. She was semi-sexually active but not slutty, on birth control, but no boyfriend for the past month or two.

Earl told me that there was a little punk ex-boyfriend sniffing around, trying to get her attention again. She was giving him the brush off. I had video of him trying to talk to her over a fence while she was in that bikini. She seemed like she could be a bit of a cock tease. She had a bit of sass but not enough to come across like a bitch. No, it was just enough to make me want to bring her to heel.

The girl hadn't had it easy; her old man was a piece of shit, by the sounds of it. She worked part-time at an ice cream shop near the foster home but she also did volunteer work at the animal shelter as well as at a nearby old age home. She wasn't a typical 19 year old girl out to party and spend and that appealed to me, too. Not a virgin but not a slut.

After way too much attention spent looking at videos of her and flipping through a file of photos and general intel I decided to stroll in and size up the potential chemistry in person. Regardless of what she looked like, I needed to know if there would be any sort of spark before moving forward.

Yeah, most would say I should just let her go, let her go live her life. If I was a nice guy that's what I'd probably do. There were girls out there that I'd already been with who'd be more than happy to wear my ring and sleep in my bed. But I guess I'm not a nice guy. The thing was that my Pop had a claim on her so either I took the gift or he'd give her to someone else. Either way, she was now Ferrano property. That was my justification, as twisted as that was. She was property of the Ferrano family so if I had to get married she'd might as well become mine. Yeah, I know; I guess I'm not even a little bit of a good guy.

BELLS JINGLED OVER the door to the small store as I walked in. Music played and it had a fifties diner theme going with a long white counter flanked by a dozen or so red and chrome stools and half a dozen little red tables, some for two, some for four, in front of a big window that looked out to the busy street. She was working alone and the shop was empty except for a prepubescent kid playing on his handheld game system at the counter while nursing a drink and making an annoying slurping sound as it was obviously just a few ice cubes rattling around in the bottom of the cup. I gave him the 'scram' stare and jerked my chin toward the door. The kid gulped, grabbed his skateboard, and took off.

I stood at the counter and watched her. She was up on a footstool stocking a shelf above her head with small boxes of ice cream cones and she was humming along to the song on the radio. Her arms over her head made her tank top ride up, showing her bare lower back and two sexy dimples at the base of her spine. My pants suddenly felt tight. She had a juicy heart-shaped ass popping from those tight low rider jeans. And the knowledge that it was mine? In that moment, with that knowledge, I had to take a deep breath to stop myself from taking her right then and there.

She turned around and smiled at me expectantly. Then she instantly blushed. Yeah, I had that effect on women. Nope, she didn't look like a teenager in person, either. She looked closer to 25. Her pictures didn't even do justice; she was fucking beautiful.

"Can I help you?" she beamed. She quickly moistened her full pink lips with the tip of her tongue and eyed me in a way that I liked. It wasn't the look of a woman hunting man prey, which was a complete turn-off for me. No, this was shyness and anticipation. This was a girl tingling at the idea that the guy in front of her could be remotely interested in her. Clearly she had no clue how beautiful she was. And obviously she liked what she saw when she looked at me.

"I hope so," I smirked at her.

She climbed down and straightened her black tank top, pulling it down slightly to cover her midriff but resulting in revealing just the scalloped tops of the cups of a lace black bra and (probably unintentionally) giving me an even better view of her cleavage. Great rack. Full C-cup, maybe even a D.

"What do you recommend?"

She flushed even pinker and it was clear she'd seen where my eyes had landed, "Umm, we have ice cream, cold drinks. If you want something hot I can do coffee, hot chocolate, cappuccino..." she trailed off.

Hot. Yeah, I'd like something hot. "Surprise me," I told her.

She chewed her lip shyly, "Well, what do you like?"

"I see plenty that I like. What do *you* like?" I asked, widening my eyes at her and then trailed my gaze from her eyes to her mouth, down to her hips, and then back up. I did this slowly, being very obvious that I was checking her out.

"Hmm," she smiled at me and eyed me up and down, too, showing me she liked what she saw, "Hungry or thirsty?"

Mmm. "Hungry," I said.

"We don't have much for food, really. Popcorn, nachos, ice cream?" she suggested.

"What flavor?" I asked her.

"There's a list up there." She motioned behind herself.

"What's your favorite flavor?" I asked.

"Call me weird but I really just love plain old vanilla." She shrugged.

I almost laughed at her. My face split into a grin. I bet she did. I bet vanilla was all she'd been exposed to so far.

"You *are* weird," I said.

She wrinkled her nose up at me and fuck, but it was adorable.

"Vanilla when there are so many flavors to choose from?" I drummed my fingertips on the counter, staring into the ice cream freezer, "Bah, vanilla sounds like a good start." I sat on a stool.

"One scoop or two?" she asked, flushing even pinker. I wondered if she picked up on the double entendre.

"Two." I was eyeing her luscious round tits.

"Cup or cone?" she asked.

"Cone." I raised a brow.

"Sugar cone?"

"Oh yeah," I said low and gave her another grin.

She gulped, fumbled, and got the ice cream for me. Then she put a cherry right in the middle of the top scoop. A fucking cherry. I could've come in my pants right then and there.

"That's three bucks," she'd said, holding it out to me with both hands demurely but something flirty in those eyes. Gorgeous eyes. Jade green, long thick black lashes.

Oh it'd be a lot more than three bucks. I could buck all fucking night if I had her in my bed. I'd put a $20 in her hand, then grabbed her wrist for a second before she could turn to the cash register and told her to keep the change and then wiggled the tip of my tongue against the cherry and winked at her before letting go of her wrist. Then, I walked out.

I used the tip of my tongue to scoop the cherry into my mouth and dropped the cone in the trash bin outside the shop and glanced in the window. She was staring at me, mouth open. After a few flicks of the tongue behind my teeth, I pulled out the stem and showed her that it was now knotted and then put it between my teeth, winked, and then I got into my car and drove directly to my father's office, tonguing that stem while I drove.

I didn't knock; I strolled right in, interrupting a phone call and ignoring the 4 other people sitting there with him at a conference table, one of them my brother.

Pop had looked up at me and put his hand over the mouthpiece of the phone.

"Tia O'Connor? Make it happen," I told him, dropping the knotted cherry stem into the trash can beside the table.

"On it," he'd answered with a huge smile and then lifted his chin at Dario, my brother. Dare got up and cracked his knuckles, "Let's go," Dare said to Bruce, Gus, and Earl, who were all sitting there with him.

Later that night, Dare called me and told me he'd visited with Greg O'Connor and told him the score. He walked in and told him Tom Ferrano was calling in his debt. If he didn't have cash on the spot, he was to hand over his daughter Tia, that Tia would be presented to Thomas Ferrano Jr. as potential marriage material and that if marriage didn't happen she'd remain Ferrano property in order to clear his debt. Dario had brought muscle with him, expecting resistance even though Pop told him not to bother.

O'Connor hadn't even seemed all that surprised, according to Dare. Said he knew that my father wasn't done with him yet and had a feeling this day would come. That my father had warned a few weeks prior that Tia might be the payback for what'd happened back in the day, whenever and whatever that was.

O'Connor had told my brother it was almost a relief that the day had come and that Tom had chosen to handle things this way because he'd been carrying around the worry for years. What the fuck? Piece of shit. Whatever the beef was between him and my Pop he wasn't even gonna try to barter or fight for his daughter? What a sorry excuse for a father, for a man.

Of course she was already mine in my head so there was nothing he could do even if he had the money to pay the debt but that the man wasn't even trying? He'd get zero respect from me.

Dare thought it was funny that Pop had done this to get me married off and said he was surprised that I was going through with it. I told him it was a means to an end and we joked about the fact that he'd be next. I'd seen Dare date plenty; he got a lot of female attention and had even been engaged already but she'd broken his heart and in return he'd broken the jaw of the guy she was fucking as well as bankrupted the guy's family's business. Since then he was about as interested in settling down as I was.

I saw my Pop the next evening at dinner at his house with him, my two sisters, their families, and Pop's wife, wife #4 if I hadn't lost count yet, and he told me on the side that he'd told O'Connor years back that he'd have his daughter someday. I tried to ask questions but again he brushed me off.

Why that son of a bitch didn't leave the country to protect his little girl was beyond me. I mean, we had reach across borders but if you'd at least tried to get out of his line of sight maybe you'd have somewhat of a chance of getting off his radar. I knew that O'Connor had left his kid to rot in foster homes right under my Pop's nose while he put cocaine up his own nose, while he repeatedly bet all his earnings on the horses and in card games, while he paid no attention to his kid whatsoever. Knowing Pop was threatening his kid, how could he stay around here?

I didn't know what the beef between Pop and O'Connor was about as Pop was being tight-lipped but it had to be a pretty big beef for Pop to let a wound fester for years and then decide that the payment would come in the form of about 120 pounds of flesh. For whatever the reason was, I'd be getting that flesh in my hands right after she graduated from high school. It was all arranged. Dare would pick her up and deliver her to me.

Tia

The SUV stopped in front of a gatehouse and then when the gates opened, it pulled up a driveway in front of a gorgeous Tudor style house. A mansion, really. I clutched my purse close and when the SUV emptied, big black scary dude reached for my hand and helped me out. He gave me a little smile. Hmm, not so scary, really. Now that he'd smiled at me, he reminded me a little of Michael Clarke Duncan. The guy from the Green Mile isn't scary, just misunderstood. Maybe this guy wasn't scary. The other two, burlies one and two *were* scary, though. Burly Number Two from the back seat looked a tad like Lou Ferrigno, the Incredible Hulk. Burly One looked like a total criminal -—Sopranos or Godfather henchman type -—angry dark eyes, uni brow, deep acne scars on his cheeks. All three of them were huge men. The blond driver in the front looked little less scary but his attitude was scarier than all the other guys. He was in maybe his mid-20's, and while he was good-looking, wearing an expensive suit, he looked pissed off and impatient. He seemed like the one in charge.

The Michael Clarke Duncan-looking dude finished helping me out of the SUV and blond angry hot guy motioned for me to follow him. I did, wondering what the heck I was walking into here. I was on a gated property with several big scary guys and I'd bet money they all carried guns. The blond guy led me through a big foyer into a room down a long hallway and rapped on a door.

"Come in," A man answered from the other side.

The two burlies and the Michael Clarke Duncan guy stopped and waited in the hall while the blond guy opened the door and signaled for me to walk ahead of him. My heart felt like it was in my throat.

I was inside a large office and a man was behind a desk. He had salt and pepper hair and light brown eyes and looked handsome for his age, kind of George Clooneyish. He wore a suit and he looked tall and muscular. He looked more businessman or hot shot lawyer than mobster.

A guy in a mansion with all these thugs or whatever was buying debts from bookies? It didn't add up. How big could Dad's debt actually be? Who would front him more than a few hundred dollars on a poker game, knowing he wasn't capable of earning more than the minimum wage?

"Athena, I'm Thomas Ferrano. Call me Tom. Please sit." He motioned toward a chair in front of his desk.

I sat. His name sounded familiar. His face sort of seemed familiar, too.

"Aren't you lovely? You graduated high school today, I hear.

Congratulations."

I stared at him. Words won't form on my lips.

He narrowed his gaze at me, "No need to be rude."

I shook my head, "I'm not trying to be rude. I'm just a bit overwhelmed. Thank you. For the congrats."

He nodded, "Dario, get a bottle of water for Athena." Angry hot blond guy nodded and left the room.

"So, I take it your father filled you in? Why don't you tell me what he said to you, ah? He used to have an unfortunate habit of leaving out important facts. Maybe he still does."

Boy, did I know that.

Blond guy, Dario, returned with a bottle of water and handed it to me, then left the office.

"Umm thanks," I took a sip, "I haven't seen much of my father in years. He turned up today at my high school graduation and then told me I had to be a marker for a few days so he could get money together to clear up a gambling debt?"

Thomas Ferrano laughed, "Interesting spin."

My heart plummeted. Spin? If that wasn't the truth, what was?

"Isn't that the truth?" I asked, starting to tremble.

"Not exactly. Your father owes me a rather large debt, one I'm not sure he can ever actually repay." He looked at me expectantly.

"Why am I here, then?"

"Let's say you've been drafted." he smirked.

Huh?

"My son Tommy needs to get married. He hasn't found Miss Perfect yet. Your father owes me a great deal. I've agreed to consider writing off the debt if my son decides you're Miss Perfect."

I started to laugh, "Am I being punk'd?"

"Excuse me?" he asked and I knew, then, that he was serious.

"I don't understand..." The room began to slowly turn. I was white-knuckled, gripping the arms of the chair I sat in.

"Simple, really. As of now you are property of the Ferrano family."

If my chin wasn't touching the floor right now, it must be awfully close. Had I been transported back to the dark ages? I didn't know what to say. I was totally and utterly gob smacked.

"So, I've arranged for you to be transported to Tommy's home. There you two can get acquainted and go from there, see if this is an amicable arrangement for him."

For him? For him?

"What?" I can't fathom this, "No."

Don't I have to agree to this? I don't agree to this. He raised his index finger and his eyes narrowed. He took on a much more menacing look, "Listen carefully. This meeting, the one between you and my son, if it doesn't go well it won't bode well for your father and it may not bode well for you, either. We have many options available for where you could go. I think you'd prefer ending up with my son over the alternatives. We're a wealthy and powerful family so you could be in a much worse position, believe me. I'd advise you to cooperate. You're in an enviable position, Athena. I'll be seeing you soon. Tommy's brother will drive you. Dario!"

Enviable? Was this man whacked in the head?

The door opened and Dario popped his head in.

"Take Athena to your brother. Athena, don't be difficult. I wouldn't advise it. It was nice to see you again. You've grown up to be a lovely girl. An almost dead ringer for your mother." He gave me a big smile. My blood ran cold.

My mother? This man knew my mother? See me again? When had he seen me before? This man was scary. The brother was scary. Their thugs or whatever they were -—really scary. Was I in the middle of the fricking dark ages or what? An arranged marriage to a mafia kingpin's son to save my father's life? This was nuts! If I was asleep I wanted to wake up right now!

Dario led me back out to the SUV and two of the other guys got in, too. One had apparently opted out of this leg of the drive. They thought they needed muscle to get me from point A to point B, evidently. Were they afraid I'd try to run? I didn't know what the heck I was dealing with here so no, I wasn't about to run now before sussing things out. I didn't want to end up dead. I didn't want Dad to end up dead. Did Dad really sell me out like this? I mean, he was a lousy father, for sure, but did he really sell me to the mafia in exchange for payment of his old gambling debts? Not a marker. Not temporarily. Sold, like chattel. Married off. No way. He was capable of a lot but this? Surely not. This was North America and the 21st century. This kind of stuff didn't happen.

I combed through my memory. The name Ferrano rang bells. Was he known in the city as a mafia guy? Where had I heard his name from? I stayed somewhat up to speed on current events and his name and face was familiar but I couldn't place it.

What might've been about ten minutes later the SUV was pulling up in front of another set of gates. The drive had been quiet, more sports, I figured out was soccer, on the radio and no talking other than a "Woo" and a "Yes!" in unison from angry driver, err

Dario and burly # two (number one had opted out) on what must've been a goal... it'd all been white noise to me due to my state of mind.

"Wait here," Dario told me after getting past the gate and then he walked into the house alone. Me and the muscle sat in awkward silence.

My purse started ringing my ringtone for Ruby, Sexy Back by Justin Timberlake.

"Hand it over," Burly #2 said gruffly and I knew he meant business.

I took my cell phone out and handed it to him.

Tommy

Dare was inside my doorway, "I come bearing gifts. I deliver your bride," he gave a gallant bow and then snickered at me. I'd just gotten here and had known they were going to be along soon.

I rolled my eyes, "Fucking Pop."

He laughed, leaning against the wall, "She's a looker, bro. He did good."

"Don't look at my bride." I pointed at him, a little smirk on my face. I punched his shoulder playfully, "And just you wait. I'm sure he's lining up someone for you to marry next."

"Since you'll be head of the family, I think that means you get to pick, doesn't it?"

I threw my head back and let out an evil laugh, "Oh yeah. And just you wait!"

"I'll go get her," He told me, grinning. He knew I'd have his back. Truth be told, he couldn't wait for Pop to head out to pasture. Dare and I had plans for taking the family business to the next level together. We were half-brothers and five years apart but we'd grown up together and were alike in many ways. He was the only other person I'd 100% trust to have my back. I didn't even trust my father 100%.

I didn't think he'd set out to do harm to me intentionally but I knew that we were all pawns, to a degree, and that his idea of having my back and Dare's idea of the same would diverge.

"Put her in my bedroom and lock the door." I said and wiggled my eyebrows. Then I walked into my office to tie up a few loose ends before the big reveal. I didn't know much about her yet but from what I did know so far, I guessed that she wouldn't have taken the news of today lightly. I was anticipating, even hoping for some resistance and looking fucking forward to it.

Tia

The guy with my phone gave it to Dario when he came back to the SUV.

"Let's go," Dario said to me with a chin lift.

Michael Clarke Duncan lookalike guy let me out and I had to walk around the back of the truck to meet up with Dario. I couldn't run. The gate was shut. Would I run, though, if it wasn't? Thomas Ferrano threatened me, pretty much saying Dad was a goner if I didn't cooperate, and maybe me, too. But what was going to happen to me here?

I followed Dario into the big house, feeling a little shaky and a lot queasy. I couldn't help but notice the architectural details of the place because it was the sort of house I'd always dreamt of living in. It looked like a pretty hacienda, had an orange terra cotta roof, white parging with archways. There were loads of flowers everywhere. Climbing vines, overflowing baskets, covering the ground, everywhere.

Inside the front door was a foyer that opened to a staircase directly to my left and a long hallway under an arch to my right. This was the kind of house Mom and I used to talk about having, a hacienda and beautiful gardens. It was her dream to live in a house like this and it'd become my dream, too. I shivered at the thought of my Mom, unable to fathom all this.

"Follow me," Dario led the way up the stairs, down a long hall with several closed doors to a set of double doors, and then opened them both and walked in. I followed inside.

"Bag?" He motioned.

I hesitated.

"I'll give your bag and phone to Tommy. He'll decide when you can have them back."

I was trembling. I couldn't help it. I was in a big master suite with a king-sized bed, about to be left for someone who thought they had a claim on me. I was supposed to be at a party celebrating the end of my childhood and the beginning of life as an adult. An adult with choices, a future, independence.

This was not that. This was something else. This something else was bad. Very bad. He nodded politely, reached over to the bedside table and picked up a cordless phone, and then he left with it. I let out a big breath, as if I'd been holding it in for hours. I had to keep my cool somehow. If I had a freak out, there was no telling what would happen to me. If I kept my coo, I could suss everything out and then make a calculated decision about what to do.

I surveyed the room. It was nice, luxurious, even. Soft dove gray walls, big dark wood furniture, lots of leather, exposed beam ceilings with ceiling fans. The room was decorated in gray and black. It didn't really match the hacienda theme outside and I wouldn't say it was my taste, really, but it was nice. There was a big difference from this room to the kind of room I was used to. The small room I'd shared with Bethany with our two twin loft beds with desks underneath and drawers for stairs was small but we'd made it our own. Here was a room I was expected to share with a man. I cringed, looking at the bed, fearing what I'd be expected to do. I knew nothing about this Tommy. All I knew was that I was in a pickle of a situation and I didn't know how I'd get myself out.

Rose, Cal, and everyone must've been worried about me right now. Or had my Dad made up an excuse? They'd probably report me missing if they didn't hear from me in a few hours. They knew how stoked I was about this party. Rose had made me my favorite artichoke and spinach dip as well as mozzarella sticks plus a plethora of appetizers that the other girls had requested. There was a huge cake for us, two thirds vanilla and a third chocolate because me and Mia preferred vanilla and Beth preferred chocolate. Cal had suggested three separate cakes or cupcakes with icing slathered all over to hold them all together but we were all so close we wanted the same cake. Rose had said she had our photos put on in icing. I never saw my cake. A tear slid down my cheek. Then I heard the doorknob turn and I dashed it away and held the others back. I put my lips together and stood still, back straight, took a deep breath, and waited.

End Sample

Visit ddprince.com to learn more about this and other DD Prince books.

Don't forget:

Like DD's Facebook page at http://www.facebook.com/ddprincebooks

More Books by DD Prince

Dark, paranormal, contemporary, and mind fuck romances.

This list may have been updated since publishing, so check ddprince.com for a full list of DD Prince & Scarlett Starkleigh books.

As of the date of publishing, the Nectar Trilogy is available from a number of retailers. Some books are available in paperback. See DD Prince's website for further information and links.

MC Romance: Romantic suspense with comedy, angst, steamy scenes, and a little bit of gritty darkness.

Detour (Beautiful Biker 1) Deacon & Ella

This alpha-male is not an alpha-hole. You're going to FLOVE Deacon Valentine.

Joyride (Beautiful Biker 2) Rider & Jenna

Rider starts out as a little bit of an alpha-hole. Jenna resists, but resistance is futile when a Valentine brother has you in his sights.

*A total of 8 books for the Beautiful Biker series are expected.

Dark Mafia Romance: dark romance with a debt flesh payment plot.

This one DD's most popular book, but it *is* dark. Non-consensual / rough sex. An anti-hero you may love to hate and hate to love.

The Dominator

The Dominator II; Truth or Dare

Sex slave rescue romance with dark themes.

The Dominator III: Unbound

More Tommy, More Dare; More Domination!

Spin off Dark Romance (maybe DD's darkest book yet):

Saved (Alessandro & Holly's story)

Dark Paranormal Romance: Vampire dark romance / kidnapping

Nectar Trilogy (Includes Nectar, Ambrosia, and Essence)

https://www.books2read.com/tristanandkyla (book 1)

https://www.books2read.com/nectar2ambrosia (book 2)

https://www.books2read.com/nectar3essence (book 3)

https://www.books2read.com/nectartrilogy (box set)

Dirty / fun / instalove alien romance (Writing as Scarlett Starkleigh)

Hot Alpha Alien Husbands: Book 1 – Daxx and Jetta

Sign up for DD Prince's free newsletter to get notified of new releases, sales, and contests - http://ddprince.com/neswletter-signup/.